THE
SCRIBE

Also by Antonio Garrido:
The Corpse Reader

THE SCRIBE

ANTONIO GARRIDO

Translated by Simon Bruni

Text copyright © 2011 Antonio Garrido
English translation copyright © 2013 Simon Bruni

The Scribe was first published in 2011 by Zeta Bolsillo as La Escriba. Translated from Spanish by Simon Bruni. Published in English by AmazonCrossing in 2013.

Published by AmazonCrossing
PO Box 400818
Las Vegas, NV 89140

ISBN-13: 978-1477848838
ISBN-10: 1477848835
Library of Congress Control Number: 2013911777

Year of Our Lord 799.
Citadel of Würzburg. Franconia.

And the Devil came to stay.

I know not why I write anymore: Theresa died yesterday, and I might join her soon. We have had nothing to eat today. What I bring from the scriptorium is barely enough. All is desolate. The city is dying.

Gorgias set his wax tablet on the ground and lay on the old bed. Before closing his eyes he prayed for his daughter's soul. Then all he could think about were the terrible days leading up to the famine.

NOVEMBER

1

There was no sunrise in Würzburg on All Saints' Day. In the half-light of morning, farm workers started to emerge from their homes. Heading for the fields, they pointed at the grubby sky, swollen like the belly of a great cow. Dogs sniffed the coming storm and howled, but the men, women, and children continued their weary, silent parade like a soulless army. A whirl of dark clouds soon obscured the heavens as if heralding the end of the world. Then, such a torrent of water came that even the most hardened country folks trembled.

Theresa's stepmother roused her from a deep sleep. The young girl listened in astonishment to the drumming of the hailstones threatening to bring down the wattle roof and immediately understood that she must hurry. In a blink, mother and daughter gathered up leftover bread and cheese from the table, wrapped a few clothes in an improvised bundle, and—securing doors and windows—left to join the desperate mob running for shelter in the high part of the city.

As they climbed the arched street, Theresa realized she had forgotten her wax tablets. "You carry on, Mother. I'll be right back."

Ignoring Rutgarda's shouting, Theresa disappeared into the crowd of peasants fleeing like sodden rats. Many of the streets had already turned to rivers cluttered with broken baskets, lumps of firewood, dead chickens, and soiled clothes. She negotiated the crowded tanners' passageway by clambering over a cart jammed between two flooded houses, then she ran down the old street to the rear of her home, where she surprised an urchin trying to break in. She gave him a shove, but—instead of fleeing—the boy merely scampered off to another house where he had better luck climbing in through a window. Cursing him, Theresa went inside. From a chest she took her writing tools, her wax tablets, and an emerald-colored bible. She crossed herself, stashed everything under her cloak, and ran back as quickly as possible through the downpour to the place where her stepmother was waiting for her.

On the way to the cathedral, streets disappeared under the mire, and roofs flew off like dead leaves. Then, a great torrent of water engulfed the maze of hovels in the poor quarter, leaving a trail of devastation in its wake.

Over the next few days, wandering the streets of Würzburg became a terrible nightmare. Townsfolk were constantly falling over in the quagmire, and they had to keep their distance from the collapsing buildings. But their prayers could not prevent the rain and blizzards from turning their fields into lakes.

Then the ice came: The Main River froze over, trapping the fishing skiffs, and the snowstorms blocked the passes that connected Würzburg to the plains of Frankfurt, preventing supplies of food and goods from getting through. Frosts decimated the crops and ravaged the herds. Gradually, provisions ran out and hunger spread like wildfire. Some villagers sold their land off cheap, and nothing more was heard of the fools who had left the protection of the city walls to make for the woods. It was rumored that some, driven by desperation, commended themselves to God and hurled themselves into the ravines.

While the older folks shut themselves in their homes and waited for a miracle, the little ones, ignoring the warnings of their elders, continued to meet at the dunghills outside the walls to search for rats to roast. When they caught one, they celebrated with songs and cries of jubilation, parading down the main street with their quarry held up high.

After two weeks, dead bodies peppered the streets of the city. The more fortunate dead were buried in the small cemetery beside the timber structure of Saint Adela's Church, but volunteers soon gave up, letting bodies lie scattered like a plague along the watercourses. Some of the corpses swelled like toads, but usually the rats would devour them before then.

Many children had grown weak, and their mothers despaired as they searched in vain for something besides a little water to put on the table. The stench of dead bodies permeated the city, as did the mournful ringing of the cathedral bells.

Fortunately, Theresa still had work in the countship's cathedral, where she had taken shelter the morning of the deluge. The cathedral had a meager yet steady need for workers. Laypeople worked in the diocesan workshops in return for a weekly ration of grain. The few women in service were there either to pleasure the men or toil in the kitchens. But Theresa had found work in the parchment-makers' workshop, a job she had mixed feelings about. Yes, she had to suffer the crude stares of the leather workers, the comments about her breasts, and the men brushing past her with varying degrees of blatancy, but the reward for these annoyances came when, at the end of the day, she was left alone with the parchments. Then she would stack the pages that had arrived from the scriptorium—and instead of stitching the quinternions, she would enjoy a few moments to read. Theresa took compensation for her hard work from the tales told in the polyptychs and patristic texts. One day she knew her skills would be put to use for more than just baking cakes and washing pots.

Her father, Gorgias, plied his trade as a scribe at the episcopal scriptorium, close to the workshop where she worked as an apprentice. Theresa had assumed the position thanks to the mis-fortune of Ferrucio, the previous apprentice who had blighted his future in a moment of carelessness by severing the tendons in his hand. That was when her father put her forward to replace him. However, from the beginning, Korne—the master parchment-maker—opposed her appointment on the basis of women's change-able natures, their inclination toward quarreling and gossip, their inability to bear heavy loads, and the frequency of their menstru-ation. All of this, in his view, was incompatible with a role that required wisdom and dexterity in equal measure. And yet Theresa could read and write fluently, a skill of unquestionable value in a place where there was too much muscle and not enough intellec-tual talent. It was thanks to her skill, and the intercession of the count, that she had been awarded the post.

When Rutgarda first found out about Theresa's appointment, she was up in arms. If Theresa had been feebleminded or sickly, she might have understood the decision. But she was an attractive young woman—perhaps a little skinny for the tastes of Frankish boys—but with wide hips and generous breasts, not to mention a full set of teeth, as white as they come. Anyone else in her position would have sought a good husband to knock her up and keep her. But no, Theresa had to throw away her youth, shut away in some old priests' workshop, working on pointless priestly things, and enduring the idle gossip of the priests' women. And worst of all, Rutgarda was certain that the person responsible for all of this was none other than Theresa's father.

In the end the girl had succumbed to Gorgias's absurd ideas. His head was always stuck in the past, yearning for his native Byzantium, and he rattled on about the benefits of knowledge and the greatness of the ancient writers as if those wise men could put food on his table. The years would go by, Rutgarda thought, and one day, all of a sudden her stepdaughter would find herself with

sagging flesh and bare gums. Then she would regret that she had
not found a man to feed and protect her.

On the second to last Friday of November, Theresa awoke earlier
than usual. She used to rise before the sun to sweep the animal
pen and take care of the hens, but for some time there had been no
food to give them and no chickens to feed. Even so, she considered
herself lucky. The storm that had laid waste to the poor quarter and
forced her to take refuge in the cathedral for a few nights had left
the walls of her house intact—and neither her stepmother nor her
father had been harmed.

As she lay in bed, waiting for the sun to rise, she curled up under
her blankets. In her head she went over the trial she would undertake in a few hours' time. The week before, Korne had expressed
his objections to her taking the entry examination to become an
official parchment-maker. When he discovered she had applied to
take the exam, he became like a bear with a sore head, arguing
that a woman had never before held the position. He grew even
angrier when she reminded him that two years had gone by, following which, under the rules of the guild, anyone could demand
entry into the trade.

"Any apprentice who is able to carry a heavy load," Korne had
responded with a look of distaste.

Nevertheless, late on Thursday, Korne had appeared in the workshop and sneeringly told her that he would accept her application,
informing her that the test would take place the following day.

Korne's haste raised Theresa's suspicions, and despite her joy at
the news, she could not help but wonder why Korne had changed
his mind so suddenly. Yet she was confident that she could pass
the test: She could distinguish between parchments of lambskin
or goat's vellum. She was able to frame and stretch the damp skins
better than even Korne, and she could mend arrow and bite marks

to leave the leather as white and as clean as a newborn's backside. And that was all that mattered to her.

Even so, when it was time to rise Friday morning, she could not stop a shiver from running down her spine. Quietly, she sat up and unhooked the worn blanket that separated her old bed from her parents'. Wrapping the blanket around her body and tying it in place with a piece of cord, she left the room, doing her best not to make any noise. After relieving herself in the animal pen, she washed with some ice-cold water and ran back into the house. She lit a little oil lamp and sat down on a chest. The flame dimly lit the only room in the house, a small rectangular space that could barely accommodate a family. In the center of the room, the fire smoldered in its pit dug into the soft, damp earth. The cold was biting and the embers were beginning to weaken, so she added a little peat and stoked the fire with a stick. Then she took a scorched pot and scraped leftover porridge from it—until she heard a voice behind her.

"What on earth are you doing? Come on! Back to bed."

Theresa turned around and looked at her father. She wished she hadn't woken him.

"It's the test. I can't sleep," she explained.

Gorgias stretched and moved closer to the fire with a begrudging grumble. Its glow lit up a bony face under a tangle of white hair. He sat next to Theresa and squeezed her against him.

"It's not that, my child. It is this cold, which will end up killing us all," he whispered as he rubbed his hands. "And forget that porridge. Not even the rats would eat it. Your mother will find you something for breakfast. Right now what you have to do is stop being bashful and use the blanket to keep warm at night instead of using it as a curtain."

"Father, I don't do it out of shyness," she lied. "I put it there so I don't bother you while I read."

"I don't care why you do it. One day we will find you stiff as an icicle, and there will be nothing to agree or disagree about."

Theresa smiled and went back to scraping the porridge. She served some for her father, who devoured it as he listened to her.

"I can't sleep because of the examination. Yesterday, when Korne agreed to test me, there was a strange look in his eyes. I don't know . . . something that worried me."

Gorgias smiled and ruffled her hair. He promised her that all would be well. "You know more about parchments than Korne himself. What vexes that old man is that his sons, after ten years in the trade, can't tell a donkey's hide from one of Saint Augustine's codices. He'll give you some documents to bind, you will do it perfectly, and you will become Würzburg's first official female parchment-maker. Whether Korne likes it or not."

"I don't know, Father . . . he won't permit a newcomer to . . ."

"So what if he's not willing? Korne might be a master parchment-maker, but the owner of the workshop is Wilfred, and don't forget that he will be present, too."

"Let's hope so!" said Theresa as she rose.

The sun was starting to rise. Gorgias stood up and stretched out like a cat. "Well, wait for me to dry the styluses and I'll come with you to the workshop. At this hour, a pretty young girl should not be wandering about the citadel alone."

While Gorgias prepared his tools, Theresa amused herself admiring the beautiful snowy maze of rooftops. Sunlight was starting to pour into the alleyways, tingeing the buildings with a soft amber glow. In the part of the poor quarter sheltered by city walls, the timber hovels were cramped together as if they were competing for the one piece of land they could cling to—unlike in the high area, where fortified structures proudly festooned the streets and squares. Theresa was perplexed at how such a beautiful city could be transformed so quickly into a place of death and misery.

"By the Archangel Gabriel!" exclaimed Gorgias. "Your new dress makes an appearance at last!"

Theresa smiled. Several months before, her father had given her a lovely dress, blue like the summer sky. It was for her nineteenth birthday, but she had been saving it for the right occasion. Before leaving, she approached the straw mattress where her stepmother still slept and kissed her on the cheek.

"Wish me luck," Theresa whispered into her ear.

Rutgarda grumbled and nodded, but as her family left the house, she prayed that Theresa would fail the test.

Father and daughter climbed the blacksmith's road in double time, with Gorgias occupying the center of the street to avoid the nooks and crannies where all manner of undesirable might be lurking. In his right hand he clutched a torch and with his other arm he held Theresa to him, his cape wrapped around her. As they reached the watchtower, they passed a group of guards who were heading down toward the city walls. Then they came to the top of the hill and turned down the knights' street toward the central square. There they skirted around the church until they could make out the workshop building, a squat but ample timber structure situated behind the baptistery.

They were a few steps from the entrance when a shadow swooped down on them from out of the darkness. Gorgias tried to react, but he barely had time to push Theresa to one side. A knife flashed, and Gorgias's torch rolled down the street and off the edge.

Theresa screamed as the two men rolled around on the ground. Desperate, she ran to find help, pounding on the door to the workshop with all her strength. She felt the skin on her knuckles tearing, but she kept screaming and hitting the door. Behind her she heard the two men struggling, fighting for their lives. She kicked the accursed door again, but nobody answered. Had she been able, she would have knocked it down and dragged out the workshop's occupants herself. Exasperated, she turned and ran, calling for help. Then she heard her father's voice telling her to stay away.

Theresa stopped, not knowing what to do. The two men suddenly disappeared down an embankment. The young woman remembered the soldiers they had passed a few moments earlier, and she shot off down the street to find them. But as she approached the watchtower, she stopped again, uncertain she could reach them in time and even less sure she would be able to persuade them to help. She quickly retraced her steps to the workshop, where she found two men doing their best to help a blood-soaked figure. She recognized Korne and one of his sons, trying to lift her father's limp and bloody body.

"For God's sake!" cried Korne to Theresa. "Run inside and tell my wife to prepare a cauldron of hot water. Your father is badly wounded."

Theresa did not stop to think. Calling out for help as she went, she rushed up to the attic where the parchment-maker lived. The space had been used as a storeroom until the previous year when Korne turned it into a home by adding some solid scaffolding.

Bertharda, the parchment-maker's wife and a rather stout woman, peered out half-dressed with a sleepy face and a candle in her hands. "For heaven's sake! What's all this racket about?" she exclaimed, crossing herself.

"It's my father. Quick, for the love of God!" Theresa implored.

The woman bounded down the stairs, trying to cover her intimate parts. As she reached the bottom, Korne and his son were coming in through the door.

"The water, woman—have you not prepared it yet?" Korne bellowed. "And light. We need more light."

Theresa ran to the workshop and fumbled through the tools scattered over the workbenches. She found some oil lamps, but they were empty. Finally, she found a couple of candles under a pile of oddments, but one of them rolled under the table and disappeared into the darkness. Theresa picked up the other, has-tening to light it. Meanwhile, Korne and his son had moved the skins off one of the tables and placed Gorgias on it. The parchment-maker ordered Theresa to clean the wounds while he went to find some knives, but the girl did not listen to him. In a daze, she held the candle closer and looked in horror at the awful gash on her father's wrist. She had never seen such a terrible wound. The blood was gushing out, soaking clothes, skins, and codices—and Theresa did not know how to stop it.

One of Korne's dogs came over and started lapping up the blood dripping onto the floor, but then Korne returned and kicked the dog aside.

"Light, here," he blurted.

Theresa moved the flame where he indicated. Then the parchment-maker tore a skin from a nearby frame and spread it out on the ground. Using a knife and a piece of wood, he cut the skin into strips and tied the ends together to make a long cord.

"Get his clothes off," he ordered Theresa. "And you, woman, bring that bloody water."

"Good God! What has happened?" asked his frightened wife. "Are you all right?"

"Stop your chitchat and bring the damned pot," Korne cursed, slamming his fist on the table.

Theresa started to undress her father, but Korne's wife uncer-emoniously shoved her aside to take over. Once Gorgias was unclothed, Bertharda washed him carefully using a scrap of leather and warm water. Korne examined the wounds at length, noticing several cuts on the back and one or two more on the shoulders. The one that worried him most was on the right arm.

"Hold this here," Korne said, lifting Gorgias's arm.

Theresa obeyed, ignoring the trickle of blood soaking her own dress.

"Boy," the parchment-maker said to his son, "run to the fort and alert the physician. Tell him it's urgent."

The young lad ran off, and Korne turned to Theresa.

"Now, when I tell you, I want you to bend his arm at the elbow and press it against his chest. Got it?"

With tears streaming down her cheeks, Theresa nodded without looking away from her father.

The parchment-maker fastened the leather cord above the wound and wrapped it round several times before tightening it. Gorgias seemed to regain consciousness, but it was merely a spasm. Soon, however, he did stop bleeding. Korne gestured to Theresa, and she folded her father's arm as she had been told.

"Well, the worst is over," Korne said. "The other cuts seem less serious, but we will have to wait for the physician to give us his opinion. He also has bruising, but the bones all seem to be in place. Let's cover him to keep him warm."

At that moment, Gorgias coughed violently and started to heave as he winced with pain. Through his half-opened eyes, he saw Theresa sobbing.

"Thank the heavens," he said, his voice choked with emotion. "Are you all right, my child?"

"Yes, Father," she sobbed. "I thought I could get help from the soldiers and I ran off to find them, but I couldn't reach them, and then when I turned back . . ."

Theresa was unable to finish the sentence, choked up by her own weeping. Gorgias took her hand in his and pulled it toward him approvingly. He tried to say something but instead coughed again and fell unconscious.

"He should rest now," said the woman, delicately leading Theresa away. "And stop crying—those tears won't solve anything."

Theresa nodded. For a moment she thought about returning to her house to let her stepmother know, but she quickly ruled out the idea. She would tidy the workshop while they waited for the physician. When she knew the extent of the injuries, then she would tell Rutgarda.

With a bowl of oil, Korne set about filling the lamps. "If you only knew the number of times I've almost dipped some old bread in this oil," the parchment-maker grumbled.

When he finished lighting the lamps, the room looked like a torch-lit cavern. Theresa started clearing up the morass of needles, knives, lunella mallets, parchments, and jars of glue strewn between the tables and frames. As usual, she divided the tools according to their purpose, and after carefully cleaning them, she placed them on their corresponding shelves. Then she went to her workbench to check her pounce box, polish levels, and to ensure all surfaces were clean. Having finished her tasks, she returned to her father's side.

She did not know how long it was before the surgeon Zeno arrived. He was a grubby and disheveled man whose potent body odor was matched only by the fumes of cheap wine emanating from his breath. On his back, he carried a sack. And he appeared to be in a half stupor as he walked into the room without a greeting. With a quick look around, he went over to where Gorgias lay unconscious. Opening his bag, he pulled out a small metal saw, several knives, and a tiny box from which he took some needles and a roll of string. The surgeon placed the instruments on Gorgias's stomach and asked for more light. He spat on his hands several times, paying particular attention to the blood dried to his fingernails, and then he grasped the saw firmly.

Theresa went pale as the little man positioned his instrument over Gorgias's elbow, but mercifully he only used it to cut the tourniquet Korne had made. The blood started flowing again, but Zeno didn't seem alarmed.

"Good job, though it was too tight," said the surgeon. "Do you have any more strips of leather?"

Korne brought him a long one, which the physician grabbed without looking away from Gorgias. He knotted it expertly and began working on the wounded arm with the indifference of someone stuffing a pheasant.

"It's the same every day," he said without lifting his eyes from the wound. "Yesterday someone found old Marta on the low road with her guts cut open. And two days ago they found Siderico, the cooper, at the gate to his animal pen with his head bashed in. And for what? To steal God knows what from him? The poor wretch couldn't even feed his children."

Zeno seemed to know his trade well. He stitched flesh and sutured veins with the dexterity of a seamstress, spitting on the knife to keep it clean. He finished with the arm and moved on to the rest of the wounds, to which he applied a dark ointment that he took from a wooden bowl. Finally, he bandaged the limb in some linen rags that he declared to be newly washed, despite the visible stains.

"Well," he said, wiping his hands on his chest, "all done. Take care of him, and in a couple of days—"

"Will he recover?" Theresa butted in.

"He might. Though, of course, he might not."

The man roared with laughter, then rummaged in his sack until he found a vial containing a dark liquid. Theresa thought it might be some kind of tonic, but the physician uncorked it and took a long draft.

"By Saint Pancras! This liquor could revive a corpse. Would you like some?" the little man offered, waving the flask under Theresa's nose.

She shook her head. The surgeon repeated the gesture with Korne, who responded by taking a couple of good swigs.

"Knife wounds are like children: They're all made in the same way, but no two are ever the same," he sniggered. "It's not up to me whether he lives or dies. The arm's well stitched, but the cut is deep and it may have reached the tendons. All we can do now is wait, and if in a week's time there are no pustules or abscesses . . ."

"Here," said the surgeon, taking a little bag from his sash. "Apply this powder four times a day, and do not wash the wound too much."

Theresa nodded.

"As for my fee . . ." he said as he slapped Theresa's backside, "don't worry, Count Wilfred will pay me." And he continued laughing as he gathered his instruments.

Theresa reddened in indignation. She despised men taking that kind of liberty with her, and if Zeno had not just helped her father, God knows she would have smashed the flask of wine over his ugly head. But before she could protest, the surgeon flung open the door and left, humming to himself.

In the meantime, Korne's wife returned from the attic with some lard cakes.

"I brought one for your father," she said with a smile.

"Thank you. Yesterday we had barely a bowl of porridge to eat between us," Theresa lamented. "We're receiving less and less food. Mother says we're fortunate, but the truth is she can barely lift herself from the bed she's so weak."

"Well, child, it's the same for all of us," the woman answered. "If it wasn't for Wilfred's love of books, we'd be eating our fingernails by now."

Theresa took a cake and nibbled it delicately, as though she didn't want to cause it pain. Then she took a bigger bite, savoring the sweetness of the honey and cinnamon. She breathed in its aroma deeply, trying to trap it inside her, and she slid her tongue into the corners of her mouth so as not to waste even the tiniest crumb. Then she put the remaining piece in her skirt pocket to take to her stepmother. Part of her felt ashamed to enjoy such a delicious morsel while her father lay unconscious on the table, but her accumulated hunger got the better of her conscience and she succumbed to the comforting taste of warm lard. Suddenly, the sound of coughing distracted her from her indulgence.

Theresa's father was coming round. She ran to his side to stop him from sitting up, but Gorgias would not listen to reason. As he moved, he grunted and winced with pain. After he managed to sit up, he briefly rested before opening his bag. With his healthy arm, he nervously rummaged through his writing instruments. Cursing, he kept looking around as though something was missing. His irritation growing, he tipped the contents of the bag onto the floor. Quills and styluses scattered across the pavement.

"Who took it? Where is it?" he cried.

"Where is what?" Korne asked.

Gorgias stared at him with a wild look, but he bit his tongue and turned his head. He rifled through the instruments again and then turned the bag on its head. When he was sure nothing was left in it, he walked over to a nearby chair, slumping into it. Closing his eyes, he whispered a prayer for his soul.

2

By early afternoon, the boys' voices brought Gorgias back to the land of the living after spending all morning in a dreamlike state. He had remained lying down, his head to one side and his gaze absent, oblivious to Korne's suggestions and Theresa's gestures of affection. But gradually awareness crept back into his face, and after a few moments of confusion he lifted his head to call for Korne. The parchment-maker seemed pleased to see Gorgias's health improving, but when Gorgias asked him about his assailant, Korne's countenance changed, and he declared he could not remember anything.

"When we went to help you, whoever it was had already fled."

Gorgias screwed up his face and spluttered a curse as he grimaced with pain. Then he stood and began pacing around the workshop like a tormented animal. As he walked up and down, he tried to recall his attacker's face, but his efforts were in vain. The darkness and the suddenness of the attack had masked the identity of the assailant. He was weak and confused, so he asked Korne to allow one of his sons to accompany him to the scriptorium.

Once Gorgias left, the workshop gradually resumed its usual bustle. The younger workers spread earth over the blood on the ground and cleaned the table, while the craftsmen complained about the mess that had been created. Theresa said a brief prayer for her father's recovery before diligently returning to her daily tasks. First, she cleaned and picked up the rubbish from the day before. Then she separated the more damaged pieces of leather and placed them in the scrap barrel, where they would rot. Unfortunately, the keg was overflowing. She had to decant its contents into maceration jars so that once the leather had been soaked, mashed, and boiled, they could make the glue that the master craftsmen used as an adhesive. When she had finished, she covered herself with a sack to keep the rain off and made for the outdoor pools in the dilapidated inner courtyard.

Theresa examined the quadrangular pools closely. Seven pools were distributed in a disorderly fashion around the central well so that the flayed skins could be easily transferred between them after the usual process of cutting, shaving, and scraping. The young woman observed the whitish skins floating on the water like scrawny corpses. She hated the penetrating acid stench that came from the defleshed pelts.

On one occasion, when she had had a severe chill, she asked Korne to relieve her for a few days because the dampness and causticity of the pools were aggravating her lungs, but all she received was a cuff around the head and a scornful guffaw. She never complained again. When Korne ordered her to turn over the sticky, wrinkled skins, she hiked up her skirt, and—holding her breath—stepped into the pools.

She was still looking over the pools when someone came up behind her.

"They still repulse you? Or perhaps you think it's not a task a parchment-maker's nose should have to endure?"

Theresa turned to find Korne smiling sardonically. The rain ran down his grotesque face and over his bare, exposed gums. He stank of incense, which he used to mask his usual rancid stench.

She would have happily told Korne the nature of her thoughts, but remembering the past, she bit her tongue and bowed her head. After so much sacrifice, she was not about to give in to provocation. If he was trying to find an excuse to reproach her, he would have to try a lot harder.

"No matter," continued the parchment-maker. "I must admit, I feel sorry for you: Your father has been hurt . . . you have had a fright . . . you're nervous, of course. Evidently it is not the right time to undertake such an important test. So in consideration of your father, I am prepared to postpone the examination for a sensible length of time."

Theresa breathed a sigh of relief. It was true that she still had the image of her blood-soaked father in her head. Her hands trembled, and though she felt strong enough, a postponement would give her the chance to calm down.

"I'm grateful for your offer, but I don't wish to disrupt preparations. However, I would welcome a few days to rest," she admitted.

"A few days? Oh, no!" he said with a smile. "Postponing the trial would mean waiting until next year. It's the rules, you see. But in your state . . . look at you: trembling, frightened . . . I have no doubt that postponing it is the right thing to do."

Theresa feared that Korne was right. Candidates who withdrew from the examination could not reapply for admission until a full year later. However, for a moment she had thought that given the circumstances the parchment-maker would make an exception.

"So?" Korne pressed.

Theresa was unable to respond. Her hands were sweating and her heart thumped in her chest. Korne's offer was not unreasonable, but nobody could foresee what would happen in twelve months. However, if she attempted the test and failed, she would never again be allowed to retake it. Or at least, not while Korne was head of the parchment-makers, for he would use her failure as proof of what he had so frequently proclaimed: that women and animals are merely there to bear children and transport loads.

As Korne waited for her response, he tapped his fingers on a barrel. Theresa considered withdrawing, but at the last moment she resolved to show Korne that she was better qualified than any of his sons to be a parchment-maker. And what's more: If she really wanted to become a master parchment-maker, she must get used to dealing with problems as they arose. And if for any reason she did not pass the test, perhaps in a few years' time, she would be able to attempt it again. After all, she told herself, Korne was old, and by then he might have died or fallen ill. So she lifted her head, and with determination in her voice, she informed him that she would take the examination that morning and accept the consequences. The parchment-maker looked unperturbed.

"Very well. If that is what you wish, let the show begin."

Theresa nodded and turned to head back into the workshop. As she was about to go through the entrance, the parchment-maker called out:

"May I ask where you are going?" he said with nostrils flaring like a horse's.

Theresa looked at him, perplexed. She was going to her workbench to check the equipment she would use in the test. "I thought I would sharpen the knives before the count arrived, prepare the—"

"The count? What has the count got to do with this?" he interrupted, feigning surprise.

Theresa lost the will to speak. Her father had assured her that Wilfred would be present.

"Ah, yes!" Korne continued with an affected grimace. "Gorgias said something about that. But yesterday, when I visited the count, he was so busy I judged that we should not disturb him for such a trivial thing. I presumed, and I think rightly, that if you are capable of coping with any turn of events, the count's absence from your examination should not be an impediment. Or should it?"

Theresa then understood that Korne had not assisted her father out of kindness, nor had he suggested postponing the examination out of consideration of her circumstances. He had helped Gorgias knowing that the fate of the workshop, and therefore his own, was bound to the scriptorium's activity. What a fool she had been! To think that for a few moments she had believed he had good intentions. Now she was at the mercy of this moron, and all her skills would be as much use as a pile of sodden firewood. The young woman bowed her head and prepared to accept the inevitable, but just as she had lost all hope, an idea lit up her face.

"It's curious," she said confidently. "My father not only assured me that Wilfred would witness the examination, but also that, aware of my progress, he wanted to keep my first parchment for himself. A parchment that—as you know—I must mark with my seal," she pointed out. She prayed that Korne would swallow her lie. If he did, perhaps she would have a chance.

The parchment-maker's stupid smile immediately disappeared from his face. Ultimately, he did not know whether what she was saying was true, but if they were Wilfred's wishes, he could hardly risk going against them. In any event, he could not care less what the count said or thought, because the girl would not pass the test. Not, at least, while he was master of the parchment-makers.

Theresa was still waiting to hear whether she would be allowed to take the test when Korne summoned the rest of the workers. Laborers and craftsmen immediately stopped their work filling the courtyard and turning it into a sort of arena. The youngest workers nabbed the front spots, spreading out around the yard. One boy shoved another lad, who fell into a pool, making the crowd cheer with approval. The craftsmen made themselves comfortable in the corners out of the rain, but the laborers were unfazed by a little water. One of them came out with a basket of apples to share with those who were waiting impatiently as if for the beginning of the show. It seemed like everyone except Theresa knew what was about to happen. Korne clapped his hands and addressed the improvised audience.

"As you all know, young Theresa has applied for admission to the guild." There was a roar of laughter.

"The lass," he said, pointing at her as he clutched his groin, "thinks she is cleverer than you, cleverer than my sons, and cleverer than me. This woman! A woman who shits her skirt and hides under a blanket when she hears a dog bark! But she has some courage, I'll give her that. Ha! The audacity to ask for a job that by its very nature is for men."

The laborers laughed in unison. One joker threw an apple core, which flew across the yard and hit Theresa in the face. Another flailed about, imitating a girl running scared, and the rest applauded until Korne interrupted the jesting to continue his tirade.

"Women doing men's work . . . can someone explain to me how a woman could work here and also tend to her husband? Who would cook and clean for him? Who would take care of his children? Or perhaps she would bring her brood of little girls here to join the guild, too?"

Laughter rippled around the yard again.

"And when summer comes and the heat arrives, when sweat soaks her body and her smock presses tight against her breasts, will she expect us to look elsewhere and repress our desires—or perhaps she will offer us her fruits as a reward for our efforts?"

The crowd continued laughing, shoving each other and winking as they applauded Korne's witticisms.

At that moment, Theresa stepped forward. Until then she had kept quiet, but she was not going to put up with any more jeering. "If I have a husband one day, how I look after him will be my business. And as for my breasts," she said, "given the attention you pay them, I will be only too pleased to inform your wives of your lecherous desires so they can make up for the lack that you so clearly suffer from. And now, if you don't mind, I would like to start the test."

Korne reddened with rage. He had not expected such a feisty reaction, let alone the derisive snickers her words provoked among the youngsters—snickers that he imagined were aimed at him. The parchment-maker went over to the basket of apples and picked out the most damaged one. Then he turned and walked over to Theresa. Planting himself a few inches from her, he slowly bit into the apple. After slobbering all over the fruit, he held it out in front of the girl's lips.

"Want some?"

He smiled at Theresa's disgust. Looking at the fruit again, he saw a worm squirming in its rotten center. Without batting an eye, he bit through the core and the worm, casting the rest of the apple into one of the pools. As he chewed, he gathered his unkempt hair into a grotesque ponytail. Then he went over to the pool where he had discarded the apple.

"Here you have your test," he said, and he opened the lattice-work lid that protected the pool. "Make ready the skin and you will earn the qualification you so crave."

Theresa's lips tightened. Scraping and preparing the skins was not a task befitting a craftsman, but if that was what Korne wanted, she would not disappoint him. She walked over to the edge of the pool and observed the layer of blood and fat floating on its surface. Taking a spade, she pushed the remains left by the caustics to one side and fished around for the skin that she would work on. But after several attempts, she still could not find one. She turned with a look of puzzlement on her face, demanding an explanation.

"It's in there," Korne indicated toward the deepest pool.

Theresa walked over to the pool that received the skins just as they had been torn from the animals. Carefully, she took off her boots. Then she gathered up her skirt and stepped into the water, holding her breath.

Scraps of skin and clots of blood floated in the bath, intermingling with the filth of the maceration pool. Under the attentive gaze of the crowd, she lowered herself until the liquid reached her stomach. The cold made her groan.

She waited a moment before taking another deep breath and letting herself sink into the depths of the pool. For a blink of an eye she disappeared underwater, but she quickly emerged with her head veiled in grease. Spitting, she wiped the filth from her face. Then she plunged further into the center of the bath, pushing away the floating detritus. The lime stung her skin under her clothes and the ice numbed her bones. Under her bare feet she could feel a bed of slime. And she groped the surface like a blind woman looking for a rail to cling to. But she kept going, feeling her way forward as the water lapped against her chin.

Suddenly she bumped into something under the water, and her heart missed a beat. When she managed to calm herself down, she felt the object with her foot to try to identify it. For a moment she thought about giving up, but she remembered her father and everyone who had believed in her. She filled her lungs with air and submerged herself into the water. The cold made her temples throb as her hands touched the object. Its sticky feel made her retch, but she suppressed her revulsion and continued to run her hands over the thing until she found a string of beads that felt like little shingles. She felt along the line and after a moment of uncertainty, she realized with horror she was grasping a row of teeth. She almost opened her eyes in fright and would have been blinded forever by the lime, but she kept control of herself. She let go of the jawbone and went up for air, gasping, her face flushed red as the Devil's. As she coughed and spluttered, vomiting water, the remains of a putrid and deformed cow's head bobbed up in front of her.

The laborers immediately came to the edge of the pool to taunt the young woman. One offered her his hand, but as Theresa grasped it, he let go, making her fall back into the water. At that moment, the parchment-maker's wife appeared in the courtyard. She had witnessed the scene and come with dry clothes. The woman pushed past the laborers and pulled Theresa—who was quivering like a puppy—out of the pool. She covered her with a blanket and took her into her home, but as they were about to go through the door they heard Korne say, "She can get changed and get back to work."

When Theresa returned to the workshop, she found the wrinkled remains of the cowhide on her bench. She spread it out with the help of a wooden trowel and then removed the excess water. After examining the skin, she deduced that the animal must have been flayed that very week, since the lime had barely begun to dislodge the hair, and scraps of meat and fat were stuck to the inside. The cow must have been devoured by wolves, because the skin had many bite marks. Aside from that, there were signs of the abscesses and blemishes typical of older beasts. She wouldn't even throw that skin to the rats, she thought.

"You want to be a parchment-maker, do you not? Well, there's your test," Korne smirked from the doorway. "Prepare the parchment that you are so keen for Wilfred to see."

Though she knew what he asked was impossible, Theresa did not protest. Rendering and cleaning an animal skin required several days of work with time to rest in between so the caustics and washing could take effect. Still, she was not about to give up. With a stiff brush, she scrubbed the skin to remove the remnants of meat that the worms had not managed to devour. When she finished with the flesh side of the skin, she turned her attention to the hair side. She brushed and scraped the hair energetically. Then she wrung out the leather and spread it over the bench to better see the areas that still had hair. Finally, she looked around for the box that contained the broom bundle used to apply the acid—but she was surprised to find it had disappeared.

Korne observed the whole process, a smile appearing on his lips from time to time. Occasionally he would turn away, as though he had more important things to do, but he would soon return to check the young woman's progress. Theresa did her best to ignore him. She assumed that the broom's disappearance was no coincidence, so she did not bother searching for it. Instead she scooped up a trowelful of ash, mixed it with some dung that the mules had deposited at the entrance, and applied the resulting paste to the pores in the skin. Then, with the help of a blunt, curved knife, she continued to work on the thick hair until she achieved the desired result.

Then she stretched the skin over a frame to form a gigantic tambourine—a delicate step, for she ran the risk of tearing the leather at its most damaged points. She skillfully positioned some pebbles around the skin and wrapped them in pinches of the leather to form little sacks resembling thick teats, which she fastened with some cord. Then she attached the leather to the frame and stretched it using the cords coming from the teats. When she saw that the tears on the skin were holding, she sighed with relief. Now all she had to do was dry the skin by the fire and wait for it to tighten before scraping it. She moved the frame over to the fire blazing in the center of the workshop. Not only was it the warmest part of the room, it was also the brightest, so the benches where the most valuable codices were repaired were located there.

As she waited for the moisture to exude from the taut leather, she warmed herself by the fire and wondered where the skin had come from. Cattle had been in short supply for some time, and as far as she knew, only Wilfred had a few animals, so Korne had probably obtained it from one of his intendants. And judging by its condition, he had done so with the sole intention of making her life difficult.

The parchment-maker came over to the fire. He ran his finger over the skin, which was oozing moisture. He turned to Theresa with a look of indifference.

"I can see you are applying yourself. You may yet get something out of it," he said, pointing at the taut skin.

"I'm doing my best, sir," she responded.

"And this pig's ear is the best you can do?" Korne sneered as he drew his knife and waved it at the skin. "Have you seen these marks? The skin will break here."

Theresa knew that would not happen. She had checked the tears and tightened the cords in a way that would prevent breakage.

"That won't happen," she retorted.

Korne seemed barely able to contain his rage. Very slowly, he passed the point of his knife over the taut leather, like someone sliding a dagger over the throat of his victim. The blade scraped against the skin, roughening it ever so slightly. Theresa watched, aghast, as the blade's point stopped near a mark Korne had indicated earlier. With flashing eyes and his mouth opened enough to show his bare gums, Korne started to press the point into the surface.

"No!" Theresa implored.

At that moment, Korne sunk the knife into the skin, making it tear into a thousand pieces that flew over their heads and floated down like dead leaves onto the fire.

"Oh, dear!" Korne said. "It would seem that you did not calculate the required tension for the skin, which regrettably reverts you to your miserable life as an apprentice."

Theresa clenched her fists, her face contorting with anger. She had endured cold and humiliation. She had tended to that unusable skin and made it into something acceptable. She had put her heart and soul into preparing for the test. And now, for the sole reason that she was a woman, Korne was condemning her forever.

She was seething as he grabbed her arm and put his lips to her ear. "You could always earn a living massaging some drunk's skin," he sniggered.

Theresa could not take any more. She jerked her arm away and was about to leave the workshop, but the parchment-maker stopped her. "No harlot disrespects me like that," he muttered, dealing her a blow to the cheek.

Theresa tried to defend herself, but Korne pushed her again and she slipped, falling against the frame she had been working on. The structure wobbled heavily, swaying for few prolonged moments before finally collapsing onto the fire with a great crash. On impact, a swarm of embers flew out into the workshop, turning it into a furnace. Sparks flared and landed on the nearest benches. A few of the cinders set fire to the codices, and in the blink of an eye, the flames had reached the shelving.

Before Korne could react, a dimwitted laborer rushed to open all the windows. Fueled by the draft, the flames licked at the timber and wattle roofing, making the dead leaves catch fire. Korne had just enough time to snatch a bundle of parchment away before a burning branch fell, close to where Theresa stood in a daze.

Ignoring her, Korne ordered the laborers to quickly grab anything of value they could find and flee the building. They obeyed, bumping into each other as they gathered objects and bolted outside. One of them started to drag Theresa away from the flames, but when he saw that she was regaining her senses, he left her to her own fate.

When Theresa came round, she thought she was on the threshold of Hell. She looked around in desperation to see the flames devouring everything in their path and threatening to surround her. A creaking above made her look at the ceiling. For a moment she thought the roof would fall in, but then she could see that the flames were not spreading across the wattle, probably because of the damp and the accumulated snow.

She scanned the room and saw that her only hope of escape was to reach the inner courtyard, for the way out to the street seemed impassable. On her left she discovered a group of codices that had been stored under a ledge. Without hesitation, she wrapped herself in her dress, still damp from the pool, and gathered up as many codices as she could carry. Then she ran out into the courtyard, where she noticed a chestnut tree climbing up the easternmost corner to the rooftop that adjoined the cathedral's eaves. She took off her wet garment and used it as a sack for the codices, but as she was about to climb the vine, a cry from inside made her stop.

Theresa dropped the codices and ran toward the workshop. As she entered the room, smoke blinded her. She advanced toward the fire, unable to breathe with the heat burning her insides. Huddled behind a wall of fire, she discovered Korne's wife, crying out in desperation. The fire must have caught her by surprise while she was up in the attic and for some reason prevented her escape. As she approached, the woman was squealing like a hog about to be slaughtered, and suddenly Theresa noticed that the woman's clothes were already on fire.

Theresa moved toward her, but a wall of fire between them kept her from getting close. Above the fireplace the roof creaked. The branches of the latticework were beginning to give way under the thick layer of snow piled on top of it. Looking around, Theresa found a long spade lying on the ground. She picked it up and thrust it with all her might into the branches above that were starting to break. The roof creaked again, but she kept jabbing at it, until suddenly a great cracking sound made her stop. The latticework was on the verge of collapse. With the smoke asphyxiating her, she needed air. With her remaining strength she rammed the spade into the ceiling as hard as she could.

A flood of snow suddenly burst through the hole that had opened up to the roof. When the avalanche subsided, the flames between her and Korne's wife were extinguished.

"Your hand! For God's sake, give me your hand!" Theresa cried.

The woman stopped screaming and opened her eyes. She stood, kissed Theresa's hand, and moving as quickly as the woman's thick legs would allow, they ran together toward the baths.

3

When Gorgias arrived at the scriptorium, he realized with horror that he had left his bag in the parchment-maker's workshop. He cursed his stupidity, but he was comforted by the fact that he had hid the parchment that he was working on in a secret compartment inside the bag. He was certain that the man who had attacked him knew the incalculable value of the parchment and had been after it. If he had not taken this extra precaution, his assailant would now have his hands on a document more valuable than even he probably knew. However, the assailant had stolen a draft from out of his bag that contained some of the most delicate passages, and it would cause Gorgias a significant delay.

He looked at his arm and saw blood had soaked through the bandage that Zeno had made. Using his healthy hand he undid the dressing and rested his wounded limb on a table. He tried to move his fingers, but they would hardly bend. The wound was still bleeding, so he tightened the stitches that kept the cut from opening, but the pain made him give up. He could feel his raw flesh palpitating in time with his racing heart. Worried, he asked a servant to call the physician again. While he waited he lay back in his chair and reflected on all that had happened.

The creaking of the door roused Gorgias from his thoughts. The same servant reappeared and asked for permission to enter. With him was the surgeon, visibly annoyed.

"Save me, Lord, from scholars," he grumbled. "They think themselves so learned, yet at the slightest discomfort they moan like old women at a wake." The physician brought a lamp over to Gorgias's wounded arm.

"I can hardly move my fingers and it won't stop bleeding," Gorgias said, showing him the cut.

The surgeon examined the limb with the same scrutiny a butcher might examine a chicken he was about to dismember. Its stitching had nearly come completely undone. "Dear God! What have you been doing? Writing out the Bible in Greek? You should be grateful if I don't have to amputate."

Gorgias did not answer. The physician rummaged around in his workbag. "Well, I'll be damned! I'm out of knotgrass. Do you have the powders I prescribed for you here?"

"I left them in the workshop. I'll send someone to collect them later."

"As you please, but I must warn you—your other wounds do not concern me, but this arm . . . If you don't look after it, in one week, it will not be fit to feed to the pigs. And if you lose the arm, you can bet that you will lose your life. Now I'm going to strengthen the stitching to stop the hemorrhage. It will hurt."

Gorgias grimaced, not just from the pain but also because he sensed the dire truth in what the physician said. "But how can a surface wound—"

"Whether you like it or not, that's how it is. It is not just king's evil and pestilence that kills people. In fact the cemeteries are stuffed with healthy people who croaked because of minor cuts and scrapes: a slight fever, some strange spasms . . . and farewell to them and their suffering. Perhaps you don't know Galen's methods, but I have seen enough people die to know who the likely candidates are months before they go to the grave."

Having finished the dressing, the little man gathered up his implements and put them untidily in his bag. Gorgias ordered the servant to leave the scriptorium and wait outside before he said to the physician, "One moment, please. I need you to do me a favor."

"If it's in my power . . ."

Gorgias made sure the servant was out of earshot.

"The thing is, I would rather the count did not hear about this. I mean, the severity of my injury. I'm working on a codex, a document that he has a special interest in, and no doubt he will be displeased if he learned that the job were to be delayed."

"Well, I don't see that you have any other option. You will not be able to hold a pen in that hand for at least three weeks. And that's if it doesn't worsen. Since it is the count who is paying my fee, you will agree that I should not lie to him."

"But I am not asking you to lie, just to keep quiet. As for your fee . . ."

Gorgias put his left hand in his shirt pocket and pulled out some coins.

"It is more than the count will pay you," he added.

The physician took the coins and examined them closely. His eyes flashed with greed. He kissed them and put them away among his belongings. Then, without a word, he walked off toward the exit.

At the door he stopped and turned toward Gorgias.

"Rest and allow the wound to heal. Health is lost at a gallop, but it returns at walking pace. If you see abscesses or cysts, send notice to me immediately."

"Don't worry, I will follow your advice. And now, if you don't mind, send the servant in."

The physician nodded and said good-bye with a wink. When the servant came into the scriptorium, Gorgias looked him up and down. He was a scrawny, beardless young man, with a dimwitted, ungainly look about him.

"I need you to run over to the parchment-makers' workshop and ask my daughter for the remedy that the physician prescribed for me. She will know what to do. But first, alert the count that I'm waiting for him in the scriptorium."

"But, sir, the count is still resting," he stammered.

"Then wake him!" Gorgias shouted. "Tell him it's urgent."

The servant drew back, nodding his head. When he left, he closed the door behind him, and Gorgias could hear his footsteps as he rushed away.

Gorgias looked around the scriptorium and saw that everything in the room was damp. The flames from the lamps barely lit the benches they rested on, giving the room a dreamlike appearance. Only a narrow window protected by solid bars provided some weak light for the gigantic wooden lectern, where there was a jumbled collection of codices, inkwells, pens and styluses, intermingling with awls, scrapers, and blotters. The room had another lectern and, in stark contrast, it was completely bare. On the north wall, a sturdy cabinet flanked by two lamps housed the most valuable codices, which had chains running through the rings on their spines to secure them to the wall. On the lower shelves, separate from the rest, there were psalters for communal use, beside both books of the Bible in Aramaic. On the rest of the shelves, dozens of unbound volumes stacked on top of missives, epistolaries, and cartularies of various kinds competed for space with the polyptychs and the censuses that recorded accounts and transactions.

He was still thinking about that morning's attack when the door slowly creaked open and the light of a torch blinded him. When the servant moved aside, a strange, squat figure stood silhouetted against the torchlight. After a moment, Gorgias heard a faltering voice from the doorway.

"Tell me, Gorgias—what is this emergency that ails us so?"

At that moment a low, sustained growl interrupted. Gorgias recognized one of Wilfred's dogs clenching its jaw and advancing toward him, with the other hound close behind. But they were retrained by harnesses that Gorgias saw tighten as they pulled along the familiar but strange contraption that screeched along on its crude wooden wheels. Hearing their master command them to stop, the dogs lay down and the cart came to a standstill.

Gorgias could see Wilfred's grotesque face cocked awkwardly to one side. The man let go of the reins and held his hands out to the dogs, who rushed over to lick them.

"Every day I find it harder to handle these devils," said Wilfred, his voice choked with emotion, "but the Lord knows that without them, I would live like a dry old olive tree."

Despite the years that had gone by, Gorgias was still shocked by the extraordinary appearance of the count. For as long as he'd known him, Wilfred had been a prisoner of that wheeled device—where he'd slept, ate, and emptied his bowels ever since both his legs were amputated as a boy.

Gorgias bowed in greeting.

"Dispense with the formalities and tell me—what has happened?"

The scribe looked from side to side. He had been so anxious to speak with the count, and now he did not know where to start. At that moment a dog moved and the contraption suddenly rolled along. One of the wheels was squeaking and Gorgias went down on his knees to examine it as he tried to find the right words.

"It's one of the rivets," Gorgias said. "It must have come out with all the jolting. The boards are misaligned and could come off. You would do well to take the chair to the carpenter."

"I hope you haven't woken me to examine my cart."

When Gorgias lifted his hand apologetically, Wilfred saw the bulky, bloody bandage wrapped around it.

"Good heavens! What have you done to your arm?"

"Oh, it's nothing! A small incident," he lied. "On the way to the workshops some poor wretch gave me a scratch or two. They fetched the physician and he insisted on dressing it, but you know these quacks, they're worried they won't get paid unless they wrap you in bandages."

"True, but tell me: Are you able to move your hand?"

"With some difficulty. But a little work will loosen it up."

"So what was the emergency?"

"Allow me to sit down. It's about the codex. It's not progressing as quickly as I would have hoped."

"Well, *aliquando bonus dormitat Deux*. It is not a question of going quickly, but of finishing on time. Tell me, what has caused the delay? You haven't told me anything about it," he said, trying to conceal his annoyance.

"To be honest I didn't wish to concern you. I thought I could make do with the pens I have, but I have sharpened them so much I can barely make the ink flow."

"I fail to understand. You have dozens of quills."

"Yes, but not of goose feather. And as you know, there are no geese left in Würzburg."

"Then continue with the ones that you have, I don't see the issue."

"The problem lies with the flow. The ink descends too rapidly, and this could cause leaks that would ruin the entire document. Remember that I am using unborn calf's vellum. The surface is so soft that any mistake handling the pen would have irreparable consequences."

"Then why don't you just use another type of parchment?"

"Not possible. At least, not for your purposes."

Wilfred shifted in his seat. "So what do you propose?"

"My idea is to thicken the ink. Using the right binding agent, I could ensure that it flows more slowly, while maintaining the required glide. I could do it in a couple of weeks, I think."

"Do what you must, but if you value your head, make sure the codex is ready by the agreed day."

"I have already begun the preparations, don't worry."

"Very well. And since I'm here, I would like to take a look at the parchment. If you would be so kind as to bring it to me."

Gorgias clenched his teeth. He did not want to explain that he faced a delay because the attacker had stolen a valuable copy and the original was tucked away in the bag that he had left behind in the workshop.

"I'm afraid that won't be possible."

"Excuse me? What do you mean it's not possible?"

"I don't have it here. I left it in Korne's workshop."

"And what in hell's name is it doing there, at the risk that anyone could discover it?" roared the count. The dogs fidgeted restlessly.

"I'm sorry, Father. I know I should have consulted you, but late last night I noticed that one of the pages was starting to peel. I don't know the cause, but when it happens it is vital that the problem is dealt with immediately. I needed an acid that Korne uses, and knowing how distrustful he is, I thought that it would be best to take the codex there, rather than ask him for the acid. At any rate, aside from Theresa, no one at the workshop can read, and one more parchment among the hundreds they have there would not attract anyone's attention."

"I don't know . . . that all seems reasonable, but I don't understand why you are here instead of at the workshop applying that acid. Finish what you have to do and bring the document back to the scriptorium. And for God's sake, do not call me *Father*! I haven't worn a habit for years!"

"As you wish. I will leave as soon as I have tidied the lectern and gathered my blades. However, there was one more thing."

"Yes?"

"The time that I will need to prepare the new ink . . ."

"Yes?"

"If Your Grace will allow it, I would like to be excused from coming to the scriptorium. At home I have all the required tools, and there I could carry out tests in peace and quiet. I also need to find certain ingredients in the forest, so I will have to stay outside the city walls overnight."

"In that case, I will tell a soldier to escort you. If you were attacked just this morning inside the shelter of the walls, just imagine what might happen to you on the other side."

"I don't think that will be necessary. I know the area well, and Theresa can accompany me."

"Ha!" bellowed Wilfred. "You still look at Theresa with a first-time father's eyes, but that young woman attracts men as if they were in heat. If bandits get a whiff of her you won't have time to cross yourselves. You worry about the codex, and I will take care of you. The soldier will be at your house this afternoon."

Gorgias decided not to persist. He had planned to spend the next two days looking for the man who had attacked him, but with the soldier at his heels it would be too difficult. Still, he decided to end the conversation to avoid alarming Wilfred any further.

Gathering his belongings, he changed the subject. "How long do you think the king will take?" asked Gorgias.

"Charlemagne? I don't know. A month. Maybe two. The last letter announced that a convoy with supplies was to set off immediately"

"But the passes are blocked."

"Indeed. But sooner or later they will arrive. The pantries will be completely empty before long."

Gorgias nodded. Rations were becoming meager, and soon there would be nothing left.

"Very well. If there is nothing else," added Wilfred. The count took his reins, tightening the harnesses on the dogs. He cracked his whip, and the beasts labored to turn the heavy contraption around.

He was about to leave the scriptorium when a servant burst into the room, screaming as though he had seen the Devil himself:

"The *factoriae*! For the love of God! Fire is devouring them!"

4

When Gorgias saw what was left of the workshop, he prayed to God that Theresa wouldn't be found under the wreckage. The flames had consumed the exterior walls, leading to the collapse of the roof, which in turn only fueled the fire, turning the place into a gigantic pyre.

Onlookers arrived in throngs to watch the spectacle, while the bolder ones toiled to assist the wounded, rescue anything of use, and smother the embers. After a few moments of confusion, Gorgias recognized Korne, lying on some wooden boards. He looked ragged, his clothes blackened and a wild look in his face.

Gorgias ran over to him. "Thank God I've found you. Have you seen Theresa?"

The parchment-maker recoiled as though Gorgias had spoken of the Devil. Then he jumped up and lunged for Gorgias's throat.

"That dammed daughter of yours! I hope she burns to the last bone!"

Gorgias threw Korne off just as two neighbors attempted to separate them. The men apologized for Korne's behavior, but Gorgias suspected his words stemmed from more than some common fit of anger. He thanked them for their intervention and left to continue his search.

After walking around the perimeter of the site, he observed that the fire had not only devastated the workshops and Korne's home, but also the storerooms and adjoining stables. Fortunately, there were no animals in the stables, and as far as he knew the storerooms contained no grain, so the losses would be limited to the value of the buildings. Both buildings would surely be condemned, for the fire had started to vent its rage on their roofs.

He noticed that the wall between the courtyard and the workshops was still standing, and he remembered that Korne, fed up with so many thefts, had ordered the primitive palisade to be replaced with a stone wall. Thanks to that decision, it appeared that the area between the wall and the pools had been saved from the flames.

A trembling hand touched Gorgias on the shoulder. It was Bertharda.

"What a tragedy. Such a great tragedy!" she said, tears in her eyes.

"Bertharda, for the love of God, have you seen my daughter?" he asked with desperation in his voice.

"She saved my life. Do you hear me? She saved me."

"Yes, yes, I hear you. But where is she? Is she hurt?"

"I told her not to go in. To forget the books. But she ignored me."

"For goodness' sake, Bertharda, tell me where my daughter is," Gorgias insisted, shaking the woman by the shoulders.

The woman stared at him but it was as if her red eyes were focused on another world.

"We came out of the workshop, escaping the flames," she explained. "In the courtyard she helped me scale the wall. She helped me until she could see I was safe, and then she said she had to go back for the codices. I shouted at her not to go, to climb the wall with me, but you know how headstrong she is," she sobbed. "She went back into the workshop among those terrible flames and then suddenly there was a crashing sound and the roof fell in. Do you hear me? She saved me and then everything collapsed."

Gorgias turned in horror and ran headlong into the wreckage. The embers sizzled and crackled as the grayish smoke spread slowly into the sky like a sign announcing the macabre event.

If he had been thinking clearly, he would have waited for the fire to die out, but he could not wait another second. He dodged the rafters that were in his way and went deeper into the chaos of crossbeams, stanchions, and buttresses, ignoring the flames that licked his limbs. His eyes were stinging and the heat burned his lungs. He could barely see his own hands in the cloud of ash and embers floating in the air, but it did not stop him. Striding on, he shoved aside uprights, corbels, and frames, screaming Theresa's name over and over.

Suddenly, as he was trying to find his bearings in the smoke, he heard a cry for help behind him. He turned and ran across the embers, but as he reached some earthenware jars he saw the cry for help came from Johan Shortfoot, son of Hans the tanner. The youngster was just eleven years of age and his torso was severely burned. Gorgias cursed his bad luck, but quickly bent over the boy only to see that he was trapped under a crossbeam.

A quick glance was enough to understand that if he did not help him at once he would inevitably die, so he gathered his strength and pulled on the boards that pinned him to the ground. But as fate would have it, the beam would not budge. He tore a piece from the bandage on his arm and used it to wipe the sweat from the boy's face.

"Johan. Listen to me. I'm going to need help to get you out of here. My arm is wounded and I cannot move these boards alone. I'll tell you what we're going to do. Can you count?"

"Yes, sir. I can count to ten," he said with pride.

"Well, that's marvelous. Now I want you to breathe through this bandage, and every five breaths, shout your name as loud as you can. Understood?"

"Yes, sir."

"Good. So, I will go to seek help, and when I return, I'll bring you a slice of cake and a good apple. Do you like apples?"

"No, please. Don't leave me," he sobbed.

"I'm not going to leave you, Johan. I'll be back with help."

"Don't go, sir, I beg you!" he said, grasping Gorgias's hand.

Gorgias looked at the boy and cursed. He knew that even if he managed to find help, the youngster would not last that long. It was already impossible to breathe in that place. Burned or asphyxiated, one way or the other Johan would die. Even so, seeking help was surely all he could do for him.

He crouched down and again grabbed the beam with both hands, bending his legs and tensing his arms until his back creaked, but he continued to pull as if his own life depended on it. He could feel his injured arm tearing and the stitches popping out, his skin and tendons cleaved open, but he persisted with excruciating effort.

"Come on, you son of a bitch, move!" he cried.

Suddenly there was a cracking noise and the beam lifted, creating a space the width of a few fingers. Gorgias breathed in a mouthful of smoke, heaved once more and the beam moved again, now there was a palm's width of space between the boy and the beam.

"Now, Johan! Get out of there!"

The youngster rolled to one side, just as Gorgias's strength left him and the beam went crashing to the floor. Puffing with exertion, he lifted the enfeebled boy onto his shoulders and quickly fled the inferno.

In the courtyard, where neighbors tended to the injured, Gorgias saw Zeno helping a man with blister-covered legs. The physician brandished a lancet that he used to burst the blisters at great speed before squashing them like grapes. He was assisted by a helper who, with panic in his eyes, was applying oil-based ointments with questionable skill.

Gorgias headed toward him with Johan on his back. As he reached Zeno, he lay the boy down on the ground and asked the physician to help.

But with one quick glance, Zeno turned toward Gorgias and shook his head. "Nothing to be done," he said with resolve.

Gorgias took Zeno by the arm and pulled him away from the boy. "You could at least make sure he can't hear," he whispered. "Tend to him at any rate, and let God decide his fate."

Zeno gave him a scornful smile. "You should look after yourself," he said, pointing at his blood-soaked arm. "Let me have a look."

"First the boy."

Zeno grimaced and squatted beside the youngster. He called over a helper and snatched the ointment from his hands.

"Pig fat—the best thing for burns," he announced as he smeared the substance on Johan's wounds. "The count will not be pleased if it is wasted on someone with no hope of recovery."

Gorgias did not respond. All he could think about was finding Theresa. "Are there more wounded?" he asked.

"Of course. The most seriously injured have been taken to Saint Damian's," the surgeon answered without lifting his gaze.

Gorgias crouched beside Johan and stroked his brow. The boy responded with a hint of a smile. "Pay no heed to this meatcutter," he said. "You will get better, you'll see." And without giving him time to respond, he stood and set off toward the basilica in search of his daughter.

Despite its squat appearance, Saint Damian's Church was a solid, sturdy structure. It had been built from good masonry stone and Charlemagne himself had expressed his satisfaction when he learned that a building consecrated to God had been erected on foundations as robust as the faith of its subjects. Before going in, Gorgias crossed himself and prayed to God that Theresa was safe.

As he walked through the door, he was struck by an unbearable stench of burned flesh. Without stopping he took one of the torches secured to the walls and continued toward the transept, using the torch to illuminate the little chapels that flanked the lateral naves. When he reached the presbytery, he noticed a row of straw sacks arranged behind the altar for the injured to lie on.

Gorgias promptly recognized Hahn, a bright boy who would hang about the workshop waiting for someone to give him an odd job. Now his legs were scorched and he was wailing bitterly. Beside him lay a man who Gorgias was unable to identify since burns had transformed his face into a dark scab. By the central apse he spotted Nicodemus, one of Korne's craftsmen, confessing his sins. Beyond the transept there was a stout man, his head in bandages with only his ears showing, and behind him, the prostrate figure of a naked boy. Gorgias noted that it was Caelius, youngest son of the master parchment-maker. The youngster's body was lying there with half-open, unseeing eyes, his neck twisted round. He had undoubtedly died in terrible agony.

Nobody there was able to tell him the whereabouts of his daughter.

Gorgias went down on his knees and prayed to God for Theresa's soul. As he prepared to continue his search, he felt his strength leave his body. A shiver ran through his insides, shaking him until his vision blurred. He tried to hold himself up against a column, but blackness overcame him. Swaying from side to side, he fell to the ground, unconscious.

By midmorning, pealing bells roused Gorgias from his slumber. Slowly the hazy veil that had clouded his vision dissipated, until vague forms took clear shape again, as if they were being rinsed with clean water. He soon recognized his wife, Rutgarda, with a hint of a smile on her face that did little to disguise the fact she had been weeping. Farther back he could see Zeno, busy with some vials of tincture. Suddenly he felt a pain so intense that he feared they had cut off his arm, but when he lifted it, he saw that once again it had been carefully bandaged. Rutgarda sat him up, positioning a large cushion behind his back. Then Gorgias realized he was still in Saint Damian's, resting against the wall of one of the little chapels.

"And Theresa? Has she turned up?" he managed to ask.

Rutgarda looked at him with sadness in her eyes. Tears welled up as she hid her face in her arms.

"What has happened?" he cried. "For God's sake, where is my daughter? Where is Theresa?"

Gorgias looked around, but there was no response. Then, just a few steps away, he noticed a lifeless body, covered by a cloth.

"Zeno found her in the workshop, huddled under a wall," Rutgarda sobbed.

"No! No! God almighty! It cannot be."

Gorgias clambered to his feet and ran to where the body lay. The shroud that covered it was marked with a grotesque white cross, a charred limb protruding from one end. Gorgias pulled back the cloth and his pupils dilated in horror. Flames had devoured her body, turning it into an unrecognizable mass of flesh and scorched skin. He did not want to believe his eyes, but his hopes were shattered when he recognized the remains of his daughter's blue dress, the one she had adored so much.

By early afternoon, folks started gathering outside of the locked doors of Saint Damian's Church for the funerals. Children were laughing and chattering, playing at dodging the jostling grownups, while the more irreverent ones mocked the women by imitating their weeping. A group of old women wrapped in dark fur-lined cloaks congregated around Brynhildr, a widow purported to run a brothel who tended to know everything that happened in the city. She had piqued the interest of the other women by suggesting that it was the scribe's daughter who had caused the fire and that it was not only the victims' lives that the flames had claimed but also, perhaps most regrettably, some provisions that Korne had kept hidden in his storerooms.

People were forming rings to discuss the number of wounded, dramatize the severity of their burns, and speculate on the cause of the fire. Now and then a woman would run from one place to another with a smile on her face, eager to share the latest bit of idle gossip. However, despite all the excitement, the rain was growing worse and there were not enough places in the street to take shelter. So the arrival of Wilfred and his team of dogs was welcomed with relief.

As soon as the gate opened, the crowd rushed in to grab the best spots. As usual, the men positioned themselves nearest the altar, leaving the women and children at the back. The front row, reserved for the parents of the deceased, was occupied by the parchment-maker and his wife. Their two children who had been injured in the fire rested on sacks of straw beside them. The remains of the youngest, Caelius, lay wrapped in a linen burial cloth next to Theresa's body. The dead lay on a table in front of the main altar. Gorgias and Rutgarda had declined Wilfred's invitation to sit up front, instead sitting farther back to avoid any confrontation with Korne.

The count waited in the doorway for the last of the parishioners to take their places. When the murmuring subsided, he cracked his whip and made the dogs pull him down a side nave to the transept. There, two tonsured acolytes helped him position himself behind the altar, covered the dogs' heads with leather hoods, then freed the count from the belts that kept him secured to his wooden contraption. The subdeacon then removed the cope that Wilfred was wearing and replaced it with a *tunica albata*, which he tightened with a *cingulum*. Over it he placed an embroidered *indumentum* with a string of silver bells hanging from its lower edging, and finally he crowned him with an impressive damask headdress. Once the count was appropriately dressed, the ostiarius washed his hands in a lavabo and placed a modest funerary chalice beside the chrismatories that contained the holy anointing oils. Two candelabras shed their weak light on the shrouds of the deceased.

A chubby cleric with an awkward gait approached the altar equipped with a psaltery. He calmly opened the volume. After wetting his index finger, he began the service, reciting the fourteen verses required by the Rule of Saint Benedict. He then intoned four psalms with antiphons, and chanted another eight, before offering a litany and the vigil of the dead. Then Wilfred took the floor, his mere presence ended the first murmurings. The count scrutinized the congregation as though he were looking for the perpetrator of the tragedy. It had been two years since he had worn the vestments of a priest.

"Be grateful to God that in His boundless mercy He has taken pity on us today," he decreed. "Accustomed to living in complacency, to abandoning yourselves to the pleasures of your desires, you forget with despicable ease the reason why you were put on this earth. Your pious appearances, your prayers and offerings, your clouded understanding. These things make you believe that what you possess is the result of your own efforts. You insist on desiring women who are not your own. You envy others' good fortune. And you allow your ears to be pulled from your head if it means obtaining the wealth that you so covet. You think that life is a banquet that you have been invited to, a feast in which to savor the finest meats and liqueurs. But only a selfish brain, a weak soul oozing ignorance, is capable of forgetting that nobody but the Holy Father is the owner of our lives. And just as a father thrashes his children when they disobey—and just as a bailiff cuts the tongue from a liar or severs the limbs of a poacher—God corrects those who forget His commandments with the most terrible of punishments."

The church was filled with murmuring.

"Hunger calls at our door," he continued. "It seeps into our homes and devours our children. The rain floods our crops. Disease decimates our livestock. And still you complain? God sends us signs, and you lament His ways? Pray! Pray until your souls cough up the phlegm of your greed and hatred. Pray for the glory of the Lord. He has taken lives today, including Caelius and Theresa, freeing them from the sinful world that you have built. Now that their souls have left the corruption of the flesh, you tear your hair out and cry like women. Heed His warnings, I say, for they will not be the last. God is showing you the way. Forget your hardships and fear Him, for you will not find the feast that you crave in this world. Pray! Beg for forgiveness, and perhaps one day you will sit at His table, for those who renounce the Lord will be consumed in the abyss of damnation, until the end of time."

Wilfred went silent. Over the years he had come to understand that, whatever the cause, the best argument was eternal damnation. Nonetheless, Korne frowned and stepped forward.

"If you will allow me," he said, raising his voice. "Since my conversion, I have always thought myself a good Christian: I pray when I rise in the morning. I fast every Friday, and I follow the Lord's commandments." He looked around at those gathered as if seeking their approval. "Today God has taken my son Caelius: a healthy and robust boy, a good child. I accept the ways of the Lord, and I pray to Him for my son's soul. I also pray for my own, for my family's, and for those of almost everyone present." He swallowed and turned to Gorgias. "But the culprit of this tragedy does not deserve a single prayer to ease her punishment. That girl should never have set foot in my workshop. If God uses death to teach us, perhaps we should use His teachings. And if it is God that judges the dead, let us be the ones to judge the living."

The church filled with shouts and cries: "*Nihil est tam volucre quam maledictum—nihil facilius emiltitur, nihil citius excipitur, nihil latius dissipatur.*"

Wilfred interjected at the top of his voice. "Poor *illitterati*: Nothing moves quicker than slander. Nothing issues forth from us so easily. Nothing is accepted so readily. And nothing spreads farther across the face of the earth. I have already heard the rumors surrounding Theresa. You all say the same thing, yet none of you know the truth of what happened. Give up this falseness and ignominy—because there are no secrets that do not come out sooner or later. *Nihil est opertum quod non revelavitur, et ocultum quod non scietur.*"

"Lies, you say?" responded Korne, waving his arms around. "I suffered the wrath of that daughter of Cain myself. Her hatred caused the fire that has destroyed my life. And I will say it here, in God's house. My son Caelius would have borne witness to it had he not died because of that girl. Everyone who was there can attest to it and I swear before the Almighty that they will do so when Gorgias and his family face judgment." And without waiting for Wilfred's consent, he lifted Caelius's body onto his shoulders and left the church with his family following.

Gorgias waited until the rest of the congregation had left the building. He wanted to talk to Wilfred about Theresa's burial and he knew that there would not be a better time. Wilfred's words had come as a great surprise to him. Rutgarda had told him about the rumors that pointed to Theresa as the perpetrator of the fire, but the count's warning seemed to suggest it was far from an established fact. While Rutgarda waited outside, discussing preparations for the burial with some neighbors, Gorgias approached

Wilfred and was surprised to see him stroking the backs of his hounds. He wondered how a man without legs could handle those ferocious beasts with such ease.

"I am sorry about your daughter," said Wilfred, shaking his head. "In truth she was a good girl."

"She was all I had —my whole life." His eyes filled with tears.

"People think there is only one death, but that is not entirely true. Every time a child dies, the death is also felt by the parents, and this in turn gives rise to a painful irony: The emptier life is, the heavier it becomes. But your wife is still young. Perhaps you could yet . . ."

Gorgias shook his head. They had tried many times, but God did not want to bless them with another child.

"My only desire is that Theresa receives a burial worthy of the Christian that she always was. I know that what I ask of you may be difficult now, but I beg you to heed my request."

"If it is within my power."

"I have seen terrible things of late: unclothed bodies lying in ruts, corpses thrown in dung heaps, remains dug from graves by desperate starvelings. I don't want these things happening to my daughter."

"Naturally. But I do not see how—"

"The cloister cemetery. I know only clerics and important men rest in that garden, but I ask you as a special favor. You know how much I have done for you."

"And I for you, Gorgias, but what you ask of me is impossible. Not another soul will fit in the cloister, and the chapel tombs belong to the church."

"I know, but I was thinking about the area near the well. It's unused."

"That place is almost pure rock."

"It doesn't matter. I will dig."

"With that arm?"

"I'll find someone to help me."

"Regardless, I don't think it's a good idea. The people would not comprehend why a girl accused of murder should lie to rest in a cloister surrounded by saints."

"I do not understand. You defended her yourself just a few moments ago."

"True," he said, shaking his head. "Nicodemus, one of the injured workers, asked for confession. He must have felt the presence of death and between confessing his sins he spoke of what happened. It would seem that events did not occur as Korne described them."

"What are you saying? That it was not Theresa who caused the fire?"

"Let us say that it is not clear what happened. Nonetheless, even if Korne's accusation was false, it would be very difficult to prove it. Nicodemus spoke under the secrecy of confession, and we can assume that the rest of the workers will confirm Korne's version. I do not think Nicodemus will survive much longer in his condition, and even if he does, no doubt he will take back what he said. Remember that he works for Korne."

"And Korne works for you."

"My good fellow, sometimes you underestimate Korne's power. People do not respect him for his work. They fear his family. Many townsfolk have suffered his wrath. His sons are as quick to draw their swords as an adolescent is to unsheathe his member."

"But you know that my daughter could not have done it. You know Theresa. She was a kind and generous soul." His tears began to flow.

"And stubborn as a mulc. Look, Gorgias: I hold you in great esteem, but I cannot grant what you ask. I am truly sorry."

Gorgias could understand Wilfred's position, but he was not going to allow his daughter's body to be defiled in some old dunghill.

"Then you leave me no option, Your Grace. If I cannot bury my daughter in Würzburg, I will take her body to Aquis-Granum."

"To Aquis-Granum you say? You must be jesting. The passes are blocked, as are the relay posts. Even if you had a cart with oxen, the bandits would tear you to pieces."

"I tell you that I will do it if it costs me my life."

Gorgias held Wilfred's gaze. He knew the count needed his services and would not permit anything to happen.

Wilfred took his time to respond. "You forget that there is a manuscript that needs finishing," he eventually said.

"And you that there is a body that needs burying."

"Don't tempt fate. Until now I have protected you like a son, but that does not entitle you to behave like an insolent child," he said, and resumed stroking the dogs' heads. "Remember that it was me who took you in when you arrived in Würzburg begging for a scrap of bread. It was me who secured your place on the registry of free men, despite the fact that you lacked the required documents or weapons. And it was me who offered you the work that you have benefited from until now."

"I would be an ingrate if I forgot it. But that was six years ago, and I believe my work has more than compensated you for your help."

Wilfred gave him a stern look, but then his face softened. "I'm sorry, but I cannot help you. By now Korne will already have been to the judge to report what has happened. It would be reckless for me to accept the body of a person who might be found guilty of murder. And there is more. I would advise you to start worrying about yourself. You can be certain that Korne will go after you."

"But why? During the fire I was with you in the scriptorium."

"Hmm . . . I see that you still have no understanding of the complexities of Carolingian Law, something you will have to remedy if you value your head."

Wilfred cracked his whip and the dogs moved obediently, dragging the wheeled contraption to one of the lavishly decorated chambers. Gorgias followed, obeying the count's gesture to follow.

"This is where the optimates are given lodging," Wilfred explained. "Princes, nobles, bishops, kings. And in this little room we keep the capitula that our king has been publishing since his coronation. Archived with these are the codices of Salic and Ripuarian Law, decretals and acts of the May Assembly—in short, the rules that govern the Franks, the Saxons, the Burgundians, and the Lombards. Now let me see . . ."

Wilfred brought his wheelchair up to a bookcase built low to the ground and, one by one, examined the volumes organized and protected in wooden covers. The cleric stopped in front of a threadbare tome. He removed it with difficulty, then leafed through it, wetting his finger with the tip of his tongue.

"Aha. Here it is: *Capitular de Vilbis. Poitiers, anno domine 768. Karolus rex francorum.* Allow me to read it to you: 'If a free man inflicts material or personal damage on another man of equal status, and if due to any circumstances he is unable to compensate for his offense, the punishment that justly befits the offender will fall upon his family.'"

Wilfred closed the book and returned it to the shelf.

"My life is in danger?" asked Gorgias.

"Perhaps. I have known the parchment-maker for a long time. He is an egotistical man. Dangerous, perhaps, and shrewd as they come. You are no good to him dead. I imagine he will go after your assets. But what his family wants is another matter. They are from Saxony. Their customs are different from those of the Franks."

"If what he seeks is wealth . . ." said Gorgias with a bitter smile.

"That is precisely your biggest problem. The trial could finish you. You could end up being sold on the slave market."

"I don't care about that now. After I have buried my daughter, I will find a way to remedy this situation."

"For God's sake, Gorgias, think it over. Or at least consider Rutgarda. Your wife is innocent. You should concentrate on preparing your defense. And do not even think about running away. Korne's men will hunt you like a rabbit."

Gorgias lowered his head. If Wilfred did not authorize the interment, his only option was to take the body to Aquis-Granum. But this would be impossible if—as the count warned—Korne's relatives were prepared to hunt him down. "Theresa will be buried tonight in the cloister," Gorgias said, "and it will be you who oversees the trial. After all, Your Grace needs my freedom much more than me."

The count flicked the reins and the dogs growled menacingly. "Look, Gorgias, since you started copying the parchment for me, I have given you food that many would kill for. Now you are pushing me too far. In fact, perhaps I should reconsider the scope of our agreement. Your skills are to a certain extent essential to me, but if an accident, illness, or even this trial prevented you from completing the task we have agreed to, do you think my plans would go on hold? That your absence would prevent me from completing my undertaking?"

Gorgias knew that he was treading on thin ice, but his only chance was to put pressure on Wilfred. Otherwise his head would end up on a dung heap alongside Theresa's.

"I don't doubt that you will be able to find someone. Of course you could. All you would have to do is find a scribe whose mother tongue is Greek, who knows the customs of the ancient Byzantine court, who has equal mastery of both diplomatics and calligraphy, who can distinguish an unborn calf's vellum from a lambskin parchment, and, who of course, knows how to keep his mouth shut. Tell me, Your Grace, how many men like that do you know? Two scribes? Three perhaps? And how many of them would be prepared to undertake such a risky commission?"

Wilfred growled like one of his animals. His head tilted to one side, aglow with rage. He was more grotesque than ever.

"I could find that man," he said defiantly as he turned away.

"And what would he copy? A charred piece of parchment?"

The count stopped dead. "What do you mean?"

"You heard me, my Lord. The only complete copy in existence went up in flames, so unless you know someone who can read ashes, you will have to accept my conditions."

"What do you want? For us all to end up in hell?"

"That is not my intention, for luckily I remember the contents of the document word for word."

"And how exactly in the Devil's name do you think I can help you? I represent the law in Würzburg. I owe obedience to Charlemagne."

"You tell me. Or is the powerful Wilfred, count and guardian of the greatest of secrets, unable to arrange for a simple burial?"

* * *

As soon as they heard the news, Reinold and Lotharia rushed to Saint Damian's to help with Theresa's interment. Lotharia was Rutgarda's older sister, and after her marriage to Reinold, the ties between the two families had only grown stronger. Once the arrangements had been made to bury the body in the cloister cemetery, Gorgias and Reinold left to retrieve the body.

Arriving home, Gorgias placed the body on the straw mattress that his daughter slept on. He looked upon her with tenderness and his eyes reddened. He could not accept that he would never again enjoy her smile, never again see her bright eyes or glowing cheeks. He could not understand how all that remained of her sweet features was a disfigured face.

It was going to be a long night of digging and the cold would numb their limbs, so Rutgarda suggested they have something hot beforehand. Gorgias agreed and he lit a fire. Once it was burning brightly, Rutgarda heated the turnip soup she had prepared the day before, topping it up with water and thickening it with a piece of lard that Lotharia had brought, while her friend busied herself tidying a corner that she thought would be appropriate for shrouding Theresa. The woman, despite her ample size, worked with the agility of a squirrel, and in a blink of the eye she had cleared the area of clutter.

"Do your children know you are spending the night away from them?" Rutgarda asked.

"Lotharia told them," Reinold replied before whispering to Gorgias, "I shouldn't say it, but that woman is a gem. As soon as she heard what happened to Theresa, she ran to the midwife's house to ask for a vial of essence. I know it's improper for me to say this, but sometimes I think she has more sense than some men."

"It must be a family thing. Rutgarda is sensible, too," Gorgias confirmed.

Rutgarda smiled. Gorgias did not say nice things to her often, but he was a good man, and it made her proud.

"Stop your flattery and go chop some firewood. I have to prepare the shroud. I'll let you know when I've finished," Lotharia grumbled.

Rutgarda filled a bowl with soup and handed it to Gorgias.

"See what I mean. They have more sense than some men," Reinold repeated.

The two men drank their broth eagerly. Before going out, Gorgias's eyes turned to the single chest in the room. He examined it closely and after a moment's hesitation he opened and started to empty it.

"What are you looking for?"

"I think I'll be able to turn it into a casket. Outside I've got some planks that might work."

"But it's our only chest. We can't just throw our belongings on the floor," said Rutgarda.

"We'll leave our clothes on Theresa's bed—and don't worry, I'll buy another better one soon," said Gorgias as he pulled out the last garment. "When you've finished shrouding her, wrap these things in a blanket. Then gather up everything of value: food, pots, dresses, tools . . . I will take care of the books."

"Good God! But why?"

"Don't ask, just do as I say."

Gorgias seized a torch and asked Reinold to help him with the task. His friend lit another torch and together they dragged the chest outside.

Lotharia left Rutgarda to gather their belongings while she undressed Theresa's charred body. Naturally it was not the first time she had shrouded a body, but until then she had never had to deal with one whose skin came off in pieces like willow bark. She carefully removed the remains of her dress and cleaned the blackened body with hot water. Then she doused it in perfume, splashing it with cardamom essence. To wrap her she used a linen sheet, swathing her from feet to shoulders. Afterward she selected an old dress, which she tore with a knife to use as decoration for the shroud. By the time Lotharia had finished, Rutgarda had gathered up practically all of their valuable things.

"Though she was not my daughter, I always loved her as my own," Rutgarda said with tears in her eyes.

Lotharia thought it best not to say anything. It was already enough that Rutgarda could not conceive, and now she had lost her only stepdaughter.

"We all loved her," Lotharia said at length. "She was a good girl. Different, but good . . . I'll get the men." She dried her hands and called out to Gorgias and Reinold.

The two of them appeared with the chest transformed into a strange coffin.

"It's not pretty, but it will do," Gorgias declared. He dragged the chest near to where the body lay, looked sadly upon his daughter and turned to Rutgarda. "I've been talking to Wilfred. He warned me that Korne is likely to lodge a complaint against us."

"Why us? What does that rat want? Does he want us to be exiled? Does he want us to admit that Theresa should never have set foot in the workshop? For the love of God! Have we not been punished enough?"

"Not enough for him, it would seem. I presume he wants to get his dues for the losses caused by the fire."

"But what is he going to achieve? We barely have enough to eat."

"That's what I said to Wilfred, but under Frankish law, they can take everything we have."

"Oh? And what do we have? All our possessions are there, wrapped up in a tiny bundle on the bed."

"They could take your home," suggested Lotharia.

"The house is rented," Gorgias responded. "And that is precisely the problem."

"Why's that a problem?" Rutgarda asked anxiously.

Gorgias looked hard at Rutgarda and sucked in his breath. "Because they could sell us at the slave market."

Rutgarda's eyes opened almost as wide as her mouth. Then she buried her head in her lap and broke into tears. Lotharia shook her head and reproached Gorgias for his words.

"I said they *could* do it, not that they *will* do it," he explained. "First they must prove that Theresa is guilty, and Wilfred says he will help us."

"Help us?" Rutgarda sounded doubtful as she sobbed. "That cripple?"

"I promise he will. In the meantime I want you to take all our belongings to Reinold's house. That way nobody will be able to take justice into his own hands. Leave some old junk here, and a couple of worn blankets. Don't forget the mattresses. Empty out the straw and use the covers to transport everything. That way we won't arouse suspicion. Then you and Lotharia must shut yourselves in with the children at their house while Reinold and I take care of the burial. We'll return at dawn."

Gorgias sat alone on the casket and waited for nightfall. He had agreed with Reinold that they would head to the cloister after sundown, so all he had to do now was keep vigil over his daughter's body and wait for the first stars to appear. Soon his mind was painting a picture of Theresa. He remembered Constantinople, the pearl of the Bosphorus, the land where he was born. Those were times of good fortune and abundance, of enjoyment and happiness. How life had changed, and how cruel his memories had become. Nobody in Würzburg could have imagined that Gorgias, the man who worked as a simple scribe in the scriptorium, had once held the title of patrician in the city of all cities, far-off Constantinople.

He recalled the birth of his daughter, that little peach, that bundle of life trembling in his arms. The wine and honey had flowed for weeks. He sent news to all the empire's forums, commissioned an altar be built behind the villa, and had his slaves mark her birth with offerings on that happy day. Not even his appointment as optimas of Bithynia had brought him greater satisfaction. His wife Otiana lamented that they had not had a boy, but he was in no hurry. The girl had his blood running through her veins, the blood of the Theolopouloses, the most renowned merchant family in Byzantium, from the Danube to Dalmatia, from Carthage to the Exarchate of Ravenna, respected and feared beyond Theodosius's walls. There would be time for more children to fill their home with their mischief. They were young and had their whole lives ahead of them. Or at least, that's what he had thought.

The second pregnancy was ill-fated. The physicians attributed Otiana's death to the damp softness of the fetus. Damned fools!

They could have at least prevented all her suffering. For months, desperation had become his only companion. He could see his wife in every corner of the house, smell her perfume, hear her laughter. In the end, on his brothers' advice, he decided to put some distance between himself and the melancholy that consumed him, and he moved to old Constantinople. There he bought a villa, surrounded by gardens, close to Trajan's forum, where he made a home for himself with his slaves and a wet nurse.

Several years went by in which he watched Theresa grow surrounded by books and writing, which were his only passion, and the only remedy for his grief that no physician could prescribe. His title of patrician and his friendship with the Cubicularius of the Basileus gave him access to the library of the Hagia Sophia, the greatest repository of wisdom in Christendom. Every morning he would visit the hall at the cathedral accompanied by Theresa, and while she played, he would reread Virgil, copy passages from Pliny or recite verses by Lucian. After her sixth birthday, the child took an interest in her father's activities. She would sit between his legs and bother him until he let her have one of the codices he was reading. At first, to distract her, he would offer her damaged documents, but he noticed that, as he wrote, Theresa would imitate each of his movements with extraordinary delicateness.

In time, what had started as a pastime became her preoccupation. The little girl hardly ever played with other children and when she did, she would amuse herself by scribbling on their clothes with feathers she'd stolen from the henhouses. The librarian Petrus had told him about Theresa's behavior with the other children and persuaded him to introduce her to the secrets of writing, putting himself forward as the girl's tutor. That was how Theresa learned to read and, later on, to make her first inscriptions on wax tablets.

He reminisced with sorrow how her passion for reading had been interrupted when she was sixteen years old, following the assassination of the Emperor Leo IV at the hands of his wife, the

Empress Irene. The death of the Basileus triggered an endless cycle of feuds and revenge, ending in the arrest and execution of anyone who dared oppose the new monarch. But it was not just dissenters who ended up in the cemeteries. Anyone who had forged political or commercial ties with the Basileus while he was alive also suffered the wrath of the empress.

One winter night, the Cubicularius turned up at Gorgias's home in disguise with a warning and a couple of horses. The next day he and his daughter were to be put to death. They fled on horseback to Salonika. Then they undertook a pilgrimage to Rome before journeying to the cold Germanic lands.

But why was his mind preoccupied with the past at this precise moment? Why bring back memories that only fueled his pain? *Accursed destiny. Cruel torment. Meandering caprices that tear the flesh that was mine from my soul, leaving me empty. Loathsome hair shirt, path of punishment. Take me with you so that I may give you my hatred. Come and embrace me.* He closed his eyes and began to weep.

* * *

Despite the stony soil, Gorgias and Reinold finished digging the grave just after midnight when the clerics were resting in their chambers and Wilfred could officiate the funeral in complete secrecy. Afterward, he told Gorgias to cover the casket without a cross or any sign that would betray their act.

"The manuscript . . ." the count reminded him when it was all done.

Gorgias nodded in understanding with reddened eyes.

Then Wilfred lowered his head and left Gorgias to be alone in his bitter sadness.

5

That night chilling winds from the north covered Würzburg in a blanket of ice. The men busied themselves sealing off cracks and stoking the fires in their homes, while the women pressed their children between straw mattresses. They all prayed for the firewood to last until dawn.

Those who slept within reach of the embers' warmth bore the cold with resignation, but Theresa was far from any heat and could not fall asleep. Her weeping had inflamed her eyelids until they were swollen like wineskins, and her feverish eyes could hardly make out the pigsty that she had found shelter in. Her skin was still ash gray from the smoke, and the charred smell of her clothes constantly reminded her of the hellish nightmare she had experienced. Again, she broke into tears and asked God to forgive her sins.

The images of all that had happened flashed through her mind again: the mocking laughter of the workshop boys, the rotten skin floating in the pool, the test that she had fought so hard to take, the argument with Korne, and finally, the terrifying fire. Just thinking about it gave her goose bumps, but she thanked the heavens that she had been able to escape the flames with her life.

Lord, if only you could have prevented Clotilda's death!

Once or twice she had stumbled upon Clotilda as she skulked around the workshop's storerooms or rummaged through the waste. Theresa thought her parents must have died at the onset of winter since she wandered alone about the cathedral, with nobody taking pity on her. She calculated that Clotilda must have been the same age as herself or even a bit younger. The girl eventually disappeared, and was never heard from again until the day of the fire.

She remembered the moment that she decided to return to the workshop, right after making sure Korne's wife had reached the top of the courtyard wall safely. As she went in, the fire was crackling on the roof, turning the place into a great forest of flames. She was looking for her latest books when she had seen her. Clotilda, curled up in a corner, was waving her arms around in an attempt to fend off the embers that rained down on her from the ceiling. At her feet apples were strewn across the ground. No doubt the girl had taken advantage of the mayhem to enter the workshop and find some food.

Theresa tried to get her out, but the girl resisted, her face etched with pain. That was when Theresa saw that her reddened skin looked as if it were already burning. At that moment, Theresa saw her blue dress under one of the tables, the one she wore when she had submerged herself in the pool. She picked it up and—discovering that it was still soaking wet—she offered it to the girl, who threw off her rags and pulled on the dress. The water soothed her, but at that moment the roof creaked and the beams began to cave in. Theresa remembered trying to drag her out, but the girl was too terrified and ran in the opposite direction. Then everything collapsed, and Clotilda was buried under the wreckage.

Theresa managed to escape, fleeing down the hill—running, stumbling, feeling the Devil's breath on her neck. She took the path that ran around the walls, running deep into the undergrowth, until she reached a chestnut grove where pigs would often be put to forage. There she took shelter in the swineherds' hut. She closed the door hard as if wanting to shut out all the sorrow and pain left behind, and then fell to the ground, resting her back against the wall of mud and bramble.

The burned books, the workshop ruined and consumed, that poor girl dead. She would never be able to look Gorgias in the eye again. She had dishonored him in the worst way a daughter could dishonor her father, and though it pained her to admit it, letting him down was what caused her the most grief. She cried inconsolably until the tears made her cheeks raw. She sobbed, deeply releasing mournful cries from her throat over and over, asking God for forgiveness, praying that none of it had actually happened. It was all her fault. All because of her stupid desire to be someone she was not. They were right, those who said that a woman's place was in the home—with her husband, bearing children, and looking after the family. And now God was punishing her for her greed.

Theresa woke up shivering, her body numb and her temples thumping against her head. As she stood, her legs wobbled as if she had been walking all night. The cold tightened her chest and her throat felt lined with thorns. When she had managed to clear her head, she opened the door and saw that dawn had already arrived. The hut seemed deserted, but still she scanned it carefully.

A flock of starlings took flight, their fluttering making a great clamor. In the light of a new day, Theresa admired the green of the fir trees, the purity of the sky. The chestnut wood clumped as if a neatly arranged garden and for a moment she lost herself in the scent of damp earth and the soft whispering of the wind.

Her stomach grumbled, reminding her that she had not had a bite to eat since the previous day. She untied the leather bag that her father had left behind in the parchment-maker's workshop before he was carried away, and she spread its contents on the ground. Wrapped in a linen cloth, she discovered a wax tablet and a bronze stylus. Also wrapped in cloth was a ripe apple. She bit into it with relish. As she munched on the fruit, she looked through the rest of her belongings: a little steel for lighting fires, a crucifix cut from bone, a vial of essence for perfuming parchments, and a reel of hemp thread, which Gorgias used to sew quinternions. Then she put everything back in its place.

She thought hard for a while about what to do next before coming to a decision: She would flee far from Würzburg, to a place where no one could find her. Perhaps to the south, to Aquitania— or the west, to Neustria, where she had heard there were abbeys run by women. If the opportunity arose, she would even travel to Byzantium. Her father always said that one day she would meet her grandparents, the Theolopouloses. She could barely remember them, but if she reached Constantinople, no doubt she would find them. She could work there until she was a woman of standing. She would study grammar and verse, as Gorgias would have wanted, and perhaps one day she would have the courage to return to Würzburg to find her father and beg his forgiveness for her sins.

Frightened, she picked up her father's bag and turned to look upon the city's walls for the last time. Now, in her nineteenth year, she would have to build a new life for herself.

She prayed to God for the strength she would need and set off purposefully on the path that wound through the vegetation.

By the midmorning she dropped her bag on the ground, exhausted. She had traveled five miles along the path between Würzburg and the roads to the north, but as she climbed the first foothills, the path had disappeared under the snow. Wherever she looked, everything from the smallest stone to the most distant hill was covered in a white blanket, obscuring any landmark she might use to guide her. Every tree was identical to the last and every outcrop a reflection of the next.

She needed to rest. Sitting on a fallen trunk, she looked to the sky with concern, for the weather was changing quickly and the threat of a storm loomed. She had thought she would find nuts and berries on the way, but ice had ravaged the shrubs, so she had to make do with the apple core that thankfully she'd had the foresight to keep. As she opened her bag and took it out, a bolt of lightning suddenly lit up the horizon. The wind began to shake the treetops and gradually the sky turned a somber gray. Before long it started to rain. Theresa sought shelter among some crags, but soon she was soaked through.

As she huddled under a projection, she grasped the naivety of her decisions. No matter how much she wanted it, she would never reach Aquitania or Neustria, let alone far-flung Byzantium. She had neither food nor money, nor relatives to turn to. She had no knowledge of the hoe or plow. She had never harvested crops nor even made a rudimentary stewpot. She only knew about useless parchments that would never help her make a living for herself. What a fool she had been not to listen to her stepmother! She should have devoted herself to cooking or some other women's trade: spinner, seamstress, washerwoman . . . any of them would have enabled her to earn a crust in Aquis-Granum, and even save enough to pay her passage to Neustria with a caravan.

Even given her predicament, she resolved to learn. She would work as a farm laborer or find a job as a tanner's apprentice. Anything but end up in a brothel covered in boils and riddled with disease.

With the rain growing heavier, she considered whether she should move somewhere safer. What's more, she thought, in Würzburg they had probably started searching for her by now, and if she stayed near the path, they would soon find her. Then she remembered the old lime kiln, a building in a small quarry half an hour's walk away. She knew the place because she'd been there on several occasions to collect the lime they used to tan the skins. The kiln belonged to the Larsson widow, a burly woman who worked the quarry with the help of her sons. In winter, when the builders' orders stopped, they closed the kiln and plied their trade in Würzburg, so she knew she could take shelter in one of the sheds and wait for the storm to ease without running into anyone.

Not long before midday, Theresa approached the quarry. She was desperate to get out of the rain, but rather than rush in, she pricked up her ears and cautiously listened. The pit was dug into the side of the mountain like a great gap-toothed mouth, boulders strewn down the slopes like fallen teeth. At the foot of the mountain stood the lime kiln, a sort of squat, tapered tower slightly larger than a bread oven. At the top there was a circular hole that served as a chimney, while on the side were four vents. The house stood on the riverbank, away from the vapors of burning lime, and farther on, behind it, were the sheds used as storehouses.

Theresa waited to make sure neither the Larsson widow nor her sons were in the area. She was holding on to the hope that she was alone, but as she approached the house, she saw the door ajar and wondered whether she had made the wrong decision. Still she knocked, but there was no answer. She knew it was foolish but decided to go in nonetheless. Picking up a stick from the ground, she pushed the door open with her shoulder. It was jammed. On the third attempt it flew open with a loud crash, revealing an empty room. Theresa went in, leaving the door ajar the way she found it. Then she closed her eyes, savoring a moment of peace. The bitter odor of lime burned her throat, but she welcomed it in exchange for a bit of rest. She heard the rain beating against the roof and the wind battering the timber, and she felt comforted in her newfound shelter.

Similar to other buildings in the area, the house had no windows, so the only light was from the hole in the wattle that served as a chimney. As her eyes grew accustomed to the half-light, she could see that the room was a mess, with stools tipped over and belongings and pans scattered on the floor. She assumed some animal had been the cause of the chaos and so thought nothing of it. After establishing that there was no food or warm clothes, she decided to amuse herself by tidying up the room. In one corner she piled up the offcuts of logs and timber that the Larsson widow would use to make clogs. Like so many other families, the Larssons had found woodcutting to be an additional trade they could ply while they waited for a batch of lime to be baked.

Theresa gazed at the impressive tool that lay on one of the workbenches, a sort of giant machete articulated with a ring nailed to the bench. This enabled the blade to pivot on its end like a guillotine, which reminded Theresa of a drawbridge.

On occasions she had seen the Larsson widow operating the implement with great skill. She would lift the handle and rest it on a support, place a piece of wood under the blade, and with precise up-and-down movements she would hew the timber until she had carved the outside of the clog.

Driven by curiosity, Theresa decided to try it out. She found a piece of wood the right size and positioned it beside the blade. Then she took hold of the guillotine's handle and with both hands she lifted it to rest it on the support, but the handle slipped and the blade fell violently onto the bench. Theresa was glad she had used two hands, for otherwise she surely would have lost one. More carefully this time, she raised the blade once more and placed it on the rest. Securing it in place, she decided that her career as a clog-cutter was over and picked up the overturned stools instead.

While she worked she pictured her arrival in Aquis-Granum. First she would go to the market and trade her steel and stylus for food. No doubt she could get a pound of bread and several eggs, or even barter for a slice of smoked meat. Then she would seek work as a tanner in the artisans' quarter. She had never been to Aquis-Granum, but she assumed there must be an artisans' quarter in the city King Charlemagne had chosen for his residence.

Suddenly her heart gave a leap upon hearing voices outside, and those voices were growing ever nearer. Horrified, she stopped what she was doing and ran to the door. Was it the Larssons? She pressed her head against the wall, peering through a crack, and saw two blurred figures approaching the house. Oh, Lord! They looked like armed men and in a few seconds they would be inside the room.

She had to find somewhere to hide. Remembering the pile of wood by the guillotine, she ran and crouched behind it, just as the men burst in. She tucked her head between her legs and prayed they would not discover her. But the two men, instead of searching the place, went to the middle of the room and set about lighting the fire.

Hidden behind the firewood, Theresa could see what was happening. What were they waiting for? Why were they not searching for her? From her hiding place she peered around the woodpile to watch the men remove their weapons and skewer a pair of squirrels to roast on the fire. They laughed and gesticulated like two drunks, shoving each other and turning their spits with indifference. She examined the bulkiest one, a mountain of fat covered in furs, whose mere girth made simply standing upright and not falling flat on his face seem laudable. The skinny one would not stay still and was constantly scratching his freckled face and turning up his nose to sniff his prey. Theresa thought that if a rat could walk on two legs, it would look just like this man.

At one point, the bigger one blurted something to the freckled man, who then made a motion as if to grab his knife. But he suddenly stopped, and they both burst out in noisy laughter. When they had calmed down, Theresa realized they were speaking in an unintelligible dialect, and then it dawned on her that only a miracle could save her. Those men were not soldiers, nor were they from Würzburg. They looked like Saxons: pagans ready to kill the first unlucky soul to cross their paths.

At that moment Theresa leaned against a piece of timber, knocking it onto the ground with a crash. She held her breath as the big man's stupid eyes fell upon the log, but instead of investigating the source of the noise, he turned back to the fire to continue his cooking. The freckled man, however, gazed toward the woodpile. Then he picked up a burning branch, gripped his knife, and slowly advanced toward the logs. Theresa closed her eyes and curled up so tightly her bones hurt. Suddenly a hand grabbed her hair and pulled her up onto her feet. She kicked and screamed, trying to shake off her captor, but a brutal punch to her face took her breath away. The taste of blood made her realize that the last thing she would see would be the faces of these murderous Saxons.

The freckled man held the torch near Theresa and examined her like someone who had found a vixen in a rabbit trap. He smiled when he noticed her fair skin, its only imperfection the mark from his punch. He slowly looked down to her breasts, which he could see were firm and generous, before continuing down to her hips, wide and well-defined.

Sheathing his knife, he dragged her by the arm to the center of the room. There, Theresa watched in horror as he undid his trousers to reveal a hairy, palpitating member. The young woman stood paralyzed. She could never imagine such a horrible thing could be hiding under a pair of trousers. She was so terrified that her bladder spontaneously emptied itself, making her feel she might die of shame. The two men, however, celebrated her accident with a guffaw. Then the big man held her, while the other tore at her dress.

A grotesque smile spread across the freckled man's face as Theresa's stomach was exposed in the glow of the embers. He admired how her pale flesh contrasted with the triangle that crowned the top her legs and felt desire ferociously gnawing at him. He spat on his member, rubbed it, and guided it toward Theresa.

The young woman cried out and struggled furiously. She cursed them over and over and, somehow amidst her thrashing about, managed to free herself, taking the opportunity to run toward the pile of logs. Frantically she groped for the stylus she had in her bag, thinking she might have a chance if she could find it. But her hands rummaged in the dim light, seemingly in vain.

Just as the freckled one was about to jump on her, Theresa grasped her father's stylus and held it out in front of her, hands trembling. The skinny man stopped, the implement just a hand's width from his face.

The big man looked on in astonishment, waiting like a dog for his master's command, but the freckled one said nothing and merely burst into laughter. Then he picked up a jug and drank until the liquid streamed down his chin over his clothes. Without letting go of the jug, he slapped Theresa with his other hand, making the stylus fly through the air.

Theresa suddenly found herself lying on the clog-covered bench, with the Saxon on top of her drooling over her face. The smell of alcohol filled her nostrils. Fevered from the wine, the Saxon fumbled for his organ, pinning Theresa's arms down above her head. Theresa tried to close her legs, but the man pulled them violently apart. At that moment she noticed that her assailant's right hand was resting under the gigantic blade. He was so drunk he hadn't even realized. If she could just get her arms free for an instant . . . She lifted her head and kissed the Saxon on the mouth, taking him by surprise.

Theresa took advantage of his confusion. In an instant, she pushed away the support under the guillotine, making it drop down onto the Saxon's hand with such violence that his fingers flew through the air, blood gushing as they were severed clean off.

Theresa took her chance and ran for the door while the wounded man rolled around like a hog. She would have escaped were it not for the big one, who stood in her path. She tried to sidestep him, but with unexpected speed the man grabbed her by the hair and raised his knife.

Theresa closed her eyes and screamed. Yet, right when she expected to feel the Saxon's killer blow, he instead let out a strange groan. His eyes turned white and he began to stagger, falling to his knees right in front of Theresa, before collapsing face-first onto the floor. In the bandit's back, she saw a large dagger. And behind him, young Hoos Larsson offered her his hand.

Hoos took her safely outside, then went back into the house from where Theresa heard more gut-wrenching screams. Before long he returned, his hands bloody. He went to Theresa and wrapped her in his woolen cloak.

"It's all over now," he said awkwardly.

She looked at him with tears in her eyes. Then she realized that she was half-naked and flushed. She covered herself up as best she could, and Hoos helped her.

Hoos Larsson looked more attractive than she remembered. A bit too stout, perhaps, but with an honest face and restrained manner. She had not heard anything about him for some time, though it had not bothered her. She was grateful to him for saving her, even if he would surely now take her to Würzburg to hand her over to the authorities. But she no longer cared. All she wanted was for her father to forgive her.

"We should go in. We'll freeze out here," he said.

Theresa looked over to the house and shook her head.

"You have nothing to fear. They're dead."

She shook her head again. She would rather die of cold than go back in there.

"By God!" said Hoos gruffly. "Then let's go to the shed. There's no fire there, but at least we can get out of the rain."

Without giving her time to respond, he took the young woman in his arms and carried her to the shed. There he arranged some straw on the ground with his feet and gently laid Theresa down on it.

"I must take care of those bodies," he told her.

"Please, don't go."

"I can't leave them. The blood will attract the wolves."

"What will you do with them?"

"Bury them, I suppose."

"Bury those murderers? You should cast them in the river," she suggested with a frown.

Hoos burst into laughter. But on seeing the look of reproach on Theresa's face, he tried to contain himself. "Sorry for laughing, but I don't think that's a good idea. The river's so frozen I'd need a pick first in order to make a hole to throw them through."

Theresa went quiet with embarrassment. The fact is she knew a fair bit about parchments, but almost naught about anything else.

"And even if the water was flowing," he added, "throwing them into the river wouldn't solve the problem. No doubt those men were part of a scouting party, and sooner or later the river might carry the bodies to their companions."

"There are more Saxons?" she asked in fright.

"Just a small band—but fierce as wild animals. To be honest, I don't know how they got through, but the passes are infested with them. In fact, I lost three days skirting the mountains to avoid them."

Skirting the mountains . . . that could only mean Hoos had come from Fulda, so he wouldn't know what had happened in Würzburg. She gave a sigh of relief. "Anyway, your arrival was heaven-sent," she said, watching Hoos clean the blood from his hands by rubbing them on the snow.

"Well, the truth is I've been here for a couple of days," he replied. "Yesterday, I had decided to spend the night in the kiln, but as I approached the site, I noticed light in the house and saw that it was those Saxons. I didn't want any trouble, so I thought I would sleep in the shed instead and just wait for them to leave. When I awoke this morning they had gone. However, I searched the forest to make sure. After a while, I decided to head back home and that was when I saw that they'd caught you."

"They must have gone out to hunt. They came in with squirrels."

"Probably. But tell me . . . what were you doing in the house?"

Theresa blushed. She hadn't expected that question.

"I was near the kiln when the storm took me by surprise." She cleared her throat. "I remembered the house and I went to take shelter there. Then those men came out of nowhere."

Hoos furrowed his brow. He still could not understand what a young woman was doing alone in these parts.

"What will we do now?" she asked, trying to change the subject.

"I need to start digging. As for you," he suggested, "you should take care of that bruise on your face."

Theresa watched Hoos go back into the house. She had not seen him for some time, and though his face had hardened, he still had his curly hair and kind countenance. Hoos was the Larsson widow's only son to give up the trade of quarryman. She knew this because the woman was constantly boasting about his appointment as *fortior* of King Charlemagne, a position she knew nothing about, except for its strange name. She estimated that Hoos was around thirty years old. At that age a man would normally have fathered a couple of offspring. But she had never heard the Larsson widow mention any grandchildren.

Hoos eventually returned to the shed with the spade he had used to dig up the earth. With a weary gesture he threw it to the ground beside Theresa. "Those men won't be causing us any more problems," he said.

"You're soaked."

"Yes, the rain's pouring down out there."

She screwed up her face but didn't know what to say.

"Are you hungry?" asked Hoos.

She nodded. She could have happily eaten a whole cow.

"I lost my mount crossing a gorge," he grumbled. "The horse and my supplies are gone, but in there," he said, pointing at the house, "I've seen a brace of squirrels that could ease our hunger, so you decide. Either we go back in the house, get warm, and fill our bellies, or we stay out here until the cold takes us to our graves."

Theresa pursed her lips. She did not want to go back into the cabin, but Hoos was right: They would not last much longer in that shed. She stood and followed him to the house, but at the front door she stopped in her tracks as a shiver ran down her spine.

Hoos looked at her out of the corner of his eye. He felt sorry for her but didn't want her to notice. Kicking open the door, he showed her the empty room. Then he put his arm over her shoulders and they walked in together.

The warmth from the firewood comforted them like a hot broth. Hoos added an armful of logs to the fire, which was spluttering away lighting the room with a soft glow. The fragrance of hot chestnuts filled her lungs and the smell of roasting meat piqued her appetite. Theresa looked at the tidied belongings and blanket near the hearth. For the first time since the fire, she felt safe.

She hadn't yet fully settled in before Hoos had the squirrels and chestnuts ready. "Those men knew where to look for food," he said. "Wait a minute." He went off and soon returned with some clothes. "I took them from the Saxons before burying them. Take a look. There might be something you could use."

Theresa wolfed down some food before turning her attention to the garments. She examined them closely before choosing a scruffy-looking dark woolen coat, which she used to cover her legs. Hoos chided her for discarding a thicker fur because it had bloodstains on it, but he was pleased that she decided to keep the knife that the big Saxon had tried to stab her with.

When they finished eating, they fell silent for a while, listening to the rat-a-tat of the rain on the wattle roof. Then Hoos went to peer through a crack in the wall. He guessed that it would be night soon, though a gray darkness had already settled over the heavens some time ago.

"If the weather keeps getting worse, the Saxons will stay in their hideouts."

She nodded.

"Aren't you the scribe's daughter? Your name is . . ."

"Theresa."

"That's it. Theresa. You would come to the kiln sometimes to collect lime for tanning parchments. I remember the last time I saw you. You had so many pimples on your face you looked like a bilberry cake. You've changed a lot. Do you still work as an apprentice at the parchment-maker's workshop?"

Theresa's face hardened, annoyed at being compared to a cake. "Yes. But I'm not an apprentice anymore," she lied. "I took the examination to become craftswoman."

"A woman in such a position? Good God! Is that possible?"

Theresa fell silent. She was accustomed to talking to laborers whose greatest talent was pelting dogs with stones, so she merely lowered her head and curled up under the coat. After a while, she slowly stood up again and looked at Hoos more intently. From close up, it was apparent that he was taller than she had first thought. Perhaps even a full head taller than any of the laborers she could remember. He seemed strong and sinewy, probably from his work in the quarry. As Hoos continued to look out through the crack in the wall, she imagined him as one of those great shaggy dogs that lick children affectionately, enduring their mischief with patience, but then could tear anyone to pieces in an instant if they tried to lay a finger on him.

"And what do you do?" she asked. "Your mother boasts about your position in the court."

"Well," he smiled, "you know what mothers are like when they talk about their sons. You would be wise to believe only half of what they say. Give them some words of admiration, and then quickly dismiss the other half."

Theresa laughed. Her father spoke so highly of her that she would redden with embarrassment.

"Three years ago," Hoos continued, "as fortune would have it I did well in one of the military campaigns undertaken by

Charlemagne. The news reached him, and on my return, he offered me the chance to swear an oath. Which many see as a great privilege."

"And what does that mean?"

"Well, to put it simply, it means being a vassal of the king. A trusted soldier. Someone to turn to at any time."

"A soldier? Like those of the *praefectus* of Würzburg?"

"Not exactly," he laughed. "Those men are poor devils who have to obey orders without so much as a murmur for a paltry day's pay. But I have my own land."

"I didn't think soldiers owned land," she said with surprise.

"Let me see if I can explain. When the king takes your oath, you pledge to serve him loyally, but the oath establishes a mutual agreement which the king usually honors generously. I received twenty arpents of farmland, another fifteen of vines, and forty more of uncultivated land that I will soon begin to plough, so in reality, my life is not so different to that of a comfortable landowner."

"And on top of that, you must go to war."

"That's right. Though generally the levies only go into combat when summer arrives, after the harvest. That's when I get my gear ready, summon those who will accompany me on the campaign, and respond to the king's call to arms."

"And you have serfs, too?" she asked with surprise.

"No, not serfs. Tenant farmers, freedmen, or *mancipia*, call them what you will, but they are not serfs. They are free men, numbering twenty or so, including men and women. Obviously, I could not work the land alone. Fortunately, Aquis-Granum is overrun with dispossessed folks from every corner of the kingdom: Aquitanians, Neustrians, Austrasians, and Lombards . . . They come to the court believing they will make their fortune and end up destitute, begging for a crust of bread to ease their hunger. With so many, all you have to do is use your best judgment determining who to lease the land to."

"So, you're rich?"

"Good Lord, no. I wish!" he laughed. "The tenant farmers are humble folks. As payment for their use of the land, they give me part of the harvest, plus certain weekly corvées: you know, clearing paths, repairing fences and such. Sometimes they help me plough the lands that I keep for my own use, but as I was saying, it's not much compensation. My wealth is not even close to that of a king's *antrustion*."

"Tell me, Hoos, is Aquis-Granum as beautiful as they say?"

"It certainly is! As beautiful as a great bazaar to anyone with enough denarii. I can tell you that on just one street in Aquis-Granum there are more people crowded together than in all Würzburg. So many people that you will lose yourself among them. At each step there are traders selling meat or harnessing buckles or stews. Beside them stalls are filled with fabrics and silk, and pressed between these—where there is barely space for a rug—you'll find merchants offering everything from jars of honey to a still-bloody swords."

He told her how the streets wind their way round like a tangle of old threads woven by trembling hands, intertwining a mesh of hovels, taverns, and brothels; how crowds would gather in small squares with countless nooks and crannies, where pickpockets and cripples competed with drunks, outsiders, and animals—all looking for the best place to do their business; and about how all the alleys finally converge upon a boulevard that a mounted regiment could ride along. At the end of this avenue, beside the great basilica, an imposing black brick building stands majestically: King Charlemagne's palace.

Theresa was spellbound. For a moment she thought she was seeing far-off Constantinople.

"And are there games, a forum, a circus?"

"What do you mean?"

"Like in Byzantium: buildings of marble, paved avenues, gardens and fountains, theatres, libraries . . ."

Hoos raised an eyebrow. He thought Theresa was joking. He told her places like that only existed in fables.

"You're wrong," she answered, slightly put out and stood up, turning away. She did not care whether Aquis-Granum had gardens with fountains, but it hurt that Hoos should doubt her word.

"You should see Constantinople," she added. "I remember the Hagia Sofia, a cathedral like you couldn't imagine. So tall and wide you could fit a mountain inside it. Or Constantine's hippodrome, two stadia in length, where games and chariot racing took place every month. I remember walking along Theodosius's walls." Her eyes lit up. "Stone defenses that could withstand the onslaught of any army. The illuminated fountains, making water sprout from the ground. The magnificent imperial parades with endless legions of troops led by columns of exquisitely festooned elephants . . . yes, you should see Constantinople. Then you will know what paradise is like."

Hoos's mouth gaped. Though it was nothing but fantasy, he admired the girl's prodigious imagination. "Naturally I would like to see paradise," he said to her mockingly, "but I don't wish to die so soon. By the way . . . what are chariots?"

"They're carriages pulled by several horses. But not like the ones to which oxen are yoked. They're smaller and lighter and fast as the wind."

"Aha! Like wind, eh? And elephants?"

"Oh, elephants! You should see them," she laughed. "They're animals as huge as houses, with skin so hard it stops arrows. They have legs as thick as tree trunks and two giant tusks thrust out from their mouths that they wield like lances when they charge. Under their eyes sways a nose like a great snake." She smiled at Hoos's disbelief. "And yet, despite their fierce appearance, they obey their masters—and mounted by six riders they become as docile as a pony."

Hoos tried to contain his mirth, but before long he burst out laughing. "Well, that's enough for today. We should get some rest. Tomorrow we have a trek to Würzburg," he said.

"So what's the reason for your visit?" Theresa asked, choosing to ignore him.

"Go to sleep."

"It's just that I don't want to go back to Würzburg."

"You don't? So what do you intend to do? Wait here for more Saxons to arrive?"

"No, of course not." Her expression darkened.

"So stop talking nonsense and get some sleep. I don't want to have to pull you along tomorrow."

"You haven't answered me yet," she insisted.

Hoos, who had already settled down by the fire, sat up annoyed.

"Two ships loaded with food are soon to leave Frankfurt for Würzburg. Two important people will travel on them. The king wishes them to be received in accord with their rank, which is why he sent me as an emissary."

"But will they come even now, with the storms?"

"Look, it's business that doesn't concern you," he snapped. "It doesn't even concern me, so lie down and sleep until morning."

Theresa lay quietly, but she could not get to sleep. The young man had helped her, yes, but he was no different than the laborers, and no doubt the fact that he had saved her was merely due to Providence. It also seemed odd that someone in his position should cross the mountains unarmed and unaccompanied. Almost instinctively, she clutched her knife she had hidden under her clothes and half closed her eyes. Then, after some time imagining her beloved Constantinople, she began to drift to sleep.

In the morning she woke before Hoos. The young man was fast asleep, so she rose carefully. Tiptoeing to the door, she pushed her face against a crack and was greeted by the chill of the morning. Disregarding any danger, she slowly opened the door and went out onto the blanket of fresh snow that covered the path. It smelled peaceful, and there was no threat of rain.

Hoos was still sleeping when she returned. Without knowing why, she lay down next to him, pressed against his back, and felt comforted by the warmth of his body. For a moment she surprised herself by imagining a life with him in some distant city—a warm and bright place where nobody would give her grief for her interest in writing; a place where she would converse with this young man with his honest face—so far from the problems that had unexpectedly entered her life. But in the next moment she remembered her father, and she scolded herself for being so selfish and cowardly. She asked herself what kind of daughter she was to be fantasizing about a happy world while her father bore the dishonor of her sins. She did not want to be such a daughter and swore to herself that one day she would return to Würzburg to confess her sins and give her father back the dignity that she should never have taken from him.

Then she turned her gaze to Hoos. She thought for a moment about waking him and asking him to take her to Aquis-Granum, but she resisted the temptation, knowing that, no matter how hard she pleaded with him, he would not approve of such a plan.

With trembling fingers she stroked his hair, before whispering a farewell wrought with guilt. Taking care not to wake him, she stood up and looked around. By the window rested the belongings that Hoos had taken off the bodies: hunting equipment mostly, and a disorderly pile of clothes. Although the young man had already scoured their contents for anything useful, she decided to examine them herself.

Among the folds of a cloak, she found a little wooden box containing a sharpened piece of steel, a small piece of flint, and some tinder. She also found several amber beads on a thread and a portion of dried roe, which she quickly put in her bag along with the box. She threw aside a half-rotten belt but kept a small skin of water and a couple of enormous boots, which she pulled over her own shoes. Then she turned to the weapons that Hoos himself had cleaned and sorted according to type. As he had done so, he told her about the Saxons' skill with the scramasax, a broad dagger sometimes used as a short sword, and their ineptitude with the francisca, the throwing axe used by the Frankish armies. She looked over the assortment, passing over the yew bows and stopping in front of the deadly scramasax. As she took it in her hand, a tremor ran down her spine. Weapons frightened her, but if she intended to make it through the passes, she would have to carry something. Finally she decided on a shorter and lighter sheath knife, but as she picked it up, she noticed a dagger that Hoos had set slightly aside.

Unlike the crude Saxon knives, this dagger had intricate carvings running down both sides of the blade, interweaving into a silver handle crowned with an emerald. It was light and cold. Its delicate edge glistened in the glow of the embers. It looked priceless.

Glancing at Hoos sleeping peacefully, her heart filled with shame. He had saved her life and in return she was stealing from him. She hesitated, but then discarded the knife's sheath and secured the ornate dagger to her belt. Whispering an imperceptible apology to Hoos, she wrapped herself in her new furs, picked up her bag, and went out into the biting cold of the early morning.

At dawn Hoos was taken by surprise, with Theresa already far from the cabin. He searched for her around the quarry and the adjoining woods, and even followed the river upstream, before giving up the hunt. As he returned to the house he was saddened at the fate that awaited the girl, but even more grieved by the fact that she had stolen his emerald-studded dagger.

6

Gorgias woke up in terror, shivering from the sweat that soaked him. He was still unable to accept that he had buried his only daughter a few days ago. He saw Rutgarda by his side and put his arms around her. Then he pictured Theresa when she was alive, smiling, wearing her new dress, ready to take the test that would make her a master parchment-maker. He remembered the attack, and how she had saved him. Then the terrible fire, his desperate search for her, all the wounded and the dead . . . He cried as he relived the moment when he looked upon Theresa's body. All that was left of his daughter were the tatters of that blue dress she so adored.

Curled up beside Rutgarda, he sobbed until he had no tears left. After a while he asked himself how long they could live crammed into his sister-in-law's home like salt herrings, with no straw to lie on, sleeping instead on the wooden boards that Reinold arranged each night on the dirt floor.

He thought how his sister-in-law and her husband made a wonderful family. Despite the inconvenience of his and Rutgarda's presence, both had welcomed them into their house with affection, and each of them did their best to ensure that neither he nor Rutgarda missed the comforts of their old home. Gorgias was gladdened by Reinold's good fortune. His work as a carpenter did not depend on the weather—so even in difficult times, repairing a rotten roof or fixing a broken wheel kept hunger at bay for his family.

For a moment he felt overcome with jealousy, envying Reinold's simple life. His only concern was to find enough bread to feed his offspring, and every evening he slept with the warmth of his wife beside him. Reinold always said that happiness did not depend on the size of one's estate, but on who awaits your return home—and judging by his family, his assertion could not have been more true.

Since their arrival at Reinold's home, Rutgarda had looked after the couple's children, taken charge of the cleaning and the sewing—and even of the cooking when there was enough food to make a meal. This had enabled Lotharia to concentrate on her work as a servant of Arno, one of the wealthy men of the region. Gorgias tried to help Reinold in his wood workshop when his injured arm prevented him from working in the scriptorium. However, despite his brother-in-law's hospitality, he knew that they would have to soon find elsewhere to stay, for their presence might cause Reinold or his family to become the victims of some wicked act.

The whimpering of the littlest one made both Lotharia and Rutgarda jump up, just as the child broke into a full wail. Between the two of them they tended to the infant and also the other little ones, who were shivering as though they had fallen into a river. They washed their eyes with a little water and dressed them in robes of clean wool. Then they lit the fire and heated some dried-out porridge, which in better times would have been thrown to the pigs.

Gorgias rose. Still half-asleep, he grunted a good morning and rummaged through a rickety chest for his scribe's apron. As he did so, he swore at the pain radiating from his wounded arm.

"You should watch your language," Rutgarda said reproachfully, pointing at the children.

Gorgias murmured something and yawned as he went over to the fire, picking his way through the odds and ends scattered all over the room. He washed his face and moved closer to the smell of porridge.

"Another foul day," Gorgias complained.

"At least it's not so cold in the scriptorium," Rutgarda said.

"I'm not sure I will go there today."

"You won't? So where will you go?" she asked, raising her eyebrows.

Gorgias did not answer straightaway. He had intended to investigate the attack on him before the fire had happened, as he still intended, but he didn't want to worry Rutgarda.

"I've run out of ink at the scriptorium, so I'll go by the walnut grove and gather some nuts."

"So early?"

"If I go any later, there won't be a single walnut left after the kids have at them."

"Wrap up warm," Rutgarda ordered.

Gorgias looked at his wife affectionately. She was a good woman. He held her in his arms and kissed her on the lips. Then he picked up his bag of writing equipment and set off toward the cathedral buildings.

As he climbed the narrow, still-quiet streets, Gorgias's mind turned to the assailant who a few days earlier had stolen an incomplete draft of the valuable parchment, remembering the event as if he were reliving it: The crouching shadow pouncing on him. The icy eyes peering through the scarf that hid his face. Then the sharp pain running through his arm. And finally, nothing but darkness.

"Eyes of ice," he said to himself bitterly. If he had a handful of wheat for every pair of blue eyes he saw in Würzburg, he could fill a granary in a week.

For a moment he hoped that the mugging might merely have been some random, unfortunate twist of fate. The desperate actions of a starving man looking for a crust to eat. If that were the case, the draft would have been dumped somewhere, ruined by the rain or gnawed at by rodents. However, it was foolish to think such a thing. In all certainty, the thief already knew its incalculable value. So Gorgias began ruminating on who might have coveted that parchment.

Several clerics and servants had access to the scriptorium, but it was unlikely they could have conceived of the value of the document—unless they had overheard something from Wilfred, the only person who knew its secret. At that moment he decided to make an actual list of suspects.

Gorgias walked into the basilica through the side entrance that led directly to the cloister. He stopped there for a while to pray for Theresa. After shedding some tears, he traced the sign of the cross on the ground. Then he went through the kitchens, not bothering to greet the cellarer, making haste for the scriptorium.

He found the room empty, so he would be able to work until Terce without interruption. Closing the door, he shuttered the windows and carefully lit the mass of candles spread around on the desks. When their flames had cut through the darkness, he took his writing instruments and a wax tablet from a small chest, erasing his previous annotations with the blunt end of a stylus. He made himself comfortable on a stool—and, loosening up his hands, he started composing the list.

For a while he scribbled away at the tablet, noting and deleting names of suspects without being convinced of any of them. His arm was smarting again, but he hardly paid any attention. All that mattered was recovering the parchment. Once he had completed his list, one by one he reviewed the names.

First there was Genseric, Wilfred's coadjutor and secretary, a wizened old man, who, if not for his persistent odor of urine, could have been mistaken for one of the sculptures that flanked the ambulatories of the cloister. Genseric acted as vicar-general, which meant that, alongside Wilfred, he was responsible for the everyday administration and accounts of the district.

Then there was Bernardino, a Hispanic monk of tiny stature who ran the household with a firm hand. His role enabled him to come in and out of every room, so it would come as no surprise if he had got wind of the existence of the parchment.

Next in the list was Cassiano, the young precentor, a Tuscan whose honeyed voice, to Gorgias, reminded him of a woman of ill repute. As the head of the choir, Cassiano would often visit the part of the library where the psalters, tetragrams, and antiphons were kept. He was also one of the few adept at reading, which made him a serious suspect.

Finally, he had included Theodor, a giant man who, though of kindly demeanor, had the bluest eyes that Gorgias could remember seeing. Theodor worked as a general factotum, but because of his strength he often helped Wilfred with his relocations around the fortress.

He had erased Jeremiah, his personal assistant, and Emilius, his predecessor as a scribe, as well as the *cubicularius* Boniface, and Cyril, the novice master. The latter three could all read, but Boniface had almost entirely lost his sight, and both Cyril and Emilius had his complete trust.

The rest of the domestic staff and Wilfred's men were either illiterate or did not have access to the scriptorium.

Gorgias reread the tablet as he massaged his wounded forearm: Genseric, the old coadjutor; Bernardino, the midget; Cassiano, the precentor; Theodor, the giant. Any of them could have been behind the attack—as could have Korne, whom he had not forgotten.

He was trying to solve the mystery when there was a resounding knock on the door. Gorgias hid the tablet and hurried to open it. However, as he took hold of the bolt, he found that it was jammed into its housing. The knocking continued, accompanied by an urgent voice, so Gorgias pushed up on the latch again until the door gave way with a piercing squeak. Genseric, the old coadjutor, was waiting on the other side. His liquid gaze scanned the room.

"May I ask what all the fuss is about?" asked Gorgias in irritation.

"I am sorry to bother you, but Wilfred asked me to speak with you. I was surprised to find the door locked, and I thought that perhaps there was a problem."

"For the love of God, does nobody understand that my only problem is finding the time to do all the work that piles up in the scriptorium? What does Wilfred want now?"

"The count needs to see you. In his chambers," he elaborated.

In his chambers. A shiver ran down Gorgias's spine. To the best of his knowledge, no one had access to Wilfred's private rooms. In fact, the servants often said that aside from the coadjutor nobody knew the way. He frowned, sensing that the count's summons could not lead to anything good.

Gorgias took his time cleaning his instruments and gathering up all the documents that he presumed he would need for the meeting with Wilfred. When he was ready, the coadjutor turned around and started the walk back with weary steps. Gorgias followed him at a safe distance, still trying to guess the reason for the summons.

From the scriptorium they took the corridor that flanked the refectory, past the grain stores, across the cloister's portico where they entered the chapter house located behind the narthex, between the stone choir and the novices' chapel. At the back of the chapel was a passageway leading to the chapter house, normally closed off by a sturdy door. At that point Genseric stopped.

"Before continuing, you must swear that nothing will leave your lips about anything you see here," he warned.

Gorgias kissed the crucifix that hung from his neck. "I swear before Christ."

Genseric nodded, then removed a hood from his sleeve and offered it to Gorgias.

"I must ask you to cover your eyes," he ordered.

Gorgias did not protest. He took the hood and pulled it over his head.

"Now hold the end of this rope and follow my directions," he added.

Gorgias held out his hands until he grasped the rope that Genseric offered. He felt the old man tie it to his arm and then check to see if the hood was properly in place.

Moments later, Gorgias heard the squeaking of hinges and they departed, the rope suddenly tightening, forcing him to stumble forward with no means of support other than his unsteady feet. In the darkness, he followed the tugging of the rope, probing the wall with his injured arm, aided now and then by Genseric's terse warnings.

As he walked, he could feel the walls begin to ooze some greasy substance, which was not usual for those buildings. Gorgias wondered what part of the fortress he could possibly be in, for they had walked a fair stretch already. He had heard no fewer than four doors being opened so far. They had climbed a narrow staircase, and there was an unpleasant smell of excrement, which must have come from some nearby latrine. Then he felt as if they were descending a long slope, before climbing again on uneven, slippery ground. Before long, the rope that guided him slackened, signaling their arrival at their destination. He heard another bolt being opened, and the count's rasping voice resounded in his ears. "Please come in, Gorgias."

Genseric led Gorgias in, still wearing the hood. The door closed behind him and an unnerving silence descended upon the place.

"I should imagine, my good Gorgias, that you are wondering why I have summoned you."

"Indeed, Your Grace." The hood was suffocating.

"Well, I shall tell you. It seems paradoxical, does it not, that sometimes, the more diligently we serve God, the more He tests us. Last night," he continued, "not long after retiring, I began to feel out of sorts. It is not the first time it has happened to me, yet on this occasion the pain became so unbearable that I had to request the presence of our physician. Zeno believes that the malady in what is left of my legs is spreading to the rest of my body. It would seem there is no cure, or if there is, he doesn't know of it, so all I can do is try to rest before the pains return. But for goodness' sake! Take off that hood—you look like a condemned man!"

Gorgias obeyed.

As he removed the cloth, he could make out they were standing in what once must have been an armory. He saw bare walls of stone blocks arranged in neat lines, the order broken only by an alabaster window, a weak glow filtering through it. On the main wall, carved into the ashlars, he noticed the remnants of a crucifix, which seemed to be watching over the great four-poster bed. Wilfred lay among plump cushions, breathing with difficulty as though an intolerable weight bore down on his chest. This had the effect of transforming his face into a bloated mask. To his left were a side table with the remains of his breakfast and a chest holding a pair of chasubles with a coarse woolen habit lying on top. On the other side of the room Gorgias saw a clean chamber pot, a table, writing instruments, and a small alcove carved into the stone. There was no other furniture adorning the chamber. Only a single flimsy chair at the foot of the bed.

He was surprised not to see a single codex, or even a copy of the Bible. However, as his eyes became accustomed to the darkness, he could make out another room: Wilfred's private scriptorium.

Some menacing growls suddenly made Gorgias take a step back.

"Do not be alarmed," said the count with a smile. "The poor dogs are a little restless, but they aren't dangerous. Come and make yourself comfortable."

Before accepting his invitation, Gorgias made sure that the animals were tied to Wilfred's wheeled contraption. He also noticed that Genseric had left the room.

"So tell me the reason for this summons," said Gorgias, his eyes still fixed on the dogs.

"In fact it is you who must talk to me. It has been six days since we spoke and I haven't heard anything of your progress. Have you brought the parchment?"

"My Lord, I am not sure where to start!" he sputtered. "The truth is I must confess a matter that troubles me. Do you remember the problem with the ink?"

"Not exactly. Something to do with its fluidity?"

"That's right. As I said, the pens I have do not retain ink for very long. The excess flow causes splattering and sometimes leaves big trails of ink. Hence, I attempted to make a new mixture to solve the problem."

"Yes, I vaguely remember now. So?"

"After several days of reflection, I decided to test my theory last night. I charred a bit of walnut shell, which I added to the ink, and I mixed it with a drop of oil to thicken it. I also tried it with ash, a little tallow, and a pinch of alum. Naturally, before using it, I tested the mixture on a different parchment."

"Of course," the count said.

"Straightaway I noticed that the pen slid across the parchment as if floating on a pool of oil. The letters appeared bright and silky before my eyes, as smooth as a young girl's skin, and jet black. But, on the document, as I went back over the uncial letters, I had the accident."

"Accident? What accident?"

"These letters, the uncials, required a finish in accord with the importance of the document. I had to retouch them to ensure clean and well-defined edges. Unfortunately this process must take place before the final layer of pounce is applied."

"For the love of God! Stop beating about the bush and explain to me what has happened!"

Gorgias grimaced. The moment had come to fabricate some kind of mistake that would explain why he didn't have the document ready.

"I am sorry. I have no excuse for my ineptitude. The truth is that, through lack of sleep, I forgot that I had applied the pounce a few days earlier. The powder waterproofed the surface, and when I went back over the capital letters—"

"What?"

"Well, the whole thing was ruined. The whole damned document went to hell!"

"By God Almighty! But didn't you say you had resolved the problem?" asked Wilfred, making as if to get up.

"I was so pleased with my solution that I didn't notice the gypsum," he explained. "Because the pounce had covered the pores, the material could not absorb the ink, which spread to the point of ruining the entire parchment."

"This cannot be," Wilfred responded in disbelief. "And what about a palimpsest? Did you not prepare a palimpsest?"

"I could attempt it, but if I were to scrape the skin, it would make marks that would reveal the nature of the repair, and that of course would be unacceptable for this particular manuscript."

"Show me the document. What are you waiting for? Show it to me!" he screamed.

Gorgias clumsily produced a piece of crumpled parchment, which he held out to Wilfred. But before the count grasped it, Gorgias took a few steps back and tore it into pieces.

The horrified count thrashed about as though on fire. "Have you lost your mind!"

"I can see that you haven't fully understood," responded Gorgias in desperation. "It's ruined, don't you see? Ruined!"

Wilfred let out a guttural sound, his face contorted by rage. From the bed he tried to collect the pieces of parchment scattered over the rug, but in doing so he lost his balance and fell. Fortunately, Gorgias managed to catch him before he landed on the floor.

"Let go of me! Do you think the fact I don't have legs makes me a useless fool like you? Get your filthy hands off me, you damned squanderer!" he roared.

"Please try to calm down, Your Grace. That document is lost, but I am already working on a new parchment."

"A new parchment you say? And what will you do this time? Give it to a dog to keep between its jaws? Boil it? Shred it with a knife?"

"Your Grace, I beg you. Have faith. I will work day and night if necessary. I swear that you will have the document soon."

"And who says I have time for that?" replied Wilfred as he tried to make himself comfortable again. "The papal envoy could arrive at any moment, and if I do not have the document ready—by God! You do not know that prelate! I cannot bear to think what might happen to us."

Gorgias cursed his stupidity, but the fact was that his injured arm prevented him from proceeding with the required diligence. If the Roman legation arrived before it was ready, Wilfred could explain its absence by saying that it had been burned in the fire. Gorgias took a deep breath and turned to Wilfred once more. "When do you say the prelate will arrive?"

"I do not know. In his last letter he informed me that he would set sail from Frankfurt at the end of the year."

"The storm might delay them."

"Of course! Or they might arrive right now and catch me with my breeches down!"

For a moment, Gorgias didn't know whether he should suggest just relaying the truth, but he had little choice, so he presented the idea.

"What are you saying?" the count asked incredulously.

"I'm saying that if the envoy arrives before the document is ready, perhaps you could tell him that the original was burned in Korne's workshop. It would give us the time we need."

"I see. And tell me: Aside from convincing the prelate of your ineptitude—and also mine—do you have any other ingenious ideas?"

"I was merely trying."

"Well, for the love of God, Gorgias, stop trying and do something for once!"

Gorgias lowered his head, accepting that he had been foolish. He lifted his gaze and observed the count's pensive expression.

"Well, perhaps I have judged you too harshly. I do hope your intention is not to allow so many hours of work to go to waste."

"Of course not, Father."

"And your idea—about the fire," added the count. "It is truly what happened?"

"Indeed," said Gorgias, his nerves calming a little.

"Very well. And you think you could have the document ready in three weeks?"

"I am certain of it."

"Then this conversation is over. Begin work immediately. Put your hood back on."

Gorgias acquiesced. He went down on his knees, kissed Wilfred's wrinkled hands, and awkwardly donned the hood. As he waited for Genseric to arrive, he was finally able to breathe without feeling his heartbeat in his throat.

Though Gorgias was blinded again, the walk back seemed shorter than the way there. At first he attributed this to Genseric's haste, but as they walked he realized that the coadjutor was taking him down a different path. Indeed, he did not notice the stench of the latrines or the stairs that he had climbed on the way there. For a moment he thought the change might be attributed to Genseric's zealousness, for at that time the whole building would be crawling with servants, but when the coadjutor told him to remove the hood, he was surprised to find that he still didn't know where he was.

Gorgias examined the small circular room closely. An altar was situated at the center, and on it a torch crackled away. The flickering light cast a yellow glow on the hewn stone and the timber roof, which had been eaten away by rot. Between the beams there were blurry liturgical images, blackened slightly by the smoke from the candles. He deduced that the room must have been a Christian crypt, though judging by its state, it would be easy to mistake it for the dungeons of the Hagia Sofia.

To one side he saw a second door, bolted shut.

"What is this place?" he asked in surprise.

"An old chapel."

"I can see that. An interesting place, no doubt, but you will understand that I have other duties to get on with," he said, losing his patience.

"All in good time, Gorgias, all in good time." The coadjutor gave a hint of a smile as he took a candle from a bag, lit it, and placed it at one end of the stone altar. Then he went over to the door that Gorgias had spotted and drew back the enormous bolt that kept it closed. "Please, this way."

Gorgias did not trust him.

"Or follow me if you prefer," he added.

He let the old man go in first before hesitantly following.

"Allow me to sit," Genseric continued. "It's the damp. It gnaws at my bones. You sit, too, please."

Gorgias reluctantly complied. The smell of dry urine that Genseric exuded made him retch.

"I suppose you are wondering why I brought you here."

"Well, yes," Gorgias answered, his irritation growing.

Genseric smiled again, taking his time to respond.

"It's about the fire. An ugly affair, Gorgias. Too many dead . . . and what's worse: too many losses. I believe Wilfred has already spoken to you about the intentions of Korne, the parchment-maker."

"You mean his determination to hold me responsible?"

"Believe me, it is not just intentions. The parchment-maker might be a thoughtless individual, a primitive man without restraint, but I can assure you that his tenacity is inhuman. He blames you blindly for what has happened, and he will do anything to see you pay with your blood. And forget about compensation. His desire for revenge obeys reasons that you will never comprehend."

"That's not what the count told me," Gorgias answered, his concern growing.

"And what did he tell you? That a reparation would appease his anger? That he will be content with whatever he makes from selling you as a slave? No, my friend. No. That is not Korne's way. I might not have Wilfred's refined learning, but I know a rat when I smell one. Have you heard about the rats of the Main?"

Gorgias shook his head, nonplussed.

"The rats of the Main band together to form ferocious packs. The eldest rat selects her prey without a care for its size or any difficulty it presents. She patiently stalks it, and when the time is right, she leads the clan to kill—and they devour it. Korne is a Main rat. The worst kind of rat you can imagine."

Gorgias fell silent. Wilfred had told him about the Carolingian code, the fines he might have to pay by way of compensation, and the possibility that Korne might bring the weight of the law down upon him, but he didn't mention all that Genseric seemed to be insinuating.

"Perhaps Korne should try to understand that I have also received my punishment. Moreover, the law obliges him to—"

"Korne? Understand?" Genseric interrupted with a guffaw. "For Christ's sake, Gorgias, do not delude yourself! Since when has a law protected the destitute? Even if the foundations of the Ripuarian Code underpin our justice system, and even if the reforms undertaken by Charlemagne abound with Christian charity, I can assure you that none of them will free you from Korne's hatred."

Gorgias could feel his stomach turning. The deranged old man kept blurting out absurd stories of rats and meaningless prophecies, while he had work to do—work that would take an incomprehensible amount of time to finish. He felt on edge and so signaled that the conversation was over by standing. "Sorry, but I do not share your fears. And now, if you don't mind, I would like to return to the scriptorium."

Genseric shook his head. "Gorgias, Gorgias . . . you must try to understand. Give me another moment and you will be grateful for it—you'll see," he said condescendingly. "Did you know that Korne was a Saxon?"

"A Saxon? I thought his children were baptized."

"A convert, but Saxon nonetheless. When Charlemagne conquered the lands of the north, he forced the Saxons to choose between the cross and the gallows. Since then I have attended to many of these converts, and though they come to my mass and fast at Lent, I can assure you that the poison of sin still runs through their veins."

Gorgias rapped his knuckles on the chair. Genseric's words were making him increasingly worried.

"Did you know that they still practice ritual sacrifice?" he added. "They meet at crossroads to slit calves' throats. They perform sodomy. They even engage their sisters in the most appalling incestuous acts. Korne is one of them, and Wilfred knows it. But the count does not know about their ancestral traditions—customs like the *faide*, by which the death of a son is avenged with the murder of the person responsible. That is the *faide*, Gorgias. Saxon vengeance."

"But how many times do I have to say it? The fire was an accident," said Gorgias in irritation. "Wilfred can confirm it."

"Calm down, Gorgias. It does not matter what you say, or even what really happened that morning. All that matters is that Korne blames your daughter. She is dead, and soon you will follow her."

Gorgias looked at him. Genseric's liquid gaze seemed to cut right through him.

"You brought me here for this? To announce my death?"

"To help you, Gorgias. I brought you here to help you."

The old man paused. Then stood up. He gestured to Gorgias to wait and went out of the cell, in the direction of the crypt. "Wait there, I must fetch something."

Gorgias obeyed. From inside the cell he could see Genseric wandering back and forth in the crypt. Then he returned with a lit candle, which he placed on a ledge near the doorway.

"Take this," he said, tossing an object to Gorgias.

"A wax tablet?"

Genseric's only response was to retreat a few steps before, in one quick movement, he slammed the door shut, leaving Gorgias alone inside.

"What in God's name are you doing? Open this door immediately!"

He realized after some time that all he would achieve by pounding on the door was tearing his knuckles. When he finally stopped banging on the door, he heard Genseric's voice, softer than ever.

"Believe me, it's better for you. You will be safe here," the elderly man whispered.

"You demented old fool—you can't keep me here. The count will flay you alive when he finds out."

"Poor, deluded Gorgias," he said. "Do you not see that Wilfred himself conceived all this?"

Gorgias did not believe him.

"You must be insane. He would never—"

"Shut up and listen! On the table you will find a stylus. Note the items you need: books, ink, documents . . . I will return after Terce to collect the list. Until then you may do as you wish. It looks like you will have time to complete the task, after all."

7

Not long before midday, Theresa savored her last mouthful of salt roe. She foraged in her bag for any remaining crumbs and then sucked her fingers until they were glistening. She took a gulp of water and sat down to rest. She knew the terrain well, but looking ahead the snow hid any distinguishing landmarks, creating an immaculate landscape that obscured the routes that ran through it.

Since she had left the cabin, she had endeavored to follow Hoos Larsson's advice when he had told her about his journey. She recalled his description of the Saxons as lazy brutes, careless folks whose singing and extravagant campfires were usually enough to betray their whereabouts. According to Hoos, staying alive was not difficult: All she needed to do was behave with the cunning of a hunted animal, move stealthily, refrain from lighting fires, avoid startling flocks of birds, and watch for footprints in the snow. He had also declared that, with enough care, anyone who knew the way could make it through the passes.

"Anyone who knows the way," she grumbled.

Normally, to reach Aquis-Granum travelers had to take the western route, which meant crossing the River Main in the direction of Frankfurt, following its course for four days to its confluence with the Rhine, and then journeying for three more days to the capital. But according to Hoos, with the bandits prowling both banks of the river, that route meant certain capture.

On the other hand, in the middle of winter, with the snow growing worse on the paths, going south to the Alps would be an act of insanity.

She decided that her only option was to travel via Fulda.

She looked skyward to contemplate the impregnable wall of mountains. The Rhön range marked the northern boundary of the countship of Würzburg. It was the road that Hoos had taken from Aquis-Granum. Once she reached Fulda, she would continue along the Lahn, a river that, according to Hoos, was easy to negotiate.

Though she had never traveled to Fulda, Theresa estimated that it would take her two days to reach the abbatial city, which meant she would have to spend the night on the road. She crossed herself, took a deep breath of air and set off toward the mountains.

She walked in double time, fixing her sights on the peaks that seemed more distant with every stride. Drinking her remaining water, she ate whatever berries and nuts she could find on the way. For several miles she marched without incident, but within three hours she started to hobble. What began as a slight tingling quickly became a sharp pain that finally stopped her in her tracks. With snow up to her knees, she looked at the mountains and sighed. Dusk had arrived. If she wanted to reach the Rhön pass, she would have to pick up the pace considerably.

She was about to get moving again when a whinny made her start. She turned slowly, expecting to find an enemy, but to her surprise there was nothing there. Soon she heard another whinny, followed by some barking. She kicked away the snow that confined her and ran to crouch behind some rocks, but as she hid, she noticed with horror that she had left a trail of footprints in the snow. Whoever came through would undoubtedly discover her. She tucked in her head and waited, hunched over, as the barking grew louder until it became the clamor of a pack of dogs. Slowly she lifted her head and scanned the surroundings. The place was still deserted, but she noticed that the racket came from the gully flanking the path.

She hesitated for a moment but then decided to leave her hiding place, and she crawled to the edge of the precipice, where she lay flat on her stomach. She edged forward to poke her head out and was immediately transfixed by the scene in front of her: A pack of wolves were devouring the innards of a horse, which lay at the bottom of the gully. The poor horse was puffing and snorting, struggling and kicking in desperation. She could see its guts already strewn across the snow.

Without giving it a second thought, she shouted and waved her arms as if she were the one being attacked. Upon hearing her, the wolves stopped feasting and immediately started growling with menace. For a moment she thought they would attack her, so she bent down and picked up a dry branch at her feet. Wielding it above her head, she threw it at the pack with all her strength. The stick flew until it hit the crown of a tree. The snow that had piled high on its branches dislodged, falling to the ground. A gray wolf was startled and fled. The others hesitated, but then quickly followed.

After making sure they weren't returning, Theresa decided to head down the gully. Descending was more difficult than she expected, and when she arrived at the bottom, she could see that the horse was in the throes of death. She found it peppered with wounds—and not all of them had been inflicted with teeth. She tried to loosen its girth, but it was impossible. It shuddered as though it were being flayed, whinnied a couple of times, and then—after several spasms—it lay lifeless in the snow.

A tear of compassion rolled down Theresa's cheek. Calming herself, she untied the saddlebags and inspected them. In the first she found a blanket, a lump of cheese, and a leather bag with the name Hoos scrawled on it. For a moment she froze, stunned by the coincidence of her discovery. The horse undoubtedly belonged to the Larsson boy. He had mentioned that his mount had fallen headlong down a ravine, which explained the other injuries. She bit into the cheese and continued to search eagerly. In the same saddlebag she found a tanned boar skin, a pot of jam, another of oil, two metal traps, and a flask containing a stinking essence. She kept the jam and left everything else. In the other saddlebag, there were several more skins that she could not identify, a sealed amphora, a handful of peacock feathers, and a box of beauty ointments. She assumed they were gifts that Hoos had been taking to his relatives, and that he may have decided to leave behind when he lost his mount.

She knew that some of these objects might come in useful, yet they would also be a burden. What's more, if someone found them on her, they might accuse her of theft, so she decided to take just the food. She closed the saddlebags, and glancing back at the horse for the last time, continued her journey.

She reached the entrance to the pass with enough light remaining to see that it was impassable in the dark, so she decided to spend the night on the mountain. The next day she would continue to the east in search of the path to Fulda. All she knew was that there was a peculiar rock formation that, according to Hoos, marked the beginning of the route.

At first she thought she could endure the cold, but when her feet started to freeze, she decided to light a campfire. She arranged some firewood under a handful of tinder before striking her steel against the pieces of flint. The tinder ignited, but just as easily as it caught fire, it also extinguished before the branches could start to burn.

She knew that the damp wood was the problem and she would have to position the drier branches on top of the damp ones. She restacked the firewood, placed another little pile of tinder upon it, and repeated the operation, with the same result. Distraught, she saw there was only enough tinder left for a couple more attempts. Perhaps if she used it all at once instead of little by little, she might have a chance.

She pulled out the flask of oil and poured a little onto the branches. Once they were soaked, she put the tinder onto a piece of leather and stamped on the little box until it was shattered into pieces. Then she arranged the splinters under the tinder and prayed that they would catch.

For the third time, she struck the flint, which spat out sparks as if by magic. On the fourth attempt the tinder caught. She quickly blew on the flames that licked against the splinters. For a moment they faded until they had almost died, but gradually they began to gain strength until they spread to the oiled branches.

That night she slept peacefully. In the warmth of the fire she imagined her father watching over her. She dreamed of her family, of her work as a parchment-maker, and of Hoos Larsson. She pictured him noble, strong, valiant. At the end of the dream, he was kissing her.

The storm woke Theresa just before dawn. She gathered her belongings and ran to take shelter under a nearby oak tree. When it stopped raining, she felt like the cold would return. But gradually the clouds dispersed and the sun timidly cast its rays on the mountain peaks. She took it as a good omen.

Before setting off again she prayed to God for the good health of her father and her stepmother, and also for the soul of Hoos's unfortunate horse. She also thanked him for allowing her to live another day. Then she wrapped herself in her cloak, bit into a piece of cheese, and started walking, still wet from the rain.

Three miles later, she began to wonder whether she had taken the right route. The tracks had narrowed to footpaths, appearing and disappearing in the endless white surroundings. Yet she went on undaunted, on a course that appeared to lead to nowhere.

At midday she came across a fast-flowing stream that blocked her path. She walked along the bank for a while, looking for somewhere to wade across, until she reached a section where the water had formed a large pool. There she stopped to admire the scenery, the fir trees and mountain peaks reflected in the clear surface of the water as though it were a mirror, doubling their beauty. She was captivated by how the trees bunched together like a vast army, with snow dotting their olive-green foliage. The water gurgled peacefully and the intense aroma of resin mixed with the cold to clear her lungs.

Hunger growled softly in her stomach.

Though she knew she would find nothing, she rummaged through her bag once again before deciding to do something she had sometimes seen the village boys do: She looked for a shady bend in the stream and lifted up some rocks until she found a seething mass of worms. Then she made a hook by taking a clasp from her hair and bending it over a branch before threading a couple of worms. She tied one end to a string of wool that she pulled from her dress and cast it as far into the water as she could. If she was lucky, she would be having roast trout for lunch.

No sooner had she cast her line, she saw something unsettling. Half-hidden in the undergrowth, a few paces away, she noticed some sort of grounded craft. Hoos wouldn't have bothered to mention something like that to her, but no doubt it was one of those ferries used to transport goods back and forth over the river.

She pushed aside the thicket and jumped onto the boat, which creaked under her weight. Near the bow she found a pole, resting on a rope that formed a bridge from one bank to the other. She thought it was probably used to prevent the current from dragging the ferry off during loading. After checking that the hull was intact, she decided to use it to cross to the other side of the bank.

Walking around to the grounded end, she pressed her back against the stern and pushed with all her weight, her feet sinking into the mud. The ferry didn't budge. She attempted it several more times, until her legs and arms were trembling. Exhausted, she finally fell to the ground, crying bitterly.

Since fleeing Würzburg, she had lost count of the times she had cried. Wiping away her tears, she thought about giving up and wondered if she should return and beg Wilfred, God, or whoever necessary for mercy. At least then she could be with her family, and perhaps with their help she could prove that she had not caused the fire. However, she remembered the dead girl and shuddered. Her idea was surely deluded. She decided that if she were to make any sort of life for herself, it would have to be on the other side of this river.

Dismayed, she looked around until she found a medium-sized pebble, which she threw with all her strength toward the opposite bank. The stone flew a quarter of the way across the pool before sinking, so she estimated that it was around a hundred paces wide. In that cold water she would never make it across by swimming. She thought there might be a bridge farther on. But just as she was about to continue on her way, it occurred to her that if she hung from the rope, perhaps she could claw her way to the other side. On either side of the bank the rope was knotted to a tree, and the trees seemed secure enough to support a man's weight. She could also see that, though the rope dipped halfway across, at no point would she be entirely submerged.

Persuaded by the idea, she waded into the water. The cold made her flinch, but she kept going. When she started to lose her footing, she swung up onto the rope and maneuvered herself until she was hanging belly-up. She advanced toward the other side by stretching and contracting like a caterpillar.

She completed the first stretch without difficulty, but a third of the way across, the rope dipped, dropping her dangerously close to the water. When the water finally touched her back, she dropped off and started swimming, holding on to the rope as a guide. When the rope started to rise again, she pulled herself back up. That was when her bag came open and the steel fell out. She tried to grab the little box, but the current dragged it down until it disappeared under the water. Swearing, she pressed on, until at last, after what seemed like an eternity, she reached the other shore.

As soon as she arrived, shivering, she pulled off her wet clothes, in order to wring them out. As she was doing so, she noticed a strange glimmer that seemed to come from an indeterminate point nearby. She thought it might be the steel she had just lost, and though it was highly unlikely, she quickly dressed anyway and headed toward the spot. However, as she approached, she could see that it was a mass of crayfish, swarming over the disfigured body of a dead soldier. She assumed it was a Saxon, though it could also have been a Frank.

Theresa noticed the great gash running from the soldier's left ear to the base of his neck. His face was worm-eaten and blood had accumulated under the skin, turning it purple. His ankles seemed dislocated and from under his clothes, his stomach protruded, swollen like an old wineskin. She noticed that the glint she had seen came from the scramasax that he wore on his belt. She briefly thought about taking it, but then gave up on the idea, for everyone knew that the souls of the dead kept vigil over their bodies for three days.

She stepped back to watch the spectacle, repulsed and astounded. And she imagined what the crayfish would taste like once they had been roasted over a fire. Then she remembered that she had lost her steel and wondered whether one could be found on the body. Using a stick, she flicked aside several crayfish, but all she found underneath were entrails and more creatures.

As she became absorbed rummaging through his clothes, someone suddenly grabbed her from behind. Theresa screamed and kicked as if the Devil himself had seized her, but a hand was pressed over her mouth. In response she sunk her nails into the arm with such force that she thought they would come clean off. Then she received a blow to her face and was shaken like a rag doll.

"Damned bitch! Scream again and I'll tear out your tongue!"

Theresa tried to scream, but she was unable to with his hand still covering her mouth.

The figure before her seemed more like a creature from Hell than a human. The old man's face was mouse-bitten and devoured by rot. His thin hair revealed several bald patches dotted with wounds and grime, and his menacing gray eyes seemed to stare right through her. Her gaze fell on the fangs of the dog that accompanied him.

"Don't worry, lass, Satan only bites people who ask for it. You alone?"

"Yes," she stammered, immediately regretting her response.

"What were you searching that dead man for?"

"Nothing." She bit her tongue at such a stupid answer.

"Nothing, eh? Well! Get those shoes off and throw them over there," he ordered. "What's your name?"

"Theresa," she answered, following his instructions.

"Good. Give me that," he said, pointing at the bag she had on her shoulder. "May I know what you're doing here?"

Theresa did not respond.

The man opened her bag and inspected its contents. "And this dagger?"

It was the knife she had stolen from Hoos Larsson. "Give it back." Theresa snatched it from him and stuffed it in her dress.

The man didn't protest, but continued to rummage.

"What's this?" he asked. He had already pulled out the stylus and wax tablets.

"What?"

"Don't play the fool. This parchment that you were hiding in a secret compartment."

Theresa was surprised. She imagined that her father, for some reason, had hidden it there.

"A poem by Virgil. I always keep it protected so it doesn't get dirty," she improvised.

"Poems," he muttered as he returned the parchment to her. "What sentimentality! Now pay attention," he continued. "This place is crawling with bandits, so I don't care what you do, where you come from, whether you're alone or what you were searching that body for, but I warn you: If you try to scream or do anything silly, Satan will tear your throat open before you know what's happening. Got it?"

Theresa nodded. She would've tried to escape, but without shoes it would've been stupid. She presumed that was why he had told her to remove them. She took a few steps back and examined the old man. He wore a threadbare cloak tied around his waist, revealing long, bony legs. When he had finished rummaging through her bag, he bent down and picked up a stick with a bell hanging from one end. Theresa looked at his wounds more closely and realized he was a leper.

With this realization, she didn't give it a second thought. As soon as the old man glanced elsewhere, she turned and ran, but before she could even take a few steps, she lost her footing and slipped. No sooner had she hit the ground, she felt the dog's breath on her back. She waited, stock-still, for its fatal blow, but the animal didn't move. The man approached and held out a scab-covered hand toward her. Theresa moved away.

"You're frightened by my sores?" he laughed. "So are the bandits. Come on, get up. It's just dye."

Theresa examined the ulcers, which close-up looked like blotches, yet even so, she did not trust the man. Noticing this, the man rubbed his hands and the wounds disappeared.

"See? I'm not lying. Come now: Sit there and stay still." He gave her back her bag. "You won't get far with what you have in there."

"You're not a leper?" she stammered.

"Of course not," he laughed. "But it's a disguise that has saved my skin more than once. Watch carefully."

The man took a fistful of sand from the river, draining the water from it. He then took out a flask of dark dye and poured it on the sand, making a uniform mixture. He added another substance and applied the poultice to his arms.

"I mix it with a paste of flour and water so that it sticks to me when it dries. The bandits fear a leper more than any army." He glanced at the dead man. "Except this one," he said nodding at him. "The bastard tried to steal my furs. Now he can try to thieve from the Devil. So . . . since when have you been robbing corpses?"

As Theresa was about to answer, the old man bent down and—ignoring the crayfish—he searched the body. He found a bag tied inside some sort of sash. He smiled upon seeing its contents and stashed the bag in his clothes. Next he pulled necklaces with strange, dark stones off the man's throat. Then he picked up the scramasax, sheathed it next to his own, and, finally, turned over the dead body. Finding nothing else of interest, he left it lying among the pebbles.

"Well, he won't be needing it anymore. And now, are you going to tell me what you're doing here?"

"You killed him?"

"Not me. It was this," he said, touching his knife. "I suppose he had been watching me for some time. He must have been an imbecile because instead of dispatching me he went straight for the furs."

"Furs?"

"The ones I have back there, in the cart," he said, pointing.

Theresa turned to where the old man indicated and the sight of it cheered her: If there was a cart, there had to be a road.

"A wheel's broken and I'm going to see if I can repair it. But you should get away from here. I doubt this man was traveling alone."

He gave Theresa back her shoes. Then he turned and walked off toward the woods.

"Wait," said Theresa, pulling her shoes on and running after him. "Are you going to Fulda?"

"I have little reason to visit that city of priests."

"But, do you know the way?"

"Of course. As well as the bandits."

Theresa didn't know what to say. She followed him to the cart, observing his walk: He had the gait of a younger man. Then she saw his teeth, which though large and crooked, were gapless and extraordinarily white. She thought he might be her father's age. He bent down near the split wheel and started to work on it. Then he stopped and looked at Theresa.

"You haven't answered me. What were you searching for on the body?" Then before she could respond he looked down at himself. "Damnation! Look what you've done to my arm," he said as he cleaned the scratches from Theresa's fingernails. "Did you think the Devil was coming to get you?"

"I was on my way to Fulda." She cleared her throat. "I saw a dead man and I thought he might have a steel. I lost mine when I crossed the lake."

"Crossed the lake you say? Let's see . . . pass me that mallet. So you came from Erfurt?"

"That's right," she lied, handing him the tool.

"Then you must know the Petersohns. They run the bakery just a few buildings down from the cathedral."

"Of course," she fibbed again.

"How are they? I haven't seen them since summer."

"They're well . . . as far as I know. My parents live some way from the town."

"Is that right?" he said, grimacing. He hit the wedge hard and the wheel came away from its axle.

Theresa gave a start, thinking maybe he didn't believe her.

"Now comes the difficult part," the man continued. "See this spoke? It's split. And so is this other one. Lousy damned timber! I'll change the most damaged one and repair the other with a couple strips of wood. Take this. Hold it—and when I hit it, ring the bell. If the bandits have to hear us, then let them hear the music of the lepers, too."

Theresa noticed that the old man had unhitched the horse and arranged several rocks under the cart to stop it from toppling. He pulled a stick out from the back, which turned out to be a spare spoke. He kept talking, saying that he always carried one with him because carving oak was very difficult. He compared the new spoke to the broken ones before adjusting the end with an adze.

"Will it take long?"

"I hope not. If I bothered to do it properly, I'd be here all night: I'd have to take off the iron rim, remove the four surrounds, and replace the spokes. It's not difficult, because the surrounds are of ash, but then you have to mount the pivots, the tongue, and the ends of the spokes." He stood back to look at his work. "A devilish job! I'll saw the ends and adjust them with the mallet. Now shake the bell."

Theresa swayed the stick until the bell jingled. The hammer blow resounded all around the forest. The young woman tried to drown out the echo by shaking the bell harder, but try as she might, the blows could be heard all morning.

They talked. He said his name was Althar. He was a trapper who lived in a log cabin in the woods with his wife and their dog, Satan. In winter he hunted and in summer he sold the furs in Aquis-Granum. Theresa said that she had fled a marriage of convenience and asked for his help to reach Fulda. But he refused, and when he had finished mending the cart, he said farewell.

"You're going?" Theresa asked.

"Yes, I'm going home."

"What about me?"

"What *about* you?"

"What will I do?"

Althar shrugged. "What you should have done from the beginning: Go back to Erfurt and marry that man you say you hate. I bet he's not so bad."

"I would rather go to the Saxons," she said, with such conviction that she admired her own acting skills.

"You can do whatever you want as far as I'm concerned." Althar hitched the horse to the harness and began removing the stones that held the cart in place. "But hurry. There might be more bandits looking for him," he said, pointing at the dead man. "I'll lead the horse to the river. After she has drunk, I'll be off like the clappers."

Theresa walked off. As she went, she saw the forest as dense and cold as a cemetery, and tears came to her eyes. She stopped, knowing that if she continued alone she would die. Althar seemed like a good man, for he had done her no harm. Besides, he was married and knew the Petersohns. Perhaps he would allow her to accompany him.

She pleaded with him to let her stay and talked of her skill as a seamstress, and lied about her ability to cook, but Althar did not seem impressed.

"I can also tan skins," she added.

The old man looked at her out of the corner of his eye, indicating this was an area where he could use a little help. Leatherwork required dexterity, and his wife, since the last of her fevers, could barely move her hands. He looked at her again and shook his head.

No doubt this ill-bred lass would only make his life difficult. What's more, his wife would be suspicious of a young woman.

He moved the last stone away and climbed on the cart.

"Look, lass, I like you, but you'd be a burden. Another mouth to feed. I'm sorry. Go back to your town and ask that man to forgive you."

"I won't go back."

"Then do what you want." He urged the horse on.

Theresa didn't know what to say. But suddenly she remembered the traps she had found by Hoos's mount.

"I'll make it worth your while."

Althar raised an eyebrow and glanced at her. "I don't think you could. I'm too old to get my cock moving."

The young woman pretended not to hear him. "Look at your traps . . . they're old and rusty," she observed, walking alongside the cart.

"So am I, but I can still look after myself."

"But I can get you some new ones. I know where to find them."

Althar stopped the horse. Some new traps would of course be useful, and in truth he felt sorry for the poor girl. Theresa told him about the incident with the wolves and the contents of the saddlebags. She also described the place where it happened.

"Are you sure it was in that gully?"

She nodded. Althar seemed to be considering it.

"Pox on you! Come on, get in the cart. I know a path that will take us to that precipice. And change your clothes, or you'll die before you can show me the exact place."

The young woman leaped onto the cart and made herself comfortable in the heap of furs. The dozens of bundles in the cart began to jump about with the trotting of the horse. Theresa recognized pelts of beaver and deer, and even one or two wolf pelts. Most of them looked to be in a fairly poor state. Several skins looked like they had been tanned, but most were teeming with insects that crawled among the dried out fur and remnants of blood as though the skins had been flayed that very morning. She positioned herself as far away as possible from them, for they gave off an unbreathable stench, and she covered herself with a dry skin she found acceptable. Behind her, she discovered an earthenware jar covered with a greasy mesh that let off the delicious aroma of cheese.

Theresa squeezed her belly, trying to calm her complaining intestines. Then she lay back and closed her eyes. In her mind's eye, she journeyed back to Würzburg, to the winter mornings when Gorgias would wake her with a kiss so she could help him light the oven they had built. She recalled looking out over the snow-covered fields, and how thankful she was for the warmth of the embers on those early mornings when she accompanied her father, reading some manuscript to him. She wondered whether Althar had ever seen a book.

She looked at Satan. The animal followed behind the cart by about a stone's throw. He looked like he had more intelligence in his little darting eyes than some of the boys she knew. Once in a while he would come closer to the horse to jump into the air and catch the pieces of meat that Althar threw him. Theresa heard her belly rumble again and asked Althar when they would eat.

"Do you think I'm made of food? Patience, lass. Now get cleaning those skins. The brush is there, by the bow."

Theresa made no complaints. She took one of the bulkiest bundles, untied the tendons that held it together, and boldly started to clean one of the grotesque furs on her lap. On the first stroke, a swarm of insects flew from the skin, falling to the floor of the cart and scattering across the boards. She kept brushing, her eyes fixed firmly on the pelts, until she had brushed the whole bundle. Without respite she continued to do the same with a second wad of furs. When she had finished, Althar pointed at a third.

"After that, clean the traps till they're gleaming," he said.

Theresa grabbed the traps, spat on the filth, and got started with her new task. Then, as she scrubbed the contraptions, she reflected that Althar must have a special gift for the art of hunting, for how else could he have amassed such a collection of furs? When at last she finished her work, she informed Althar, who, surprised at her diligence, stopped the cart to check her handiwork.

"Right then, lass, time to fill our bellies," he said with a smile before clambering off.

He went to the back of the cart and rooted around until he produced a small sack, which he dropped on the ground. Satan approached for a sniff, but Althar kicked him away. Then he turned to Theresa. "Climb up to that hillock and take a good look around. If you see anything out of the ordinary: a fire, horses, men, anything out of place, bark like a dog."

"Bark?" asked Theresa incredulously.

"Yes, bark . . . you know how to bark, don't you?"

Theresa practiced barking with varying success. She thought it sounded awful, but Althar seemed satisfied.

"Hurry, then. And take the bell with you."

While she climbed the slope, he prepared some slices of cheese with pieces of hard bread. Then he cut open a couple of onions. He commandeered the biggest portion and then beckoned Theresa.

"All quiet," said the young woman.

"Good. At this rate we'll reach the gully before midday. We'll eat now because we won't stop again. Back there, behind the traps, you'll find some wine. And put some more clothes on, if you want. You must be freezing."

The trapper clambered back onto the cart and urged the horse on. Theresa followed his lead, and dispensing with any prayers of thanks, she set about her food, washing it down with a gulp of wine that tasted of heaven.

Before long they were traveling over a strip of woodland surrounded by a quagmire. Althar's countenance changed, and he seemed more cautious. Any noise that they heard would make him give a start. He glanced around continuously, and every now and again he stopped the cart to stand up and scan the surroundings. There were moments when he thought Satan was sniffing danger. The hound was no longer straying very far from the cart. With his ears pricked and tail extended, he followed his master's movements closely.

They must have gone a hundred paces when the dog began to bark. Althar stopped the cart dead, clambered down and walked on ahead. With a worried expression he ordered Theresa to be silent, his hand slowly moving to his scramasax. Then, without a word, he straightened and disappeared into the undergrowth, leaving Theresa in the cart in the middle of the road.

Theresa's nerves started to get the better of her. She tried to stand on tiptoes to see farther than her stature permitted, but the sores on her feet prevented her. She didn't know why, exactly, but in her bones she felt that something terrible was about to happen.

A few moments later Althar reappeared looking shaken. "Come with me. Quickly."

Theresa jumped down from the cart and followed him into the vegetation. The trapper walked bent over like a cat stalking its prey, while the young woman floundered behind him, dodging the branches that he pushed aside. They progressed with difficulty through the dead leaves and mud from the recent rains. In some places the undergrowth was so thick that all Theresa could see was Althar's behind, a hand's width from her face.

Suddenly he turned his head to signal that she should be silent, and slowly he moved aside to reveal a scene of death and devastation. Two blood-soaked bodies lay on top of one another in a macabre embrace, half-hidden under a mantle of slime. A few paces ahead, half-submerged in a ditch, the mutilated corpse of a third man could be made out.

"This one's no Saxon," said Althar, nudging one of the men with his foot.

Theresa didn't respond. Despite the mud, she recognized those clothes. She had seen them in the Larssons' cabin. With her heart in her throat, she approached the grotesquely conjoined bodies. Slowly she pulled away the one on top and suddenly her vision clouded over and she would have fallen to the ground if Althar hadn't held her up. The body lying under that shroud of blood was none other than Hoos Larsson, the young man who had a few days prior saved her life.

* * *

After a few moments, Althar realized that Hoos Larsson was still breathing. He immediately informed Theresa, and they carried him to the cart to tend to his wounds. The old man examined him with concern. Theresa questioned Althar with her eyes as to the seriousness of his injuries, but he didn't answer.

"You say he saved you?" he asked.

She nodded, tears rolling down her cheeks.

"Well, I'm sorry for him, but we can't take him with us."

"We can't leave him, he'll die."

"He's going to die anyway. What's more, look at that wheel," he said, pointing at the repaired spoke. "You two, me, and the load—with so much weight, it won't last a mile."

"Then get rid of the furs," Theresa suggested.

"The skins? Don't make me laugh! They're my living for the next year."

Althar's words seemed final. Theresa hesitated. She knew that if she was to help Hoos, she would have to be convincing.

"The man you want to abandon to his fate is called Hoos Larsson. He's an antrustion of the king," she lied. "If he survives he could feed you and your family for the rest of your lives."

Althar looked at Hoos's near-lifeless body and spat in surprise. He was at pains to admit it, but perhaps the girl was right. Upon examining the young man, he had already noticed his fine clothes, and though he had thought them stolen, perhaps that was a rash conclusion. After all, he could see how well tailored his robes were and the perfect fit of his shoes; he doubted that a thief would have had such good luck.

He cursed. Perhaps the man was indeed who Theresa claimed he was, though that did not change his fragile state or his own predicament. He might not be able to save him, but maybe he would last long enough to reach Aquis-Granum alive. He cursed again and took the reins of the horse, which had been grazing through the layer of snow. Carefully reconsidering it, he spat and grumbled, "He might live, I suppose."

Theresa nodded, relieved.

"Until I get my reward, at least," Althar muttered to himself.

With the additional weight of Hoos, Theresa was forced to walk. Althar urged on the mount, using the whip as readily as he uttered oaths. He forbade Theresa from holding on to the cart because, he said, it couldn't bear the weight. And he made Theresa push with all her might whenever they had to climb a slope.

Most of the time Althar drove alongside and in pace with Theresa. She confessed that the traps she had spoken of actually belonged to Hoos Larsson, but this fact did not seem to bother him. They kept moving, stopping only when they had to readjust the repaired wheel. When they reached the gully, the traps were still next to the horse's carcass, nearly licked clean by the pack of obstinate wolves.

As Althar retrieved the equipment, she attended to Hoos. The old man had said that Hoos had several broken ribs and that they might have pierced his lungs, which is why he laid him face up on some bundles of fur.

He was still breathing weakly. After moistening his face, she wondered what had made Hoos deviate from his planned route. She thought he might have followed her to reclaim the dagger, which she suddenly became aware of again under her skirt where she had concealed it. She continued to clean Hoos until Althar returned, laden with equipment.

"There was more than you promised," he announced with a smile. "Now let's see how we're going to carry it."

"You're not intending to leave him."

"Don't you worry, lass. If it's true that these valuable things are this man's possessions, I'll do everything in my power to save him."

After some food, they continued their journey headed toward the mountains and Althar spoke of the past. Years ago he said he had lived in Fulda, working like the rest of its inhabitants in the service of the abbey. He and his wife, Leonora, managed to rent a plot, where they built a nice cabin. In the morning they would work the land, and in the afternoon they would move onto the abbey's fields to pay their *corvées*. That tenure gave them enough to buy a small piece of land, not much, around forty unplowed arpents, but enough to grow their own crops. He explained that they didn't have children. The Lord's punishment, he reasoned, for the little faith he professed. Like most simple folks he learned several trades without mastering any. He was skilled with the axe and the adze. He built his own furniture, and in autumn, with his wife's help, he repaired the roof.

The years went by and he thought he would spend the rest of his days in Fulda, but then one autumn night a man raided his smallholding and tried to steal his only ox. He took an axe and without saying a word sunk it into his head. The thief turned out to be the abbot's son, a wild young man who was a slave to wine. After the burial, they came to his house, seized him and took him to trial. His statement was worthless, for twelve men swore that the young man had jumped over the fence looking only for a little water. Althar couldn't prove that they were lying. They took everything he had and condemned him to exile.

"The sentence made Leonora sick with melancholy," he continued. "Fortunately, her sisters offered to look after her while I waited for her to join me in the mountains. A couple of neighbors who knew me well also helped me. Rudolph gave me an old adze, and Vicus lent me some traps, provided I return them along with any furs I could collect. I found refuge in the south, in the Rhön foothills," he said, pointing at a nearby mountain, "in an abandoned bear cave. I closed up the entrance, made it as homely as possible and spent the winter trapping.

When I went back for Leonora, I learned that some of the bastards who had wrongly accused me had confessed to their false testimony, but by then they had already sowed my land with salt. Even then, the abbot refused to sell me seeds or rent new land to me, and he we went so far as to threaten anyone who helped me with the same treatment. That was when Leonora and I decided to move to the bear cave and live alone there forever."

"And you haven't been back to Fulda since then?" Theresa probed.

"Of course I have. Where else would I sell my furs? The abbot died not long afterward," he said with a smile. "He exploded like a cockroach. The one who succeeded him forgot about the threats, but nothing would be the same again. I travel to Fulda frequently to trade honey for salt—or when I need it, tallow, which is nowhere to be found round here. Leonora used to come with me, but her feet are in a bad state now and she seems to struggle with everything."

At sundown they left the green of the forest behind them and the land grew rugged. Trees became scarce and the wind grew fierce.

It was nightfall by the time they approached the bear cave, an area so stony that Theresa was surprised the two wheels of the cart remained intact. Althar told her to hold Hoos tightly, but despite her efforts, all the jolting made the young man moan for the first time.

At the foot of a great wall of granite, Althar stopped the cart and gave a couple of whoops as he clambered down. "You can come out, my dear," he said, whistling a silly tune. "We have company."

A plump face appeared among some bushes. It let out a funny little cry and intoned the same melody. A large, squat body moving with surprising swagger followed the woman's contagious smile.

"What has my prince brought for me?" asked Althar's wife, running into her husband's arms. "Jewelry or some perfume from the Orient?"

"Here are your jewels," he joked, pressing his crotch against the woman's stomach and making her laugh wildly.

"And these two?" she asked motioning behind him.

"Well," Althar murmured, raising an eyebrow. "I mistook him for a deer, and she fell in love with my flowing locks."

"I see." She laughed. "In that case, come in and we'll talk inside. It's getting cold as hell out here."

They left the goods outside, then took Hoos into the bear cave and lay him on a bed of furs. Theresa noticed that they had made a hole in the ceiling to serve as a chimney and around it they had set up a cooking area. A roaring fire kept the cave warm. Leonora offered them some apple cake, which they accepted with pleasure. There was hardly any furniture, but even so, Theresa felt like she was in a palace.

As they ate their dinner, Althar explained that they had another cave that they used for storage, and a cabin where they went when the weather improved. When they had finished, Theresa helped Leonora clear the table. Then she turned to Hoos to wrap him in more furs.

"You'll sleep here," Leonora indicated. She kicked aside a goat and cuffed away some hens. "And don't worry about the young man. If God wanted to, He would have taken him already."

Theresa nodded. When she lay down to sleep, she wondered again if Hoos had really followed her to retrieve his dagger.

That night Theresa barely slept, pondering the significance of the parchment that had been tucked away in her father's bag. Before going to bed, she had taken it out and read through it quickly. It appeared to be a legal document detailing the legacy left by Constantine, the Roman emperor who founded Constantinople. She assumed it was very important or her father wouldn't have bothered to hide it. Then her mind bubbled over with thoughts of the fire in Würzburg; the flames devouring Korne's workshop; the parchment-maker's loathsome smile; and the inferno swallowing up that poor girl. As she drifted to sleep she dreamed of the two terrifying Saxons, half men, half monsters, holding her down and violating her. Then it was the wolves, which, after devouring Hoos's mount, were trying to tear her to pieces. In her delirium she thought she saw Hoos himself in front of her, slowly raising the emerald-studded dagger to her throat. Several times she didn't know if she was sleeping or daydreaming. When she managed to open her eyes, she would evoke the protective image of her father. Though that calmed her for a while, yet another demon would come through the darkness at the mouth of the cave to torment her once more.

In that bear cave, where all was silent except for the hooting of an owl and the crackling of flames, she found it difficult to think. Awaiting the new day, she concluded that so much ill fate could only be part of some greater design: God was sending her a message. She reflected on what her sin might have been, and decided that perhaps everything bad that had befallen her was a consequence of her lies.

She recalled lying to Korne when she made him think the count wanted to personally check her entrance examination. She had deceived Hoos, telling him that she worked as a master parchment-maker rather than admitting she was a simple apprentice. And she had proceeded in the same manner with Althar, claiming that she had fled an arranged marriage, when she was merely escaping from the consequences of her deeds.

She wondered whether the master parchment-maker was right about women being the broth in which the filth of lies is boiled; whether in truth she had been a corrupt soul since birth, at the mercy of the compassion of the Almighty. Many times she had refuted those who proclaimed that the daughters of Eve embodied all the vices: weak, impulsive, changing at the whim of their flows, tempted by lust . . . and yet, at that moment, she began to doubt her convictions. She asked herself whether her lies were the Devil's doing. After all, it was he that used his trickery to seduce the first woman created by God. In which case, wasn't it the same demonic force that took Korne's hatred and transformed it into fire?

Who was she trying to fool? As much as it pained her, she could not deny what she had become. And what would she do when Hoos awoke? Tell him that she had picked up the wrong dagger by mistake? That in the darkness, she had mistaken it for the crude scramasax that he had offered her? Every lie was followed by another, each one a little bit bigger than the last.

She cried inconsolably, but when she felt she had no more tears left, she promised herself that she would never lie again. She promised it for her father. Even if he could not see her, this time she would not fail him.

8

With the first light filtering through the roof of the cave, Theresa decided it was time to rise. She was surprised to find Althar and Leonora still asleep, but she would soon understand that things went at a different pace up there in the hills. She wrapped herself in the cloak she had slept under and silently approached the bed where Hoos was resting. His breathing sounded deep, which put her mind at ease. It was cold, so she turned to the fireplace and stoked the embers. The noise woke Althar, who came round with a clamorous fart. With his eyes half-closed, he huddled affectionately against Leonora.

"Mmm . . . you're up already?" he grumbled to Theresa as he finished scratching his crotch. "If you need water, just up the path you'll find a stream."

Theresa thanked him. Dodging the nag that like the rest of the animals had spent the night in the cave, she pushed open the door that sealed the entrance and went outside. Satan barked but then followed behind her, tail wagging. She noticed that the temperature had fallen since yesterday, just as Leonora had predicted. Holding her cloak tightly around her, she examined the surroundings.

In front of the entrance to the bear cave there was the empty cart, which she assumed Althar must have unloaded. Wandering a little farther up the path she discovered a hawthorn animal pen, with signs that it had recently been emptied. All around there were woodchips, interspersed with chopped firewood, used wedges, logs of various sizes, mounds of shavings and several mallets, piled into a strange heap. There was no sign of a vegetable patch or anything resembling one.

As she was about to wash she realized she was bleeding down below. Satan came over to sniff her and, annoyed, she shouted at him to go away. Her flow was abundant, so she washed herself thoroughly in the stream before positioning the folded cloth that she always carried with her for this purpose. She crossed herself and ran back to the bear cave.

By then, Althar had already taken the animals outside and Leonora was attending to Hoos.

"How is he?" Theresa inquired.

"He's breathing better, and seems at ease. I'm heating water to wash him. Come on, give me a hand."

Theresa obeyed. She took the pot from the embers and brought over the soap made from boiled animal fat, blushing when she realized that Leonora was starting to undress him.

"Don't just stand there gawking, pull his trousers down," she ordered.

Theresa tugged them off to reveal a pair of tight woolen long johns. She looked away as it became apparent that Leonora was taking these down, too.

"Right, then, pass me the soap—and be quick about it, or he'll freeze."

The young woman turned red. Aside from her little cousins, she had never seen a man with so few clothes on. She passed the soap to Leonora, who scrubbed Hoos as though she were washing a chicken. When she asked Theresa to hold him while she continued to clean, she couldn't help glancing toward his groin. Her gaze fell on the soft hair that surrounded his member, and she felt flushed when it occurred to her that she would never have imagined it so

big. She thought Leonora would chide her if she caught her looking and so tried to be as discreet as possible, but while they were
wringing out the cloths, she was able to reexamine him less surreptitiously.

"It looks like he's broken a rib, see?" said Leonora, pointing at
a reddish bump on his chest. She rested her right ear against his
torso and listened. "But I can't hear any whistling, which is a good
sign, at least."

"Will he be all right?"

"I should think so. Bring some more water and I'll turn him
over. A year or so ago a trunk fell on Althar and almost cut him
in two. He was cursing and raving like a madman, but within two
weeks the lucky sod was already scuttling around like a lizard."

"It's true," said Althar, who had just walked in. "How's he looking, my queen?"

"A cracked rib and a bad knock to the head."

"Well, then, nothing that one of your breakfasts won't cure," he
declared.

"That's your solution to everything: food." She laughed and gave
him a shove.

They finished washing him and then sat down at the table.

Breakfast proved to be quite an event. Leonora prepared slices
of salt meat, which she covered with pork fat, mushrooms, and
onion. Then she added some slabs of goat's cheese, which she
browned by placing some embers on top of the stewpot. Finally,
she added a splash of wine, which, she said, settled the belly.

"And you haven't tried her pastries yet," said Althar.

Theresa licked her lips as she sampled the honey and almond
creation that Leonora served afterward. Theresa liked them so
much she asked for the recipe. Then she looked at Hoos despon-
dently.

"Don't worry about him," said Althar. "Leonora will take care of
him. Now come with me—we've work to do outside."

He explained that in winter there was less game to hunt, and that fishing became impossible. They had a small sown field on more fertile land some distance from the bear cave, which did not need any attention until the onset of spring. Although he did some hunting in the winter, he explained that the bulk of his time was spent doing carpentry, making repairs and crafting tools until spring arrived.

"And above all, stuffing animals," he added with pride.

They walked up the slope to a crevice in the mountain that looked as if a great axe had cleaved it open. The second cave had a narrower mouth and Theresa had to bend down to follow Althar, who, equipped with a torch, went on ahead as though he knew the way by memory.

Soon the tunnel widened into a spacious chamber, like a church nave.

"Nice, eh?" he bragged. "We used to live here, but when Leonora fell ill we moved to the bear cave. A shame, but its sheer size made it impossible to heat. However, the cold is good for the pelts, so I set up my storeroom here."

He used the torch to show her his trophies. In the half-light emerged a pack of foxes, a brace of ferrets, and deer, owls, and beavers—all strangely immobile, frozen in grotesque positions that made it hard to believe they had once been alive. Theresa observed their twisted jaws, gleaming eyes, and claws spread in a macabre dance. Althar explained that in his youth he had learned the art of taxidermy—and that many nobles liked to display the beasts whose lives they claimed on their hunts.

"All I need now is a bear," he added. "And that's where you come in."

Theresa nodded, assuming he was referring to the stuffing process, but when Althar told her that they would have to hunt it first, she prayed to God he was jesting. They spent the morning getting the cave in order.

Althar cleaned the skins while Theresa concentrated on cleaning the various instruments. The old man brushed the stuffed animals until they shone, explaining that in Fulda he would earn two denarii for a ferret and a fox, enough to buy five pecks of wheat. For an owl they would pay him less—because birds were easier animals to stuff—yet even so, selling one would enable him to buy a couple of knives and a pot or two. A bear, however, was different. If he could hunt and stuff a bear, he would take it to Aquis-Granum and sell it to Charlemagne himself.

"And how will you capture one?"

"I don't know. When I locate one we'll find out."

At midday they returned to the smaller bear cave. They were hungry when they arrived, and Leonora greeted them with a cup of wine and a hunk of cheese.

"Don't eat too much. Leave some room for the rest," she warned and proceeded to bring out meatballs with preserved figs, bird pie, and hot compote. Halfway through the banquet, Leonora informed them that Hoos had woken up, taken some broth, and gone back to sleep.

"Did he say anything?" asked Theresa.

"He just moaned. Perhaps he'll be more talkative tonight."

When they had finished, Althar went out to relieve himself and check on the animals. Theresa helped clear the table, taking off the top and tidying away the trestle. She did not have time to sweep up before Satan cleaned the floor with his tongue. When she was about to throw the scraps out, Leonora stopped her with a gesture of disapproval.

"I don't know how you spent most of your time while growing up, but it certainly couldn't have been doing any cooking," she said.

Theresa told her about her passion for reading and Leonora looked at her as though she were the oddest of creatures. The young woman explained that she had frequented schools and scriptoria since she was a child, and once she had grown up, she had gone to work as a parchment-maker's assistant.

"A great help to your mother, then," she reproached.

"But since trying your dishes, I'm eager to learn how to make them," she said, seeking her approval.

Leonora laughed heartily. She consented that, in the eyes of men, if a girl could not cook, it was worse than if she were flat chested.

"Although, you have nothing to worry about in that department," she noted.

Theresa looked at herself and then at Hoos and felt a fluttering in her stomach. She pulled her loose dress tight to her body, seeing the fabric mold to her breasts.

Leonora seemed to read her thoughts. "He's certainly handsome," the woman said, "and shapely." She winked at Theresa and flashed a wily smile.

Theresa reddened and smiled back, but she quickly steered the conversation back to recipes.

In the afternoon, Leonora listed the dishes that each season favored. In winter, the weaker of the animals they kept would be slaughtered before they died from the cold. She would have to learn not just how to cook the various cuts of meat, but also how to smoke, salt, and cure them. However, most of the meat was hunted, so it was only plentiful with the arrival of spring. As for vegetables, she described the mushrooms that grew in the forest, and the importance of knowing what they were before cooking them, and she extolled the virtues of cabbage—red and white—cauliflower, and thistle. Finally, she described the benefits of pulses.

"They might give you wind, but they make for good eating," she laughed, letting out a timely fart that reverberated around the cave.

She spoke of the importance of leftovers. In her experience, a good cook must know how to turn a handful of scraps into a delicious dish, and she discussed the many resources for this task. Her favorite tip involved using *garum*, a condiment that could turn the most insipid stew into an explosion of flavor.

"The best *garum* comes from Hispania," she explained, "but it is so expensive that only the rich can afford it. Years ago, a Roman merchant taught me how to prepare this relish using salt, oil, and fish tripe. But don't think it can be any old fish guts: Tuna or sturgeon give good results, but I use herring tripe, which has a lot more flavor. Once it has been macerated and dried, it can be mixed with wine, vinegar, or even pepper—if you have the money to buy that, of course."

"But if this *garum* is so good, why mix it?"

"Heavens, lass, for some variety of course! *Garum* is like sex: At the beginning it's always good, but the best thing is knowing how to mix it up. Look at us," she said with a smile, "married for thirty years and we still chase each other about. It's like everything: Wear the same dress for three days and even a blind man will grow tired of you. Add a flower or change your hair, and just watch how they run after you."

"I don't want men running after me," she responded dismissively.

"You don't? So what does a young girl think about then?"

"I don't know. My job. My family . . . I don't need men," she said, keeping to herself that she had already celebrated her nineteenth birthday.

"I see. And that's why you were staring at that young man's dangler when I was washing it."

Theresa blushed so fiercely she thought her face would stay red for the rest of her life. "Will you teach me?" Theresa said, trying to conceal her embarrassment.

"Teach you what? How to wash a prick?"

"No, good God. To make *garum!*"

"Ah, of course. I'll teach you that, and other things you need to know," she said with a grin.

While some turnips were roasting, Leonora took the opportunity to talk to Theresa about wine. Not the everyday stuff, drunk to quench the thirst, always young and watery, but the type that was served for important celebrations: pure, fragrant, glossy, ruby red . . . the drink that made the timid eloquent, that strengthened the hearts of the cowardly . . . every drop of that wine was a sin.

"I've never tried that kind," Theresa admitted.

"Well, we have an amphora we're keeping for a special occasion. If you catch the bear, we'll open it tomorrow."

At dusk, Althar returned, sporting a broad smile. He had found the beast's trail.

"He's still there, the big brute. Shitting in the same cave as last year," he announced euphorically. Dropping his gear, he laughed as he slapped Leonora on the backside.

Together they sat down to eat vegetable soup and salted rib of boar accompanied by watered-down wine. Althar slurped down his soup eagerly and quickly served himself another helping, for after setting traps all afternoon, he felt he could have eaten a cow.

"The girl cooked it," Leonora informed him.

"Well, I never! So I did well to take her on then?" he laughed. "How's the patient? Has he woken yet?"

"He opened his eyes for a moment, but I don't know. He seems groggy. The blow to the head, perhaps."

"He must be confused. I'll go and take a look at him."

They soon finished eating. While Leonora cleared up, Althar and Theresa went over to Hoos, who opened his eyes when he felt the damp cloth on his brow. He looked at Theresa and seemed to recognize her, but his eyelids closed and he resumed his rest.

Althar dug a blob of wax out of his ear and pressed the side of his head to Hoos's chest. "I can't hear any whistling."

"And that's good?"

"Of course. If the rib had perforated the lung he would have snuffed it by now. Tomorrow we'll try to get him up and walking round for a while."

They carefully covered him, brought the animals into the cave and barred the door, then said goodnight and went to bed.

A few hours later, Theresa woke to feel Satan licking her face. It was not yet dawn, but Leonora was already warming the stewpot and Althar was singing softly to himself, pacing around the cave.

"Little bear, your time is up. Althar's going to eat you up," he intoned with a wide smile.

They ate breakfast and wrapped themselves in furs. Althar armed himself with bow and quiver, slung a net over his shoulder, and picked up three iron traps. Then he handed a crossbow to Theresa.

"This will do," he declared. "My dear! This evening you'll have a new overcoat!"

Leonora laughed and planted several kisses on him. Then she cuffed Theresa around the head and wished her luck.

The sun was starting to rise as they left the cave. It was a clear, crisp day, which Althar took as a good omen. They left the horse behind, since Althar said it could alert the bear to their presence. While they walked, Theresa confessed that she was scared.

The old man reassured her, "You won't have to do anything. Just keep watch."

"And what about this strange bow?"

"You mean the crossbow? I won it from a soldier in Aquis-Granum. I'd never seen such a thing, to be honest, but it's effective. I'll show you how to use it."

He drove one end of the bow into the ground and put his foot on it. Then he pulled the string up with both hands until it slotted into a notch.

"It's not a toy, so be careful. This is the nut," he indicated, "and the thing underneath is the trigger. Insert the dart in the groove. See? Then hold it firmly in both hands and aim."

Theresa lifted the weapon but was unable to keep it up. "It's too heavy," she complained.

"Rest it on the ground," he grumbled. "And listen to me carefully: If the time comes when you need to use it, you will only have one chance. You will not be able to reload, so aim well and shoot at the stomach, agreed?"

Theresa nodded. She went down on the ground and aimed the weapon.

"Hold it steady."

Althar pointed at a rotting tree trunk, the width of two men. On his signal Theresa pressed the trigger purposefully. The dart whistled through the air and was lost in the undergrowth.

"Try again," Althar grumbled. She attempted it twice more with varying success. On the fourth attempt Althar declared the training over.

"Let's get going, or the morning will run away from us."

As they walked, Althar explained that bears normally hibernate from the end of November until the thaw. "People think they sleep like logs, but they're actually light sleepers. That's why we have to be very careful."

"And what if there's more than one?" asked the young woman.

"Unlikely. Bears hibernate alone, so that shouldn't worry us."

They continued walking until Althar noticed the fixation that Satan had for Theresa's crotch. He noticed that, despite the girl's efforts, the mutt kept sniffing her as though she were hiding something under her skirts. Curious, he asked her whether she had stolen some food.

"No, sir," she responded awkwardly.

"So what the devil is the dog smelling?"

"I don't know," she answered, blushing.

"Well, you can start talking, because if the dog can smell it, the beast will, too."

Theresa didn't know what to say, not wanting to confess that it was that time of the month, but in the end there was no need, for Althar guessed it.

"Pox on you! The one day we go out hunting, you have to be bleeding," he said, but he didn't look as if he was ready to turn back.

Before long they arrived at the area where the bear was taking shelter. Althar indicated the location of the bear cave, which was at the top of a steep slope. Theresa noticed that a ditch below the entrance would make the approach difficult.

"We'll position the net over the mouth of the cave. Then I'll set fire to some branches and Satan will bark. With the smoke and the noise, the bear will wake and try to escape, but he'll run straight into the net. Once it's trapped, I'll bring it down with the bow. You wait somewhere it won't smell you. Up there, above the entrance, just in case."

"Just in case?"

"If I get in trouble, shoot the beast. And for the love of God, make sure you hit the target this time."

He stayed to gather branches, while Theresa climbed toward the mouth of the cave. Halfway there, the young woman stumbled, making several stones roll down the slope. Althar cursed her, gesturing to be silent. When Theresa had scrambled to the top of the entrance, she signaled to Althar, who by then had piled all manner of brushwood by the cave's mouth. Then he quickly covered the entrance with the net. After securing it in place, he stepped back to light the fire, retrieving one burning branch.

Theresa watched him take up position behind a rock and signal to her to be on the alert. The smell of burning wood soon told her that it was nearly time, so she took a deep breath and lay down. Suddenly, Satan started barking like a dog possessed, scratching about among the stones and spinning round several times. She thought the hound had lost its senses, but promptly a roar could be heard from inside the cave.

Her heart missed a beat. She held the crossbow as firmly as she could and aimed it at the entrance, but even lying down the weapon was unsteady. A few moments of quiet passed by until suddenly a gigantic mass of fur appeared from nowhere, snorting as it exited the cave and ran straight into the net. Finding himself trapped, the animal bellowed with fury, swiping and biting at the mesh. Satan howled excitedly, barking and attacking the beast with a complete disregard for the bear's snapping jaws.

Unexpectedly, the fire spread to the net and then to the bear's belly, making the animal howl in pain and try to free itself by rearing onto its hind legs. For a moment Theresa thought the beast would scale the rock face to reach her, but it slipped and fell back into the cave. The bear then turned and let out a terrifying roar, exposing its great jaws. Theresa closed her eyes, but another bellow made her open them again, just as Althar took his shot. The arrow cleaved through the air, embedding itself in the sole of the bear's hind foot. Althar knew he had to hurry before the fire could ruin the beast's pelt. He drew the bow and fired once more. The second arrow disappeared into the animal's belly. The bear howled in pain, twisted round and then clumsily reared up, before finally crashing to the ground like a mountain collapsing.

Theresa waited a few seconds and then stood up. She was still trembling, but at least she was breathing. She looked at the motionless bear, lying flat out on the ground. It was an imposing animal, its fur glossy and its claws sharp. She was about to go down, but Althar stopped her.

"Wait there till I say," he told her sharply. "They're dangerous even after they've been flayed."

He approached the animal with an axe in one hand and a long stick in the other. Three paces away, he stopped. He prodded the bear with the stick, but it didn't move. Then he raised the axe with both hands and let it fall with all his strength onto the beast's neck. Afterward, he just stood admiring the dead bear for a while.

Fortunately, the flames had barely damaged the hindquarters. The neck, furthermore, had been cut cleanly, and the marks from the arrows were almost imperceptible. He told Theresa she could come down and help him skin the animal. In the end the hunt had been easier than expected.

Before descending, the young woman removed the dart from the crossbow and sheathed it in a cloth as Althar had shown her. She was halfway down the slope when another roar stopped her in her tracks.

For a moment she couldn't believe her ears. She had watched the animal die, and yet another bellow was thundering around the mountain. With all the speed she could muster she ran toward the promontory where she had been positioned. She watched in horror as another bear came out of the cave and attacked Althar. The old man stepped back. Gripping the axe with two hands, he lashed out—but the animal kept coming. In his desperation, Althar backed up all the way to the precipice. He was trapped. The bear seemed to understand this, and it paused before launching its final attack. Althar tried to escape to one side, but he slipped and the axe tumbled to the bottom of the ravine.

He knew death was certain.

The beast reared up until it was twice Althar's size. It advanced a couple of paces and roared as though it had the Devil inside it, but just before dealing its final blow, Satan appeared between the beast and his master, barking as if he were the one possessed. The bear hesitated before suddenly swiping at the hound with its giant paw, and Satan was dispatched, his neck broken.

Theresa realized that she had to act. She took out a dart and positioned it in the groove of the crossbow. Lying flat on her stomach, she aimed carefully at the animal's head. Then she remembered Althar's words and pointed the weapon at the great brown belly.

She told herself that she only had one chance. Taking aim, she then closed her eyes and fired. The dart flew through the air and disappeared from sight before a bellow could be heard. For a moment she thought she had hit her target, but then she noticed with horror that the dart had hit the animal above one of its hind legs.

She thought Althar would certainly perish. Yet something strange happened. As the beast tried to move forward, its injured leg caused it to lose balance, and it fell heavily onto its left side. For a moment it seemed like it would stumble to its feet again, but it slipped yet again and slid toward the edge of the precipice. The bear kicked out desperately as if it could sense what was about to happen. All of a sudden the rocks that were supporting it came away, and despite its efforts, it fell with them to the bottom of the ravine.

It was some time before Theresa managed to react. When she came to, she ran down to Althar who, in a daze, also appeared to be unaware of quite what had happened.

"Two bears. There were two damned bears."

"I aimed like you said, but I couldn't . . ."

"Don't worry, lass, you did well . . . two of the bastards," he repeated.

He scratched his head and looked at Satan with sorrow in his eyes. Removing his cloak, he wrapped it around him carefully. "He was a good dog. I'll stuff him so he's with me always."

They spent the afternoon skinning the first bear. When they had finished, it occurred to Althar that they could recover the skin from the second one, too. "At the end of the day, all we have to do is climb down into the ravine."

"Won't it be dangerous?"

"You wait here," he said.

He set down his load and started along the path on the hillside that seemed to descend to the bottom of the precipice. After a while he returned along the same route, with something loaded onto his shoulders.

"The skin was no use, eaten away by the mange," he explained. "But it had nice eyes, so I brought them back with me. Along with the rest of the head."

When they arrived home, Leonora welcomed them with good tidings: Hoos had risen and was waiting for them at the table.

As they ate their dinner, Theresa thought Hoos seemed more interested in his pottage than their story of the hunt. However, when he had wolfed down the last spoonful, he thanked Althar for saving his life.

"Thank the lass. She's the one who insisted I put you on the cart."

Hoos looked at Theresa and his expression hardened. Leonora sensed that something was amiss. "I am grateful," he said drily. "But after I saved her life, it's the least I would expect."

"That's right," Althar conceded. "It's clear the girl can be relied upon." He laughed and gave Theresa a shove.

Hoos changed the subject. "Your wife tells me you've lived here a long time."

"Verily. I can assure you we don't miss the filth of the city: the scandalmongers, the false accusations, the gossip—bah! We're happy here. Just the two of us, doing and eating what we please." He took a slug on his wine. "Tell me, how are you feeling?"

"Not good, to be honest, but I couldn't remain lying down any longer."

"Then you should rest. Until those ribs heal, at least. Otherwise any movement could ruin your lungs."

Hoos nodded. Every time he swallowed he felt as if barbs were tearing at his insides. He downed his wine, excused himself, and went back to bed. While the women cleared up, Althar spread out the bear skin, placing the two heads on top of some buckets. When he ushered the animals into the cave for the evening, he realized that he missed the scurrying of Satan, who would always help him with the task.

The next day started gloomily, with a blustery wind. A bad day for venturing out, Althar thought to himself, but not so bad for stuffing trophies. Before breakfast he took the animals outside to water them and took the opportunity to empty his bladder. On his return, Theresa and Leonora were up and about. They ate breakfast in silence so as not to wake Hoos. Then Althar picked up the pelt and the bear heads and asked Theresa to accompany him.

"I still need to wash," said the girl.

Althar assumed she still had her period, so he didn't insist.

"When you've finished, come to the other cave. I'll need your help."

Althar swung the skin over his shoulder and walked out with her. Theresa went to the stream to wash with the cloths that Leonora had given her. When she returned she saw that Hoos had woken and was glaring at her.

Leonora seemed to notice this, too, and said, "I'm off to feed the animals. Just call if you need anything."

They both nodded. When she had gone, Hoos made as if to get up, but he felt a stabbing in his chest and lay back down again. Theresa sat down beside him.

"Do you feel better?" she asked timidly. They were the first words she had said to him. Hoos hesitated before answering.

"You weren't so concerned when you took off with my dagger," he said.

Theresa didn't know what to say. She went to her bag and returned red-faced. "I don't know how I could have done it," she said, tears in her eyes.

Hoos's expression changed. He took the dagger and stuffed it under the blanket. Then he closed his eyes and turned away.

Theresa understood that nothing she could say or do would change his mind. After all, if it had been the other way round, she would have reacted the same. She wiped away her tears and with a trembling voice asked him to forgive her. Finally, faced with the young man's indifference, she left the cave with her head bowed.

On the way to the second cave she came across Leonora, who noticed the young woman's reddened eyes. But Theresa walked past, not giving her a chance to say anything. Leonora went back to the bear cave. When she questioned Hoos about what had happened, he replied with a terse, "It's none of your business."

Leonora was affronted by his response. "Listen to me, young man: I don't care where you come from or what titles you have. You should know that you are only alive because that girl, who you've just made cry, made sure of it, so you had better start behaving like a prince toward her or it'll be me who breaks your ribs."

Hoos didn't answer. He thought to himself that nobody would know or care about the impulse he had to follow the girl in the first place.

DECEMBER

9

First it was just a slight tingling. Then the wound stabbed at him. Gorgias threw the wax tablet that Genseric had given him onto the old bed and approached the light that sifted through the little window high up in the cell. He undid the bandage around his arm, taking care not to pull off the scab. When he looked at his flesh underneath he noticed that his entire arm was violet and a cluster of pustules was starting to appear between the stitches. If it had been possible he would have had the physician Zeno take a look at it, though the absence of a foul smell was reassuring. With the point of his stylus, he flicked off the driest scabs and cleaned out the yellowish pus underneath. Then he tightened the bandage and prayed that his arm would scar without further complications.

For the first hour of his confinement, he merely waited, examining the little window that not even a small child could have squeezed through. Try as he might, he could not see anything through the alabaster. He thought about breaking it, but controlled his urge. When he heard the bells signaling Sext, he knew his wife would have probably come to the chapter by now, worried about his absence.

He imagined the lies they would tell her.

Gorgias wanted to believe that Genseric was telling the truth: That it was Wilfred who was responsible for his imprisonment.

Perhaps he did want to protect him from the parchment-maker. Or was it more that he wanted to watch over his progress with the document? But, why in such a place of confinement where he had so little control? He could have chosen the scriptorium, where all the necessary equipment could be found, or even his own chambers, to keep him under close scrutiny. After all, Wilfred didn't know about the attack, so if he was being sequestered for his own safety, as the coadjutor claimed, Wilfred probably would have thought the scriptorium sufficient.

As night fell, he heard the sound of the bolt announcing someone's entrance. He thought it might be the count, but the stench of urine announced the arrival of the coadjutor. Then he heard his slow, deliberate voice ordering him to go to the back of the room.

Gorgias did so and asked after his wife, but received no answer. The hatch at the foot of the door started to revolve, and when it stopped turning, he went to investigate and found Genseric had placed inside his cell a hunk of bread and a jug of water. From the other side of the door, he heard the coadjutor tell him to take the food and put the list of the items that he would need to complete his work in the hatch.

"Not until you answer me," he insisted.

A few moments went by, which felt like an eternity to Gorgias. Then the hatch turned again, taking with it the bread and water. Gorgias thought he could hear Genseric retrieving the food from the hatch on the other side. Then he heard a door slamming, and then silence, a silence that lasted until deep into the early hours.

Midmorning, Genseric returned, this time humming a tune. After checking to see if Gorgias was awake, he informed him that Rutgarda was well. He had visited her at her sister's house.

"I told her you would be spending a few days in the scriptorium, working, and you know what? She was perfectly understanding. I gave her two loaves and some wine, and I promised her that while you remain with us, she will have the same every day. She asked me to give this to you."

Gorgias watched the hatch revolve. Along with the bread and water that he had taken away the day before, there was a little embroidered scarf. It was Rutgarda's—she wore it all the time.

Gorgias held it gingerly against his chest. Then he took the bread, which he eagerly began to eat. From the other side Genseric pressed him for the list of things he would need. Still wolfing down the bread, Gorgias wrote a long list on the tablet. Next he pretended to go over the notes before leaving the tablet in the hatch and rotating it back to its initial position. Genseric grasped the tablet, read it closely and disappeared without saying a word.

An hour later he returned laden with sheets of parchment, inkwells, and other writing utensils. He told Gorgias that he would visit him every day to check on his progress, bring food, and remove his excrement. Before leaving he also assured him that he would visit Rutgarda. Then he said farewell and left the crypt, leaving Gorgias with his equipment.

When Gorgias was sure he was alone, he began work. He took one of the codices from among those that Genseric had brought and turned his back to the door to hide his movements as an extra precaution. With the utmost care, he unfolded a blank parchment. Spreading it out on the desk, he brought the words to mind as if he were reading them:

IN-NOMINE-SANCTAE-ET-INDIVIDUAL-TRINITATIS-
PATRIS-SCILICET-ET-FILII-ET-SPIRITUS-SANCTI

- - -

IMPERATOR-CAESAR-FLAVIUS-CONSTANTINUS

He knew the text by heart. He had read the heading a hundred times and transcribed it just as many. He crossed himself before beginning and checked the quality of the skin on which he would make the copy. Despite its rather large size, it was still too small for the twenty-three pages in Latin and twenty in Greek that he would need. He ran his fingers over the imperial seal printed at the foot of the parchment that depicted a Greek cross over a Roman head. Encircling the seal was the name *Gaius Flavius Valerius Aurelius Constantinus*—Constantine the Great, the first Christian emperor and founder of Constantinople.

Legend had it that Constantine's conversion had taken place four centuries ago, during the Battle of the Milvian Bridge. It was said that, shortly before the attack, the Roman emperor saw a cross floating in the sky. Inspired by the image he embroidered the Christian symbol onto his standards. The battle ended in victory for Constantine and in gratitude he renounced paganism.

Gorgias reflected on the document, which was divided into two different texts. The first part, or the *Confessio*, recounted that Constantine, now afflicted with leprosy, went to see the pagan priests at the Capitol in Rome, who advised him to dig a ditch, fill it with the blood of newly sacrificed children, and then bathe in it while the blood was still warm. However, the night before he was to do this, Constantine had a vision in which he was told to turn to Pope Sylvester and give up paganism. Constantine decided to obey his dream, so he converted and was cured.

The second part, entitled *Donatio*, spoke of the honors and privileges that, as payment for his cure, Constantine would grant the Church. The preeminence of the Roman Papacy over the patriarchates of Antioch, Alexandria, Constantinople, and Jerusalem was thus recognized. Moreover, to guarantee that the pontifical dignitaries held lands and possessions befitting their rank, he also donated the Lateran Palace, the city of Rome, all of Italy, and the entire West. Finally, so that he would not infringe upon the rights he had granted, Constantine declared he would build a new capital in Byzantium, where he and his descendants would limit themselves to governing the eastern territories. There was no doubt: That donation represented a great leap in the expansion of Christendom.

With the utmost care, he divided the parchment into the gatherings that would form the quinternions. Next he split the sheets into bifolios of an identical size and ensured that there were enough of them. Then he dipped his quill in the ink and began to transcribe the text on the sealed parchment from memory. Despite the persistent pain in his arm, he did not stop until the day's end.

10

Theresa was surprised to find she wasn't disturbed by the taxidermic process, and it even made her forget for a moment about the dagger. She could see that Althar had started building the frame for the bear's great pelt. The structure had a central trunk, with two thinner poles serving as legs. The old man asked her to remove the skin to test the balance of the frame. Then he changed the position of the legs and shored them up with nails and wedges.

"We can always keep it together with some rope," he said, unconvinced.

He assigned Theresa the job of separating the skin from the remains of fat, delousing it properly, and washing it with soap. She was accustomed to doing these same tasks in Korne's workshop so it didn't prove to be difficult. When she had finished, she dried the skin and hung it on the frame to air it out.

"Shall I clean the heads, too?" she asked.

"No. Not for now." Althar climbed down from the stall and threw his mallet on the ground. "That's a another matter entirely."

He sat on a rock with the head between his legs to better examine it. After confirming that the blood had stopped flowing, he made a vertical incision with his knife from the crown to the back of the neck, and then added a second, horizontal line on the nape, forming an inverted *T*. He then removed the skin by pulling hard from the vertices, revealing the skull.

"Chuck the head in the cask," Althar ordered.

Theresa did as she was told. As Althar added the hot water, the boiling lime ate away at the tissue still stuck to the skull. Althar repeated the operation with the other head.

By midmorning they had finished preparing the frame. Althar took one of the perfectly clean heads and patted it dry. Then he positioned it at the end of a branch, which served as a kind of spinal column, with the wooden poles sticking out like legs. The frame took on the appearance of a horrendous scarecrow. But Althar seemed satisfied with the work.

"When the skin's been cured, we'll be able to finish the job," he declared.

On their way back to the cave, they passed some strange, very dirty-looking wooden chests. Theresa asked what they were used for.

"They're beehives," Althar informed her. "The boxes are covered in mud because bees are fragile in winter. Sealing the structure, it keeps them warm."

"So where are the bees?"

"Inside. When winter is over I'll open the hives and then we'll have honey again before long."

"I love honey."

"Who doesn't?" he said, laughing. "The little creatures sting like bastards, but they give us enough honey to sweeten our puddings for a whole season. And not just honey. You see that old honeycomb?" He went over to one of the chests that appeared abandoned and lifted the lid. "It's pure wax. Ideal for candles."

"I didn't see any candles in the cave."

"That's because we sell nearly all of them. We only burn them with good reason: when we're sick and whatnot. God created night so we could sleep, otherwise He would have made us like owls."

Theresa wondered if she might take some wax to fill the tablets she still had in her bag so she could practice her writing. However, when she suggested it to Althar, he roundly refused.

"But I'd return it to you intact," the young woman argued.

"In that case, you will have to earn it."

They closed the lid and walked back toward the cave where Leonora welcomed them with an appetizing hare stew. They all ate together, for Hoos was already up and about, and they drank heartily to celebrate their successful hunt. When they had finished, Althar said he was delighted with the return from the new traps, and announced that he would stuff Satan that afternoon, a task he would do alone because of the considerable patience it required. Before he set off, he told Theresa he would let her have some beeswax if she could find some suitable eyes.

"Eyes?" she asked in astonishment.

"For the bears," he explained. "The real ones rot, so we need false ones. Some amber would be perfect, but I don't have any. I'll have to make do with whatever round pebbles you can find at the river." He took some stones from his bag and showed her. "Like these, more or less, but smoother. Varnished with a little resin, they'll appear genuine."

Theresa nodded. When she finished washing the dishes, she told Leonora that she intended to head to the river.

"Why doesn't Hoos go with you? A bit of fresh air won't do him any harm."

He seemed surprised at the suggestion, and Theresa was surprised that he gladly accepted. They left the bear cave together, but soon she walked on ahead, keeping her distance until they reached the stream where she bent down to search among the stones.

"This one might do," said Hoos.

Theresa took the pebble he held out and compared it to one she had chosen. She was loath to admit that Hoos's stone was smoother and more uniform.

"Too small," she objected, and gave it back, barely giving it a second glance.

He put it in his bag. Looking at Theresa, he remembered again the day the young woman fled the cabin. He continued to observe her closely, the delicacy with which she examined the texture and color of the stones. He watched her fingers move deftly over the pebbles to feel how smooth they were, how she wetted them to bring out their color, delicately tested their weight, and categorized them according to some system that only she seemed to know. At that moment, she turned around and he saw her eyes blaze like amber.

He was deep in thought when Theresa lost her footing and fell into the river. Hoos ran to help her and, as he pulled her out, he felt his chest constrict followed by a strange burning sensation. They finished collecting the stones and made for the cave. Hoos asked about the pebbles she had collected, and she said she was quite pleased with what she'd found. They walked on in silence until they reached the beehives.

"In the winter they cover them in mud. It stops the bees from dying," Theresa declared.

"I didn't know that." He did not mention that his chest was throbbing.

"Neither did I," she admitted with a smile. "Althar told me. He seems like a good man, don't you think?"

"We are here thanks to him."

"See that chest over there?" Theresa pointed to the abandoned chest. "Althar said I could use its wax to fill my tablet." She approached it and lifted the lid.

"What's a tablet? Some kind of lamp?"

"No," she laughed. "A flat box, the size of a loaf of bread. Well, there are bigger ones, and smaller ones, too. Mine is wooden and once it's filled with wax, I use it to write on."

"Aha!" said Hoos as if he understood—though he was none the wiser.

"When I'm finished drying off, I'll go to the cave where Althar keeps his trophies. That place is amazing! Do you want to come with me?"

"I've done enough walking for one day," he complained. "You go. I'll lie down for a while and change my bandages."

"Hoos . . ."

"Yes?"

"I don't know why I stole it from you. I am truly sorry."

"It's all right. Just don't do it again."

Theresa changed her clothes before setting off for the cave of trophies, but not before she had inspected the stones and chosen four lenticular pebbles of a similar size. She thought that once they had been painted they would without a doubt resemble real eyeballs.

When she reached the cave she found that the door was closed. She assumed Althar was inside, so she pushed it open and went in without knocking. Sure enough she found the old man working on the bear's frame, to which he had added two branches as front legs, in a downward direction.

"Oh! I didn't expect you so soon," he said in surprise. "So, tell me, what do you think?"

The young woman looked at the bizarre structure. "Horrible," she said without thinking.

Althar took it as a compliment. "As it should be," he asserted. "It will sell for more that way. What are you doing here?"

"I've brought the stones for the eyes," she said, showing him.

Althar examined them carefully. He put them on the box that contained the scalpels, scrapers, and awls.

"They'll do," he confirmed.

Between them they mounted the treated skin on the crude frame, sewing the seams and filling the cavities with hay and rags.

Finally, they attached the skull, pulling the skin of the head over it. When they had finished, the bear resembled a gigantic and rather battered toy.

"It doesn't look very fierce," Althar complained.

They changed the filling several times, but the result was worse still. It was the first time Althar had attempted such a large specimen. After a while, the old man cursed and went outside to clear his head.

Meanwhile, Theresa thought about the pitiful appearance of the bear. It was clear that, in its standing position, the weight of the hay made it accumulate in the belly, making the torso and shoulders sag. The front legs flopped down weakly, and the head, its mouth closed, seemed permanently stooped. Instead of it looking ferocious, she thought the animal looked like it had just been hanged.

She went out to look for Althar and tell him her thoughts, but she couldn't find him, so she went back inside the cave to continue to ponder the problem without him.

When the old man finally returned he was speechless. Theresa had changed the position of the front legs so they were now raised ferociously above the animal's head. In this pose, the hay accumulated around the shoulders, bulking them up. For the rear legs she replaced the hay with backstitched rags to keep them tight.

"And if we insert hay between the skin and the fabric, you won't be able to see the bumps," she explained.

Althar continued to survey her work, completely absorbed. He could see that Theresa had also positioned a dark stick in the mouth to keep the jaws open, giving the beast a menacing expression. It seemed impossible that this magnificent animal was the same pitiful scarecrow he had cast aside in frustration a little earlier.

They returned together to the bear cave at nightfall, tired but happy. On the way they stopped at the beehives to collect Theresa's promised wax. When they arrived back at the cave, Althar greeted

Leonora with a loud kiss before telling her about the progress they'd made.

"My news is not so good," the woman lamented. "The young man has taken a turn for the worse."

Hoos lay in the corner, trembling and struggling to breathe. Leonora showed them a bloody cloth, and told them he had spat it out.

"Did he vomit or cough it up?" Althar tried to ascertain.

"How do I know? It all happened at once."

"If he coughed it up, it's bad news. Hoos, can you hear me?" he said into his ear. The young man nodded. Althar put his hand on his chest. "Does it hurt here?" He nodded again.

Althar grimaced and shook his head. The presence of blood in the young man's spit could only mean a rib had pierced a lung and was now tearing at it. He cursed unceremoniously when he found out that Hoos had been exerting himself earlier in the day.

"If what I fear has happened, there will be nothing we can do," he said to his wife as an aside. "Except pray, perhaps, and wait until tomorrow."

Hoos spent the night coughing and moaning. Leonora and Theresa took turns tending to him, but even with their attention and care, he hardly improved. By morning, he was consumed by a fever. Althar knew that without the help of a physician he would die.

"Wife: Prepare some food for the road. We're going to Fulda," he announced.

They were ready by midmorning. Althar loaded the cart with the stuffed bear, the half-finished head, and the pebbles for the eye sockets. They lay Hoos Larsson on a pallet among the goods. Then Theresa gathered her belongings, and Althar packed up the food, as well as a bundle of skins to sell, and they said farewell to Leonora.

"I hope to see you again," said Theresa, her eyes welling up.

"He'll get better," she said, giving her an equally teary kiss.

Their first day on the road went by without incident. They stopped only to eat some venison pie and empty their bladders. Hoos slipped in and out of consciousness, his fever still high. They spent the night by a stream, taking turns to keep watch. Theresa used this time to finish sewing the second bear head. When she inserted the false eyes it acquired a formidable appearance—or, at least in the dim light, that's how it seemed. The next morning they set out again, and just after midday, they could make out plumes of smoke indicating that Fulda was near.

Though they were still some distance away, Theresa could make out the abbey and was impressed. On top of a large hill, dozens of buildings of all different colors crowded together. It appeared that for every inch of land where timber could be driven into the ground or a fence built, that's what had been done. In the town center at the top of the hill stood the walls that protected the monastery, a cheerless, dark structure that blended into the mountain it was erected on. Lower down, on the slopes, scores of hovels, shacks, storehouses, and barns were jammed together alongside workshops and animal pens. It was such a jumbled confusion that it was difficult distinguishing where one structure began and another ended.

As they approached, the path grew wider until it became a broad road, with peasants and animals trudging up and down in a disorderly fashion. Outlying farmhouses, with their roofs of wattle and mud, lay scattered around the fields with hawthorn fences protecting the owner's land. Eventually they reached the banks of the River Fulda, the boundary between the tortuous road and the entrance to the city.

An endless line of peasants waited their turn to cross the bridge into and out of the city. Althar covered his face with a hood and urged the horse on until they reached the end of the queue.

They crossed the viaduct after paying their toll to the guard in the form of a jar of honey. Althar grumbled, for he could have saved the expense had they forded the river a couple of miles downstream, but with the cart loaded down with the bears, and with Hoos in a bad way, he decided it would be best to use the bridge.

Entering the city walls, Theresa remained silent, entranced by the coming and going of people, the constant clamor, and the smell of pottage and unwashed bodies, intermingling with the stench of sheep, chickens, and mules that seemed to be wandering about with more freedom than their owners. For a moment she forgot her worries, distracted by cloth merchants, food hawkers, improvised taverns, and groups of street urchins scampering among the apple stands that festooned the great city gates. It all seemed so different and vast that for a moment she thought she had returned to her beloved Constantinople.

Althar guided the cart toward a side entrance to avoid the busy artisans' quarter. They left the market behind them and climbed an empty alleyway until they came to a square where a web of streets converged. There they were forced to stop and make way for a procession from the abbey and then some other carts that had been waiting to continue toward the hill.

As they waited, Althar told Theresa that he knew a person in the city who would put them up. "But don't tell Leonora," he laughed, which took Theresa by surprise because they seemed to share everything with each other. Althar stopped the cart and told her to keep an eye on it while he made some inquiries. He made for a group of men, joking with each other around a jug of wine. After greeting them as if they were old friends, he returned looking down in the mouth. Apparently, the person he was looking for had moved to the outskirts of town. At that moment there was a crack of the whip from the cart in front of them, and they all set off again.

In the vicinity of the abbey, he turned down a narrow street, scraping the sides with the cart's wheels, and continued along a road that led east. Gradually the houses became older and darker, and the smell of cooking and spices gave way to a persistent stench of sour wine. When they reached a dilapidated home, Althar stopped the horse. But Althar dismounted and walked up to the house opposite with a door daubed in bright colors. It wasn't in ruins, but it certainly needed some attention. The old man walked in without knocking. He soon returned, sporting a cheerful smile.

"Come on, they're making us some lunch," he said.

They unloaded the bears and their baggage and made themselves comfortable in the hostelry.

11

Helga the Black proved to be a most entertaining prostitute. As soon as she recognized Althar, she stuck her tongue out at him impudently, lifted her skirt to show him her knees, and said "sweetheart, come here!" before planting a loud kiss on his cheek. Then she turned to Theresa and asked about his prissy girlfriend. She continued to jest until she noticed the wounded man with them, which caused her to immediately stop her fooling around to start fussing over Hoos as though her life, and perhaps his, too, depended on it.

While she fussed, she told Theresa her story. She had worked as a barmaid until the day she discovered that sucking off a neighbor was more lucrative than doing it to her drunkard of a husband. So as soon as he died, she sold her house and opened a tavern to earn her living. They called her "the Black" because her hair was dark as charcoal and so were her fingernails. As she spoke, she frequently burst into laughter, her smile revealing several conspicuous gaps between her teeth. Theresa noticed that the rouge on her cheeks worked hard to hide her wrinkles, but despite this, she was still an attractive woman. As she changed Hoos's bandages, Helga asked after Althar's wife, and Theresa understood now why the old man had told her to keep his secret.

Theresa had never dealt with prostitutes before. In Würzburg she knew none, and indeed she was surprised there should be one so close to the abbey in Fulda. When the woman had finished fussing with Hoos's dressings, she asked Althar about the severity of his injuries. He told her what he thought and she appeared to ponder deeply before responding. Finally, she said, "The only physician here is a monk who lives in the monastery, but he only attends to the Benedictines. The rest of us are at the mercy of the dentist-barber."

"This isn't just any old casualty," said Althar irritably. "He needs someone who knows what he's doing."

"Well, let me know how you get on, my dear. I can't turn up with a man at the abbey gate. And you can't just turn up either: As soon as they realize who it is, you can be sure they'll set the dogs on you."

Althar stroked his beard. Helga the Black was right: In the monastery there were many who thought him responsible for the death of the abbot's son. The only option was to call for the barber.

"His name is Maurer," said Helga. "In the morning he tends to the sick and cuts hair, but by midday he's already in the market tavern spending every penny he's just earned."

Althar nodded as if he understood. Then he asked Theresa to put her things under Hoos's bed and accompany him. Helga would look after the patient.

"We're going to the market," he announced with a smile. "I almost forgot we have some bears to sell."

When they arrived at the market, they had to set up shop on its periphery, for the best spots had already been claimed. The crowds thronged around stands selling food, ceramics, tools, implements, seeds, fabrics, and basketwork. It was market day and everyone was there to shop, gossip, and chatter about the mercantile, even though the same things were sold every week.

Althar parked the cart against a wall so he would only have to guard one side from the street urchins who took every opportunity to steal from him behind his back. In the cart, he lifted the bear up into a standing position, propping the other head beside it with some sticks.

He asked Theresa if she knew how to dance. She said she didn't, but the old man didn't seem to care. He ordered her to climb onto the cart and shake her behind anyway she pleased. Then he took out a hunting horn and blew on it.

First a few young lads appeared to imitate Theresa's wiggling, but soon more onlookers arrived, drawn to the unusual spectacle before them, and before long a ring of people had formed around the cart.

"I'll swap my wife for that bear," a toothless peasant proffered. "Her claws are just as long and sharp."

"Sorry, but I already have a wild beast for a wife," said Althar with a laugh.

"That creature's a bear you say?" said another man from the back. "You can't even see its balls."

The crowd guffawed.

"Come closer to its jaws and yours will shrivel up, too."

The people laughed again.

"How much for the girl?" someone else asked.

"It was the girl who killed the bear, so imagine what she could do to you."

There was another roar of laughter.

A boy threw a cabbage at them, but Althar swiftly grabbed him by the hair and gave him a shove that sent him scuttling back to the other youngsters. An ale merchant decided to take advantage of the situation and pulled his barrel up near the cart. Some drunks followed him, hoping for a handout

"This bear devoured two Saxons before we made the kill," Althar announced. "Their skeletons were in his cave. He killed my dog and wounded me," he said, showing them an old scar on his leg from some unrelated accident. "And now he can be yours for just a pound of silver."

Hearing the price, several onlookers turned away and walked off. Anyone in their right mind in possession of a pound of silver would buy six cows, three mares, or even a couple of slaves before the patched-up skin of a dead bear. The ones who stayed seemed more transfixed by Theresa, who was still dancing.

But there was one woman, wearing a coat of fine furs, who seemed to be admiring the animal quite a bit. She was accompanied by a little man of an elegant appearance who, upon seeing her interest, sent a servant to inquire about the price.

"Tell your master what he already knows," said Althar. "One pound for the animal," and he blew the horn again.

The servant went pale, but his owner appeared unperturbed when he learned the cost. He sent the servant back to offer half.

"Tell him I wouldn't sell him a vixen for that price," Althar responded. "If he wants to impress his lady, he can get his coin pouch out or risk his own backside and kill one himself."

This time, when the couple heard his response, they turned away and disappeared into the crowds. However, when they had walked a few steps, Althar saw the woman look back at them. The old man smiled and starting packing up. "Time for a drink," he announced to Theresa.

Before leaving, he managed to make a few deals: He sold a beaver pelt to a silk merchant for a gold solidus, and exchanged another with a baker for three pecks of wheat. Then he paid two boys to guard the bear, though not without warning them that he would skin them alive himself if he returned to find anything missing.

Althar and Theresa walked into a nearby inn, and sat near the window to keep an eye on the cart. Althar ordered two cups of wine and some bread and sausages, which were served to them immediately. While they drank, Theresa asked him why he had refused to negotiate on the price for the bear.

"You need to learn the language of business," he replied as he scoffed down his food. "And the first lesson is know your customer, which luckily for me I do. The man who showed an interest is one of the richest men in Fulda: He could buy a hundred bears and still have the money for a thousand slaves. And as for her, I don't know what she must have between her legs, but she always gets what she wants."

"Well, I might not speak your language of trade, but the bear is still out there and if you had lowered the price then we might be celebrating a sale right now."

"And that's what we'll do," Althar laughed, winking and pointing at the door just as the little rich man walked in. The woman who was with him earlier accompanied him now, but stayed outside, admiring the stuffed animal.

The newcomer approached them. "May I?" he asked.

Althar consented almost without a glance and the man sat down unhurriedly. The innkeeper soon came over and as he served them wine and cheese, Theresa took the opportunity to examine their guest more closely. He wore rings on all his fingers and under his nose hung a limp, recently oiled moustache. She noticed that his clothes, though ostentatious, seemed to be covered in bits of food. The man grabbed the wine jug, and after filling his own cup, he filled Althar's until it was brimming over.

"Do you not *want* my money?" he asked bluntly.

"As much as you want my bear," Althar answered without lifting his eyes from his cup.

The man pulled out a pouch and deposited it on the table. Althar picked it up and felt its weight in his hand before placing it back down in front of its owner.

"Half a pound is what one of my laborers earns in a year," the man pointed out.

"That's why I'm not a laborer," said Althar, brushing aside the comment.

The man picked up the bag and stood, irritated, before going outside and speaking to the woman. Then he returned and kicked the table, making Theresa and Althar's food scatter across its surface. He took out two pouches and threw them down onto the mess he had just created. "A pound of silver. I hope you and your whore enjoy it," he said, glancing at Theresa.

"That we will, sir. Thank you!" said Althar, downing the last of his wine without batting an eyelid.

Outside, the woman fluttered about, kissing her man and laughing, while a pair of servants transferred the bear to another cart. One of the kids who Althar had paid to ward off thieves tried to stop them, receiving a slap in return. When Althar came out of the tavern, he called the boy over and gave him an obol for his bravery.

"Tell me, lad, do you know where I can find Maurer—the barber?"

The boy bit into the obol and ground it between his teeth before eagerly stuffing it in his pocket. He said he did, so they all climbed onto the cart and the boy guided them down a few streets to another tavern a couple of blocks away. Jumping off and running ahead, the boy disappeared into the inn, soon reappearing accompanied by a pot-bellied man with a pockmarked face.

Althar clambered down from the cart and after telling the barber the reason for their visit, they agreed on a price for a consultation. The barber went back into the tavern and returned carrying a bag. Climbing onto the driver's seat with Althar, they all set off to Helga the Black's hostelry.

Though he stank of wine, the barber set to work with obvious skill. As soon as they arrived, he shaved Hoos's torso and cleaned it with oils. Then he examined the hardened skin on his chest near the nipples, remarking on the redness, heat, and swelling. His bruises made the barber shake his head. He listened to his breathing using a bone ear trumpet, which he positioned over the wound, and inhaled Hoos's breath, which he found thick and sour. He prescribed a poultice, deciding that bleeding him would be unnecessary.

"It's the fever that worries me," he explained, gathering up his razors and the colored stones he had used to sharpen them. "He has three broken ribs. Two seem to be healing, but the third has punctured his lung. Fortunately it went in and out. The wound is scarring well, and the murmurs are weak. But the fever—that's bad news."

"Will he die?" asked Althar, prompting Helga to give him a slap on the head. "I mean . . . will he live?" he corrected himself.

"The problem is the swelling. If it persists, the fever will grow worse. There are plants . . . potions that can alleviate the illness, but unfortunately I don't have any."

"If it's money you need . . ."

"Regrettably, no. You've paid me well, and I've done what I can," he said.

"And these plants you speak of?" Helga inquired.

"I shouldn't have mentioned them. Aside from fennel for constipation and chervil for hemorrhages, I don't know much more about them."

"So who does?" asked Theresa. "The monastery physician? Come with us and we'll speak to him. Perhaps you can get him to help us."

He scratched his bald patch and looked at Theresa with pity. "I don't think he will be much help. That physician died last month."

Upon hearing that, Helga dropped the pot she was holding, which fell with a clatter to the floor. The news surprised Althar, too, and it hit Theresa even harder. Though no one had said it, all three of them were secretly hoping that the abbey physician would come to Hoos Larsson's rescue.

"Although, perhaps you could visit the apothecary," Maurer said. "The one they call Brother Herbalist. He's stubborn as a mule, but he'll often take pity on those who accompany their entreaties with some kind of food. Tell him I sent you. I do business with him and he regards me well."

"But could you not come with us?" Theresa persisted.

"It's not a good time for me to be associated with plants. At the beginning of the month a church legation sent by Charlemagne arrived in Fulda. They're led by a friar from Britannia the king has entrusted to reform the church, and from what I hear, he has come with whip in hand." He took a slug of wine. "All it would take is for someone to tell him that from time to time I earn a few coins warding off evil spirits and he'll accuse me of heresy and hang me from a very tall pine tree. That Briton has the whole monastery in a frenzy, so be careful."

Maurer finished applying the poultice and covered Hoos with a blanket. Before leaving he told them how to find the apothecary and showed Helga how to repeat the treatment without pressing too hard. Then, with a grave expression, he shook Althar's hand and left.

For a while they sat in a silence that felt as solid and heavy as stone. Then, Helga the Black powdered her face and tidied the room where she would begin work later on that evening, and Althar decided that it was a good time to visit the smithy and have the cart's axle casing repaired. Theresa stayed with Hoos to keep him cool with a damp cloth. She passed the cloth across his face with the delicacy of a whisper, over his eyebrows and his sleeping eyelids, praying that her trembling would not disturb his sleep. She realized that though she endlessly wiped away the sweat from Hoos's body, her own eyes were becoming moist, as though in some way the two of them were sharing the same suffering. She swore to herself then that, while he depended on her, Hoos Larsson would not die. She would drag him to the monastery herself if necessary to have the apothecary cure him with his herbs.

When Theresa saw Helga a little while later, it was as though a completely different person stood before her. Her loose hair, decorated with colorful ribbons, seemed less gray. She had painted her lips blood red and accentuated her plump cheeks with an extravagant rouge. Her pronounced cleavage revealed ample breasts, which, though sagging, were pushed up by an underskirt. She wore a long overskirt and her outfit was cinched with an eye-catching belt. With every step beaded necklaces danced over her chest, clicking invitingly. The woman sat down and filled her cup to the brim.

"We'll have to wait and see," she said, looking at Hoos. A roll of flab had flopped out over her belt, which she absentmindedly pushed back into her skirt.

"I don't think this poultice is helping. We should take him to the apothecary," said Theresa.

"He must rest now. Tomorrow we'll see what dawn brings, and then decide what to do. Althar told me you intend to stay in Fulda."

"That's right."

"And he mentioned you have no family. Have you thought about how you will earn a living?"

Theresa flushed. The fact was she hadn't considered it yet.

"I see," Helga continued. "Tell me something: Are you a maiden?"

"Yes," she responded, taken aback.

"You can certainly see it in your face." She shook her head. "If you'd been a whore it would make things a lot easier, but there's still plenty of time for that. What's wrong? You don't like men?"

"They don't interest me." She looked at Hoos and realized she was lying.

"And women?"

"Of course not!" She stood up, offended.

Helga the Black laughed brazenly. "Don't be scared, princess, God isn't here to hear us." She had another sip of wine, looked her over again and then wiped her mouth with the back of her hand, smudging her lipstick. "Then you'll have to think of something. Food costs denarii, clothes cost denarii, and the bed that this young man is sleeping in, when it's not used for fucking, also costs denarii."

Theresa's head was spinning. For a moment she didn't know what to say.

"I will find work tomorrow. I'll go to the market and ask at the stalls and in the fields. I am sure to find something."

"What trades do you know? Perhaps I can help."

She explained that in Würzburg she had worked in a tanning workshop. She also knew how to cook, she said, having just learned a thing or two from Leonora. However, she didn't mention her ability to write. Helga thought the tanning workshop was intriguing and pushed for more details, so Theresa told her that she had prepared parchment, sewed quinternions, and bound codices.

"There are no leather workshops here. Everyone makes do by themselves. They might make parchments at the monastery, but I couldn't say for sure. Did you earn much doing that?"

"I was given a loaf of bread each day. Apprentices aren't paid."

"Ah! So you're still learning. And what did a day laborer earn?"

"One or two denarii a day, but usually they also received food." She didn't explain that she was as skilled with the leather as they were.

Helga the Black nodded. Payment with food or goods was normal. However, when Theresa informed her that the laborers were given a peck of wheat, which was the equivalent of a denarius, the woman burst into laughter.

"You have obviously never been to the market. Let's see." She moved the jugs to one side of the table and began making little balls of bread with the leftover crumbs. "A pound of silver is twenty solidi." She finished making the little balls and positioned two rows of ten to one side. "And a solidus is equal to twelve denarii." She did a few more calculations, but miscounted and then sent all the balls flying onto the floor with an accidental swipe of her arm. "Basically, solidi are gold and denarii are silver, right?"

Theresa looked up as though she were searching for something on the ceiling. Suddenly she responded: "If twelve denarii make a solidus, and twenty solidi make a pound"—she counted with her fingers for a moment—"then one pound is equal to two hundred and forty denarii!"

Helga looked at her in astonishment, thinking she must have already known the answer. "That's right," she conceded, and then launched into explaining how it all works in the marketplace. "Two hundred and forty denarii. With one denarius you can buy a quarter of a peck of wheat or a third of a peck of rye. Even half a peck of barley—or one of oats. The problem is that, to grind them, you need a millstone, and the old ones are expensive as hell. So if you find work, it would be best if they paid you in bread rather than grain. If you could earn one denarii a day, that would equal twelve one-pound loaves, but that would be too much for one person." She continued to speculate about how it all might work out, barely taking a pause for breath. "You really only need one loaf for your own consumption, so you would have to go to the market to trade the nine remaining loaves. And I say nine, because if you stay here, you will have to give two to me for your lodging. A pound of meat or fish costs about half a denarius—or, in other words, the equivalent of six loaves of wheat bread. After that, you will still have three to trade for salt, which doesn't go bad, so you can always trade that again at any time. If you don't like it here, I can ask around the area. You might find another room for that price."

"But there are other things I will need. I don't know . . . clothes, shoes . . ."

"Let me have a look . . . I can lend you something for now. At any rate, although woolen fabric costs one solidus per yard, you can find used fabric for three denarii. Deloused and mended, it will serve the same purpose as any new garment. In fact, yesterday I bought four or five yards' worth of old wool. That's enough for two or three garments. I'll give you a piece so you can make a beautiful new dress."

Theresa didn't know what to say—she was overwhelmed by all this new information. As she chewed on a piece of bread, she just looked at Helga the Black and thought that despite her rough language and vulgar manners, the woman had a big heart.

"As for Hoos," Helga added, "he can stay as long as necessary, but I need the bed because sometimes the customers want some fun. At the back, in the hayloft, you'll find space where you can make yourselves comfortable."

Theresa went over to Helga and kissed her on the cheek.

Helga was moved by the gesture. "You know, there was a time when I was pretty, too," she said, a bitter smile on her face. "A long, long time ago."

At dinner, Althar cursed the blacksmiths' guild, its members, and in particular the swindler who had repaired the cartwheel. "The bastard charged me a solidus," he complained. "Any more and he may as well have kept the cart." He then announced that the next day he would return to the mountains.

Helga barely said a word at dinner. Theresa noticed that as the hours passed, the way her makeup smudged made her face resemble a scarecrow's. She seemed to barely be able to keep her eyes open, having drunk more than her fair share of wine, yet she was still clutching her cup.

After clearing the table, Theresa retired to the loft to tend to Hoos. She reapplied some poultice, but the fever was still devouring him. That night Hoos vomited three times and Theresa hardly slept.

As she lay awake she thought of her father and Rutgarda and longed to be with them. Not a night went by in which she didn't miss them sorely. She imagined them sad and downtrodden, and she felt terrible for letting them down. Sometimes she considered returning, but fear and shame held her back. She often consoled herself by imagining that they were well, daydreaming about how she would let them know where she was. She promised herself that she would find a way to contact them, to explain what had happened so that one day they might forgive her.

In the morning she was woken by Althar's puffing and panting as he attempted to hitch the horse to the cart. Theresa helped Hoos, still confused and delirious, to the stable latrine. While he relieved himself, Theresa cut a slice of the pie that Helga had made for the apothecary. She asked Althar if he would take them to the abbey before he departed, and the old man happily agreed.

Theresa didn't bother to say good-bye to Helga, for she was so drunk she couldn't even get out of bed. In the stable, Theresa noticed that Althar's cart looked good as new: The blacksmith, in addition to repairing the wheel casing, had also sanded it down. In the cart she positioned herself next to Hoos, covering him up with a blanket, to protect him from the dew.

Althar cracked his whip and the animal set off at a slow trot down the crowded streets as the earliest risers were preparing to leave their homes to head for the fields. Following the barber's directions, they made for the southern side of the abbey, where, he had said, they would find the apothecary working in the orchard. It must have been still very early, because they could not see any workers in the fields yet through the wattle fence. Althar dismounted from the cart and helped position Hoos so he sat on a nearby tree stump.

"We're here," the old man announced.

A shiver ran down Theresa's spine and she didn't know whether it was because of the frosty morning or because she was about to find herself alone again. She gave Althar a look of gratitude and when he held out his arms she hugged him.

Then she stepped away with tears in her eyes. "I'll never forget you, bear hunter. Nor Leonora. Tell her."

He rubbed his eyes before rummaging around in his clothes and pulling out a pouch of coins, which he offered to Theresa.

"It's all I could get."

She was speechless.

"For your bear head," he added. Then Althar waved good-bye to Hoos and urged on the horse. Slowly he disappeared down the mud-covered streets.

It was a short while before the bells rang for Prime, announcing the beginning of activity in the monastery. Soon a door opened and several monks came out to mill around the garden paths. The younger one began to lazily rake and weed, while the eldest, a tall, gangling monk amused himself by examining the shrubs, bending down from time to time to caress them. Theresa thought the tall one must be the apothecary, not just because of his age, but also because his habit was made of serge instead of than the coarser material worn by novices. The tall monk meandered from plant to plant, inspecting them in no great hurry, until he arrived near where Theresa stood partially hidden in the shrubbery.

She called to him with a "*Psst.*"

"Who goes there?" the monk asked, trying to see through the bramble. Theresa shrank back like a frightened rabbit.

"Brother Herbalist?" she asked in a tiny voice.

"Who seeks him?"

"Maurer the barber sends me. For the love of God, help us."

Pushing aside the bramble, the monk saw Hoos slumped over, sitting on the tree stump.

The monk immediately ordered two novices to carry him into a nearby enclosure. Theresa followed without questioning, crossing through the animal pens to a squat building protected by a door with a crude padlock. The monk took a key from his sleeve and after a couple of attempts pushed open the door, which gave way with a creak. The novices cleared several bowls from a table and lay Hoos on top, then following the elderly monk's instructions they returned to the garden to continue weeding and repairing the fences. Theresa waited in the threshold.

"Don't stay out there," said the monk as he cleared away the pots, jars, flasks, and vials that were balanced precariously on either side of the table around Hoos. "So the barber sends you? And he told you I would help?"

Theresa thought she knew what he was hinting at.

"I brought you this." She offered him the meat pie that Helga the Black had prepared.

The monk glanced at it and set it aside without paying it any more attention. He turned back to the table and continued to tidy the jars while he interrogated Theresa about the cause of the fever, biting his lip when he heard about the problem with the lung.

He moved an alembic to one side, ducking under a wooden press that seemed to be tilting slightly. Then he picked up some hand scales and a flask, which he filled with water from an indoor well, carefully measuring out the quantity, and then turned to a great dresser, where he began to search through dozens of ceramic containers. By the way he squinted, Theresa could tell that he was struggling to read their written labels.

"Let's see: Salix Alba . . . Salix Alba," he said, his nose up against the jars. "You know, health is the whole body, the balance of nature based on heat and moisture. That's what blood is. Hence we say *sanitas*, as though we were saying *sanguinis status*." He picked up a jar, examined it, and put it back in its place. "All illnesses originate in the four humors: blood, bile, melancholy, and phlegm. If they exceed their natural levels, illnesses occur. Blood and bile cause acute conditions, while phlegm and melancholy are the sources of chronic ones. Where have they put the willow bark?"

"*Salix Alba*. Here it is," said Theresa.

The monk looked at her as if caught off guard. He turned toward the jar that the young woman was pointing at and saw that it was the right one. "You can read?" he asked incredulously.

"And write," she responded with pride. The monk arched an eyebrow but said nothing for a while before picking up where he left off. "He has phlegm in his lungs," he explained. "And there are multiple treatments and remedies for that problem. But there are so many tinctures, incantations, and potions that it will take some time to find the right one. Take this remedy, for instance," he said, removing a piece of bark from the jar. "It is true that willow infused in milk reduces fever, but so does barley flour dissolved in tepid water, or saffron with honey. Each remedy behaves differently, depending on the proportions of its ingredients—and each patient responds differently, just as the organs that make up the person are different in nature. Weak or badly wounded hearts sometimes heal as if by magic, while others, by all appearances more vigorous and healthy, swell without reason with the arrival of spring. Incidentally . . . what is this young man's trade?"

"He possesses lands in Aquis-Granum," she explained, and she informed him that they were staying with Helga the Black until she could find work.

"Interesting," he said and put down the jar of willow bark before crossing the room to a stove, which he lit with a candle. "God sends us illnesses, but he also provides the remedies we need to get better. Just as we must study His word to reach paradise, we must also study Empedocles, Galen, Hippocrates, and even Pliny to find cures, whether it be in the powdered mineral of an alum, or in the glands of a beaver's foreskin. Hold this tincture," he instructed.

The young woman grasped the container in which the monk had poured a dark liquid. She was concerned he was talking too much, and that the church envoy that Maurer had mentioned might appear at any moment and expel them from the monastery before the apothecary could complete the treatment.

"If there are several remedies, why not use them all?" she asked.

"*Alibi tu medicamentum obligas*. Pass me that." The monk added a pale powder to the dark liquid and whisked the solution until it was whitish in color. "*Medicine* comes from *measurement*, or in other words, from moderation, which is the premise that must guide our every action. The Greeks were the fathers of this art, which Apollo introduced, and his son Aesculapius continued. Later it was Hippocrates who adopted this wisdom and developed it with his careful, learned approach. It is to him that we owe our understanding of healing that is based on reason, experimentation, and observation."

Theresa was growing impatient. "But how will you cure him?"

"The question is not *how*, but *when*. And the answer is, it does not depend on me, but on him. He must therefore remain here until that happens. That is, if it happens at all."

"To be honest, I don't think that's a good idea. The barber told us that a foreign monk sent by Charlemagne arrived at the abbey last week, and if he's as strict as they say, I fear he may find reason to reproach you."

"And what is it that he would rebuke me for?"

"I don't know. Your behavior. Isn't the abbey supposed to only look after its own sick? If this man finds out you are helping a stranger . . ."

"What is his name?"

"I don't know. I just remember that he's a foreign friar."

"I meant the patient."

"Sorry," she answered, red-faced. "Larsson. Hoos Larsson."

"Well, then, Sir Larsson, a pleasure to meet you. And now that we have been introduced—problem solved."

Theresa gave him a smile, but she insisted: "If for any reason that man expels Hoos before he is cured, I could never forgive myself."

"And what makes you think he would do that? From what I know, this newcomer is no devil. He only wishes to impose order in the abbey."

"But the barber said—"

"For goodness' sake, forget the barber. In any event, for your own peace of mind I can assure you that this envoy of Charlemagne's will not get wind that Hoos is staying here in the apothecary."

"Please try to understand me. I'm so worried. Can you promise that if Hoos stays here, he'll get better?"

"*Ægroto dum anima est, spes est.* While there is life, there is hope."

Theresa supposed that all this kindness would not come cheap, so she offered him the pouch of coins that Althar had given her.

But the monk paid that as much attention as he did the pie. "Keep your money. You can make it up to me some other way. In fact, come back tomorrow morning after Terce and ask for the cellarer. Tell him Brother Alcuin is waiting for you. Perhaps I can find you a job."

When she told Helga what the monk had said, the woman could hardly believe her ears.

"I doubt the apothecary has good intentions," she said.

"What do you mean?"

"Wake up, lass. Bad intentions, toward you."

"He seemed honest. He didn't eat the pie himself but gave it to the novices."

"Who knows, he could have just eaten and been stuffed already."

"But he's thin as a rake!" Theresa said with a nervous laugh. "What kind of job do you think it could be?"

"Well, if the apothecary behaves like a good Christian, perhaps he will employ you as a maidservant. Monks may do a lot of praying, but they're dirty as pigs. Or you might be lucky and he'll employ you as a cook, which wouldn't do you any harm, for you could put on a pound or two. But if you want me to be honest, there are dozens of lasses prepared to clean latrines, so I don't understand his interest in hiring such a prissy young woman. So tread carefully and watch your backside."

Theresa and Helga spent the rest of the morning cooking and tidying the tavern. In the main room there were several barrels that served as tables, some stools, a long bench, and a drape to separate the customers from the kitchen. By the fireplace they arranged an iron stove, two trivets, various pans and skillets, a stewpot, wooden spatulas, some chipped pitchers and jars, and an array of tankards and plates, stacked and ready to be washed with the water from the well. Helga explained she kept the wine in the loft, since it was frequently pilfered when stored in the kitchen. She plied her other trade in the storeroom, which was located at the back—half animal pen, half henhouse.

At midday they ate some of the food they had prepared to serve in the hostelry, and their conversation turned again to the events at the monastery earlier that morning. When they finished their meal, Helga proposed going to the main square to see The Swine, a prisoner accused of a terrible crime. She suggested they do their hair and amuse themselves watching the youngsters throw cabbages and turnips at him, and on the way they could buy some perfume to scent their bodies. Theresa accepted the invitation, and singing softly to themselves they left for the market square.

12

Though the blows dealt by the guards had turned The Swine's body into a mass of battered flesh, his wrinkled, beardless face that gave him his nickname could still be made out. The man was curled up on his knees, tied to a plank of wood and guarded by two men armed with swords. Theresa thought he must be a half-wit, for his little eyes were trembling in fear, as though he were trying to understand what was happening to him. A crowd surrounded the captive, threatening and cursing him. A boy attempted to set a dog on him, but the animal turned and ran away.

Helga bought a couple of ales from a peddler and looked for some place where they could watch the spectacle, but several women were pointing fingers at her, so she finally decided to retreat somewhere more discreet. "He was born an idiot, but for thirty years nobody imagined he could be dangerous," she told Theresa, leaning against a wall.

"Dangerous? What happened?"

"He had never made any trouble before. But last week they found the girl he had a habit of pestering, naked and sprawled out on the riverbank. He'd cut her throat."

Theresa could not help but remember the incident when the Saxons had tried to violate her. She drank her beer quickly and asked Helga if they could go home. The woman reluctantly agreed.

It had been a long time since a murderer in Fulda had been taught a lesson, but she would settle for enjoying the celebrations on execution day.

On the way back they stopped to buy the fragrances that Helga used when she plied her trade. She chose a flask of pine-scented perfume and another more intense scent similar to incense. Instead of charging Helga for the perfume, Theresa noticed the merchant wink at her and arrange to see her later on.

In the afternoon two drunks visited the tavern, drinking cheap wine until they ran out of money. After they left, Theresa suggested to Helga that they visit the monastery to check on Hoos, but Helga advised her to wait until the appointment with the apothecary the next morning. A little later on, three young men turned up at the hostelry, ate some dinner, laughed among themselves, and left. Soon afterward five laborers arrived, stinking of sweat and eager for food. They sat near the fire, ordered copious amounts of beer and joked about which of the two women would be the first to end up with her underskirt around her ankles. After serving them some food, Helga left Theresa in charge of the kitchen and went out in search of some friends, for they would soon be needed. She returned arm in arm with two women, also plastered in makeup and dressed in colorful clothes. Upon arriving they sat on the laborers' laps, yelping and laughing as the men caressed them. One of them slid his hand under a skirt and the woman feigned a squeal. Another man, already the worse for drink, offered his girl a swig of wine and spilt it down her cleavage, but the young woman, far from scolding him, responded by showing him a breast.

That was when Theresa decided it was time to withdraw, but one of the laborers noticed her leaving and stood in her way. Fortunately, Helga placated him by whispering in his ear and promising him a night of abandon. Then she told Theresa to go to the storeroom and shut herself in the wine store.

Theresa soon discovered that a brothel's wine store was not a good place to spend a peaceful night. From the attic she could see the corner that one of the laborers had chosen to have a woman kneel and bring his member back to life. When the tart had achieved this, the man pushed her head away, positioned himself between her legs, and began to pump his backside up and down vigorously. Then he gave a couple of jerks and cursed the prostitute before slumping onto her pale body.

Before long Helga came in accompanied by the perfume merchant. The two of them laughed when they saw the other couple asleep on top of each other. The merchant made as if to wake them up, but Helga stopped him. They started to fondle each other on a nearby bed, and Theresa was thankful they at least covered themselves with a cloak that hid their bodies from view.

When she finally managed to sleep, Theresa dreamed of Hoos. He appeared naked—as did she. He stroked her hair, her neck, and her breasts—caressing her entire body. A strange feeling woke and alarmed Theresa. When she calmed down, she asked God to forgive her for sinning in such a way.

In the morning, Theresa tidied the tavern, which looked like a battleground. Afterward she prepared some breakfast, eating alone since Helga was still hung over. When at last she rose, the woman washed her crotch in a grubby bowl, complained about the cold, and then offered Theresa some advice before she left for the abbey. "And most important, don't mention that you know me," she impressed on her with puffy eyes.

Theresa kissed Helga good-bye, recalling that she had already told the apothecary where she was staying. Then she ran to the abbey because the bells announcing the beginning of the Terce service were already chiming.

A stout monk with a retiring demeanor met her at the main gate, and he seemed surprised to hear her intentions.

"Indeed, I am the cellarer, but explain something to me. Who have you come to see? The apothecary, or Brother Alcuin?"

Theresa was taken aback, for she had assumed that the apothecary and Brother Alcuin were the same person, but the cellarer, seeing her hesitation, closed the wicket, leaving her alone outside. She rapped on the little door again with her knuckles, but the monk did not answer until he returned to empty a bucket of scraps outside.

"If you keep making a nuisance of yourself, I'll take a stick to you," he threatened.

Theresa tried to respond but couldn't think what to say. For a moment she considered pushing the monk aside and running to the garden, but it occurred to her to offer him the meat she had brought for the apothecary. Perhaps it would persuade him.

When the cellarer saw the chops, his eyes widened. "Well, make up your mind, then, lass. Who do you want to see?" he asked, snatching the meat from her.

"Brother Alcuin." She had to assume the gatekeeper was an idiot.

The man bit into one chop, stuffing the other into the sleeve of his robe. He stepped aside to allow her through, and closing the wicket behind them, told her to follow him.

To Theresa's astonishment, rather than head toward the garden, the cellarer crossed the animal pens, kicking cocks and hens out of the way. They passed the stables, and the kitchen, and after skirting round the granaries, made for an imposing stone building that stood out majestically from the rest. The friar knocked on the door and waited. "The optimates' residence. Where important guests stay," he explained.

An acolyte answered, his dark robe contrasting with his pale face. The man looked at the cellarer and nodded as if he had been expecting them. Theresa followed the man in. They avoided the communal chambers by taking some stairs that led them to a hall, its walls lavishly decorated with woolen tapestries. The furniture was finely carved and on the main table were several volumes arranged in a circle. A thread of light filtered onto them through the alabaster window. The acolyte told her to wait and thereupon left the room. Moments later the tall figure of the apothecary entered wearing an exquisite white *penula* fastened to the waist by an embroidered belt decorated with silver plaques. Theresa felt embarrassed by her own outfit.

"You will excuse the attire I was wearing yesterday, though perhaps I should apologize more for today's outfit." The monk smiled. "Please, take a seat," he said and made himself comfortable on a wooden armchair. Theresa sat on a stool beside him. She looked at his bony face and aging white skin, thin as the layers of an onion.

At length, Theresa asked, "Why are we here? And what are you doing dressed as a bishop?"

"Well, not like a bishop, exactly." He gave her another smile. "My name is Alcuin—Alcuin of York, and in reality I am just a monk. Worse still, I haven't even been ordained as a priest, though on occasions, due to the position I hold, I am obliged to cover myself in this pretentious garb. As for this place, I reside here temporarily, along with my acolytes. Well, in truth I stay at the cathedral chapter on the other side of the city, but that detail is unimportant."

"I don't understand."

"The fact is that I owe you an apology. I should have explained to you yesterday that I am not the apothecary."

"Then who are you?"

"Well, I'm afraid I am that 'foreign newcomer' about whom you've heard such unfavorable reports."

Theresa gave a start. For a moment she thought Hoos's fate hung by a thread, but Alcuin put her mind at rest.

"You need not worry. If I wanted to cast him out, do you think I would have bothered attending to him? As for my identity, my intention was not to deceive you. The apothecary died quite suddenly the day before yesterday. It's a matter I can expound on later. By coincidence I know a great deal about herbs and poultices, so when you took me by surprise in the garden, my only thought was to aid your friend."

"But after—"

"Afterward I did not wish to worry you. I thought that given your wariness, knowing the truth would only heighten your concern."

Theresa fell silent for a while. "How is he?" she eventually asked.

"Thanks be to God, much better. We will visit him later. But for now let us talk about why I brought you here. Let us talk about your job." He picked up one of the volumes from the table and examined it with great care. *De Coelesti Hierarchia* by Pseudo-Dionysius the Areopagite. A true wonder. As far as I know, only two other copies exist—one in Alexandria and another in Northumbria. You said you can write, did you not?"

Theresa nodded.

The monk clapped his hands and soon the acolyte appeared with some implements. Alcuin carefully placed them in front of the young woman.

"I would like you to transcribe this paragraph."

Theresa bit her lip. Though it was true that she could write, recently she had only done so on wax tablets because parchment was too valuable to be wasted. She recalled that, in the words of her father, the secret to good writing resided in selecting the right quill: not too light, to avoid a loose stroke; but not too heavy, which would prevent the required fluidity and grace of movement. She wavered between several of the writing implements before her, finally opting for a pink goose quill, testing its weight in her hand a couple of times before smoothing the vane and barbules.

She checked the slit in the umbilicus through which the ink would flow, judging it to be blunt and too inclined, so she cut a new tip using a scalpel. Then she examined the parchment. Selecting the softest side to write on and using an awl and a tablet, she traced several invisible lines to use as a guide. Next, she positioned the text on a lectern and dipped the calamus in the ink until the pen was dripping. Taking a deep breath, she began to write.

The first letters, though tremulously written, were nicely joined. Then the ink flowed bright and silky, the pen sliding over the parchment with the delicacy of a swan on water. At the beginning of the eighth uncial, however, a blot appeared that ruined the entire page. It frustrated Theresa and made her think of giving up, but she clenched her teeth and continued with determination. When she had finished the text, she scraped and blew away the error, cleaned away the remains of the pounce, and finally handed it to Alcuin, who had been watching her closely the entire time.

The monk inspected the parchment and then looked at Theresa with a severe expression. "It's not perfect," he concluded. "But it will do."

Theresa watched the monk as he turned back to scrutinize the text, noticing his eyes in particular. They were a light, muted blue color—a dull tone that clouds the eyes of the elderly. They did not correspond to his apparent age, which she estimated at around fifty-five years old.

"You need a scribe?" she ventured to ask.

"Indeed. Romuald, a Benedictine monk who always accompanied me, used to help me with my work. Unfortunately he fell ill soon after we arrived in Fulda. He died the day before the apothecary passed away."

"I'm sorry." She didn't know what else to say.

"As am I. Romuald was my eyes, and at times my hands also. My eyesight has worsened of late, and though when I rise my vision is still sharp enough to discern a strand of saffron or read intricate script, as the afternoon wears on, my sight begins to cloud over and seeing becomes arduous. That was when Romuald would read for me or transcribe my comments."

"You cannot write?"

Alcuin raised his right hand, showing the back of it to Theresa. It was shaking.

"It started some four years ago. Sometimes the shaking spreads above the elbow so that I cannot even drink. That is why I need someone to write down my notes. I like to record events that I witness without omitting a single detail so I may reflect on them later. What's more, I wanted to transcribe some texts from the bishop's library."

"And there are no scribes in the abbey?"

"Of course. There are Theobald of Pisa, Balthazar the Old, and also Venancio. But they are of senior rank and too important to follow me around all day. There are also Nicholas and Maurice, but though they can write, they cannot read."

"How is that possible?"

"Reading is a complex process. Demanding. It requires effort and an ability that not all monks possess. Yet, as strange as it seems, there are copyists who can imitate symbols with great skill all without being able to understand their meaning. Though of course, they are incapable of taking dictation. So there are those who can write, or rather, transcribe, but who remain unable to read. And there are others who can read well enough but haven't learned to write. And then there also those who, though they can read and write, can only do so in Latin. If we also exclude those who confuse *L* with *F*, those who write at an exasperatingly slow pace, those who commit errors as if on purpose, and those who grow bored of the work and complain of pain in their hands, we are left with very few. And unfortunately not all of those people can or want to set aside their chores to help a newcomer."

"But you could order them."

"Well, because of my position, I could, but let's just say I have no interest in unwilling help."

"And what position is that?" she ventured, and then bit her tongue, aware her curiosity might be getting the better of her manners.

"It could be described as a teacher of teachers. Charlemagne loves learning and the Frankish kingdom lacks it, which is why the king has entrusted me with the task of ensuring that education and the Word of God reach all corners of the kingdom. At first I took it as an honor, but I must admit that it has become an arduous responsibility."

Theresa shrugged. She still couldn't understand Alcuin's true intentions regarding her role in everything, but she supposed that if she wanted to help Hoos, she would have to accept the job, whatever it was.

Then the monk said was time to visit the patient. Before they set off, he covered Theresa with a robe to hide her from wandering gazes.

"What puzzles me," Theresa said as they walked, "is that you think I can help you. You don't know anything about me."

"I wouldn't go that far . . . for instance: I know your name is Theresa, and that you can read and write Greek."

"That's not a great deal."

"Well, I could also add that you are from Byzantium, no doubt from a wealthy family, albeit fallen on bad times. I know that until a few weeks ago you lived in Würzburg, where you worked in the parchment-maker's workshop, and that you probably had to flee because of a sudden fire. And I know that you are obstinate and determined enough to bribe the cellarer with two meat chops to gain entry."

Theresa spluttered. It was impossible that Alcuin could know those things because she had not even told Hoos. For a moment she thought she was looking at the Devil himself.

"And just in case you're wondering—no, Hoos Larsson did not reveal these things to me."

Theresa grew even more frightened, suddenly stopping. "So who, then?"

"Keep walking," he said with a smile. "The question is not *who*, but *how*."

"What do you mean?" she said, picking up her pace to catch up with him.

"Anyone with the right expertise and keen observation skills could have guessed it." He stopped for a moment to explain. "For instance: Your Byzantine provenance is easy to establish from your name, Theresa, of Greek origin and unusual in these parts. Then there is your accent, an uncommon mix of Romance and Greek, which not only confirms my theory but also suggests that you have been in the region for several years. And if this were not enough evidence, your ability to read the medicine jars would have sufficed, since for reasons of security were written in Greek."

"And the fact about a wealthy family fallen on bad times?" She stopped again, but Alcuin kept walking.

"Well, it is logical to assume that if you can read and write you are not from a family of slaves. Plus, your hands do not have the typical scars of heavy manual labor. In fact, the particular kind of corrosion on your nails and the minor cuts between your left index finger and thumb, signal to me that you have been engaged in parchment-making." He stopped for a moment to allow a procession of novices to pass. "All of this tells me that your parents possessed enough wealth to prevent their daughter, an exquisitely educated young woman, from having to work in the fields. However, the clothes you wear are humble and threadbare, and you do not wear fine shoes. This means that, for some reason, your family's past affluence is no longer."

"But what made you assume I lived in Würzburg?"

The processions finished filing past and they starting walking again.

"The fact that you have not resided in Fulda for very long was obvious since you didn't know what the Brother Herbalist looked like. So the only possibility was that you were from a nearby town, for with this recent storm it would be unthinkable that you came from further afield. The three closest towns are Aquis-Granum, Erfurt, and Würzburg. If you had lived in Aquis-Granum, without doubt I would have known you, because that is where I reside. And in Erfurt there is no parchment-maker's workshop, so by a simple process of elimination, I knew you must be from Würzburg."

"And the fire?"

"I must admit, that was a riskier assumption. Or at least it was riskier to assume that was the reason you left." He turned and continued to walk and talk as if they were engaged in mundane banter about the weather. "Your clothes and arms are dotted with little burns, which though dispersed are identical in appearance: Very small and precise, they indicate their cause was a single event. Their nature and dispersion reveal that you were in a burning building or at least in the vicinity of a large fire, because the marks can be found on both the front and the back of your dress. What's more, the burns on your arms have not scarred yet, which means the incident must have taken place not much over three weeks ago."

Theresa looked at him, doubting his words. Although his explanations sounded reasonable, she could still not believe that someone could deduce so much information from a mere glance. She picked up her pace even more in order to keep up with his long strides. They skirted a little garden that led to a low building.

"But how did you find out about the chops? When I gave them to the cellarer, we were alone."

"That was the easiest bit to figure out," he said, laughing. "When that glutton accompanied you to the optimates' residence, he didn't even wait for you to go in before taking out the second chop and devouring it in three mouthfuls. I saw it from the window, where I was awaiting your arrival."

"But that doesn't mean that I gave them to him," Theresa replied defensively. Then she added, "Not to mention that it was in exchange for allowing me to pass."

"That also has an explanation: Benedictines cannot eat meat, for the Rule of Saint Benedict forbids it. Only in certain cases is it allowed, for example when one is sick, and of course, that's not the case with the cellarer. So I surmised that it must have been some-one from outside the abbey who supplied the chops. I knew he was chewing on a chop because I saw him spit out a piece of bone. What's more, yesterday you brought me a meat pie as a gift, so it would be logical to expect you to do the same again."

He bent down to straighten out a lettuce that was growing crooked. "And if that were not enough information to confirm you gave him a chop for your entry, before you started writing, I saw you wipe your hands on a cloth, leaving a trace of fat there that soon attracted a pair of flies. I do not believe a young lady so well educated would appear before a supposed apothecary dirty, even if dressed in peasant clothing."

Theresa remained silent, dazed. She still found it hard to accept that Alcuin was not calling upon the black arts to make those div-inations. But before she could think of a suitable reply, a sulfu-rous smell alerted her that they were arriving at the abbey hospital. Before going in, Alcuin asked her to make it quick.

The hospital had a large but dark hall, with two rows of beds, most of them occupied by monks too decrepit to care for them-selves. There was also a small room for the infirmarians and an adjoining chamber used for patients from outside of the monas-tery. Alcuin explained that, despite what Theresa may have heard, the abbey did indeed treat the townsfolk.

A stout friar suddenly appeared and delivered a short summary on Hoos's welfare. His fever was in remission and he had got up to visit the latrine and walk about for a while, but grew tired and went back to bed. He also told them that he had wheat bread and a little wine for breakfast.

Alcuin frowned at the monk and told him next time he must give him rye bread only. However, he was pleased to hear that he had not coughed up any blood since his last visit. While Alcuin inquired after other patients, Theresa walked over to Hoos, who lay covered in thick furs, his face bathed in a veil of sweat. She stroked his hair and the young man opened his eyes. Theresa smiled at him, but it took a few moments before he recognized her.

"They say you'll be better soon," she said.

"They also say this wine is good," Hoos responded, smiling back. "What are you doing wearing a novice's robe?"

"I had to put it on. Do you need anything? I can't stay long."

"To get better is what I need. Do you know how long they will keep me here? I hate priests almost as much as quacks."

"Until you recover, I suppose. From what I've been told at least a week, but I promise to visit you often. In fact starting from today, I work here."

"Here, in the monastery?"

"Yes, I don't know as what, exactly, as a scribe I think."

Hoos nodded. He seemed very tired.

Alcuin approached to ask after his health. "I'm glad you're improving. If you keep on this trajectory, within a week you will be hunting cats, which is the only thing that you'll find to hunt around the abbey," Alcuin informed him.

Hoos smiled again.

"Now we must go," he added.

She would have liked to kiss him, but instead Theresa said good-bye with a look that brimmed with tenderness. Before they left, Alcuin instructed the infirmarian on the treatment that the young man should receive for the rest of the day. Then he led Theresa to the abbey exit, explaining as they went that the art of medicine

rested on the foundations of a science, the *theorica*, which provided the elements required to put it into *practica*. Knowledge of
both components, *theorica* and *practica*, improved the *operatio*, or
everyday practice. "At least, in theory that's what should happen in
the art of medicine. As it should," he added, "in the art of writing."

She was surprised to meet a monk familiar with two such different arts, writing and medicine, but after witnessing his divina-
tory ability, she didn't want to ask too many questions. As they
reached the gate, Alcuin said good-bye and told her to return the
next day, first thing in the morning.

When Theresa arrived back at Helga's house, she found her lying
on her bed, crying. The room was still a mess, with upturned chairs
and pieces of broken cups and earthenware jugs scattered all over
the place. She tried to console her, but Helga hid her head in her
arms as if her greatest desire was that Theresa should not see her
face. The young woman hugged her anyway, not knowing how best
to comfort her.

"I should have killed that bastard the first time he beat me," she
finally said between sobs.

Theresa dampened a cloth with water to clean the dried blood
from her face. Helga had a gashed eyelid and split lips, but she
seemed to be crying more out of rage than pain.

"Let me wash you at least," Theresa pleaded.

"Damn him a thousand times! Damn him!"

"What happened? Who hit you?"

Helga was crying inconsolably now. "I'm with child," she
sobbed. "By a pig that almost killed me."

She said that though she took precautions, this was not the first
time she had been made pregnant. At first she had followed the
advice of the midwives. To guard against pregnancy she would
remove her clothes, smear herself with honey, roll around on a pile
of wheat, and then carefully gather up all the grain that had stuck

to her body and grind it manually in the opposite direction of normal—from left to right. The bread made from this flour she then fed to the man before copulating, whose germinal fluids would then be sterilized, but she was more fertile than a family of rabbits, she said, and despite these precautions, as soon as she let her guard down, she would fall pregnant.

After her husband passed away, she had allowed her first two children to die as soon as they were born, because that was what unwedded mothers normally did. The other pregnancies ended before birth thanks to an old woman who stuck a duck feather between her legs. However, last year she met Widukind, a married woodsman who didn't seem to mind how she made her living. He would say that he loved her, and they were like young lovers when they went to bed. Once he told her he would forsake his wife to marry her.

"Which is why, when I missed my second period, I thought it would make him get on with it. Well, you can see what happened. When I told him this morning, he flew into a rage as if he had been robbed of his soul. He laid into me, calling me a devious whore. The lying bastard. I hope his prick rots, and if one day he does want to have children, let them be born with antlers!"

Theresa stayed by her side until Helga eventually stopped crying. Later she learned that Widukind hat hit her on other occasions, too, but never as brutally as that day. She also heard about the countless women who without the means to support their children would kill their newborns rather than give them up as slaves.

"But this one I want to keep," Helga confessed, stroking her belly. "Since I lost my husband, I've had nothing but problems."

Between the two of them they tidied the tavern. Theresa told her about Alcuin of York who was not the apothecary, and how Hoos was recovering from his injuries but would need to remain at the monastery for a while. She added that Alcuin had mentioned how odd he thought the sickness that afflicted the town.

"He's right. It's a strange illness, for it only seems to affect the wealthy," said Helga.

At midday they ate a pottage of boiled pulses and rye flour. They spent the rest of the afternoon talking about childbirth, children, and pregnancy. At the end of the day, Helga admitted that she had started selling herself in order to survive. One night, not long after she had become widowed, a stranger came into her home and raped her until she was broken. When the neighbors found out they turned their backs on her, refusing to speak or break bread with her. Nobody offered her work, so she had to earn a living by humiliating herself.

They went to bed early, Helga complaining of a headache.

It was not yet dawn when Theresa left the hostelry equipped with tablets filled with fresh wax and headed out into the frost-covered streets. At the first corner, she felt the wind growing stronger and so wrapped herself in the novice's robe that Alcuin had given her. Then she ran through the streets, fearing that she would take a wrong turn and arrive late on her first day at work. When she reached the monastery, the cellarer opened up as soon as he saw her and again accompanied her to the optimates' building where Alcuin waited at the entrance.

"No chops today?" he said to Theresa with a smile, leading her to the same room as the day before. Theresa found it better lit thanks to some large candles arranged around the table. She noticed that they had added a newly oiled desk on which sat a codex, an inkwell, a knife, and several sharpened pens.

"Your workplace," announced Alcuin, signaling the desk with the palm of his hand. "For the time being you will remain here copying texts. You must not leave the room without my authorization, and of course, when you do, you will always be accompanied.

Later on, when I have informed Bishop Lothar that I have employed you as an assistant, we will move to the chapter."

He went off for a moment and returned with two cups of milk. "At midday we will pay a brief visit to Hoos. If you need anything in my absence, tell one of my acolytes. Good. Now I must attend to other matters, so before you start with the notes, I would like you to copy a few pages of this codex."

Theresa leafed through the volume with curiosity. It was a thick codex, of recent making, its leather cover wrought in gold, with beautifully illuminated miniatures. According to Alcuin it was a valuable specimen of the *Hypotyposeis* by Clement of Alexandria, a transcription of an Italian codex translated from Greek by Theodore of Pisa, which like so many other codices went from abbey to abbey, for various copyists to duplicate. She noticed that the writing was different, smaller and easier to read. Alcuin explained that it was a new type of calligraphy that he had been working on for some time.

As she examined the text, Theresa realized that she had not agreed to any kind of remuneration with Alcuin for her new employment. She knew that he was looking after Hoos, and she did not wish to appear ungrateful, but when the money she was given for the bear head was gone, she would need funds to pay for board and lodging. She didn't know how to broach the subject, but Alcuin seemed to read her thoughts.

"As for your pay," he informed her, "I promise to provide two pounds of bread every day, along with whatever vegetables you need. You may also keep the robe you are wearing, and I will give you a new pair of shoes so that you do not catch a chill."

It seemed sufficient to Theresa, who guessed she would only be kept busy until dinner time, which meant she would still have several hours to help Helga at the tavern.

He had explained to her that her schedule would fit around religious services, which took place every three hours. The monastery came to life at dawn, after the Prime service. That was when they had breakfast and afterward the monks would go about their tasks. At around midmorning during the Terce service, which coincided with Chapter Mass, was when Theresa should start her work. Three hours later, at midday, the Sext service would be held, straight after lunch. None was held midafternoon until sunset, after which came dinner, and then Vespers. By midevening they would return to the church for Compline, which lasted until midnight. He told her that what time her day ended would depend on how many pages she managed to complete.

Alcuin donned a woolen overcoat. "If you should need to visit Hoos in my absence, ask for my acolyte and show him this." He handed her a tarnished bronze ring. "He will escort you. I will return in a couple of hours to check your progress. Do you like soup?"

"Yes, of course."

"I will tell the kitchen to prepare you some food."

Then he left her alone with the text.

She dipped the pen in the ink, crossed herself, and started writing—putting her heart and soul into every letter. She copied the writing imitating the stroke, inclination, movement, and size. Perfect symbols appeared on the page. Words interlinked to form harmonious paragraphs full of meaning, and in her mind's eye she saw the image of her father, encouraging her to achieve her ambitions. She was saddened to think of him and longed to be by his side. Then with renewed resolve, she went back to writing.

13

Haec studia adolescenciam alunt, senectutem oblectant, secundas res ornant, adversis solatium et perfugium praebent, delectant domi, non impediunt foris, pernoctant nobiscum, peregrinantur, rusticantur."

"No, no, and no!" Alcuin, exasperated, said to the young assistant assigned to him by the bishop. "It has been three days and you still have not learned! How many times do I have to tell you that if you do not keep the pen perpendicular to the parchment, it will ruin the document."

The novice lowered his head as he muttered an apology. It was already the second time he had made a mistake that afternoon.

"And look here. It's not *haec*, it's *hæc*. Nor is it *praepent*, but *præpent*, lad! *Præpent*! How do you expect anyone to understand this . . . this gibberish. Oh, well, I suppose we'll leave it there for today. It's almost dinnertime anyhow, and we're both tired. We'll continue on Monday when we're both calmer."

The young man stood, his head bowed. It was clear he didn't like the work, but the bishop had ordered him to help Alcuin with whatever he asked. He sprinkled some chalk powder on the blot he had just made, but all this did was ruin it further. So he decided to give up completely for the day and gathered his implements, cleaning them sloppily before placing them into a wooden chest. He blew at the chalk remains and used a tiny brush to sweep away the lumps that had formed around the blot. Finally, he sharpened the calamus, rinsed it a little, and left it on the lectern with the original codex. Then he ran after Alcuin, who had already disappeared down the corridor that led to the old *peristylium* of the cathedral chapter.

"Master, master!" called out the young acolyte. "While I remember, we may not be able to continue on Monday, since it is the day of the execution."

"The execution? God almighty! I had forgotten," he said, scratching his tonsure. "Well, it is our duty to assist him at such a difficult juncture. Speaking of which, will the bishop be there?"

"With the whole cathedral chapter," the acolyte responded.

"Well, then, lad, I will see you at breakfast on Tuesday."

"You will not be at dinner this evening?"

"No, no. At night, food, aside from bloating my stomach, dulls my senses. And I still have to finish this *De Oratione*," he said, raising the parchment roll he carried under his arm. "God be with you."

"And you, Father. Good night."

"By the way," added Alcuin, glancing at the lectern, "don't you think you should put the codex back on its shelf?"

"Oh! Of course!" said the novice, and quickly retraced his steps. "Good night, Father, I will do that right away."

The monk set off for the boarding house at the cathedral complex with a disgruntled look. The acolyte had been working on that codex for several days and had barely managed to transcribe four complete pages. At that pace he would never have a decent copy. He decided that as soon as he saw the bishop he would announce his intention to appoint Theresa to the position, for the novice was clearly not the right person for the job.

As he crossed the *peristylium* he stopped for a moment to look around him. As far as he could see, Fulda's monastic chapter had adhered to the latest reforms instituted by Charlemagne. In his *institutio canonicorum*, he aimed to promote community life among the chapter's clergymen by regulating the system and design of the clerical buildings surrounding the cathedral and the bishop's palace.

He was fascinated by that arrangement of structures of various styles and functions that wrapped around the little cathedral, and he was even more surprised by the fact that the bishop of Fulda had chosen an old Roman *domus* as the site for his episcopal see. The palace was a two-story stone building. The upper floor had eleven small heated rooms with doors leading out to a communal gallery with views over the atrium. The ground floor housed the cellar, two porticos, two chambers with timber floors, a stable, the kitchens, a bakery, the pantry, the granary, and a small infirmary. Perhaps he was not the right man to make such a judgment, but he had the impression that the palace exceeded the humility required of a prelate of the Church. That said, he knew that he should not criticize too harshly one who had so warmly welcomed him. After all, the Bishop of Fulda had felt most complimented by his presence, especially when he learned that Alcuin was interested in the exquisite treasures of his library.

It was completely dark by the time he arrived at his cell in the boarding house. He could have stayed in the optimates' residence in the abbey, but preferred a small, private cell to a large but shared room. He thanked the heavens for a space of his own, took off his shoes, and made ready to use his brief moment of solitude to meditate on the events of the day, which had been particularly arduous, but not as bad as the days he had to endure in his far-off Northumbria. After all not in Fulda nor in Aquis-Granum did he have to rise for Matins, and after the Prime service he always had a warm breakfast of cakes with honey, cured cheese, and apple cider waiting for him. Indeed, his daily duties were nothing like those he had performed with utter devotion during his days at the episcopal school in York, where he taught rhetoric and grammar, ran the library, oversaw the scriptorium, collected codices, translated texts, oversaw the loans of books brought in from the distant monasteries of Hibernia, supervised the admission of novices, organized debates, and assessed the progress of each student. How distant were those days in York!

As if he were reliving them, his mind conjured images of his childhood in Britain. He had been born into a Christian family in Whitby, Northumbria, a tiny coastal town whose few inhabitants lived from what they could pull from the sea and from the meager orchards sprawled around an ancient fort. He remembered the rain-soaked land, an eternally damp place, but fresh, where every morning he would wake to the smell of dew and salt, and the sound of waves in constant battle.

His parents found him to be a nervous boy who was happier examining seeds or studying snails than throwing stones with the other children. A strange boy, they thought, not least when he accurately guessed how much fish a certain boat would catch—or which house would collapse after the next storm.

He found it pointless to explain that he merely observed the condition of the nets used by the fishermen or the rot that had taken hold of pillars and beams. Unfortunately, the rest of the village thought the gangly little boy was touched by the Devil, so, to right his soul, his parents decided to send him to the cathedral schools in York.

His teacher was Aelbert of York, a knock-kneed monk, the head magister at the time and disciple of the previous head, Count Egbert, who was a relative. Perhaps that was why Aelbert took him in like a son and devoted himself body and soul to channeling his strange talent. There Alcuin learned that England was a heptarchy made up of the Saxon kingdoms of Kent, Wessex, Essex, and Sussex in the south of the island, and the northern realms of the Angles of Mercia, East Anglia, and Northumbria, where he resided.

He enjoyed broadening his mind in the typical subjects of the *trivium*, which included grammar, rhetoric, and dialectic; and of the *cuadrivium*, comprising arithmetic, geometry, astronomy, and music. Along with these, in accord with the Anglo-Saxon tradition, he studied astrology, mechanics, and medicine.

"*Saeculare quoque et forasticae philosophorum disciplinae*" Aelbert insisted time and again, trying to convince Alcuin that the secular arts were nothing but the work of the Devil, handed to the Christians so they would forget the Word of God.

"But Saint Gregory the Great himself—in his *Commentary on the Book of Kings*—legitimizes these studies," Alcuin retorted when he was just sixteen years old.

"That does not give you the right to spend the entire day reading that compendium of lies that is the *Historiae Naturalis*."

"Would you be less displeased if I studied the *Etymologiae u Originum sive etymologicarum libri viginti*? Because if you compare the two, you will note that the Hispanic saint modeled the structure of some of his books on Pliny's encyclopedia. And not just on Pliny, but also on the ecclesiastical writers Cassiodorus and Boethius. And on Caelius Aurelianus's translations of Asclepiades of Bithynia and Soranus of Ephesus—and Lactantius and Solinus—and even *Prata* by Suetonius."

"You should read from the Christian point of view, not the pagan one."

"The pagans are sons of God, too."

"But at the service of the Devil, boy! And do not contradict me or I will cast all thirty-three volumes out the window one by one."

In reality Aelbert did not worry too much about what kind of texts Alcuin read, for the boy never neglected his duties as a Christian. On the contrary, he had proven himself an accomplished and diligent student, able to gain the upper hand in theological debates with the most experienced monks, so his dabbling in the pagan texts, though undesirable, had not diverted him in any way from his journey toward wisdom.

Over the years, Alcuin proved to be a true artisan of letters. He would examine texts, volumes, and codices and—like a master builder—extract fragments and passages in order to construct extraordinary and highly eloquent mosaics of knowledge. He did so with poems such as his *"De sanctus Euboriensis ecclesiae."* In more than one thousand six-hundred and fifty verses, he not only described the history of York, its bishops, and the kings of Northumbria, but he also gave overviews of authors whose works Brother Eanwald had added to the library. Those authors included the likes of Ambrose, Athanasius, Augustine, Cassiodorus, John Chrysostom, Cyprian, Gregory the Great, Jerome, Isidore, Lactantius, Sedulius, Arator, Juvencus, Venancio, Prudentius, and Virgil. Alcuin would write endlessly.

In time, his didactic works written as a student were used as educational texts, due to their clarity and rhetoric. He did so with Aristotle's *Categories*, adapted in Saint Augustine's *Categoriae decem*, or the *Disputatio de Vera Philosophia*, the canon that would later become a bedside book of Charlemagne himself. And he did not forget to attend to his liturgical texts, theological works, exegetic and dogmatic writings, poetry and hagiographies.

The day that Aelbert succeeded Egbert as archbishop of York, the position of head magister of the cathedral school became vacant. Several candidates put themselves forward for the role, but by then Alcuin was first choice for the post. He was thirty-five years old and had recently been ordained as a deacon.

Later, the Saxon king Ælfwald himself sent him to Rome, to seek the pallium for the new count and obtain the rank of metropolitan for York. In Parma, on his return journey, he met Charlemagne, and from that point forward he never returned to running the cathedral school. Even so, he did not stop taking enjoyment from his divinations or from using his unique cunning.

The case of The Swine suddenly sprang back into his mind. It was Friday and he would be put to death before nightfall on Monday.

He had learned that in Fulda the public executions took place on the main square at dusk so they could be witnessed by the greatest number of people. He imagined that the prisoner must have been found guilty of some heinous crime such as stealing from the estate of a noble or setting fire to property. Under the law, theft or destruction were the only offenses punishable by death—though of course there were exceptions, usually depending on the social status of the accused or sometimes the victims.

He understood that serious crimes had to be answered with severe punishments, but he didn't share the eagerness of some judges to deal out sentences merely to set an example for others. In fact, during his tenure at the school in York, he had participated in numerous trials, and while unfortunately some had resulted in the accused being sent to the gallows, he had never attended the executions. However, on this occasion he had promised the bishop he would accompany him. For now he concluded that it would be best to put the matter out of his mind and devote a few hours to reading Virgil.

Saturday morning was bitterly cold. After attending the Prime service, Alcuin met the bishop in the small refectory next to the accommodation. The place was warm and smelled of freshly baked bread.

"Good day to you," Lothar greeted him. "Please, sit beside me. Today we have an exquisite gourd pie."

"Good day, Father." He thanked him for his offer and served himself a small slice. "I would like to speak to you about the assistant that you assigned to me for the writing tasks, the novice who is the librarian's nephew."

"Yes. What about him? I hope he is not disobeying you."

"No, Your Eminence, on the contrary. The boy is a hard worker and also very orderly. Somewhat fussy, perhaps—but diligent enough, certainly."

"So?"

"Only, he is not suitable. And believe me that I am not saying this on the grounds of his youth. I must admit that when you suggested him as an assistant, Father, I thought him a wise choice. However, the facts indicate otherwise."

"Very well. Tell me how he has displeased you and we will see if the problem can be solved."

"A thousand things, Father. To start with, he does not know how to write in minuscule. He uses that ancient Latin alphabet, all in crude capitals, with no punctuation or spaces between the words. What's more, he ruins parchments as if he were blowing his nose on them. Only yesterday, he blotted the same page twice. Ah! And of course, he does not know Greek. Yes, he is eager to learn, but what I need is a scribe, not an apprentice."

"You can be grateful to have that boy. He is meek and has a nice hand. And you know Greek. Why do you need anyone else?"

"As I have already explained, Father, my eyesight is not what it was. At a distance I can distinguish a kite from a swift, but close up, as the hours draw on, I can barely tell a vowel from a consonant."

The bishop scratched his beard and let out a belch. "All the same, I don't know how I can help you. In the chapter there is nobody I know of who speaks Greek. Perhaps in the monastery . . ."

"I have asked there, too," said Alcuin, shaking his head.

"Then you will have to make do."

"Perhaps not." He arched his eyebrows. "A couple of days ago by coincidence I met a girl who needed help. Fortunately, not only can she read, but she can also write with an immaculate hand."

"A girl? I'm sure you are aware of the ineptitude of women in matters of knowledge. She has not caught your attention for more earthly reasons, I hope?" He winked mischievously.

"I can assure you that is not the case, Father. Rather, I need a scribe, and one who speaks Greek, so her coming is a godsend."

"Then do as you wish. But she must not be allowed in the chapter at night, lest she stir the baser desires of the clergy."

Alcuin was pleased. He drank a little wine and served himself another slice of pie. At that moment he remembered the matter of The Swine and asked Lothar about his crime.

"You seem distressed by the affair," observed the bishop after wolfing down a piece of pie larger than his mouth. "Indeed, when I invited you to the event, you didn't show much interest, and I must admit, Brother Alcuin, that it troubled me."

"You must forgive me if I do not share your enthusiasm." He served himself a thin slice of cheese. "But I have never enjoyed treating death like a special occasion. Perhaps if I knew the details of what happened, I would understand your stance better, but in any case, do not concern yourself more than necessary: I will accompany you to the execution and pray for the condemned man's soul."

Lothar pushed the bread aside with one swipe of his arm. "*Actio personalis moritur cum persona.* Here in Fulda, the clergy is respectful of the law, just as I assume it is in your own country. Our humble presence not only comforts the prisoner in his final trial on earth, but also instills the necessary respect in the common folks, who, as you know, are by nature tempted to follow examples that are contrary to the doctrine of Our Lord."

"And I admire such laudable intentions," Alcuin responded, "however, I believe that certain spectacles only serve to distract the masses and accentuate their primitive instincts. Have you not seen how their faces twist into grotesque grimaces as they applaud the agony of the condemned man? Have you not heard the boorish blasphemies they utter while the accused writhes on the rope? Have you not seen their lustful expressions, still sullied by the effects of wine?"

The bishop stopped eating and challenged Alcuin with his stare. "Listen to me carefully! That bastard murdered a girl in the prime of her life. He beheaded her with a sickle and defiled her innocent body."

Alcuin choked and spat out his mouthful. He had not imagined an offense so grave. "A truly heinous crime," he said, "which I knew nothing about. But even so, this punishment . . ."

"Dear brother, the law is not dictated by we humble servants of God. It is Charlemagne's capitularies who decide such matters. What's more, I do not understand why you would argue against giving this man the ultimate punishment."

"No, no. Please, do not misunderstand me. I believe like you that the crime must be punished, and that the punishment—so that justice prevails—must be proportionate to the offense committed. Only, this morning after the Terce service, I heard a most disconcerting comment from some chaplains."

"What did they say?"

"That this poor half-witted fellow, alluding to the condemned man, should not have been born. Do you know what they might have meant by these words?"

"You said it yourself. They were talking about that cretin. I do not see anything that should concern us in those words," replied Lothar, serving himself another slice of gourd pie.

"But when I asked them about The Swine—I believe that is what they called him—they told me that he has been a half-wit since birth, and that until the day of the murder, he had not once done anything serious. They said that on a few occasions he had scared someone, but more because of his slovenly appearance than his behavior, and that nobody would have imagined that he was capable of committing such a cruel and abominable act."

"And if everything they have told you is true, it would seem, dear Alcuin, that you know more about the case than you let on."

"Just the details that I have recounted. However, I do not know how his guilt was determined. Pray tell, was he caught attacking the young woman? Did a witness see him in the area? Or perhaps someone found his clothes covered in blood?"

The bishop rose and abruptly batted his plate aside. "*Habet aliquid ex inicuo omne magnum exemplum, quod cautra cingulos, utilitate publica rependitur.* The monster is guilty. He has been tried and sentenced. And like any good Christian, I expect you to applaud when we send him to hell."

Alcuin was taken aback by the bishop's reaction. He had not intended to pass judgment on his methods, but merely to make a comment. However, he could see that his words had been ill considered. In reality he had no reason to question Lothar's views.

"Esteemed Father, forgive me," he said. "If it is still your desire, please count on me to be there this afternoon."

Lothar looked him up and down. "I hope so, Brother Alcuin. And I suggest that you think more about victims and worry less about murderers. There is no place for them, nor those who sympathize with them, in the Kingdom of Heaven," said Lothar, departing without saying good-bye.

Alcuin realized too late how foolish he had been. Lothar would now see him as an arrogant Briton more eager to demonstrate his superiority than to concern himself with his own matters. And worst of all, he was certain that, sooner or later, their confrontation would come back to bite him.

After breakfast, he went to the kitchen to pick up a couple of apples for a midday snack. He chose them ripe and yellow, highly perfumed, just as he liked them. Then he set off for the old library located on the opposite side of the palace. They had told him that the bishop had ordered it constructed at the southern end of the building, facing the interior of the atrium, to shelter it from the wind and damp.

When he opened the door, he was surprised to find Theresa sitting on the bench that ran along the scriptorium. She wielded a pen in the air as though writing on an imaginary parchment, but she was moving it with such delicacy that, more than writing, it seemed like she was performing some sort of dance. Alcuin imagined she was practicing, but no matter what she was doing, it was clear that she undoubtedly had the skills required for the delicate art of copying.

"Good morning," he interrupted. "I didn't think you were coming to the chapter today."

The young woman gave a start and dropped the pen on the desk. She looked at Alcuin openmouthed and suddenly rose as if she had been pinched on the backside. "I was . . . I was practicing," she stammered. "My father says that if you practice enough, you can achieve anything."

"That is almost always true with a great deal of practice—and I would also say with a great deal of faith. To progress, one has to believe in what one is doing. Speaking of which, do you like your trade? I mean, do you like working as a parchment-maker?"

Theresa fell silent, and her cheeks turned red. "I do not wish to seem ungrateful, but I only do it to be near books," she finally said.

"I sense a feeling of guilt, when it should be the opposite," he replied. "Divine Providence makes sure everyone fulfills the role that She has provided for them. And yours does not have to be that of a faultless bookbinder."

The young woman remained with her head bowed for a moment. Suddenly her face lit up. "Reading! That's what I love! I read whenever I can, and when I do, I feel like I am traveling to other lands, discovering other languages, and living other lives." Her eyes were moving side-to-side as if she were picturing her words. "I don't think there is anything quite like it. Sometimes

I even imagine myself writing. But I don't mean copying like an amanuensis, but writing down my own thoughts." She stopped as if she had said something foolish. "I don't know . . . my stepmother always told me that I have my head in the clouds, that it is not good for me to be doing a man's work, and I should marry and have children instead."

"You never know. Perhaps that is the path that the Lord has laid out for you. How old are you? Twenty-two? Twenty-four? Look at me. I'm sixty years old, and I'm a simple teacher. Perhaps it is not a lot, but I am content to do the tasks that God has seen fit to entrust to me."

"So, it doesn't depend on me? I mean . . . God has decided my future?"

"I see you have not yet read *The City of God*, for otherwise you would know what the saint from Hippo Regius illustrated with dazzling clarity in his writings: The stars, as has undoubtedly been demonstrated, hold the keys to our destiny in their alignment and movements."

"And you can deduce what my fate will be?"

"It is not so easy. I would need to prepare your astral chart, know the precise moment of your birth, determine the position of the sun in the heavens and, of course, it would take many, many days of work."

Theresa looked disconcerted. Suddenly she screwed up her face and sat back down. "But if what you say is true, would that not mean that the stars are more powerful than Divine Providence?"

"Not exactly. And it is not me who says so, but Saint Augustine himself, who asks what the heavenly bodies are if not mere instruments of God. His work—the heavens—a mirror of his celestial intentions. The Maker did not give us a soul in order to be slaves to one destiny. He granted us free will to differentiate us from the quadrupeds, from the wild beasts that roam this world. And this free will is the thing inside you that tells you that you must persevere with your writing. That you will better serve God by reading and writing, instead of wasting your life sewing pages and boiling leather."

"My father always told me the same thing. With different words, of course, but more or less the same." Then something occurred to her. "Could you teach me?"

"Teach you? Teach you what?"

"You said you are a teacher. I could learn what you teach to your students."

At first the friar hesitated, but finally, he acquiesced. They agreed that after the day's writing was complete, they would devote a couple of hours to studying the *trivium* and the *cuadrivium*, for she already had a good command of reading and writing. Once they had covered the basic subjects, they would move on to the Holy Scriptures.

Suddenly Alcuin rose as if he had just remembered something. "Do you feel like going for a walk?" he proposed.

"What about the writing?"

"Bring a couple of tablets with you. You'll see what use we'll make of them."

14

Before departing for their walk, Alcuin told Theresa to wait for him while he discussed a matter with the bishop. The monk set off for the prelate's chambers, where he was received by his personal secretary. After explaining his intentions, the secretary, a hunchbacked old man who seemed as if every part of his body, even his monk's habit, was in pain, rose and disappeared behind some red curtains before returning moments later with a slow step.

"His Eminence will receive you in the evening. He is busy now with an emissary from Aquis-Granum."

"But it is essential that I see him imminently."

"He is busy, I tell you. What's more, it is not a good time. It would appear he has had to postpone The Swine's execution, and it has upset him."

"Postpone it? I do not understand."

"Charlemagne is approaching Fulda with a Roman legation, and knowing of his impending visit, it would be inconsiderate to deprive the king of the spectacle."

"Perfect," Alcuin said without hiding his satisfaction. "By the way, yesterday I broke my stylus and I need to make another. Could you tell me where I can find some goose feathers?"

"Goose feathers? I don't know. The chamberlain takes care of such matters. He is in the square now, making final preparations for the execution. But if you go to The Cat Tavern, someone there will tell you. There are several farms with ducks and hens in the area."

Ducks and hens, thought Alcuin with disdain. They already had ducks and hens in the kitchen's coop! Did nobody in the chapter know that only goose feathers are suitable for writing? He then remembered that it was not the first time he had heard of The Cat Tavern. In fact, it must be a pretty popular place, for even the bishop himself was quick to recommend the delicious mead that they served at the inn. Alcuin thanked the secretary and went to rejoin Theresa.

Together they left for The Cat Tavern, encountering a light drizzle as soon as they stepped out of the palace. The friar covered his head before descending the stairs, where the group joined the crowd thronging the cathedral square since the early hours. Theresa trailed behind Alcuin. She admired the myriad of narrow streets, abuzz with folks laden with bundles of goods, livestock traders herding animals, merchants desperate to find a space for themselves among the mass of people, and street urchins fleeing the vendors they had just stolen from—all of this amid the throng of stalls offering all manner of wares.

Alcuin took the opportunity to buy a dozen walnuts, the shells of which, he explained to Theresa, would make an excellent ink after he burned and mixed them with a quart of oil. He cracked one open and tipped it into his mouth. Then they made for the blacksmiths' street, where they would find the famous tavern.

A pleasant smell of fresh bread accompanied by a lively cacophony of voices confirmed they had found the right inn. It was located in a large house of reddish timber, with two tiny windows and a door consisting of a brightly colored blanket. As they were about to enter, the blanket parted and a woman with bare breasts appeared, stumbling and stinking of wine. Seeing Alcuin, she gave him an idiotic smile as she pushed her nipples back into the men's jerkin she wore. She apologized and ran down the road gibbering nonsense. Alcuin crossed himself, told Theresa to cover herself well, and walked decisively into the tavern.

Inside, Theresa blushed as she witnessed a spectacle like a scene from hell. An obscene mishmash of men and women with pottage and drink were giving themselves to gluttony and lust in equal measure. At the back, the blind man who was playing a wind pipe and baring his gums indecently sat barricaded behind a pair of barrels that served as a counter.

The monk lowered his gaze and walked toward a man with a bushy beard and greasy arms who appeared to be the landlord. Theresa followed him, albeit at a distance.

"Tell me, brother, what can I get for you?" asked the innkeeper as he dispensed a round of ale to some other customers.

"I come from the chapter. The bishop's secretary sends me."

"I'm sorry but we've run out of mead. Come back at the end of the day, if you will. By then we'll have had a delivery."

Alcuin presumed the clergy went there to stock up on drink. When he explained that he did not require mead, but geese, the man guffawed. "You'll find what you need at the farms by the river. Are you preparing a feast at the chapter?"

But before he could respond, there was a loud clamor. Alcuin and the innkeeper turned in surprise to see that everyone had formed a ring around a table and denarii were flitting from hand to hand.

"Fight to first blood!" cried the landlord as he ran toward the crowd.

Alcuin went over to where Theresa stood watching the events, fully engrossed. A fight to first blood. She had heard about them. She had even seen youth playfully pretend at them, but she had never witnessed a real one. As far as she knew, it was a contest of skill that ended when one of the fighters seriously injured the other with a sharp weapon. Alcuin suggested she take note of what she saw.

By then the customers had made space for the contenders: One was a ball of fat with tree trunks for forearms—and his opponent was a red-haired man who looked like he had drunk all the wine in the tavern. They paced about each other like wolves stalking their prey. The onlookers roared and cheered as the fighters stabbed at each other furiously with their blades.

Despite his corpulence, the fat one brandished his scramasax with great spirit, forcing the red-haired man to retreat, switching his knife from hand to hand. Theresa scribbled something on her tablet, believing that the contest would soon end, but neither man was able to deal the deciding blow.

Finally, the stout one lunged at his opponent in a flurry of thrusts, forcing him to withdraw to a corner. It looked like he would run him through at any moment, but the red-haired man remained calm as if, instead of fighting for his life, he were playing with a child. He limited himself to simply stepping back and feinting. Meanwhile the bets continued to flow.

The stout one started to sweat and move more slowly. He must have thought that cornering his opponent would gain him an advantage, so he pushed a table into his path. But the redheaded fighter jumped clear over it. At that moment the fat man managed to grasp his opponent's weapon-wielding arm by the wrist, but in response he received the same treatment, so they were locked in a standstill.

The red-haired one resisted for a while, the veins on his arms swelling like earthworms. The crowd kept cheering and urging them on, but suddenly the stout man's hand made a crunching sound, and the onlookers fell quiet—as though the Devil himself stood before them. The red-haired man screamed something incomprehensible, made a feint, and then his knife flashed from one hand to the other. In the blink of an eye he had attacked the fat one and then stepped back and straightened his posture as if nothing had happened.

The fat man stood still, looking at his opponent as though he wanted to say something but couldn't find the words. Suddenly a jet of blood spouted from his belly, and the man collapsed like a marionette with its strings cut. The redhead howled in triumph and spat on the fallen body, while onlookers ran to tend to the wounded man. Some men cursed their bad luck, while the more fortunate ones rushed to squander their winnings with prostitutes. The red-haired man took a seat at a table away from the crowds and calmly combed his hair, laughing with contempt as he watched them take the fat man out back. He picked up a tankard and drank from it until it was empty, then served himself some bread and sausage and ordered a round of ale for all.

Alcuin told Theresa to wait for him. He approached the winning fighter with a jug of wine he'd found unattended on a nearby table.

"An impressive display. May I offer you a drink?" said Alcuin, sitting down without waiting for a response.

The redhead looked him up and down before grasping the tankard and downing every last drop. "Spare me your sermons, monk. If you're after alms, go into the middle of the room there, grab a blade, and may God protect you." The man turned his attention to the table and started counting the coins that a friend had just delivered as part of his winnings.

"To be honest, I thought the stout fellow would do away with you, but your mastery of the dagger proved to be the stuff of legends," Alcuin said obligingly.

"Listen, I've already told you I don't give alms, so clear off before I tire of you."

Alcuin decided to be more direct. "In truth I did not want to speak to you about the fight. Rather, I am interested in the another matter: the mill."

"The mill? What about the mill?"

"You work there, do you not?"

"And what if I do? It's no secret."

"You see, the chapter wishes to acquire a batch of grain. A good bit of business for someone who knows how to handle it. With whom should I discuss the matter?"

"You're from the chapter and you don't know the answer to that? I don't take kindly to liars," he said, his hand moving to the handle of his knife.

"Relax," the monk hastened to say. "I don't know who is in charge because I'm new here. The wheat would go to the chapter, but it is a private matter. In truth I wish to replace some batches before the *missi dominici* inspect the grain stores. Nobody knows about it and that's how I want it to stay."

The redhead let go of the hilt of his dagger. He knew that the *missi dominici* were the judges Charlemagne periodically sent across his lands to resolve important legal matters. Their last visit had been in autumn, so it was possible that the friar was telling the truth. "And what's this got to do with me? Speak to the owner and see what he says."

"The owner of the mill?"

"The owner of the mill, of the stream, of this tavern, and of half the town. Ask for Kohl. You'll find him at the grain stall at the market."

"Hey, Rothaart, are you going to become a monk now?" interrupted the same man who'd brought him his coins. It was clear to Alcuin that Rothaart was the redhead's name, for that is precisely what the word meant in the language of the Germanic peoples.

"You keep joking, Gus. One of these days I'll smash in your skull and put a gourd in its place. Even your wife will appreciate the change," Rothaart retorted to his friend. "And as for you," he said to Alcuin, "if you're not going to bring more wine, you can make room for one of the whores waiting for me."

Alcuin thanked him for his time and gestured to Theresa. The two of them left the tavern and made for the market square.

"Where are we going now?" she asked.

"To speak to a man who owns a mill."

"The abbey mill?" Theresa ran to keep up with Alcuin, who walked with increasing speed.

"No, no. There are three mills in Fulda: Two belong to the chapter, though only one is located at the abbey. The third is owned by a man called Kohl who, it appears, is the local rich man."

"I thought you wanted to find some feathers."

"That was before I met Rothaart."

"But didn't you know him already? I heard you address him and say that he worked at the mill. And why do you want to buy grain?"

Alcuin looked at her as if the question irritated him. "Who told you I want to buy anything? And I didn't know the miller. I deduced that he worked at the mill from the flour that not only dusted his clothes but was also embedded deep under his fingernails."

"And what's so special about this mill?"

"If I knew that, we would not be visiting it," he said, without slowing his pace. "All I can say is that I had never seen a miller who eats rye bread. By the way, what did you write on your tablets?"

Theresa stopped to search her bag. She was about to start reading, but seeing that Alcuin was not waiting, she ran after him as she read over her notes: "The stout man was wounded in the belly. The redhead waited for him to lose his balance before attacking him. The winner's earnings totaled around twenty denarii. Ah! And I didn't note this down, but the fat one's injury could not have been serious, because he left the tavern on his own two feet," she said with self-satisfaction, expecting some recognition.

"That's what you wasted your time noting?" Alcuin looked at her for a moment, then continued walking. "Lass, I asked you to note what you saw, not the things that were so obvious any fool could have seem them. You must learn to pay attention to the minutiae, the more subtle events—the details that go almost unnoticed or that seem insubstantial or meaningless. They yield the most interesting information."

"I don't understand."

"Did you see the detail of the flour? Or notice his shoes? Did you determine which hand he used to thrust the knife?"

"No," Theresa admitted, feeling stupid.

"First, the redhead: When we arrived at the tavern, he seemed drunk but he was actually choosing his victim carefully, for when he made his bet, he counted every last denarius."

"Aha."

"He chose a strong man, but one without great skill. First, his accomplice Gus sized up the unsuspecting victim, indicating him with a clumsy hand signal. Indeed, Rothaart did not start fighting until Gus had gestured that the bets had been taken."

"I thought there was something odd about that Gus, but I didn't think it was important."

"As for the money you noted—twenty denarii . . . it's a lot."

"Enough to buy a pig," said Theresa, remembering her conversations with Helga.

"But not so much if you're paying for a round of drinks and two prostitutes. However, his shoes were of fine leather, and slightly different for each foot, which means they were made especially for him. He also wore a gold chain and a ring set with stones. Too much wealth for a miller who risks his life gambling."

"Perhaps he fights every day."

"If that were the case, and he always won, his reputation would precede him and he wouldn't find opponents prepared to die, nor gamblers willing to throw away their money. And if he didn't always win, he would probably be dead by now. No. There must be another explanation for his expensive shoes. Perhaps the same explanation that accounts for his preference for rye bread rather than wheat."

"So . . ."

"So we know he works as a miller, that he is left-handed, astute, skilled with a knife, and moneyed, too."

"You saw which hand he used to attack the fat man?"

"I didn't have to look. He held his tankard in his left hand, he counted his winnings with his left hand, and he used the same hand when he tried to threaten me."

"And why is all this important?"

"It might not be. But it might also have something to do with the sickness that is plaguing the town."

* * *

On the way to the market, Alcuin admitted that the deaths of his assistant and the apothecary did not seem accidental. Several people had died in terrible pain, and since he now had some free time, he wanted to put his mind to finding out what was happening.

The attendant working at the grain stall in the market, a haggard, one-eyed man, informed them that Hansser Kohl had already left. He said that if they hurried they would find him at the mill, for he was there taking a new shipment of barley. He gave them directions to the mill, which was located in a precipitous place that they would reach by exiting through the southern gates of the city and following the course of the river for a couple of miles toward the mountains.

Alcuin thanked the man for his explanation and set off at once. They crossed the city and left through the south gate just as directed before continuing along the riverbank, heading upstream at a good pace. If she had not been so out of breath, Theresa would have asked him how it was possible that he did not tire, but the monk didn't give her the chance to rest even once. When they finally arrived in the vicinity of the mill, she felt ready to drop to her knees. They paused only briefly to observe the scenery.

The mill stood imposingly on the crag that the river torrent had carved out from the rock. A giant water wheel was positioned in the middle of the river and Theresa was surprised by its continuous, heavy creaking, only partially masked by the murmuring of the water itself. As they approached, she could see that the paddles were not driven by the river exactly, but by the current of a channel beside it, the flow of water regulated by a rudimentary sluice gate.

Alcuin admired the mill that was constructed like almost all buildings of its type on three levels. On the ground floor were the pulleys and cogs responsible for transferring the movement of the waterwheel to the great vertical axle that passed through the mill. The main level, the milling floor, housed two slotted-stone wheels threaded on the axle—one fixed and the other mobile that ground the grain by turning in opposite directions. And on the third floor were the grain store and its loading funnel. The cereals were poured down this chute, which ran through a hollow duct to the hole bored into the upper wheel, to finish grinding it between the millstones.

Alcuin observed that there was a small, fortified house adjoined to the mill. He could also see a stable and an enclosed storehouse where, he assumed, they kept the grain.

"What surprises me is its location so far from the town," said Alcuin, looking at the building. "It's also interesting that the house is made of stone. Perhaps the mill owner and his family are seeking extra protection."

"And what have we come here for? To accuse them of something?"

"In truth I didn't want to explain it to you because it's still mere conjecture, but I suspect that the source of the sickness has been the wheat." He took some grains from his pocket and handed them to Theresa. "To confirm it, I need to examine the cereal, so my plan is to pretend to be interested in doing business so that owner will give me a sample."

"You think they're poisoning the wheat?"

"Not exactly, no. But just in case, you keep your mouth shut."

At that moment some dogs loitering around the stables started barking as though they were being thrashed, and two men appeared at the door armed with bows.

"What brings you here?" asked the better-dressed one, still aiming an arrow at them. Theresa presumed it was Kohl, and Alcuin was certain of it.

"Good morning," Alcuin said, waving with both arms to show they were unarmed. "I come to talk business. May we come in? It's freezing out here."

The two men lowered their bows.

They were taken into the house rather than the mill, because according to the more modestly dressed man, the mill was cold and—for safety reasons—they did not light fires in the mill. Once inside, Kohl ordered the servant to bring some food. Then he called for his wife, who appeared, running from room to room as though the Devil pursued her. First she brought bread and cheese, then she filled all four cups from a jug of wine.

"Not a drop of water," boasted Kohl, savoring the rich wine in his mouth. "So tell me—what business do you speak of?"

"From my attire you may have guessed that I come from the abbey." He took a moment to raise his cup to everyone. "However, I must confess that I do not represent the abbey, but King Charlemagne. You see, the monarch is to visit Fulda soon, in two weeks' time or less, and I would like to receive him with the greatest reverence. Unfortunately, our grain reserves have been considerably depleted, and what remains is starting to go bad. The chapter is also short of provisions, so I thought that perhaps I could acquire a batch from you. Let's say . . . four hundred pecks?"

Kohl choked when he heard the figure, then coughed and poured himself another cup. Four hundred pecks was enough to feed an army. Without a doubt it would be a lucrative deal. "That will cost a large sum of money. I assume you know the cost of grain: three denarii for a peck of rye, two for a peck of barley, and one for oats. If what you need is flour . . ."

"Obviously, I would prefer it as grain."

Kohl nodded. It was logical that if the abbey possessed two mills, it would want to save costs by doing its own processing.

"And by when do you need it?"

"As soon as possible. We need time to mill the wheat."

"Wheat?" Kohl rose in surprise. "As far as I know nobody here mentioned that cereal. I can supply rye, barley, and oats—even spelt, if you want—but the chapter handles the wheat crops. You should know that."

He did know it. He considered how to respond. "I also know that the abbey sometimes *mislays* batches that end up on the market," he answered. Then he reminded him: "Four hundred pecks for sixteen thousand denarii."

Kohl paced up and down, his eyes fixed on Alcuin. He knew it was risky, but it was precisely by taking risks that he had become wealthy.

"Come back tomorrow and we'll talk. I have work to do this afternoon and I won't be able to arrange anything."

"Can we visit the mill?"

"They're working in there at present. Perhaps some other time."

"Excuse me for insisting, but I would like—"

"A mill is a mill. I've told you that they're working."

"Very well. Until tomorrow, then."

When they had left the house, Theresa asked him if he had discovered anything, but Alcuin merely grumbled something about his bad luck. As they walked past the stables he told her that he needed to inspect the inside of the mill, but he had not insisted further to avoid arousing suspicion.

"Did you see the horses?" he added. "Six, not counting the ones that pull the cart."

"And what does that mean?"

"Well, that there are a minimum of six people guarding the mill."

"Too many?"

"Too many."

Then he abruptly stopped as if he had remembered something. He retraced his steps back toward the house. Theresa followed. After making sure nobody was looking, he suddenly jumped over the fence and ducked into the stables. Again Theresa did as he did. Walking over to the horses' saddlebags he rummaged through them, also inspecting the boards of the cart and the straw on the ground. He was on his knees when he called to Theresa. The young woman ran over and pulled out a wax tablet, assuming that he wanted her to write something down, but Alcuin shook his head. "Search the floor for grains like the ones I gave you."

They rooted through the dung until they heard noises coming from the mill, at which point they stood and hastily made their escape.

When they reached the abbey, their hands and feet were frozen, but in the kitchens they found hot soup, which soon warmed them. They ate quickly because Alcuin wanted to get back to work, but Theresa suggested that they visit Hoos first. The monk agreed, and after clearing their plates they made for the hospital.

At the infirmary they were greeted by the same monk as before. However, his usually cheerful face now bore a concerned expression. "I'm glad you're here. Did you receive word?"

"Word? Why? What has happened?" asked Alcuin.

"Come in, by God, come in. Two more have come down with the sickness, with the same symptoms."

"Gangrenous legs?"

"One of them has already started the convulsions."

The two monks rushed to the room where the infected patients were dying. They were a father and son who worked at the saw-mill. Alcuin observed that the father already displayed the telling signs of a black nose and ears. He tried to question them, but all he obtained was incoherent babble. All he could do was prescribe them some purgatives.

"And give them milk mixed with charcoal to drink. As much as they can take," he instructed.

While the infirmarian prepared the remedies, they went to check on Hoos. However, when they arrived at his room, they found his bed empty. No one present knew where he was either. They looked in the latrines, in the adjoining dining hall, and in the small cloister where the healthier patients went to recover, but he was nowhere. After searching so thoroughly, they had to accept that he had disappeared.

"But it's not possible," Theresa complained.

"We'll find him," was all Alcuin could say.

He advised the young woman to go home and stay calm. He had to return to the library, but he would issue an order for them to inform her as soon as Hoos appeared. They agreed to meet the next morning at the chapter gates. Theresa thanked him for his concern, but as she turned away, she couldn't stop the tears from coming.

Theresa spent the rest of the afternoon shut away in the loft so that Helga would not ask her what was wrong. However, just before nightfall she decided to go for a walk around the nearby streets. As she wandered the alleyways she wondered about the meaning of the tightness in her chest. What was the shiver that ran down her spine every time Hoos came to mind? Each morning she could not wait for the moment when she would see him, speak to him, feel his eyes on her. Her tears returned. Why was her life such a punishment? What had she done so that everything she loved ended up disappearing? She walked on aimlessly, trying to guess Hoos's whereabouts, trying to imagine what might have happened to him. She recalled that on her last visit, Hoos had barely managed a few steps around the cloister, and that was just the day before. He was still so unwell that it seemed impossible that he could have fled.

She kept walking, not realizing that gradually she was straying farther away from the busier streets. It was cold and she closed her cloak around her face, trying to shield her nose. By the time she registered her surroundings, she found herself in a dark, narrow street that smelled of something rotten. A bark made her jump.

She looked around and saw that most of the houses appeared to be abandoned, as though their owners had changed their minds about living in such a gloomy place and fled without even closing the windows. Frightened, she decided to return home. Walking quickly back, she saw a hooded figure appear at the top of the street. Theresa waited for it to pass, but it did not move. She tried to stay calm, telling herself it was nobody, that nothing would happen to her. She kept walking, but as she approached the cloaked figure, her heart accelerated. Whoever it was remained silent, watching, immobile, like a statue.

Theresa quickened her step and lowered her gaze, but as she reached the hooded figure, it swooped down on her and tried to hold her fast. She wanted to scream but a hand prevented her. All she could do was whimper in terror. In a desperate attempt to escape, she bit the hand that was gagging her. The man screamed and at that moment his voice made her freeze. "Jesus, woman!

What are you trying to do? Amputate my hand?" he said, sucking on the wound.

Theresa could not believe his voice. His accent, his intonation . . . it could only be Hoos. Without giving it a second thought she threw herself into his arms, which received her with tenderness.

Hoos pulled back his hood, revealing a good-humored smile. He stroked her hair and breathed in her perfume. Then he suggested they walk on, for it was not safe where they were.

"But where were you?" the young woman sobbed. "I thought I'd never see you again."

He told her that he had followed her. He had just fled the abbey because he needed to return immediately to Würzburg.

"If I stay at the hospital, I'll never make it in time."

"But you can hardly stand."

"Which is why I need a horse."

"You're crazy. The bandits will kill you. Have you forgotten what they did to you the last time?"

"Forget that. You have to help me."

"But I don't know—"

"Listen to me," he interrupted, "it is vital that I reach Würzburg by next week. I risked my life to save yours, and now I need your help. You have to get hold of a mount for me."

Theresa could see the desperation in his face.

"All right, but I don't know anything about horses. I will have to ask Helga."

"Helga? Who's that?"

"You don't remember? The woman who helped us when we arrived in Fulda. I live with her now."

"I don't think that's a good idea. Do you not have any money? Althar left you a pouch of coins."

"But I gave it to Helga that very day, as a down payment for board and lodging. I only have a couple of denarii left."

"Damn it." He clenched his teeth.

"I could ask Alcuin. He might help us."

Hoos gave a start when he heard the friar's name. "Have you lost your mind? Why do you think I fled the abbey? Don't trust that man, Theresa. He's not what he seems."

"Why do you say that? He's been so good to us."

"I can't explain, but you must trust me. Stay away from that friar."

Theresa did not know what to say. She believed Hoos, but Alcuin seemed like such a good person.

"So what will we do? Your dagger!" she remembered. "We could try to sell it. I'm sure it will fetch you enough to buy a horse."

"If only I still had it. Those wretched monks must have stolen it," he complained. "You don't know anybody who deals in horses? Someone who would let you borrow a mount?"

Theresa shook her head. She added that it was still too soon for him to ride, because his wound would surely open up. Hoos suddenly stopped in his tracks, trying to catch his breath. He was gasping like an old man, holding the wound on his chest.

"Are you all right?"

"That isn't important. Damn it! I need a horse," he cried as he coughed and spluttered. He sat down, dejected, on some firewood. For a moment, Theresa thought his wound would come open.

"Now that I remember," she said, "this morning I was in a place where they kept horses." She was not sure why she said it.

Hoos stood and looked at Theresa with tenderness. He took her face in his hands and then, slowly, moved in to kiss her. Theresa thought she would die. Her body trembled when she felt the heat of his mouth. She closed her eyes and surrendered to the honey that flooded her body. Her lips parted timidly, allowing his tongue to caress hers. The she slowly pulled away, looking him in the eyes, her cheeks flushed. She thought his eyes were shining more beautifully than ever.

"And what will become of me when you go?" she said.

Hoos kissed her again, and she forgot her worries as if under a spell.

They set off for Helga's tavern immediately but stopped on each corner for a quick kiss, as jumpy as thieves who might be caught. Each time they laughed and then continued more quickly. When they reached the tavern they went in the back way so that Helga wouldn't see them. They climbed up to the loft where Theresa slept, and they kissed again. Hoos caressed her breasts, but she moved away. Theresa brought him something to eat, made him comfortable with a blanket, and told him to wait. If everything went well, she would return in a few hours with a mount.

She knew it was crazy, but she left the house equipped with a candle, a steel, and some dry tinder. She also took some raw meat and a kitchen knife. Then she made for the city walls, not knowing whether the gates would be open or closed. Fortunately, the maintenance work on the southern gate was still under way, so she didn't need to identify herself when she slipped past a guard, who greeted her half-asleep.

As she walked in the direction of the mill, she remembered Hoos's lips. She felt again the warmth of his whispers and his breath on her cheeks, and her stomach tightened. She quickened her pace, her path lit up by the moon, and prayed the dogs would not discover her. She hoped the ground meat would keep them occupied while she went to the stables. When she arrived in the vicinity, she could see that there was enough light that she could dispense with the tinder. She looked for the dogs but couldn't see them. However, as a precaution, she placed half of the meat on the main track and spread the rest around the path leading to the stables.

There were just four horses in the building and they seemed to be asleep. She examined them closely, trying to figure out which would be the best, but she could not decide. Suddenly she heard some barking and her heart began thumping in her chest. She ran to a corner, where she crouched down, covered herself with straw, and waited in terror. A few seconds later the barking stopped.

Suddenly she realized the mistake she was about to make. She wondered what she was doing there. How could she have even considered committing a theft? She decided that, though she wanted to help Hoos, this was not the way. She could not betray her own morals—that was not what her father had taught her. Feeling guilty and miserable, she couldn't even understand how she had ended up at the mill. She could be caught and accused of theft, a crime that was sometimes punishable by death. She was sorry to disappoint Hoos, but she could not continue. She cried at the foolishness of her behavior, then asked God for forgiveness and prayed to Him for help.

She was scared. Every sound, from a horse snorting to the creaking of timber, made her imagine she would be discovered at any moment. Slowly, she crawled between the horses' legs, trying to reach the exit. But just as she was about to leave the stables, she was horrified to hear four men approaching the building. The dogs had probably alerted them.

She retraced her steps and buried herself under the straw again just as one of the men walked in and started slapping the backs of the animals, who whinnied with alarm. Theresa watched the hoofs of a horse fly past her face and almost cried out, but managed to contain herself. The man bridled one of them, mounted, and set off toward the scrubland at a gallop. She watched as the other three unloaded the cart just outside the stables, carrying its contents into the mill. Theresa thought it odd they appeared to be working at such an unearthly hour and without torches. It occurred to her that the sacks they were unloading had something to do with the grain that Alcuin was investigating.

Her curiosity getting the better of her fear, she took advantage of the men's absence to inspect the few sacks waiting to be unloaded. Disregarding the consequences, she took her knife and made a cut in the corner nearest to her, then sank her hand into its contents with just enough time to grab a handful of grain and run back to her corner in the stables.

The men soon returned. The first to arrive quickly discovered the torn sack and blamed the other one for the damage. They accused each other and argued until the third one, who seemed like he was the boss, arrived and separated them with a few choice blows. One of the men then left, soon returning with a lit torch, which the boss grasped, casting as soft glow on his red hair. They unloaded the remaining sacks and then set off without going back into the stable.

When she knew she was alone, Theresa ran back down the path, imagining the red-haired man breathing down her neck. She remembered him stabbing his fat opponent in the tavern and she thought that at any moment he would appear from behind a tree to cut her throat. Not even when she was inside the city walls did she feel safe.

She arrived at Helga's house with her heart in her throat. Entering through the back door, she made sure Helga was still in the tavern and quietly headed to the loft where she found Hoos half-asleep. Seeing her, the young man's face brightened, but he grimaced when he heard that she had not brought him a horse.

"I tried, I swear," she lamented.

Hoos cursed through clenched teeth but told Theresa not to worry. The following day he would find a way to escape.

Theresa kissed him on the lips and he returned the gesture. "Wait a moment!" she interrupted. She jumped up and went down to the tavern.

Before long she returned, humming a silly song to herself. She sneaked up to Hoos and kissed him again. A beautiful smile spread across her face. "You have your horse," she announced.

She told him that, though he may not approve of it, she had asked Helga about the down payment she'd given her for their board and lodgings. She explained that she needed the money, and that if Helga returned a portion of it to her, she would pay her back with interest before February.

"At first she refused, but I reminded her that I have regular work, and I promised that in addition to recouping the loan, she would receive an extra fifth part on top of it. Still, she wanted to know what the devil the money was for."

Hoos looked at her anxiously, but she put him at ease. She had told Helga that she needed a horse to accompany the friar on his country outings. Hearing that, Helga not only believed her but also recommended a merchant who would give her a good price. In total she had returned fifty denarii, half of her down payment. It would be enough to buy an old nag and enough food for the journey.

"And she didn't ask why you couldn't accompany the monk by walking alongside his horse?"

"I told her my ankles hurt. Listen, Hoos, before you go, I would like to ask you for something."

"Of course, if it's within my power."

"In a few days' time, when you arrive in Würzburg . . ."

"Yes?"

"The thing is, when you found me at the cabin—I lied to you. I wasn't just there by chance."

"Well, don't worry. If you didn't want to tell me then, you don't have to tell me now."

"I was scared, but now I want to tell you. In Würzburg there was a fire."

"A fire? Where?"

"It wasn't my fault, I swear it wasn't. It was that wretched Korne. He pushed me. The embers flew everywhere, everything caught fire, and . . ." Tears welled up.

Hoos took her in his arms. "Promise me you will find my father and tell him I'm well. Promise me."

"Of course. I promise."

"Tell them I love them, him and Rutgarda. Promise me."

Hoos stroked her face, and she felt calmer. Suddenly Theresa remembered the parchment that she had found hidden in her father's bag. For a moment she thought about entrusting it to Hoos to deliver to him, but she decided against it. Perhaps it was a private document and that was why he had hidden it.

"Take me with you," she asked.

He smiled tenderly at her. "I'll find your father and tell him not to worry, but you can't come with me. Remember the bandits."

"But—"

He stopped her with a kiss.

When the last candle had been blown out, Hoos asked her to come to him. She accepted, not fully knowing why. The young man embraced her tenderly to protect her from the cold, but though they were soon warm, they didn't want to separate.

Hoos was the attentive man she had always yearned for. His arms held her tightly while he covered her in kisses. He explored her body, traveling undiscovered paths, caressing her slowly and enveloping her in his breath. She let herself become intoxicated, noticing the shameful appetite that burned inside her. She had never felt this way before and couldn't interpret that bundle of sensations—the struggle between modesty and eagerness, between fear and desire.

"Not yet," she begged him.

Hoos kept kissing her anyway, exploring her with his lips—caressing her pubis, her belly, her erect nipples. She delighted in his firm arms as he savored the smoothness of her breasts. She trembled when he parted her legs. As she felt him enter her, her body arched with pain. Even so, desire made her press herself against him as if she wanted to possess him forever. Then she surrendered to his motion and the fire that consumed her.

He kept kissing her as he moved on top of her. He slowly caressed her, relishing being between her legs—and then as he moved faster, she felt such delirious longing, as if the Devil possessed her. Finally, she felt the urgency of his desire release, and she wanted him to stay there, embracing her forever.

"I love you," he said softly, holding her tightly.

She closed her eyes, yearning for him to tell her a thousand more times.

In the morning, when Hoos said good-bye, all she could hear was that he loved her.

15

Because she did not go to the scriptorium on Sundays, Theresa used the morning to tidy the loft and wash the pots and pans that had accumulated in the kitchen. Still, she decided that after lunch she would go to the abbey and feign an interest in Hoos's whereabouts, to avoid arousing suspicion. While she cleaned the hostelry she remembered each kiss from the night before. She was imbued with the smell of Hoos, as if she had been rubbed with a cloth soaked in his essence. Hoos Larsson . . .

Before leaving, he had promised that on his return they would travel together to Aquis-Granum, to make a home for themselves on his land.

She imagined her life on Hoos's estate, attending to the house during the day and pressing herself against his body each night. For a moment she forgot Helga and Alcuin's problems, enraptured by the thought of Hoos. She thought of nothing else all morning.

By the time Helga arose, Theresa had already cleaned the same room four times. Helga complained of a burning in her stomach, which she tempered with a gulp of wine—which, in turn, made her retch several times. Her body still reeked of sweaty men, but she didn't seem to care. She was surprised to find Theresa in the kitchen, for she didn't remember that it was Sunday. She staggered over to a washbasin where she wetted her eyes just enough to clear the sleep from them.

"You're not going to see the monks today?" she said, pouring herself some more wine.

"Sundays are for praying."

"It must be because they have nothing better to do," Helga said with envy. "I don't know what the hell I'm going to make for lunch today."

She rummaged around the pots and pans until they were as disorderly as they had been before Theresa had tidied them. Then she took out a pan and put all the vegetables she could find in it. She added a piece of fatty salt pork and covered it all with clean water from a large earthenware jar. Then she put it on the heat and added a cow's tongue.

"Nice and fresh—a customer brought it for me yesterday," she boasted.

"If you keep fattening me up like this, I'll end up having to steal your clothes," Theresa warned her with a smile.

"With how little you eat, girl, it's a surprise that anyone can see your tits."

The woman stirred the pot while Theresa went back to tidying the kitchen.

"Anyhow, remember that in my condition I have to look after myself," the woman added, stroking her stomach.

Theresa smiled. Yet she wondered whether Helga would continue to prostitute herself when her belly was like a full moon.

"How does a woman get pregnant?" she suddenly asked.

"What kind of a stupid question is that?"

"No, you know . . . what I meant was . . . well . . . if doing it the first time."

Helga looked at her in surprise and then burst out laughing. "It depends how well you got fucked, you little rascal," and she gave her a loud kiss on the cheek.

Theresa tried to conceal her embarrassment by scrubbing hard at the rust in the kitchen. As she did so, she prayed to God that it wouldn't happen to her. Fortunately Helga admitted that she was joking and that becoming pregnant depended on several factors aside from the man's aim. But her explanations did little to put Theresa's mind at rest. She kept scrubbing so that the exertion would hide the embarrassed redness in her cheeks.

They spoke at length about Hoos. When Helga asked whether she truly loved him, Theresa rebuked her for doubting her feelings. However, without batting an eye the woman kept pressing her about the boy's family, the wealth he had, and his qualities as a lover. At this point Theresa stopped answering, though a smile betrayed her thoughts.

"I bet you're pregnant," Helga jested, and she laughed again before Theresa could throw a lettuce at her head.

On her way to the monastery, Theresa reflected on Helga's pregnancy. For a moment she imagined herself round as a barrel, bearing a defenseless child in her belly without any means to raise it. She ran her hands over her flat stomach and a shiver ran down her spine. At that moment she promised herself that, as much as she desired him, she would not lie with Hoos again until they were married.

When she reached the abbey, the cellarer allowed her to pass without a fuss, having learned his lesson after it was made apparent that he had accepted chops as a bribe. Theresa was also wearing the robe Alcuin had given her so that, with the hood up, she looked no different from the novices milling around outside the buildings. The monk in charge of the infirmary was surprised to see her, but after confirming that she had Alcuin's permission, he agreed to tell her what they knew about Hoos's whereabouts.

"I will tell you again: The only explanation is that he left of his own accord."

"So why didn't he tell me?" she said, feigning indignation.

"How should I know! Do you think we hide cripples around here?"

Theresa didn't like his comment. She wondered if this was the friar who had stolen Hoos's dagger while he lay in bed. The infirmarian noticed the young woman's look of mistrust, but he was unmoved.

"If you do not like what you hear, take it up with Alcuin," he said, pointing toward the scriptorium, and deciding that he would not give her another moment of his time, he turned away to mix a poultice.

Theresa wasn't sure whether to visit the monk. Although Hoos had warned her against him, the truth was that so far Alcuin had kept all of his promises. She also needed to pay Helga back the money she had borrowed to buy the horse. Suddenly she remembered the sample of grain she had taken during her clandestine visit to the mill. It was still in her pocket, so she decided to show it to him and use it as an excuse to discuss her wages.

She found him at the door of the scriptorium, just as he was leaving. He was not expecting to see her, but greeted her with a friendly manner nonetheless.

"I'm sorry to say that your friend—"

"I know, I've just come from the infirmary."

"I don't understand what might have happened to him. If I had more time . . . but I have several matters of the utmost importance to take care of."

"And Hoos is not important?" she asked insincerely.

"Of course he is. I promise I will examine the case for a while this evening."

Theresa nodded, pretending she was satisfied, then she rummaged in her pockets and brought out a handful of the grain she had purloined from the mill. When Alcuin saw it, his eyes grew almost as wide as his mouth. "Where did you get that?" he said, looking closer at the cereal.

She told him the story, explaining she went back for the grain and leaving out the part about the horse. The friar examined the grain for a moment before picking up a twig from the ground, which he used to sift through the cereal. He told her to put it back in her pocket and thoroughly wash her hands. Then they set off for the apothecary.

After checking that nobody was there, Alcuin lit several candles and closed the doors and windows so that no one could see them. He then asked Theresa to place every last grain into a metal dish. When she had finished, he made her shake the inside of her pocket onto the same dish and instructed her to wash her hands again.

"Have you felt any discomfort in your stomach?" he asked.

She shook her head. She had some discomfort, but it was from spending the night with Hoos.

The monk arranged all the candles so they were positioned near the dish. The golden grains of wheat glowed like the sun in the light of the flames, as did Alcuin's face, which was so close to the receptacle that it reminded Theresa of an animal sniffing its fodder. He asked Theresa to bring him two white ceramic bowls and some tongs from a nearby shelf. Then he began transferring the cereal, grain by grain, from the metal dish to one of the bowls.

He continued the task at a steady but slow pace, taking time to examine each grain, smelling and touching each one in a strange ritual. With three quarters of the cereal now in one of the bowls, Alcuin suddenly jumped up, brandishing the tongs that gripped a single black grain. He proudly showed it to her and let out a laugh. But he sat down again upon seeing the blank look on the young woman's face.

Then he placed the black grain in the other empty bowl. "Come here," he said, "and observe the shape and color."

She looked closely at the grain that resembled some sort of tiny horn. It was a blackish, twisted thing, and roughly the same size as a fingernail cutting.

"What is it?" She thought it looked like any old seed.

"*When the cereal blows in the wind, Körnmutter roams the fields scattering her children, the wolves of the rye.*"

Theresa looked at him, uncomprehending.

"*Körnmutter*: the Mother Goddess of Grain," he explained. "Or, at least, that's what the pagans in the north believe. I suspected it from the outset, but the strangest thing is its presence in the wheat."

"I don't understand."

"Look closely," he said, picking the object up with the tongs again. "This is no grain of wheat. It is ergot, a hallucinogenic fungus. What you see here is the *sclerotium*, the structure in which it survives after releasing its prey." He took a knife from his belt and cut open the capsule, revealing a whitish interior. "The fungus nests in damp ears, which it consumes like a parasite, and it does the same thing to anyone unfortunate enough to eat it. The symptoms are always identical: nausea, infernal visions, gangrenous limbs, and finally a terrible death. I examined the rye a thousand times without finding a single trace of ergot, but it didn't occur to me to look in the wheat. Not until after the death of Romuald, my poor acolyte."

"Why didn't it occur to you?"

"Maybe because I am not God, or perhaps because ergot does not grow in wheat," he responded in an annoyed tone. "Observe its size. It is much smaller than rye. It was not until recently, when I recalled that the illness was only affecting the wealthier folks, that I decided I must examine the wheat."

Theresa took the knife and examined the remains of the capsule with the point, as if it were a dead insect.

"So, if this is what's causing the deaths . . ." she ventured.

"Which it undoubtedly is."

"Then these deaths can be avoided by alerting the millers."

"It may seem that simple, but unfortunately that's not sufficient enough. Whoever is selling it likely already knows that the wheat is killing people, so a mere warning would only alert the criminal to the fact that we have discovered him."

"But at least people would stop eating wheat bread."

"I can see you are unaware of the extremes a famine will push one toward. Folks will eat waste, rotten food, sick animals. And don't think that it is only the rich who have been affected, for today two beggars died. What's more, we would not just ruin the merchants, the millers, the bakers, and the hundreds of families who make a living from the cereal—but it is likely that the criminal, knowing that he is being sought, would grind all the contaminated grain and thus spread the poison irremediably. No." He gave Theresa a grim look. "All we can do is find out who the ultimate perpetrator is before the wheat kills anyone else. And to do so, you must swear to the utmost secrecy."

The young woman took the crucifix that Alcuin held out to her, pressed it against her chest, and swore to him, knowing that if she broke her promise her soul would be condemned forever.

After thoroughly cleaning the containers, they left the apothecary and made for the cathedral, dashing from porch to porch as though they feared someone was following them. Occasionally they stopped to catch their breath and Theresa would ask Alcuin what he knew about ergot. The monk informed her that during his time at the school in York, they had suffered the Plague on more than one occasion.

"But it was always in the rye," he insisted.

He told her that, coinciding with his appointment as librarian, several monks had fallen ill. It was a time of famine, he explained.

When the wheat had been used up, some batches of rye were brought in from the fields of Edinburgh. This grain produced dark, bitter-tasting bread, though it was not as bitter as spelt, and it was resistant to the cold. It did not harden so quickly, so it could be kept after baking. But then people started to die. He also managed the library's collection, but also administrated tolls, market taxes, and corvées. His access to these documents enabled him to make the connection between the arrival of the rye and the first signs of the illness. However, only after a fourth novice died did they ask for his advice and help.

"By then, half the monastery had been contaminated," he lamented. "We called it *Ignis Sacer*, or sacred fire, due to the burning sensations that it caused in the limbs. I discovered the presence of the little horns among the rye grain, and confirmed their deadly effects after feeding them to some dogs. In later years the Plague would visit us again, but by then we knew how to protect ourselves."

"Did you find a cure?"

"No, unfortunately. Once the poison penetrates the body, it spreads like sand in water. From that moment on, the fate of the sufferer depends on God's will and the amount of ergot that has been ingested. However, we prevented many deaths by thoroughly inspecting the grain before eating it."

They walked on toward the chapter, for Alcuin wanted to consult the provisioning book for its mill. He had already inspected the abbey's polyptychs and he intended to inspect Kohl's books, too.

"What I don't understand is why we have to inspect the chapter's polyptychs, when I found the ergot at Kohl's mill," said Theresa, involving herself in the investigation.

"The capsule . . . the casing of the ergot was dry. Dead," the friar responded as they climbed the steps to the cathedral. "Yet even so, it still preserves its lethal properties. We can assume that the grain was harvested over a year ago, for that is how long the ergot survives before drying out."

"But that doesn't change the fact that I found it at Kohl's mill."

"It is undeniable that a batch ended up there. Yet, as Kohl himself says, no wheat is planted on his lands, which I confirmed, naturally, by checking the various polyptychs."

"So why, when you offered to buy wheat, did he even consider your offer?"

"An interesting observation," he said with a smile. "And of course, a detail to reflect upon, as long as we do not forget that the purpose of this inquiry is to prevent more deaths. Now wait here until I return. I will be back after speaking to the bishop."

Theresa sat on the cathedral steps, away from the vagrants competing for the spaces nearest the portico. While she waited, she watched a group of soldiers dismantling some stalls in the middle of the square.

"What are those men doing?" she asked a beggar who was gazing at her, captivated.

The mendicant hesitated before opening his mouth. "Preparing for the execution. They came a while ago and started digging in the middle." He pointed at a medium-sized cavity.

"The hole is for the gallows?"

"No! They're building a pond!" he guffawed, flashing his single tooth. "Can you spare a little coin?"

Theresa took a couple of walnuts from her pocket, but upon seeing them, the beggar spat on the ground and turned away. She shrugged, put them away and headed toward where the soldiers were working. Near them, two laborers toiled to widen a ditch so large it could fit an entire horse. The workers appeared talkative, but when she asked them what the hole was for, one of the soldiers told her to move on.

* * *

Alcuin found Lothar on his way back from the refectory. After the customary greetings, the bishop inquired after the progress of his writing.

"I have not made as much headway as I would have liked," he complained, "but to be honest, the writing is the least of my concerns now."

"Oh?"

"As you know, my presence in the abbey is at the express desire of Charlemagne." Alcuin noticed Lothar assume an expression of weariness, but he continued. "Our monarch upholds an uncommon balance between devotion to the divine and rectitude in worldly affairs, which is perhaps why he has commissioned me to ensure particular observance of the Rule of Saint Benedict."

Lothar nodded. He was well aware of the king's qualities, for it was thanks to him that he held the bishopric, but he allowed Alcuin to continue his address.

"I have seen, much to my regret, that in the monastery the monks come and go, frequent the markets, speak during services, sleep instead of attending Nocturns, and sometimes even eat meat. And although we are lenient when it comes to sins like laxity or complacency—which after all, are limitations of human nature itself—we cannot approve of, let alone consent to, the depravation and impurity of those whose duty is to watch over their inferiors and set an example."

"Forgive me, my good Alcuin, but where is this leading? You know that the monastery has nothing to do with the chapter."

"The Devil resides in Fulda," Alcuin said, crossing himself. "But not Satan, or Azazel, or Asmodeus, or Belial. Lucifer does not always need princes to do his despicable work. And do not assume I speak of rituals or sacrifices: I am referring to miscreants. Subjects unfit to call themselves ministers of God who use their position of power for their own loathsome ends."

"I still fail to understand, but by the cape of Saint Martin you are starting to worry me."

"I am sorry, Father. Sometimes I talk without realizing that the person who is listening to me cannot hear all of my thoughts. I will try to be clear."

"Please do."

"A couple of months ago, Charlemagne received news of certain irregularities taking place in the monastery. As you know every abbey behaves like a small county." Alcuin looked at the bishop who nodded, but he continued anyway to build his case. "It has lands from which the abbot obtains a monthly income, generally paid in-kind. Some tenants hand over barley for brewing, others spelt, wheat, rams, ducks, or pigs. Some pay their rent in wool, others in tools or implements, and most give their labor."

"That's right. Our chapter functions in a similar way. What is your point?"

"As you are well aware, here in Fulda most of the wealthy folks grow wheat, which they grind into flour at the abbey. In exchange the monastery keeps a portion as payment."

"Go on."

"The fact is that dozens of townsfolk have fallen ill or died recently from unknown causes."

"And you believe the sickness is related to our mills?"

"That is what I intend to establish. At first I speculated that it might be some kind of pestilence, but now I'm suspecting other-wise."

"Then tell me how I may assist you."

"Thank you, Father. The truth is that I need to inspect the mills' polyptychs from the last three years."

"The chapter mills?"

"Actually, all three of Fulda's mills. I already have in my possession two books from the abbey in my cell, but I need your permission for my assistant to accompany me to the episcopal scriptorium so that I may inspect the other chapter mill books."

"You can request the polyptychs from my secretary Ludwig, but I doubt you will be able to obtain Kohl's. That man does not record his accounts in books. He has it all in his head."

Alcuin grimaced, for it was a setback he had not foreseen. "As for my assistant . . ." He omitted the fact his assistant was a woman.

"Oh, yes! Of course your assistant may accompany you. Now, if you will forgive me."

"One last thing," Alcuin paused for a moment to consider.

"Speak, I am in a hurry."

"This sickness . . . do you remember a similar event occurring before? I mean, years ago."

"No, not that I can recall. On a few occasions folks have died from gangrene, but as you know, regrettably that is quite common."

Alcuin gave the bishop his thanks, a little disappointed. Then he made for the exit where Theresa was waiting for him, still staring at the hole that had been dug in the center of the square.

Alcuin informed her that they would dine in the chapter house that evening since they would continue working through the night. Theresa was surprised by the news, but did not question it. She asked for permission to return to Helga's house for warm clothes, and they agreed to meet in the same place after the bells had rung for None.

When Theresa arrived back at Helga's tavern, she found that the door had been barred. Surprised, she checked the rear entrance and the window shutters, which were also locked. There appeared to be no one inside, so she stayed outside for a while looking through the cracks, until suddenly she felt a tugging on her robe. She turned to see a small toothless child.

"My grandmother wants to speak to you," he blurted out.

Theresa looked in the direction in which the boy was pointing and saw some small hands poking through a little door in a nearby house, beckoning to her. She picked up the infant and ran toward the house. The door opened, revealing the frightened face of an elderly woman, gesturing for her to hurry. As soon as Theresa entered, the old woman re-secured the door with a wooden bar.

"She's there," she pointed.

Despite the dark, Theresa could see Helga lying on the floor. Her eyes were closed, and her face was bloody.

"She's sleeping now," the old woman explained. "I went to ask for a little salt, and I found her like this. It was the same bastard as always. He'll end up killing her."

Theresa approached her friend, filled with dismay. There was a dreadful gash across her face, from temple to chin. She stroked her hair and told herself that it must end. She asked the old woman to look after her until the next morning and offered her a denarius for her effort, which she accepted. When she was sure there was nothing more she could do for her, she returned to the tavern, forced open the flimsiest window, and fetched her belongings.

At None she arrived at the chapter door, loaded down like a mule. On her shoulders she carried her clothes, some food, the wax tablets, and the pallet that Althar had given her before returning to the mountains. When she told Alcuin she had nowhere to go, he tried to console her.

"But you cannot stay here," he explained.

They decided that she would sleep in the chapter stables until he found somewhere to house her. Theresa then asked him to take care of Helga the Black.

"She's a prostitute. I can't help her."

She tried to persuade him that she was a good woman, that she was hurt, pregnant and in need of urgent assistance, but Alcuin remained firm.

Theresa could not contain herself. "Well, if you won't help, I will," she said, gathering up her possessions again.

Alcuin clenched his jaw. He could not employ another assistant without risking his discoveries being spread all over the chapter.

Cursing, he took Theresa by the arm. "I will speak to the woman in charge of the domestic service, but I cannot promise you anything. Now come, put your hood up."

After leaving her belongings in the stables, Theresa went with Alcuin to the episcopal scriptorium, a smaller room than the one in the monastery, furnished with upholstered desks. There Alcuin unchained four volumes secured by their spines to the bookshelf. He placed them on the central table and examined their respective indices. Handing one to Theresa, he told her to look for any entry that mentioned grain transactions.

"In truth," Alcuin admitted, "I do not know exactly what we're searching for—but I hope to find a piece of information that reveals whether at any time the abbey, the chapter, or Kohl acquired a poisoned batch."

"That would appear here?"

"The purchase would, at least. As far as I have been able to establish, Fulda's harvests have never caused an epidemic, so the sickness must have originated in a batch imported from another estate."

Theresa observed that the polyptych did not only record transactions of foodstuffs, but also acted as a record of income, land conveyances, taxes, and the allocation of roles within the chapter.

"This handwriting is incomprehensible," she complained.

They dined on onion soup while leafing through the volumes making sure to not miss even a page. Theresa found several entries mentioning the purchase of barley and spelt, and even some of wheat, but nothing suspicious or out of the ordinary.

"I don't understand," said Alcuin. "We should be able to find something."

"There are still Kohl's polyptychs."

"That's what bothers me. His transactions are not recorded."

"So?"

"There must be something here. There must be," he repeated, opening the codices again.

They went through them for a second time with the same outcome. Finally, Alcuin gave up.

"Can I stay a little longer?" Theresa asked, for all that awaited her in the stables was the stench of dung.

Alcuin looked at her in surprise. "Are you sure you want to continue?"

She nodded.

"In that case I shall sleep here," he said, signaling to a bench.

The monk lay on the rigid piece of furniture, which creaked under his weight. He half closed his watery eyes and began reciting prayers, which gradually turned into snores.

Theresa smiled watching him sleep, but she quickly turned her attention to the first volume, which she started to read with every ounce of her focus. She noted the appointments and departures of the warehouse workers, the repairs to the mills, and the profits that the sale of wheat brought in each season. However, after an hour, the letters on the page started to look like a disorderly trail of insects.

She set aside the volume and turned her mind to Hoos. No doubt he was sleeping—or perhaps like her he was awake, remembering the previous night and wanting to be back by her side as they traveled to Aquis-Granum. Was he cold? If only she could be there to embrace him. Then she remembered her father and her heart sank. With each day that went by, she missed him more.

A creaking brought her out of her daydreams. She turned to see Alcuin trying to make his willowy body more comfortable on the hard bench, all the while still snoring.

She returned to her task, interspersing her reading with a few vain attempts to mop up what was left of the soup in her dish. She progressed ever more slowly, repeating her annotations to herself, until suddenly, something strange caught her attention. But it wasn't the text.

She moved a candle closer to one of the sheets, running the tip of her finger across its surface that was a different color than the rest. She stroked it again, confirming that its texture was also different than the other pages. She brought another candle near the sheet to examine it more closely. This particular sheet appeared lighter, cleaner, and smoother.

She recognized the feel of the parchment. The sheets were sewn together in quinternions of double pages, joined by the fold where they were backstitched. She found the second page of the irregular sheet. It was the same as the rest: rough and dark. Worn in the same way.

There was only one explanation for this, and she knew it because she had done it herself dozens of times. When a parchment was smudged, it could be rescued by scraping its surface until the stained skin is removed. If the entire sheet were scraped, it would look as good as new, ready to be reused. However, after scraping, it became thinner and a slightly different color. Scribes called it *palimpsest*.

She reexamined the smooth sheet. The handwriting was also different than the writing on the rest of the pages. Without doubt it had been written some time later.

She wondered why someone would be compelled to scrape an entire page.

For a moment she thought about waking Alcuin, but she decided to wait. Then she recalled a game the scribes would play in Korne's workshop to recover deleted text. They would place damp ash on the page underneath a newly scraped page and lightly rub to reveal the pressure marks left by the quill. Sometimes it was impossible because the marks of the new text jumbled the marks of the old. However, all scribes knew that before writing on a reused page, they had to position a tablet underneath to avoid leaving marks on the sheet behind it.

She took a handful of ash from the fire and crossed herself. Then she applied it, rubbing little circles gently on the page underneath until it became a gray powder that disappeared with one blow. She lifted the codex and held it against the light of the candle. A short text in white lettering appeared before her eyes. She copied it onto her wax tablet:

On the calends of February of the year 796 of Our Lord Jesus Christ.

Under the auspices of Boethius of Nantes, Abbot of Fulda, and guaranteed by Charles known as the Great, King of the Franks and Patrician of the Romans.

Transaction of six hundred pecks of rye, two hundred of barley, and fifty of spelt, settled at a discounted price, dispatched to the county of Magdeburg.

Paid to this abbey, the sum of forty gold solidi, under the law of God.

May the Almighty protect Magdeburg from the Plague.

The rest of the paragraph referred to the opening of a minor road, and it coincided with the new writing on the scraped sheet.

A surge of joy ran from her stomach to her ears. Immediately, she called out to Alcuin, telling him to wake up.

"By God, you will wake the entire chapter," he said, half-asleep.

While she told him of her discovery, Alcuin examined the codex eagerly. Then he looked at Theresa in astonishment.

"It is not a purchase, but a sale. What's more, the price . . . forty solidi is far too low."

"But it mentions a plague, and if that weren't important, they wouldn't have taken the effort to hide it," she argued.

"It could also be that, though still significant, it bears no relation to our epidemic. Yet, let me think: Magdeburg . . . Magdeburg . . . nearly four years ago . . . Heavens above! That's it!"

He ran to the bookshelf and took down the document containing the latest capitularies published by Charlemagne. Then he examined the pages with the focus of someone who knew precisely what he was looking for. "Here it is: a decree of assistance dated January of the same year." He quickly read it and explained, "It regulates the delivery and price of food sent to the county of Magdeburg. It does not specify the reasons behind the pricing, but I recall that at that time a plague was devastating the area bordering with Eastphalia, on the banks of the Elbe."

"And what does that mean?"

"Magdeburg was besieged by the Saxons during one of the worst winters in living memory. The attackers burned the grain reserves, leading to a famine that continued after the arrival of Charlemagne's troops. To alleviate matters, the king himself ordered cereals to be sent from nearby counties at a price lower than the stipulated one. The source of the epidemic was never known."

"But why would someone remove that information from the polyptych, while leaving the capitulary intact?"

"Because they are different things. Ultimately, the capitulary only contains a decree of assistance, without specifying what gave rise to it. However, the erased page in the polyptych established a link between the Plague and the abbey."

"A link correlated to the sale of grain, and quite possibly the purchase of contaminated wheat."

"We need something to hang on to. This lead could be the Devil's tail."

Theresa concluded: "Then let's pull the tail so we can catch the Devil."

16

In a corner of the stables, Theresa dreamed of Hoos. The next morning she awoke as the animals began to shuffle around, whinnying and breaking wind with a complete disregard for their guest. Stretching and yawning, her hair entangled with straw, she parted the blankets that Alcuin had put up as curtains and made for the water troughs. The water was freezing, but it felt good on her face. When she had finished washing, she noticed Alcuin standing there looking at her with despair.

"So much cleanliness. Come on, woman! We have work to do."

He told her that after she retired to the stables he went to the abbey to awaken and question two monks who may have known something. Still half-asleep, they told him that Boethius, the previous abbot, had suffered an attack of insanity that drove him to his premature death.

"This happened shortly after the cereal transaction. A dispute broke out over the succession to the abbacy involving Richolf, the treasurer at the time and also the one responsible for provisioning, and John Chrysostom, prior of the abbey, who was ultimately elected to the position. However, Richolf has left town and Chrysostom died the following year. They didn't tell me much more, but I managed to establish who drove the cart that transported the grain. It might come as a surprise to you, but it turns out that The Swine may not be as slow-witted as we thought."

On the way back to the library they stopped at the kitchens for some porridge and milk. Theresa put the food on a tray she found among the dozens of scattered-about pots and pans. She mentioned how surprised she was that the kitchens were in such a mess.

"I would have to agree with you," said Alcuin. "Clearly there is too much work—or not enough hands."

Theresa took the opportunity to press him regarding Helga the Black. "Perhaps you could employ her here. She is good in the kitchen, and as clean and tidy as they come."

"Clean? A *prostibulae*? A loose woman who lies with men for money?"

"She's clean with food. If you accepted her here, you'd help her give up her obscene behavior. And there's also the matter of her pregnancy. Should a child have to pay for its mother's sins?"

Alcuin fell silent. It was widely believed that the offspring of prostitutes were marked by the Devil from birth, but he didn't accept such nonsense. He coughed a couple of times before announcing that he would suggest it to the bishop.

"But I cannot promise anything," he added. "And now, let us resume our work."

Once they were at the scriptorium, Alcuin discovered a huge and immaculate sheet of parchment, which he spread out on the table. He began to write on it with abandon, as if it had no value.

"Let us go over the case with a fine-tooth comb: On the one hand we are looking at some deaths, which, as far as we know, were caused by the victims ingesting contaminated cereal. Wheat that, it seems, was ground at Kohl's mill—or that passed through it at least." Theresa nodded, and Alcuin continued. "And on the other hand, we have seen evidence of the sale, nearly four years ago, of a large batch of cereal to a county where, either before or after the transaction, a strange plague was unleashed. Unfortunately, the people who could help clarify matters the most have either died, like Boethius and John Chrysostom, or have been arrested and accused of murder, like The Swine."

"And let's not forget, someone tried to hide proof of the sale not so long ago."

"That's right. Well observed." He paused for a moment to reflect. "So, my theory is that the Plague in Magdeburg, no doubt attributed to the siege by the Saxons that winter, was in actual fact caused by consumption of the wheat, contaminated due to the harsh winter conditions. This corruption would have been well known among the county's millers, who during one of their worst famines in history would've probably taken their chances with the grain rather than die of starvation. However, with the arrival of Charlemagne's troops, and the replenishment of supplies, we can assume that they would've chosen to destroy the contaminated grain."

"I'm listening."

"But what would happen if that spoiled wheat, rather than being incinerated, ended up back on the same carts that delivered the rye from Fulda? No doubt it would have been a tidy bit of business for the Magdeburg vendor, who would have made a return on unusable grain—and it would have been even better for the buyer from Fulda, who would have cereal at a rock-bottom price that could then be sold for a hefty profit."

"And do you think they were aware of its blight?"

"That's something we may never know. It might have been bought without knowledge of the poison that it contained or, if they were aware of the fact, they might have intended to thoroughly clean the grain."

"But if they had cleaned it thoroughly, wouldn't that have prevented the deaths?"

"Unless, of course, the batch of grain changed hands without that bit of knowledge."

Theresa looked at Alcuin with a sense of excitement, feeling that she was playing a part in each new discovery. However, Alcuin's brow remained furrowed as he pondered their next step. He asked Theresa to return the codices to the bookcase while he meditated for a moment. Then he finished his milk and looked out through the window as if he were observing time itself.

"You know what? I think it's time we spoke to The Swine."

* * *

On the way to the slaughterhouse, Alcuin informed Theresa that there were no dungeons in Fulda. Prisoners were chained out in the open until the day they received their punishment. However, though he was guarded, someone had thrown stones at The Swine that almost split his head open, so the prefect had ordered him locked inside the abattoir to prevent some miscreant from ruining the spectacle.

At the entrance to the slaughterhouse they came across a sentry, numb with cold and nodding off. When they tapped him on the shoulder, he blew out a lungful of alcohol fumes, and then once he had learned Alcuin's intentions, recomposed himself sufficiently to stop them from entering. But as soon as he heard that his soul ran the risk of being consumed by the fires of hell if he did not let them pass, he allowed them in.

Theresa followed Alcuin's torch as he walked ahead in the darkness. The stench of rotten meat in the damp air was so intense that the porridge she had eaten for breakfast churned in her stomach. Alcuin opened a window onto the inner courtyard. The remains of bones, feathers, and skin could be seen everywhere in the light that filtered through the cracks in the poorly sealed boards.

As they progressed, the torch illuminated the narrow corridor through which the animals were led to their slaughter. At the back of the room they saw a huddled figure—dark, deformed, covered in chains like an animal that had fallen into a trap.

When they approached, Theresa could see that the poor wretch had soiled himself. Alcuin did not seem to care. The friar moved closer and greeted him in a soft voice. The Swine did not respond.

"You have nothing to fear." He offered him an apple that he had brought from the kitchens.

The Swine remained silent. His eyes trembled in the glow of the torch. Alcuin noticed a pair of gashes in his head, no doubt caused by the stones thrown at him.

"Are you all right? Do you need anything?" Alcuin persisted.

The idiot curled up into himself even tighter, terrified.

Alcuin moved the torch nearer to examine his injuries, but suddenly The Swine leaped toward him and attempting to strike him.

But Alcuin merely stepped back so that the chains stopped the captive before he could reach him.

"We should go," Theresa suggested.

Ignoring her, Alcuin moved the torch closer once more. This time The Swine retreated. He seemed fearful again.

"Calm down. Nobody wants to hurt you. Who did this to you?"

Still he said nothing.

"Are you hungry?" Alcuin cleaned the apple and placed it on the ground within reach. The Swine hesitated for a moment, then with some difficulty he grabbed the fruit and eagerly stashed it in his clothing.

"Are you afraid to answer? Don't you want to speak?"

"I don't think he'll talk to you," the guard interrupted from behind. Theresa and Alcuin turned in surprise.

"No? How can you be so sure?" asked Alcuin challengingly.

"Because last Sunday they cut out his tongue."

* * *

On the way back to the chapter, Alcuin walked with his head bowed, kicking any stones in his path. It was the first time Theresa had heard him curse so bitterly.

At the entrance to the episcopal palace they came across Lothar, who was arguing with a richly attired woman. Alcuin tried to approach, but the bishop gestured for him to wait. Before long he took his leave from the woman and approached Alcuin.

"What brings you here? Did you not see who I was speaking to?"

Alcuin kissed his ring. "Forgive my ignorance. I did not know I was interrupting a matter of importance."

"Next time, wait until I am ready. You made me look bad in front of that lady," he grumbled.

"I'm sorry, but I need to speak to you urgently, Father, and this is not the right place," he said apologetically. "Incidentally, perhaps you can explain what the hole is for that they are digging in the square."

"You will find out in due course," he said with a smile. "Are you hungry? Accompany me to lunch and we will discuss whatever it is you wished to see me about."

Alcuin said good-bye to Theresa, agreeing to meet her afterward in the kitchens. When the friar reached the refectory, he was taken aback by the overwhelming array of food crammed onto the table.

"Please, come and sit down," said the bishop taking his seat.

Alcuin took a seat by his side and greeted the other diners.

"I hope you have a hearty appetite," said the bishop, "because as you can see, we are blessed. This lamb's head seems particularly succulent, see the sweetbreads? They are so sweet, just looking at them makes them melt."

"You already know, Father, that I am moderate in my eating habits."

"And by God does it show. You are thin as an earthworm! Look at me, plump and healthy. If some infirmity afflicts me, it will not be for want of food."

Then Lothar stood, blessed the table, and recited a prayer in chorus with the other guests. When they had finished, he took the lamb's head in his hands and broke it into several pieces, which he shared merrily among those closest to him. "This is delicious, Alcuin. Do you know the pleasure you are depriving yourself of? Rich cakes, great venison pies, cheese pastries with hazelnuts, and sweet chickpeas with quince. I am certain that you have not had the chance to sample such delicacies in your Northumbria."

"And I am certain you know that the Rule of Saint Benedict is opposed to gluttony."

"Oh, yes! The Rule of Saint Benedict! Pray and die of hunger! But fortunately, we are not in your monastery now," laughed Lothar as he served himself another piece of lamb.

Alcuin raised his eyebrows and served himself a bowl of chickpeas. As he ate, he looked round at the other diners. Opposite him, Chaplain Ambrose, with his dog's face, sucked on some pigeon heads. To his right, half-hidden behind a dish of fruit, the lector munched louder than the others were talking. Beyond him, two old men with pale eyes and few teeth argued over the last piece of cake.

The bishop cast the leftovers on his plate to the dog beside him and served himself some more.

"So tell me," he said, "what was it that you wished to speak to me about so urgently?"

"It concerns The Swine."

"Indeed? That business again? So what is it now?"

"I would rather explain in private." He studied the bishop carefully. His neatly shaven face, with hardly a wrinkle, soft and chubby, revealed as much emotion as a sunburned pig. He guessed him to be around thirty-five years old, an uncommonly young age for a role with such great responsibility, albeit no impediment for a relative of Charlemagne.

At a signal from Lothar, everyone at the table stood. Alcuin waited for the room to empty before he began.

"Be brief, Alcuin. I must dress for the execution."

"The execution? But did you not postpone it?" he asked, bewildered.

"And now I have brought it forward," the bishop responded without so much as a glance at him.

"Please forgive me, but that is precisely what I wanted to speak to you about. Were you aware that someone has cut out The Swine's tongue?"

Lothar looked him up and down. "Of course. The whole town knows it."

"And what is your opinion?"

"The same as you, I should think. That some undesirable has deprived us of the pleasure of hearing him scream."

"And also speak," he said openly.

"Yes, but who is interested in the lies of a half-witted murderer?"

"Maybe that is the crux of the matter." He paused to consider his next words. "Perhaps someone does not wish him to speak. And there's more."

"More?"

"The Swine is no criminal," he said.

Lothar looked at him with irritation. Then he turned and walked off.

"I can guarantee you that he did not kill the girl," Alcuin continued.

"Stop talking nonsense!" He turned back and walked straight back toward Alcuin until they were face to face. "How many times do I have to tell you that they found him with the victim, clutching the sickle that was used to cut her throat? Soaked in her blood!"

"That does not prove he killed her," he responded calmly.

"Would you be capable of explaining that to her mother?" Lothar retorted.

"If I knew who she was, I don't see why I couldn't."

"Then you just missed your chance! She was the woman I was speaking with when you interrupted. The mill owner Kohl's wife."

Alcuin fell silent. Though it was too early to jump to conclusions, that information upset most of his ideas. However, it didn't alter the fact that he believed an innocent man was about to be executed.

"Will you listen to me, for the love of God? You are the only person who can stop this insanity. That man would be incapable of holding a sickle. Have you seen his hands? His fingers are deformed. Deformed from birth. I have seen them with my own eyes."

"You have seen him? How? Have you visited him? Who authorized it?"

"I tried to ask your permission, but your secretary told me that you were busy. And now answer me this: If The Swine is incapable of holding even an apple with either hand, how could he have held, much less wielded, a sickle?"

"Look, Alcuin, you may be a minister of education. You may know your letters, theology, and a thousand other things. But I must remind you that you are merely a deacon. Here in Fulda, whether you like it or not, the person who has the final decision is me, so I suggest you forget your foolish theories and concentrate on that codex that so interests you."

"All I am interested in is preventing an outrage. I can assure you that The Swine did not—"

"And I assure you that he killed her! And if your only argument is that his fingers do not work, you can start praying—for there is nothing else you can do before he's marched to the gallows."

"But Your Excellency—"

"This conversation is over," he said, leaving and slamming the door to his chambers in Alcuin's face.

Alcuin returned to his cell with his head bowed. He was certain that The Swine had not murdered that young woman, but his certainty rested only on the fact that the man could not even hold an apple.

He cursed his stupidity. If instead of attempting to convince Lothar he had tried to have the execution postponed, perhaps he would have had time to find more convincing proof. Maybe he should have argued it was more appropriate to wait for Charlemagne's arrival, or perhaps he should have suggested they wait until The Swine's injuries heal, to add to the enjoyment of the spectacle. But now there was nothing he could do. Only a couple of hours remained to try to prevent the inevitable.

Then the idea came to him. He wrapped up and hurried out of his cell to get Theresa from the stables. Together they made for the abbey.

In the apothecary he asked Theresa to wash a bowl while he examined the various flasks that filled the shelves. Uncorking several, he sniffed their contents before deciding on one labeled *lactuca virosa*. Opening it, he removed a whitish block, which he placed on an earthenware plate.

It had been a long time since he had used the compound extracted from a variety of wild lettuce, the sap of which had a strong hypnotic effect. He took a walnut-sized portion, crushed it into a powder, then opened the little lid on his ring and tipped the powder into the tiny receptacle. Then he tidied the flasks, leaving everything how it was, before hurrying off to the chapter.

However, when they reached the episcopal palace they found the doors closed. Theresa parted ways, for she had promised Helga she would accompany her to The Swine's execution, and Alcuin, too, set off for the gallows.

When Theresa arrived at the tavern, Helga was ready to leave, her face painted and hair pinned up. The gash on her face had disappeared under a paste of flour, water, and colored with earth, which made Theresa think it might not be too deep. Helga seemed excited, and she had prepared some sweet pastries so they wouldn't have to buy them from the hawkers, and though they were not the most attractive things, they smelled of honey and spices. Before heading to the square, they both donned fur cloaks to protect themselves from the cold. Then they locked up properly and set off carrying their food and some wine. While they walked, Theresa told Helga about what she had seen at the slaughterhouse, but to her surprise, Helga rejoiced to hear they had cut out The Swine's tongue.

"Shame they didn't rip his balls off, too," she declared.

"Alcuin says he's innocent. That killing him will solve nothing."

"What does that priest know? I hope he doesn't spoil the party," she said, and they headed for the square arm in arm.

Not long before sundown, the cathedral bells started to chime their mournful strains. The soldiers had arranged a circular arena about thirty paces across in the center of the square, cordoning off its perimeter with a circle of stakes. Inside the arena was a hole similar in size to a grave, and in front of it were three wooden tables along with three small chairs. A dozen or so men armed with sticks were watching the crowd that was starting to gather at the fence, where traders had set up their stalls to make last-minute sales. Gradually the multitude grew, and before long, the palisade was hidden under a mass of people clamoring hysterically for the spectacle to begin.

When the bells fell silent, a long cortège paraded into the square. A rider dressed in mourning led the way, accompanied by a cohort of civilians. Most of them wore colorful outfits that contrasted with the rags worn by the serfs who followed them with cured meats hanging from their arms. Next there were several slaves announcing their arrival with the beating of drums. Then came the wagon with the prisoner, and behind him, the executioner who was busy picking up the rotten food that was thrown at the captive and then rubbing it in his face. A swarm of excited children brought up the rear of the procession.

Moments later a group of clerics appeared led by Bishop Lothar. In his right hand he brandished a golden staff, and in his left, he held up an ornate silver crucifix. He was wearing a *ciclatoun* robe of red silk, covered by a tunic of Bukharan cotton, his head crowned with a linen *infula* of dubious taste. The rest of the clergymen wore woolen *paenulae*, all of them covered with the priestly alb. The bishop took the second seat at the table where a man in black already sat. Upon the bishop's arrival, the man stood to kiss his ring. An acolyte served them wine, and then a city magistrate took the third seat.

The square erupted into a roar when the oxen transporting The Swine were driven into the arena toward the hole in the ground. As soon as they stopped, the executioner grabbed the condemned man and threw him headlong onto the ground. A cheer went up and objects rained down upon the wagon, forcing the executioner and driver to take refuge under the cart. When the crowds had calmed down, the executioner dragged the prisoner to a stake near the pit, tied him to it, and put a rope around his neck. Then he checked that the knots were tight and gave a signal to the rider who was also dressed in black. The rider nodded and looked at the pathetic sight of the captive with evident pleasure.

Alcuin was the last person to arrive at the arena. Crossing the square and elbowing his way through the crowd, he jumped over the fence, threatening to excommunicate the guard who tried to stop him. As he approached the dignitaries, he realized that the man in black was the mill owner Kohl, father of the murdered young woman. His wife, accompanied by some other women, was there, too, but she was farther back in a more discreet location, her grief evident from the dark rings around her eyes. He thought to himself that, for this family, not even the execution of the perpetrator would bring relief.

As Alcuin contemplated how to deposit the powdered drug into Lothar's wine, the drums sounded, and he tried to stand behind them—close, but out of the way. The three men stood up, and Bishop Lothar spoke. "In the name of Charlemagne—the wisest and noblest king of the Franks; ruler of Aquitania, Austrasia, and Lombardy; patrician of the Romans and conqueror of Saxony—we declare that Fredegarius, better known as The Swine, a man without light and an envoy and disciple of Lucifer, has been found guilty of an abominable murder and other dreadful crimes. I, Lothar of Reims, Bishop of Fulda, lord of these lands, and representative of the king, his power and his justice, order under God's law that the accused be punished with the greatest of torments, and that his remains be spread about the city's fields as a lesson to those who dare offend God and His Christian creatures."

The crowds screamed with fury. At Lothar's signal, the executioner untied the condemned man and, after tying his hands behind his back, ushered him with blows to the edge of the pit.

The Swine seemed dazed, as if uncomprehending of what was about to happen. When he could see the ditch he was destined for, he attempted to free himself, but the executioner cast him to the ground and kicked him in the head. By then, The Swine was little more than a mass of trembling flesh. The multitude pressed against the fence squealed like a great herd of pigs.

Two boys armed with stones evaded the guards while finding their way into the arena, though they were soon caught. When the crowds had calmed down again, the executioner lifted The Swine to his feet. Lothar stepped forward, made the sign of the cross with a gesture of contempt, and ordered the executioner to begin the torment.

The crazed onlookers screamed their approval. It seemed that at any moment they would knock down the fence and lynch the prisoner.

Alcuin took advantage of the commotion to open his ring and tip the drug into the bishop's tankard of wine. Nobody saw it, but Lothar turned to see him with his hand still gripping the handle. With no time to react, Alcuin raised it and offered it to him in a toast. "To justice!" he cried, handing him his own tankard and picking up another.

Lothar was a little surprised, but finally he took it and downed its contents in one gulp. "To justice," he repeated raising his empty cup.

The executioner grabbed hold of the prisoner and with a violent blow cast him into the bottom of the pit. The clamor became deafening. The Swine stood up, drooling, with a lost look in his tear-filled eyes. The crowds pumped their fists in the air and called for blood. At that moment, two more men approached the pit bearing large wooden spades, making the crowd delirious with excitement. They positioned themselves beside a heap of sand and without saying a word they started shoveling it onto the captive. The Swine tried to turn around to escape from the pit, but the men prevented him with blows. One of them pressed into his back with the end of his spade, immobilizing him, while the others continued to bury him alive. As if in a fit of ecstasy, the crowd egged them on with curses and oaths. The Swine attempted to wriggle away from the spade that held him down. But the weight of the earth now upon him prevented him from moving his legs, and all he could do was thrash about like a trapped rabbit.

Soon the earth was piling onto his head. He spat and started to writhe out of pure desperation, his eyes all but coming out of their sockets. Spitting again and again, the sand continued to rain down on him until, gradually, he was completely covered.

For a moment the square fell silent, but suddenly the sand moved and the prisoner's head reappeared, spewing out soil. The

Swine breathed in as though it would be his last mouthful of air, and the crowd cried out in astonishment.

The bishop stood up and gestured to Kohl, but he didn't notice. Alcuin knew that the drug was starting to take effect.

Lothar sensed his vision clouding. His legs weakened and a dry heat pricked at his throat. He tried in vain to grab hold of Kohl. He attempted to speak but was unable, and he barely had time to cross himself before he fell flat on his face, taking the chair and table with him.

Silence descended upon the crowd. Even the executioner turned his head, forgetting about The Swine for a moment.

Seeing the executioner distracted, Kohl intervened. "Finish him off, damned fool."

The executioner didn't move. Then Kohl leapt down toward the pit and snatched the spade from him.

He was about to deal the final blow when Alcuin appeared between him and the prisoner. "You dare to disobey a sign from the heavens? God wishes to prolong this criminal's suffering," cried Alcuin as loudly as he could. Then he walked over to the fallen bishop and pretended to examine him. "When Lothar recovers, we will enjoy another execution!" he added.

The crowd roared again.

"You?" exclaimed Kohl. "You're the monk who came to the mill just the other day!"

"The murderer will pay for his crime, but the law, the executive authority, must justify the punishment," he put forth.

Kohl tried to strike The Swine again, but Alcuin stopped him.

"This is not God's will," he repeated, holding the spade firmly.

The masses bellowed excitedly.

Finally, Kohl spat on the prisoner, took his wife by the arm, and departed, escorted by his entourage. The chapter's council followed him, still bewildered by what had happened to Lothar. But

Alcuin reassured them that the bishop's condition was not serious and he would soon recover.

Finally, amid insults and threats, The Swine was lifted out of the pit and reloaded onto the cart. He and his captors left the square, and headed back to the slaughterhouse.

* * *

Helga the Black seemed distraught. Not only had she not seen an execution, but in a moment of distraction, a street urchin had stolen her bag of pastries. Theresa proposed buying a hot bun made with rye from a nearby stall, an offer that Helga immediately accepted. While Theresa searched through her empty pockets, the prostitute had already approached the pastry stand and was bartering for the buns. She selected a round bread roll, agreeing with the baker that she would pay her dues when he came by the tavern. She smiled with pleasure as they both wolfed down the pastries in no time at all. They found it to be so delicious that Helga did not hesitate to buy another, bigger one, laden with honey.

When they had finished, Theresa noticed the paste of flour and earth around Helga's mouth that she had used to hide her scar. Another blob hung from her nose like a strange white wart. When she told her, Helga burst into animated laughter. Theresa was surprised it didn't make her wound bleed again. She decided to ask what had happened.

"I wasn't out of bed yet when I heard a banging on the door," she said. "I didn't even have time to ask who it was. As soon as I opened it, I felt a kick to my stomach and punches rained down on me. The animal! He slit my face and told me that if I dared keep the child, next time it wouldn't be my belly that he'd cut open."

"But why does he behave so? What does he care what you do?"

"He must fear that I'll report him."

She explained that those accused of adultery were given seven years of penance, a punishment that consisted of daily fasting for the duration of the sentence, although a sum of money could be paid in lieu of it.

"He really likes his food," she complained. "And I think he's scared that his wife will disown him. Then he'll lose the carpenter's workshop, which belongs to his father-in-law. But you know what? I'm going to do it. I'll report him even if it comes to nothing. With this scar, nobody will pay for my services anymore. Who's going to want to lie with a disfigured whore?"

"It's not that bad," Theresa reassured her. "It's barely visible. When I saw you this morning, it really seemed much better."

"It's only deep here," she said, pointing near the ear, "but they'll reject me anyway. Plus I'm getting on a bit."

Theresa stopped to look at her. It was true. She was wrinkled, with visible gray hair and sagging flesh. She thought that some men might not care that her face had been scratched.

"Anyhow," Theresa said, "you can't be thinking of continuing with that work now that you're pregnant."

"Oh no?" she said, her laugh sounding bitter. "And how will I eat every day? I don't have a priest infatuated with me who'll pay me to scrawl a few words."

"You could find another trade," she responded without taking her comment to heart. "You cook better than that third-rate baker."

Helga the Black felt flattered, but she shook her head. She knew that nobody would hire a prostitute, not to mention a pregnant one.

"Let's go to the chapter," Theresa suggested.

"Are you mad? They'll send us packing with a boot to the backside."

Theresa's only response was to take her by the hand and ask that she trust her. On the way to the episcopal palace, she told her about the conversation she had had with Alcuin about a job in the kitchen.

At the entrance to the cathedral they asked for Alcuin, who soon appeared. The monk was surprised to see Helga the Black, but once he composed himself, he inquired about the wound on Helga's face, to which she replied with all the gory details. When she had finished speaking, the monk turned away, asking them to follow.

In the kitchen, he introduced them to Favila, a woman so fat she seemed like she was wearing not one but thirty dresses. Alcuin explained that she was in charge of the cooking, and that she was as kind-hearted as she was plump. The woman smiled with mock embarrassment, but when she learned Alcuin's intentions, her expression turned hard.

"Everyone in Fulda knows Helga," she argued. "Once a whore, always a whore, so get out of my kitchen."

Helga turned to leave, but Theresa stopped her.

"Nobody has asked you to lie with her," the young woman blurted out.

Alcuin took out a couple of coins and left them on the table. Then he looked Favila in the eyes. "Have you forgotten the word *forgiveness*? Did Christ not help the lepers, did he not pardon his executioners, or take in Mary Magdalene?"

"I am not a saint like Jesus," she grumbled, though she pocketed the coins.

"While the bishop remains indisposed, this woman is now in your charge. Oh! And she's pregnant," he said, "so do not overwork her. If anyone gives you any grief for it, tell them it was my decision."

"I may be kind hearted, but I'm also fussy as hell about my kitchen. And I know a thing or two about working pregnant. I've had eight children and the last one I almost let drop out of me right here," she said, patting the table where Alcuin had placed the coins. "Come then, get that paint off your face and start peeling onions. And the girl? Is she staying too?"

"She works with me," Alcuin told her.

"But I can help if needed," offered Theresa.

Then Alcuin left the women to their cooking. He only had a couple of days before Lothar recovered, and he wanted to use every last moment to continue his investigation.

Favila proved to be one of those people who overcame her problems by grumbling and stuffing her face. She would complain about everything from her staff's lack of diligence to the cleanliness of the stoves. After each scolding, she would take a bite of a bun or of a loaf of bread dipped in pickling brine, and eventually joy would be restored to the kitchen. She loved children and began to talk about Helga's future baby with such enthusiasm that Theresa thought Favila was the pregnant one.

"Although, I will never understand how something the size of a suckling pig can come out of a tube as wide as a cherry," Favila said to Helga, and upon seeing the color drain from her face, offered her a pastry to bring the color back.

Helga, for her part, aptly demonstrated her culinary skills that first evening by preparing a delicious stew of celery and carrots using the leftovers from the midday meal. Favila enjoyed the casserole and before she had finished eating, the two women were celebrating the result as if they had known each other all their lives.

That night while Theresa made herself comfortable in the straw, she was glad that she had helped Helga the Black. Then she remembered Hoos and a pleasant shiver ran down her neck, back, and legs. She imagined the vigor of his strong, hard body, the taste of his warm lips. She felt guilty that she desired him to be inside her and longed for time to pass so that she would no longer have to sin in his absence. She missed him so much that she thought if he did not return, she would go find him wherever he was. Then she realized she had thought of nothing else since the day of his departure.

JANUARY

17

Helga the Black was not accustomed to rising with the lark, nor used to going to bed early, so when she woke, she rinsed her face and swapped her flamboyant dress from the night before for a dark serge, one that would not cling to her figure. Then she left the storeroom where they had allowed her to sleep and went into the kitchens, which were still empty. She threw a piece of cheese into her mouth and started to clean, singing softly to herself and stroking her belly. When Favila arrived, she found Helga so neat and tidy, with her hair gathered up, and not reeking of sickly sweet perfume, that she thought she was an entirely different woman. The scar across her cheek was the only giveaway that she was the same woman.

Theresa appeared as breakfast was being served, with straw still in her hair, but managed to remove it before Favila and Helga could make fun of her.

"If you're going to help, follow Helga's example. She was already cooking before dawn," Favila reproached Theresa.

Theresa was just glad the cook was beginning to discover all her friend's virtues.

Before going to Lothar's chambers, Alcuin asked God to forgive him for his conduct with the bishop. He regretted having poisoned him, but he had been unable to find another way to prevent the execution of The Swine, who, in his mind, was guilty only of low intelligence. However, now, to alleviate Lothar's symptoms, he had to counteract the effects of the toxin with a syrup of agrimony. He shook the vial vigorously so that the tincture would mix with the thinner. When he entered, he found the prelate stretched out on his four-poster bed. He was breathing heavily, with bags the size of kidney beans under his eyes. When Lothar asked him for his opinion, Alcuin pretended not to know anything. Nevertheless, Lothar accepted the medicine without reservation.

Soon after drinking it, he felt some improvement.

"I suppose you were pleased by the setback," he suggested as he sat up in bed. "But I can assure you that The Swine will meet his death all the same."

"If that is God's will," Alcuin conceded without stating his opinion on the matter. "Tell me—how are you feeling?"

"A bit better now. It's fortunate that you know medicine, especially now that we have no physician. Are you sure you don't know the cause of my indisposition?"

"It might have been something you ate."

"I will speak to the cook. She is the only person who touches my food," he responded irritably.

"Or perhaps something you drank," he said, trying to exonerate Favila.

At that moment Favila waddled in accompanied by a boy with a tray full of food. Lothar looked at the woman without accusation, and his eyes widened when he saw the assortment of delicacies on the menu. Before beginning to eat he looked toward Alcuin and though he found his expression wary, he eagerly dived into the pigeon casserole anyway with Favila proudly standing by to await his verdict. As Lothar picked at the little bones, Alcuin informed him of the situation with Helga the Black.

"A prostitute? Here in the chapter? How dare you!" he sputtered over himself.

"She was desperate. A man attacked her."

"Well, they can employ her somewhere else. By God! We have to set an example here." And he stuffed another pigeon into his mouth.

"That woman can change," the cook interjected. "Not all harlots are the same."

Hearing her speak, Lothar choked. He pulled a bone from his mouth and spat the rest onto the tray. "Of course they are not all the same! There are the *prostibulae*, who ply their trade wherever they can . . . the *ambulatarae*, who work the streets . . . the *lupae*, who offer themselves in forests . . . and even the *bastuariae*, who fornicate in cemeteries. They are all different, but all of them make money in the same way," he said, clutching his groin.

"She does not have to be employed in the clerics' kitchen. She could work here in the palace," Alcuin suggested.

"With these delicious pigeons that Favila makes, why would I need more servants?"

"It wasn't me who cooked them. It was her," the woman explained.

Lothar looked at the plate of pigeon and then at the apple cake, which he surmised must also be the work of Helga the Black since Favila had never prepared it before. He tried it cautiously, and found it sublime.

Hesitating, he muttered, "Very well. But she mustn't leave the kitchen."

Favila turned and left, barely able to contain her smile. When she had gone, the bishop rose to empty his bladder, which he did in front of Alcuin as he rambled on about forgiveness and indulgence.

At the end of the lecture, Alcuin inquired about the chapter's polyptychs, and by then Lothar had lost his energy to wax eloquent. He informed him that he was still a new bishop and so wasn't unacquainted with the details of previous food transactions. However, he referred the monk to his official treasurer for the information he needed.

Alcuin spent the rest of the morning organizing his notes in his cell. He was about go over them again when Theresa appeared, a little before their agreed upon time.

"I wanted to thank you for helping Helga," she said. "From my heart."

Alcuin didn't respond. Instead, he asked her to approach and share in his ruminations. The young woman gave him her full attention. After listening to Alcuin's thoughts, she said, "So, if I understand correctly, the person responsible for the Plague is one of these men."

"For the deaths caused by the sickness. And do not forget that the girl's murderer is also at large."

Theresa went over Alcuin's list. First there was Kohl: The contaminated grain was at his mill, which made him the prime suspect. Then there was Rothaart, the red-haired miller on Kohl's payroll who possessed objects too valuable for a man of his status. And finally there was The Swine—because even if he did not kill the girl, he still drove the cart.

"Are you not forgetting someone?" Theresa asked.

"Of course. But the abbot in charge of the abbey at the time of the Magdeburg Plague died a couple of years ago, so we are left with whoever corrected the polyptych, but all we know about him is that he must be versed in the trade of a scribe."

"So, four in total."

"There might be more, even if we do not know it yet. Now let us analyze who our fourth suspect might be." He brought the candles closer to the desk. "Even if Kohl or Rothaart—or both of them—are indeed involved, the fact remains that someone, in the episcopal palace or in the abbey, has tampered with the polyptych. My theory as to what most likely happened is this: Someone acquired the contaminated wheat cereal in Magdeburg under the premise of burning it, or making use of it despite its condition, and this is the person who is responsible for the recent deaths. The Swine knew about this dubious transaction, though obviously his idiocy meant he never appreciated its significance. However, in time, and for some reason that eludes us, those involved must have feared his tongue would loosen, which is why they cut it to pieces. What's more, I would venture that perhaps these same individuals murdered the girl with the sole intention of incriminating The Swine."

"In that case, we would have to rule out Kohl. He isn't going to kill his own daughter."

"Quite. But I said *perhaps*. It would've been easier, would it not, to eliminate that poor idiot, rather than attempt to incriminate him."

"True."

"Anyhow, we know that The Swine could not have been the perpetrator."

"Then we'll have to find a better suspect with another motive."

"Indeed. Another reason why someone would want to do away with that girl." He stood and began to pace the room.

"And the polyptych? It must have been one of the monks who can write, and who also has access to the episcopal scriptorium," Theresa suggested.

"Well, not exactly. The polyptych is kept by the abbey administrator, who is also the prior. In the episcopal palace the task falls to the subdeacon. But the chapter would also have access to it, for it is they who finalize the accounts of the mill."

"I have never understood the workings of a monastery." She leant back in her chair with disinterest.

"Generally, a monastery or abbey is always in the charge of an abbot. In his absence, the prior takes charge. If a monastery does not have an abbot, then the prior performs his duties, and the abbey is called a priory. Then there are the deans of the order, who are responsible for ensuring that the monks attend the services and perform their duties. There is also the vicar of the choir, responsible for the library and the secretariat, and the sacristan, who looks after the church."

"None of them would have been involved in provisioning?"

"Only the abbot and the priors. Any of them could have arranged the transaction without raising suspicion. Trade is handled by the treasurer, in charge of money and supplies, the cellarer, responsible for victualing, and the estate manager and guest master, who look after the land and the optimates' residence. The chamberlains just have responsibility for the monks' clothes, and as for the refectorian and the procurator, I don't think either of them would have been involved."

"And the infirmarian and apothecary?"

"You know already that the apothecary was poisoned to death. And as for the rest of the monks, well I would put my hand in fire for them."

"We could list their names."

"The truth is I only know the names of the abbey monks, the late Abbot Boethius, and the two priors, secretary Ludwig and Agrippinus. The rest of them I only know by their role."

"So what do you suggest?"

"We have a couple of days before they organize another execution. And we have a number of names to consider. We have Kohl, Rothaart, Lothar, Ludwig, Agrippinus, and The Swine, who I have no doubt harbors the key to this labyrinthine puzzle."

"If only we could speak to him."

"After what has happened, it's now impossible. But it wouldn't be a bad idea to talk to Kohl's wife about the circumstances of how she discovered her daughter's body."

They agreed that Alcuin should speak with Kohl's wife that day, while Theresa would stay to reexamine the polyptychs. She was not enamored by the idea, but neither did she protest, for she did not feel like returning to Kohl's mill, either. However, after a time leafing through the codices, she decided she would be more useful if she went to investigate The Swine.

Theresa arrived in the vicinity of the slaughterhouse with the sun spilling onto the maze of narrow streets. Around her townspeople were herding livestock toward the nearby pastures, while the women were out with their little ones, as white as snow. A neighbor greeted her, used to seeing her go past every day. The woman made a comment about the weather, and Theresa cheerfully paid her respects, feeling as if she were now a small part of Fulda, which was turning out to be a captivating town.

As she arrived at the slaughterhouse, she recognized the same guard who had stood in their way on the Saturday morning. He was sitting in the same spot by the door, a stick in one hand and a piece of pork belly in the other, which he gnawed on with his few remaining teeth. When she came close, she noticed that he still reeked of wine. The man, on the other hand, did not seem to recognize her, for he glanced at her and then continued to chew on the pork belly as if his life depended on it. After a moment's hesitation, Theresa took out a slice of oat cake and offered it to the guard.

"I'll give it to you if you let me see The Swine," she proposed.

The guard looked greedily at the cake. Then he snatched it from her and bit into it eagerly. He kept munching as if the young woman was transparent, and when he had finished, he ordered her to leave. Theresa was infuriated.

"Go away or you'll get the end of my stick," the guard snapped.

Theresa understood that he would never let her in. She decided to wait in the area until someone came to relieve him, but while she walked she remembered the little window that Alcuin had opened on their last visit. If no one was on guard, perhaps she could enter through it.

She circled the slaughterhouse looking for the window. At the rear, a dozen tiny buildings were packed together as if they had been smashed together. They were the old huts that once belonged to the butchers, but most of them now were occupied by carpentry, cooperage, and cart-repair workshops. She went into a half-collapsed building that looked like it might lead into the slaughterhouse. Upon entering, she was greeted by a one-eyed man wearing a leather apron, who turned out to be the owner of the smithy. Theresa asked him to sharpen her scramasax and feigned an interest in the objects lying about in the inner courtyard. She asked for permission to take a look and went deeper into the smithy with her eyes fixed on the timber walls covered in mallets, wedges, hammers, and cold chisels hanging from hooks like sausages. There was a smell of hot metal, which she welcomed given the cold. To one side, a great door connected the storeroom to an enclosure, which Theresa assumed belonged to the slaughterhouse. Suddenly she felt an arm on her shoulder.

"What is it?" she asked, surprised by the blacksmith.

"That there?" he said looking at the enclosure. "The pen where they kept the animals before they cut their throats," he said with a laugh. "Here, your scramasax."

He did not charge her for sharpening the blade, but told her to bring money the next time. When Theresa exited the smithy, she jumped with joy. She had found the window into the slaughterhouse, and best of all she could see that it was still open. Now she just had to find a way to distract the blacksmith.

She was about to bite into her last piece of oat cake when a young lad with an old man's face planted himself directly in front of her. Aside from his bangs, the youngster was all skin and bones.

"Do you want a piece?" she offered, a plan formulating in her mind.

Luckily the boy was both hungry and gullible. He eagerly took the cake and said he was delighted to come to the rescue of a great lady traveling in disguise. He ran into the smithy, reappearing with the one-eyed blacksmith, and together they headed for the place where Theresa had said her carriage and footmen had come to a halt. When they had left, Theresa dashed into the courtyard, but as she arrived at the window she froze, second-guessing whether it was a good idea to enter the slaughterhouse. She wasn't sure she was doing the right thing. The Swine might be unchained and decide to attack her, and it was even possible that the monk was wrong about his innocence and he really was a murderer. Yet, something inside her drove her to continue. She wanted to be useful, to find out who was behind it all. She looked back, fearing that the blacksmith might return at any moment.

Scanning her surroundings, her eyes fell on the tools hanging from the wall. She noticed a heavy hammer, which she ruled out taking after realizing she could not even unhook it, so she appropriated a light poker, which she tied to her belt. Then she stacked several planks of wood under the window and climbed to the top so she could just reach the window ledge.

At that moment she heard someone returning, so she lifted herself up, making the pile of timber under her feet collapse. She clambered up the wall, managed to pull the rest of her body through the window, and then plunged into the terrifying darkness of the slaughterhouse.

When she stood, she felt a pain in her bones as if she had slept on a bed of stone all night. She must have hurt her left elbow, for she could hardly move it. At that moment she heard someone handling the window she had just come through. When she looked up, she saw the blacksmith's face appear, so she quickly curled up in the darkest corner and waited for fear he might see her. The man looked inside but couldn't see anything in the pitch black. Raising his eyebrow, he suddenly left. Theresa supposed the one-eyed smith was returning to his workshop, but some banging told her he intended to seal the window. When the hammer blows stopped, there was a gloomy silence broken only by the thumping of her heart. She had never been anywhere so dark and imagined this was what it was like to be blind. Then she mentally kicked herself, thinking that not even the most brainless buffoon would have committed such a stupid act. She was alone, in the dark. Locked in a building with a half-wit who might be a murderer. How could she have been so foolish? She didn't even have any tinder or a steel to light a torch.

She crouched there in silence, listening to her own heavy breathing that sounded labored, like an old woman with a scraping wheeze. She soon realized the blacksmith was long gone. She stood, sliding her hands along the wall in an attempt to feel something that would help orient herself. Again, she felt the greasiness of the walls and she suddenly retched. After several attempts she located the window, nailed shut with some boards.

She was a prisoner: trapped.

Gripping the poker, she brandished it in front of her as she walked on blindly, waving the implement in the air while the other arm felt for the shackles and chains that covered the walls of the corridor. As she advanced she was gradually able to make out the end of the corridor. First she saw just a shadow, then a squat figure in the half-light, huddled into a ball—and finally she could tell it was him. In the scant light filtering through the roof, The Swine lay curled up on the ground, hugging his deformed legs as if he were a great fetus.

He seemed to be sleeping, but Theresa could not see any chains restraining him. That filled her with fear. The thought occurred to her that she could still back out, call the guard, and explain everything. She would be scolded and might even receive a couple of blows from his stick, but at least she would escape with her life. The Swine gave a sudden jerk, and Theresa managed to stifle a scream.

She looked at him again more closely and saw that indeed he was sleeping, but when he moved a little, she saw a glint at his ankles, and thanked the heavens when she realized it was the reflection of chains.

She took a deep breath before continuing, then moved forward until she was within a step of his broken bowl that still contained some scraps of food in it. If she were any closer, The Swine might be able to reach her. She crouched down to observe him more closely. His tangled hair was covered in filth, his clothes were in tatters, and his skin was covered in dried blood. In his sleep, his eyelids remained half-open, revealing expressionless little eyes, like a pig whose life had been cut short. He was breathing with difficulty and from time to time he coughed, giving Theresa a fright.

Using the poker she probed one of The Swine's feet, which shrank back as though it had been stung by a bee. Theresa gave a start, but she poked him again until he woke. He seemed dazed, as if he could not understand what was happening. But before long his eyes fell on her. He was surprised to see her and retreated as far as his chains would allow. Theresa was glad he feared her, but even so, she kept wielding the poker purposefully. If he tried to attack her, she would sink it into his head.

After observing her for a while, The Swine moved closer. He was hobbling like an old drunk, dragging a lifeless foot. Theresa saw that his eyes contained no malice.

They remained silently watching each other for a while. Finally, Theresa rummaged around in her pockets.

"It's all I have," she said, offering him the remains of the oat cake.

The Swine held out his trembling hands, but Theresa decided to leave the pieces on the bowl and step back a few paces. She watched the man try to pick them up without success before sinking his face into the dish and licking it like an animal. When he had finished, he uttered something unintelligible that Theresa interpreted as some kind of thanks.

"We will get you out of here," she said, not knowing how she would fulfill such a promise. "But first I need your help. Do you understand?"

The man nodded, making a guttural sound. Theresa repeated question after question until she was convinced that the poor wretch was truly a half-wit. He responded with meaningless gestures, poked about in the bowl with his deformed hands or simply glanced from side to side. However, when he heard the name of the redhead, he started hitting himself on the head as if he had lost his senses. When Theresa repeated the name Rothaart, The Swine showed her the raw stump of his severed tongue.

At that moment she heard the screech of a bolt at the other end of the passage. She hid in a cubbyhole just in time to avoid being seen by the guard who approached bearing a torch. Theresa gestured to The Swine to be silent and remained out of sight until the guard passed. Then she ran with all the speed she could muster toward the exit. She did not stop until she reached the abbey.

When she found Alcuin, she had to wait to catch her breath before she could inform him of her findings. She tried to tell him everything all at once, gesticulating with her arms and stumbling over her words, while Alcuin attempted to make sense out of her blather. Theresa sucked in some air before blurting out, "I know who the culprit is," she announced with a triumphant smile.

She told him again, this time more slowly, the events that had transpired at the slaughterhouse, taking pleasure in recounting the most gory details and leaving the big surprise to the end. Alcuin listened attentively.

"You should not have gone alone," he reproached her.

"And that was when," she added, ignoring him, "hearing the redhead's name, he hit himself with such force I thought he would split open his head. He showed me what that man did to his tongue. It was horrible."

"Did he tell you that Rothaart did it?"

"Well, not exactly. But I'm certain of it."

"Even so, he's not the one we're looking for."

"I don't understand. What do you mean?"

"Rothaart was found dead this morning. At Kohl's mill. Ergot poisoning."

Theresa let herself flop, dejected. It was not possible. She had risked her life for nothing. She was about to argue with him when the monk cut in.

"And not just that. It would seem that our man is rushing to sell all the flour. Since this morning people have been falling sick all over the place. Saint John's Church is crammed full, and the hospital is overrun."

"But in that case it'll be easy to catch him."

"And how do you propose we do that? He is clearly very cunning, and is most likely selling batches of putrid flour alongside batches in good condition. What's more, remember that nobody is aware that wheat is the source of the illness."

"Even so, we can question the sick. Or their relatives, if necessary."

"Do you think I have not already done so? But people don't just buy their flour from the mills. They also acquire it from the market, from houses, from farms. They eat it in taverns, at bakeries or at peddlers' stalls. They share bread at work, use flour to pay for their purchases, or trade it for meat or wine. Sometimes they even mix wheat with rye flour so that it holds up longer in the oven." He paused to reflect. "Each sick person told me a different story. It's as if the entire town has been infected."

"It's all very odd. If this man is as clever as you say—"

"He is, I'm sure of it."

"Then he will have contact with the various flour traders. And they trust him."

"Presumably."

"So, perhaps he has distributed the contaminated batches far and wide so that there are more suspects."

"You mean more accomplices?"

"Not necessarily." Theresa was feeling important. "He could have deposited the batches in various storehouses without their owners knowing. This would explain why there are so many more getting sick from purchasing flour at so many different outlets."

"Perhaps," Alcuin admitted.

"And what's more, there's the matter of The Swine."

"What of him?"

"Well, the fact that it was the redhead who cut his tongue out."

* * *

The redhead cut out his tongue. Alcuin pondered the idea as he and Theresa made their way to the hospital. What if he had been rash in drawing his conclusions? In truth he had only seen Rothaart's body from a distance, and though he thought he had seen signs of gangrene on his limbs, perhaps his death had not been due to ergot. In fact, it was difficult to believe that a healthy and well-fed man could succumb so quickly to rot.

"I must return to Kohl's mill," he announced to Theresa. "You continue to the hospital. Record the names of those who have recently fallen sick. Note everything—where they come from and where they buy their bread, what they have recently eaten, and when they started to feel unwell. Anything you can think of that may help us. Then go back to the chapter. We will meet at the cathedral after Sext." And without giving her time to respond, he turned and ran off into the narrow streets.

When Theresa reached the monastery, she came across crowds of people streaming in through its open gates. It seemed that the influx of sick was so great that the cellarer and other monks had been sent to the hospital to help in whatever way they could. Theresa used Alcuin's ring that he had given her, in order to jump ahead of the long lines of relatives of the sick who were waiting for news. Entering the hospital she was received by an infirmarian, who, after recognizing her, impressed on her that she should not get in the way of the monks desperately running to and fro like bees in a hive.

Theresa did not know where to begin. The sick filled the room, scattered around on improvised beds, while outside in the courtyard, the less severe patients awaited anything that might alleviate their pain. Some of them seemed seriously ill, with pain in their limbs or afflicted by hallucinations, but many of them were mostly terrified.

Speaking to them, she discovered that the bishop and his secretary had met to discuss the possibility of burning houses and closing the city walls. She was surprised. On other occasions she had heard of such measures, but in this case, the pestilence was limited to the flour that was poisoned with the ergot fungus. She thought that she must convince Alcuin to change his mind about not revealing the cause of the sickness.

Within two hours, Theresa had gathered enough information to determine that at least eleven of the patients had not ingested any wheat bread. When she completed her questioning, she gathered her things and returned to the chapter kitchens. There she found Helga the Black busy polishing some pans that looked like they had been used as plant pots. Seeing Theresa, the woman stopped what she was doing and ran to greet her. She told her that the entire city was in a state of anxiety because of the Plague.

"Don't even think about eating wheat bread," she said, and then immediately thought that Alcuin would be angry that she had revealed their secret. She realized that, actually, they should not consume any kind of bread.

Helga the Black told Theresa that Alcuin had just deposited a sack of wheat from Kohl's mill in the pantry and told her that nobody must touch it. As soon as she heard this, Theresa disobeyed his instruction. She went to the sack and took a handful using a linen cloth. Then she examined one of the grains. On the fourth handful she found the first ergot. She assumed Alcuin had discovered this, too.

Just before Sext, Alcuin appeared bearing news. He said he had visited Kohl's mill, but—it would appear—they had taken the red-head's body far from the city, to the hollow where they burned the corpses of lepers. Fortunately, he located the body before it had been cast into the fire.

"He was not killed by the ergot," he said triumphantly. "They painted his legs to look gangrenous. They must have poisoned him because a few witnesses said he died in terrible agony. That was what misled me."

Painted. Theresa remembered Althar's ruse to feign leprosy. "But who would do that?"

"I don't know yet. The only thing that is clear to me is that whoever killed him wanted his death to go unnoticed. However, I established a couple of things: First, Kohl's wife did not catch The Swine finishing off his victim. It was another woman—Lorraine, one of the family's servants. I spoke to her, and she confirmed that she saw the half-wit over the dead girl, but not clearly enough to assert that he had killed her. She also gave me a vital piece of information: The gash on the young woman's face was on the left side, from her ear to the middle of her throat. She remembered it because she had to seal the wound in order to shroud her."

"And what does that mean?"

"Quite simply, someone left-handed must have dealt the lethal blow."

"Like Rothaart, for instance."

Alcuin nodded. "And Kohl provided me with a sample sack of wheat, but without accounting for its provenance. After apologizing for my behavior on the day of the execution, I pressed him to sell me some wheat, which he agreed to do without too many objections. But he did say that it would take him a couple of days to procure. To my surprise, he gave me a sack so that I could verify its quality."

"I've seen it. It's riddled with ergot," Theresa confirmed.

"You should not have touched it," he protested.

Theresa pulled out the cloth and showed him the little black capsules. Alcuin shook his head. "At any rate, our list of suspects continues to narrow," he added. "Now it consists only of Kohl and the priors Ludwig and Agrippinus."

"And Lothar?"

"I ruled out the bishop some time ago. Remember that Lothar did not object to us checking the chapter's polyptychs. No. His innocence is beyond doubt. As for Agrippinus, we should remove him from the list: He has also fallen sick, and I do not think he will live."

"At this rate, all of our suspects will die."

"It would be a solution," he said with bitterness.

Theresa fiddled with her hair. The list of suspects now consisted of just Kohl and the prior Ludwig. She could not understand why Alcuin would not take action once and for all.

"You should reveal the source of the illness," she finally said. "Dozens are sick now. Women and children will soon fill the cemeteries," she pleaded.

"We have already talked about that," he responded with a grim expression. "As soon as people know ergot is the cause of the Plague, the culprit will mill all the contaminated grain and hide it, and we will never know who it is."

"But by warning them, we will save people's lives."

"Save them from what? Dying of sickness rather than hunger? What do you think they will eat if they cannot have wheat or rye?"

"At least they could decide the manner of their death," she retorted in irritation.

Alcuin took a deep breath, his teeth clenched. The girl was the most pigheaded creature he had ever come up against. She would never understand that not even closing the mills would stop the murderer. Such a killer would just grind the grain manually or sell it immediately to some unscrupulous person—or even take it to another city to continue his business. Alcuin tried to explain, but it was useless.

"People are dying now," she continued. "Not tomorrow, not in a month's time. Do you not see? It is now or never," she insisted.

"These deaths are like God's eyes," explained Alcuin. "Or do you think that the lives lost now are more valuable than those that will be lost in a few months?"

"All I know is that the abbey is full of sick people who don't understand what their sin has been," said Theresa, now crying with rage. "For that is what they believe: that they have sinned and that God is punishing them."

"Clearly you are still too young to understand certain matters. If you wish to help, go back to the scriptorium and continue copying the *Hypotyposeis* texts."

"But Father—"

"Go back to the scriptorium."

"But—"

"Or would you rather return to the tavern?"

Theresa bit her tongue. She thought to herself that were it not for Helga the Black's pregnancy, she would've told Alcuin he could go take his texts and sleep in the dung tonight. Finally, she walked off without saying a word.

* * *

After reproducing several paragraphs, Theresa absentmindedly screwed up the parchment. Why shouldn't she ask for help, she thought. If the bishop wasn't a prime suspect, why not tell him what was happening? She was sure that Lothar could contribute to solving the problem. He knew the suspects, he was familiar with how the abbey operated, and he knew how a mill was run. She simply couldn't understand Alcuin's behavior, yet she had no option but to abide by his decisions.

She took out a new parchment and began again until the quill broke under the pressure. When she went to find another, she discovered that none remained in the little chest where Alcuin kept his writing materials. So she went to the kitchen to procure a new one. There she found that Favila was a bundle of nerves. She asked after Helga the Black, but the woman did not seem to hear her. She just stood there scratching her legs and arms.

"What's the matter?" Theresa asked, speaking up.

"It's this damned plague. I think your friend may have infected me," she answered, still scratching herself.

"Helga?" Theresa's hands pressed against her mouth.

"Don't even think about going near her," Favila said, pointing to an adjoining room before submerging her arms in a basin of cold water. Theresa ignored her and ran toward the chamber. She found Helga the Black prostrate on the floor. She was trembling like a fawn and her legs were turning blue.

"God almighty! Helga! What has happened to you?"

The woman did not respond. She merely carried on sobbing.

"Get up! You must go to the abbey. They will look after you there." She tried to pull her up but could not. "He told me not to bother. That they would not take in a prostitute."

"Who told you that?"

"Your friend the monk. That damned Alcuin. He ordered me to stay here until he found me somewhere to go."

Theresa returned to the kitchen and asked Favila for her help, but the woman refused, still washing her arms in cold water. Theresa snatched the basin and threw it against the wall, making it smash into pieces.

"Alcuin said—" Favila began.

"I don't care what Alcuin said. I'm fed up with that man," she cried. Then she turned and left the kitchen. As she walked in the direction of the palace, she cursed the British monk over and over again. Now she better understood Hoos Larsson's warning about him. Alcuin was a cold-blooded man, concerned only with his books and nothing else. She remembered that if she hadn't refused to continue writing, he would never have agreed to help her friend Helga the Black. But all of that was about to end. It was about time Lothar knew just what kind of a man Brother Alcuin was.

When the old secretary saw her appear, he tried to stop her, but he was unable to prevent her from bursting into the bishop's chamber. Theresa stumbled upon Lothar urinating with his back to her. She turned to avoid seeing him but did not leave the room. When she heard the trickle subside, she counted to three and then wheeled back around.

Lothar turned around and looked at her with a mixture of astonishment and irritation. "May I ask what the devil you are doing here?"

"Forgive me, Your Eminence, but I needed to see you."

"But who . . . ? You're not that girl who follows Alcuin around everywhere, I hope! Get out of here immediately!"

"Father. You must listen to me." An acolyte tried to expel her, but Theresa shoved him away. "I must speak to you about the Plague."

On hearing the word *plague*, Lothar simmered down. He arched an eyebrow and adjusted his breeches. Then he donned a robe and looked at her skeptically.

"What plague are you referring to?"

"The one that has gripped the city. Alcuin has uncovered its source and we know how to stop it."

"Sin is the source of the Plague, and this is our only cure," he said, signaling toward a crucifix.

"You are wrong. It's the wheat."

"The wheat?" He gestured for the secretary to leave them. "What do you mean the wheat?"

"According to the chapter's polyptychs, some batches of contaminated wheat were acquired and transported to Fulda nearly four years ago—during the pestilence of Magdeburg. Until recently whoever acquired it was selling it at long intervals so that nobody would link the illness to the wheat, but lately the perpetrator has flooded the markets. The sick and dying are rapidly increasing and nobody is doing anything to prevent it."

"But what you're telling me is . . . are you sure?"

"We found something at Kohl's mill. A poison that corrupts the cereal."

"And Kohl is responsible?"

"I don't know. Alcuin suspects two individuals: the prior Ludwig and Kohl himself."

"By God's bones! And why didn't he come to me himself?"

"That is what I asked him. He mistrusts even you. He is obsessed with catching the culprit, but all he does is wait while folks continue to die." She broke into tears. "Even my friend Helga the Black has fallen ill."

"I will speak to him immediately," he said, putting on his shoes.

"No, please. If he finds out that I told you, I don't know what he'll do to me."

"But we must do something. Did you say Boethius, Kohl, and Ludwig? Why those three and no one else?"

Theresa told him everything she knew. After answering Lothar's questions, she felt better, for the bishop seemed like he was keen to put an end to the problem. "I will give the order to arrest the suspects. As for your friend . . . what did you say her name was?"

"Helga the Black."

"That's it, Helga. I will request that she is taken to the chapter infirmary with orders that they do everything they can for her there."

They agreed that Theresa would return to the scriptorium but remain in the episcopal palace should Lothar need her. When she came out of the bishop's chambers, she noticed the secretary looking at her as if he wanted to thrash her.

Before going back to the scriptorium, Theresa decided to check up on Helga. She didn't know whether they would be able to find a cure for the sickness, but she assumed that the news of her imminent transfer to the hospital would at least console her a little. However, when she arrived at the kitchen, Helga was not in the room. She asked everyone she could find, but nobody knew where she had gone.

* * *

The rest of Theresa's day proceeded without her hearing from either Lothar or Alcuin. She was relieved not to see the monk. But Helga the Black's disappearance concerned her greatly. Before dinner she decided to leave the palace to wander for a while. She had not eaten for some time, but the truth was that pangs of remorse had taken away her appetite. She didn't know whether *she* had done the right thing, but at least she could hope that Lothar would do the right thing and close the mills, making the Plague disappear forever.

As she walked she could not stop thinking about her friend Helga. She had searched for her in the kitchens, in the pantries, at the infirmary. She went back to her abandoned tavern and to the house of the neighbor who had taken her in the day that Widukind had beaten her so severely. She even asked around the streets where the most bedraggled prostitutes plied their trade, but there was no trace of her to be found.

Nothing. It was as if the earth had swallowed her up. Then she remembered Alcuin, and her stomach tightened. She didn't know why she was filled with so much unease since she had acted out of good conscience.

Suddenly, she longed to be with Hoos Larsson. She missed his smile, his sky-blue eyes, his little jokes about the size of her hips, and his entertaining stories about Aquis-Granum. He was the only person who made her feel good, and the only person she could trust. She yearned for him so much she would have given everything she had to feel his caresses for even one moment.

Her walk ended in front of the city's great gates, an impressive lattice of timber, hawthorn, and metal beams that protected the main entrance into Fulda. At the top, sharpened tree trunks stood in a line like a row of teeth flickering in the reddish glow of the torches. The many repairs that had been made to the gates gave them the appearance of a dying structure.

Though there were other entrances, they were less well defended. On either side of the gates, a stone wall was erected to protect the city. Inside the walls, numerous homes were built directly up against it so that the city's fortifications served simultaneously as one of the walls of their home. This design made it difficult for the garrison to guard the wall with ease. However, the defenses only encircled part of the town, the oldest quarter. The original wall was built when the town was just the monastery and its orchards.

But with the city's continual expansion, a proliferation of buildings had spilled into previously empty fields. The new expansion of the wall would protect the extensive suburbs from any possible attack.

Each night the secondary gates were barred and only the main entrance was left open. However, that evening the main gates were also closed, turning the city into an impregnable bastion. Theresa thought that perhaps the bishop had ordered them shut to prevent the criminal from escaping. But one of the guards told her that late in the day several peasants had spotted armed strangers, and though they were probably just bandits, they had decided to take precautions.

Lost in thought, Theresa suddenly became aware of a clamor of frightened folks banging on the other side of the gate, demanding entry to the town. She watched as the guards discussed it with their superior. Then one of the guards left the turret and went down to open the gate. Theresa watched as another guard threw buckets of water on the people who were trying to squeeze through before the gates were opened. Another two guards positioned themselves on each side of the gate armed with spears. The guard on top of the gate shouted down to the unruly mob, warning them that he would not open the gates if they didn't settle down. This seemed to have a temporary calming effect. But as soon as the bolts were released, the mob pushed through the entry, making the sentries retreat in alarm. Theresa stood aside as a flood of people shoved their way past. Men, women, and children loaded with belongings and animals stormed into the enclosure as if the Devil were pursuing them. When the last person was inside, the guards closed the gates and went back up to the turret.

One of the townsfolk approached Theresa, eager for conversation. "Many have stayed outside thinking they won't attack, but they won't catch me unawares again," he said, showing her an old scar on his belly.

Theresa didn't know what to think. Those who had just gained entry seemed like they were fleeing the Apocalypse, and yet they were only a small fraction of everyone who lived outside the protection of the city walls. When she asked the man why everybody didn't want entry, he told her that not everyone believed an attack was imminent.

Fear made Theresa decide to return to the abbey. But first she went by Helga's old tavern, in case she had decided to return to her former home. She found it still empty, so she made for the episcopal palace to check the kitchens before retiring for the night. But, yet again, there was no sign of her friend. She only found Favila, who reproached her for bringing a prostitute to the chapter. "I knew that she would do the dirty on us at the first opportunity," she declared, without giving her a chance to reply.

Theresa left without saying a word. In the stables, she pondered the events: a young woman murdered, dozens of townspeople poisoned, a monk she didn't know whether to trust, and her only friend suddenly gone as if by magic. In her prayers she remembered her family. She thought of Hoos and Helga the Black. Then she made herself comfortable among the hay bales and waited for dawn.

But at midnight she was awakened by a sudden racket. From every direction she heard shouting and hurried footsteps, some running. Several clerics came into the stables bearing torches to saddle a couple of the animals.

Frightened, Theresa rose and ran to Favila's chambers, where she found the woman pacing up and down, her flesh dancing about under a simple robe. She was about to ask what was happening when the banging of drums interrupted. The two women ran upstairs to the roof terrace with views of the entire city and found themselves looking down on a surprising scene: All along the main street, which was illuminated by dozens of torches, amid cheers and applause, rode a procession of riders led by a man clad in steel, escorted by a troupe of drummers. Despite the late hour, dozens of onlookers greeted the horseman as if he were God Himself and His cohorts. Favila crossed herself and ran downstairs crying out with joy, while Theresa followed behind, still feeling clueless.

Back in the kitchen while lighting the stoves, Favila said, "Don't you know? The great monarch has arrived. Our King Charlemagne."

18

Theresa had never imagined that the king's presence could cause such a stir. That night she had to vacate the stables, since the clergy used it to accommodate the royal horses and servants. She moved to the room that Favila had in the palace pantries. However, not long after she tried to retire for the second time that night, the king's cooks took over the kitchens, filling them with geese, pheasants, and ducks that honked and quacked like demons for the rest of the night.

The next morning, the chapter was a hive of activity. Clerics ran to and fro, laden with plants with which to adorn the cathedral for the holy services. The busy kitchen staff prepared dishes of roasted meats, vegetables, and delicate pastries. The maidservants cleaned every nook and cranny. And Lothar's acolytes rushed to move the bishop's belongings to an adjoining chamber—for his room would be occupied by Charlemagne.

When Favila ordered Theresa to join the other servants in the refectory, Theresa felt there was little point in trying to explain that she only received orders from Alcuin. She tried anyway, but her argument fell on deaf ears. With a shove Favila ushered her into the refectory to help the others.

When Theresa walked into the dining hall she found it decked out with religious tapestries in sumptuous reds and blues. The central table had been replaced by three long boards laid on U-shaped trestles, opposite the entrance. Theresa arranged a row of green apples on the colorful linen tablecloths, already adorned with centerpieces of cyclamens, garlands, and violets—the winter flowers that were cultivated in the gardens. Several rows of stools lined each side of the tables, except for the central area, cleared to accommodate the throne and other armchairs that the king and his favorites would use.

The cooks had prepared a feast for a legion of hungry men, with no shortage of capon and duck still with their plumage, scrambled pheasant eggs, grilled ox, lamb shoulders, pork ribs and fillets, kidney stews, offal, accompaniments of cabbage, turnip, and radish dressed in garlic and pepper, boiled artichokes, an array of sausages and cold meats, bean salads, roast rabbit, pickled quails, strudels, and a myriad of desserts made with honey and rye flour.

On the way back to the kitchen, Theresa heard the head cook asking Favila if she had any *garum*. Seemingly, the monarch loved the condiment, but the expedition had left their stocks behind in Aquis-Granum. Favila explained hesitantly that she had started the process some time ago, but then gave up when she tasted it. Bringing it out, the head cook, Theresa, and Favila all took a sample and all three immediately spit it out.

"I know how to fix it," Theresa said, remembering what Leonora had taught her about how it could be doctored up with spices. "With your permission, of course."

Before the man could object, Theresa ran to the pantry and returned laden with aromatic herbs from the garden along with some salt. After following the steps just as Leonora had shown her, she poured the liquid into a large spoon, which she then handed to the cook.

"How is it now?"

The man tried it and looked at her in amazement.

"Well, blow me down! Charlemagne will be pleased! Let's see, you two," he snapped, addressing a couple of servants. "Leave those dressings and come and help this girl prepare more *garum*. I must say, if your stews are as good as your condiments, I'm sure you will have no trouble finding a wealthy husband."

Theresa blushed and thought of Hoos Larsson. She hoped that he would be her husband. Even though she wasn't sure if he had money, her heart fluttered when she thought about how handsome he was.

When the cook told Favila that Charlemagne wanted to congratulate the person who had made the condiment, Favila started trembling, insisting it was Theresa who should get the credit. She smoothed Theresa's hair, pinched her cheeks until they lit up like a newborn's, and gave her a clean apron to wear. Then she ushered her off, calling her a cheeky rascal. However, Theresa took her by the hand and forced her to go to the refectory with her.

As the women approached, they were surprised by the sheer number of waiters, maids, and servants milling about near the entrance. The cook showing them the way pushed past some glaring onlookers, clearing a path through the crowd to the door of the dining hall. He told them to wait until the lector had recited the psalms.

While the cleric read, Theresa observed Charlemagne standing in the center of the hall. The monarch's colossal stature made the young woman next to him seem like a dwarf. Charlemagne was dressed in a short cloak as substantial as a napkin on his great body, a woolen overcoat, baggy trousers, and leather boots. His face, shaven in the Frankish way, sported a large unruly moustache that contrasted with the rest of his hair, neatly gathered into a long ponytail. Behind him, Alcuin and Lothar waited patiently at the front of his retinue, which included a cohort of elegantly attired prelates.

When the lector finished, they all sat and started to breakfast, which was when the cook asked Theresa to follow him. They crossed the room and he introduced her to the king, whom Theresa acknowledged with a ridiculous curtsy. Charlemagne regarded her as though he did not understand what was happening.

"The *garum* girl," the cooked informed him.

Charlemagne's eyes widened, surprised by her youth. Then he congratulated her and continued to eat as if nothing had happened. Before she could even think of something to say, Theresa felt the cook grasp her arm and pull her toward the exit.

She was about to return to the kitchens when Favila suggested she wait and help her clear the tables. The two women stood together at one end of the room, observing the dignitaries devouring their feast as if it were their last meal. While the guests breakfasted, dozens of clerics, vassals, landowners, and artisans paraded through the refectory to pay tribute to the monarch.

Theresa noticed the entrance of the refined, little man who had bought Althar's bear. Behind him followed a rosy-cheeked servant holding a tray as if it were a dish of food, but on it was the head of the beast that she had hunted herself during her time at the bear caves. The little man crossed the hall and bowed before the king. Then, after a brief explanation, he stepped aside so the servant could place the animal's head among the plates of food. Charlemagne stood to admire its beauty. He said something about the bear's eyes, to which the little man responded with more bows. The king thanked him for his gift, which he had someone position at one end of the table, and then he dismissed the man who retreated backward, bowing repeatedly.

Since the head had ended up near Theresa, she decided to examine it to see what had caught Charlemagne's attention. She could see that one of the eyes had come loose in its socket, making it appear a little less fierce. She thought that it wouldn't be difficult to repair, so she took hold of a knife and—without waiting for permission—started to cut the stitching that ran to the damaged eye. She had almost opened it fully when someone grabbed her from behind.

"May I ask what the devil you are doing?" It was the little, rich man, shouting so that everyone could hear him.

Theresa explained that she was trying to fix the eye, but the man gave her a slap that made her fall flat on her face. One of the cooks ran toward Theresa to drag her out before the little man could do her any more harm. But right then, the king stood and asked them to pick her up. "Come here," he ordered.

Theresa obeyed, trembling.

"I was only . . ." she fell silent, ashamed.

"She was trying to ruin my bear head," the little man interrupted.

"You mean, *my* head," Charlemagne corrected him. "Is that true? You wanted to ruin it?" he asked Theresa.

When the young woman tried to answer, all she could manage was a thin, little voice. "I was just trying to put the eye back in place."

"And that's why you were slitting the face open?" said the king in surprise.

"I was not slitting it, Your Highness. I was just cutting the stitching."

"And a liar, too!" interjected the little man. At that moment, Alcuin whispered something to the king, who nodded.

"Cutting the stitching . . ." Charlemagne examined the head closely. "How could you have cut it, if the stitching isn't even visible?"

"I know where it is because it was me who sewed it," she declared.

Hearing her response, everyone except Alcuin burst into laughter.

"I see that I will have to agree with you," the king said to the little man who had branded her a liar.

"I promise you I am not lying. First I hunted the bear, then I sewed it," Theresa insisted. The laughter stopped, replaced by a stunned silence. Not even those closest to the king would dare to make such a joke. Charlemagne himself changed his condescending expression.

"And I can prove it," she added.

The monarch arched an eyebrow. Until then the young woman had seemed likeable, but her effrontery was starting to verge on foolishness. He could not decide whether to order her flogged, or to simply dismiss her, but something in her eyes stopped him.

"In that case, show me," said the king, ordering silence. Only the chewing of food could be heard in the hall.

Theresa looked at Charlemagne with resolve. Then, in front of the amazed faces of everyone present, she told in full detail the story of the hunt in which she helped Althar bring down the animal. When she had finished the story, not even a belch could be heard in the room.

"So you killed the bear by shooting it with a crossbow? I must admit that your fable is truly fabulous, but all it proves is that you are a bare-faced liar," declared Charlemagne sententiously.

Theresa understood that she had to convince him soon or they would remove her from there with force. She quickly took the animal's head in her arms. "If what I am saying is false, then how is it possible that I know what it contains?"

"Inside?" Charlemagne asked, intrigued.

"Inside the head. It is filled with beaver skin."

Without waiting for permission, she broke the stitching and pulled out a ball of fur, which she let fall onto the table. She unrolled it so that everyone could see that it was a damaged beaver pelt. Charlemagne looked at her gravely.

"So it was you who killed it."

Theresa bit her lip. She looked around her until her eyes fell on the pile of weapons where the men-at-arms had left them before eating. Without saying a word, she crossed the hall and took hold of a crossbow that was lying on a chest. A soldier drew his sword, but Charlemagne gestured for him to hold off. Theresa knew she had just one chance. She recalled how, after the bear hunt, she had practiced with Althar and developed some skill in handling the weapon. However, she had never managed to load one by herself. She placed the end on the floor and held it down purposefully with her foot. She grasped the string and tensed it with all her strength. When the string was a mere whisker from being secured into place, it slipped through her fingers.

There was some commotion from the onlookers, but Theresa didn't give them time to react. She clasped it again and pulled hard, feeling the fibers digging into her fingers. She thought of the fire in the workshop; of her father Gorgias; of Althar; of Helga the Black and of Hoos Larsson. There had been too many mistakes in her life. She clenched her teeth and pulled harder. The string snapped loose, resting safely in its slot.

Theresa smiled with satisfaction. Finally, she loaded a dart. Then she looked at the king, awaiting his approval. Upon receiving it, she raised the weapon, aimed carefully at an empty plot of ground, and released the arrow. The dart cut through the air, whizzing across the room and landing with a thump into the ground between the legs of the rich man himself.

A murmur of astonishment ran through the refectory. Charlemagne stood and called the young woman over. "Impressive. I can see that Alcuin was right to advise me to believe you." He looked at the woman sitting to his right. "After breakfast, come to my chambers. It would be my pleasure to introduce you to my daughter."

At that moment Lothar stood and asked for silence. He donned his miter and raised his cup in a solemn gesture. "I think it is time for a toast," he proposed. Everyone at the table also lifted their drinks. "It is always an honor to welcome our beloved monarch, Charlemagne, who as you all know I am bound to by blood and friendship. However, we are also honored by the presence of the Roman legation that accompanies him, led by his eminence Flavio Diacono, the pope's holy prelate. I am therefore pleased to announce that, as a gesture of respect and loyalty toward human fortitude," he bowed toward Charlemagne, "unconditional submission to divine justice," he did the same to the Roman Curia, "this afternoon we will finally hold the execution of The Swine."

At the conclusion of his speech, those present toasted without their cups coming into contact with each other. Theresa thought this strange.

Favila explained to her that not touching cups was a sign of trust. "In the olden days, when a king wanted to control another nation, he would marry his son to the princess of his coveted kingdom and invite the father of the bride to a feast in which he would offer him a poisoned cup of wine. To prevent this barbaric practice, they would touch cups, mixing their wine together so that if one should die, so would the other. That's why it's the custom here, as a sign of trust, to never touch cups."

Upon hearing this, Theresa looked over at Alcuin and felt ashamed, knowing deep down that she had betrayed him. At that moment, the monk took his leave from Lothar and went over to Theresa. When he reached her he greeted her quite naturally. "I did not know about your expertise with condiments. Is there anything else I should know that you have not yet told me about?"

Theresa froze, seeing that Alcuin had read her thoughts. The monk suggested they talk in private.

"I don't suppose it's a good day to go to the scriptorium," Theresa said while they walked down the corridor. "I mean, because of the execution."

Alcuin merely nodded. They continued past the scriptorium and made for the cathedral. Inside, he walked past the crossing, heading for the sacristy. There, he took a key from a small alcove and opened the gate that led to a damp smelling room presided over by a great crucifix. Alcuin took a seat on the only bench and invited the young woman to do the same. Then he waited for Theresa to calm down.

"When did you last confess?" asked the monk softly. "A month ago? More than two months? Too long, if something should happen to you."

Theresa started to panic. She glanced at the gate but knew that Alcuin would stop her if she tried to escape.

"Naturally, I trust that you have kept your word," the monk continued. "I'm referring to the secrets I have shared with you. Do you know what happens to those who break their promises?"

Theresa shook her head and started to cry. The monk offered her a handkerchief, but she refused it.

"Perhaps you would like to confess."

Theresa then accepted the rag and rubbed her eyes, leaving them red. When she had mustered enough courage, she began confessing her sins. The young woman left out the incident with the fire in Würzburg, but she told him about her sinful union with Hoos. The monk reproached her, but when Theresa admitted that she had been to see the bishop, Alcuin became infuriated.

"Please forgive me. There were so many sick, so many dead." She burst into tears again. "And then there was Helga the Black. I know she was a prostitute, but she loved me. When she fell ill and disappeared . . . I didn't want to deceive you, but I couldn't just stand by."

"And that's why you went to Lothar with what I had discovered?"

The young woman wept, but Alcuin did not seem affected. "Theresa, listen to me. It is essential that you answer truthfully. Did you tell Lothar who the suspects were?"

"Yes. The prior Ludwig, and Kohl, the miller."

Alcuin clenched his teeth. "And the cause of the poisoning? Did you speak to him of the ergot?"

Theresa shook her head no and explained that she had told him of a poison, but that she had not remembered the name of the fungus at that moment.

"Are you sure of this?"

"Yes," she said emphatically.

"All right. Now close your eyes and I will absolve you."

By the time Theresa opened them, all she saw was Alcuin leaving through the gate before turning to lock her in the sacristy.

* * *

Theresa quickly realized that nobody was coming to free her. She tried to pick the lock using her steel, but she only wore the tool down and hurt her fingers. After breaking the steel in two, she decided to give up.

She sat back on the bench and looked around. The sacristy occupied a small lateral apse that opened onto the transept's ambulatory through a corridor sealed off by a second door. She observed that it had a circular alabaster window whose peculiar appearance suggested it was on the exterior wall. She remembered seeing a similar shape of window from the square. She noticed that the bottom of the alabaster window seemed to have been damaged by a stone, creating a little hole in the wall. She moved the bench under the window, and—standing on top—she was just tall enough to peer through the hole. Sure enough, the wall looked down on the main square, giving her a commanding view. She climbed down and sat on the bench to wait for someone to release her.

While she waited, she pondered Alcuin's behavior. Hoos had warned her about him. Locking her in a room and refusing to inform Lothar about the cause of the sickness only served to give credence to his suspicion. She didn't know what to think.

The monk had helped her. And, though reluctantly, he had also arranged for Helga the Black to work in the kitchens. Even though it didn't do her a lot of good. The last time she had seen Helga, she already showed symptoms of the sickness, and at that moment Theresa had no idea where she was.

Most importantly, why had Alcuin locked her up?

Suddenly the bells started ringing, announcing the approaching execution. Through the hole in the window Theresa watched as dozens of people congregated around the hole where, the week before, they had attempted to bury The Swine alive. Most of the crowd were elderly folks arriving laden with food to secure the best places, but there were also many unemployed youth and the usual beggars who inhabited the square and its surrounding area. A few paces from the wall, almost directly under her, were the chairs and stools where the dignitaries would undoubtedly sit. These, she imagined, would include the Roman delegation, Charlemagne, Bishop Lothar, and Alcuin himself. It was still early. She guessed that there were still three hours to go before the execution.

She stepped down from the window and searched the furniture. In one of the chests she discovered a store of liturgical textiles: embroidered altar cloths, curtains for the entrance to the presbytery, rugs, capes, tunics, Easter and Pentecost habits, and endless other garments—enough to dress the entire cathedral congregation.

She tidied the clothing and then continued to wait for Alcuin's return, but after some time, she went back to the chests and tried on a purple habit with a gold edging. She enjoyed its smell of incense but soon removed it because it was very heavy. She left the cassock on the chest and stretched herself out on the bench.

She thought about her father and what he might be doing. Perhaps she should return to Würzburg. Then she closed her eyes and let her mind wander. She didn't notice she had fallen asleep until the beating of drums announced that the spectacle was about to begin.

She ran to the window. Among the mob that filled the square she could make out The Swine, awaiting his punishment at the edge of the pit. Directly below her, a mere stone's throw away, Charlemagne and his retinue had taken their seats. She could see Alcuin and Lothar, but not Kohl.

She was about to come away from the window when she saw Alcuin stand and take a few paces toward a woman whose face Theresa couldn't see because her head was stooped down. He spoke to her for a moment and then returned. When the woman lifted her head, Theresa recognized her. It was Helga the Black— walking as if fully recovered!

Theresa had not yet recovered from her shock when she heard voices. She ran to the railings and saw that two clerics were cleaning the transept. As she stepped back she tripped over the bench and the clatter rang out through the church. She peered out again and saw that the novices were coming to discover what had happened.

She was gripped by panic thinking she might be in more trouble if discovered. Acting quickly, she threw on the purple cassock she had tried on earlier, and she lay on the floor face down, with the hood up over her head. When the clerics peered into the room through the railings, all they could see was what looked like a prostrate priest. Alarmed, they called out to wake him, but Theresa didn't move. Then they did as she hoped they would: Seeing that she did not respond, one of the clerics fetched the key and put it into the lock. Theresa waited until the cleric had entered and was bent down over her. Then she jumped up, pushed the first cleric out of the way and slipped past the second one so quickly that the two men thought they had seen the Devil.

She sprinted to the exit with ease, for aside from those two clerics, everyone was in the square. Once she joined the crowd, she elbowed her way through, aided by her striking attire. However, as she approached the gallows, a soldier ordered her to halt. It dawned on the young woman that if they caught her dressed as a priest, they would accuse her of heresy. Petrified, and without a second thought she took off the habit and let it fall onto the ground, causing several women to swoop down on to the garment and begin to fight over it like wild animals. Theresa took advantage of the confusion to hide behind a peasant who was twice her size. By the time the soldier had managed to separate the women, Theresa had vanished. It wasn't long before she reached the dignitaries' podium, but to her surprise, it was empty.

"They suddenly stood and left in a hurry," said a sausage vendor.

Theresa bought half a sausage from him and the peddler told her all that he knew, stating that the bishop and a skinny monk had started an argument that made the king lose his patience.

"The monarch was incensed and told them to resolve their differences somewhere else. Then he left the podium and they all followed him like sheep."

"And where did they go?"

"To the cathedral, I think." He suddenly grew animated. "Damn them! If they don't return, who will I sell all these expensive bloody sausages to?" He turned away and continued to cry his wares.

Theresa looked toward the cathedral and saw Helga the Black. This time, the recognition was mutual. Theresa tried to signal to her, but Helga hid herself, lowering her head as she made for an entrance to the episcopal palace. Theresa ran after her, but when she arrived at the door Helga entered through, she discovered it bolted.

Perhaps she should wait outside, Theresa thought briefly, but something drove her on so she jumped in through a window.

Inside, she heard Helga's footsteps fading somewhere in the distance. She thought she could catch up with her if she cut across through the choir, so she opened the little door that led to the balcony and scanned the interior. She could see the altar, where a group of clergymen were having a heated argument. Then she saw Lothar and Alcuin, who stood in front of the clergymen. To the left of them Kohl was gagged and bound, looking as if he had been tortured.

She was so shocked that she momentarily forgot about Helga the Black and crawled to a corner where she could listen in. She thought she heard Alcuin defending the miller, when suddenly Lothar stood and angrily interrupted him. "Enough of your lectures! With the king's permission, with the permission of the vicar of the holy see, with God's blessing . . ." He stepped forward until he was directly in front of Alcuin. "The fact is that dozens of people have died from a sickness for which neither our physicians nor our prayers have found a cure. And the remarkable thing about these events is not that the perpetrator of the Plague, who anyone in their right mind would have attributed to the Devil, is in reality an abominable being of flesh and bone." He stopped and pointed a finger at Kohl. "No. What is truly astounding is that this scum is being is defended by a monk, Alcuin of York, responsible for the safeguarding of our church."

Astonished murmurs ran through the cathedral.

The bishop continued. "As I have already announced, this morning an official found a batch of cereal hidden on Kohl's property, which, it would seem, is the cause of the poisoning. Grain that Kohl could not explain until torture cleansed his abominable soul. But now, after he has confessed to his vile crime, I ask myself: How far does the miller's guilt stretch? A simple man, accustomed to luxury and plenty, with no education other than what he has learned working in the fields. For we might understand how greed could take hold of an ignorant soul like Kohl's. We might even forgive and exonerate him, given his generosity toward this congregation, and that he will no doubt continue to make. But how can we accept that an educated man, a monk like Alcuin of York, with his influence, his knowledge, and his position, should attempt to contradict what evidence and reason prove to be true?"

Theresa was surprised to hear Lothar attack Alcuin more than Kohl, but she was glad, at least, that someone had revealed the identity of the culprit.

"As I say, venerable brothers," he went on, "Kohl is a murderer, and Alcuin is his protector. And while it's true that Kohl has profited from the sale of his poisonous wheat, it is no less true that Alcuin has manipulated, obstructed, and distorted everything he knew about all of these deaths so that now, perhaps in a desperate attempt to cover up his own involvement, he stands as champion of this confessed criminal."

Alcuin snorted in indignation. "Very good. Now if you have finished with your slander . . ."

"Slander, you say? Several members of this congregation have heard Kohl confess his guilt."

Two nearby clerics nodded.

"Are they delirious, too?"

"A confession obtained through torture, if I heard correctly," remarked Alcuin.

"What would you have recommended? That we offer him cake?"

Alcuin grimaced. "It would not be the first time an innocent man confessed guilt to escape the torturer's implements," the monk rebutted.

"And you propose that this is the case?" Lothar seemed to meditate for a moment. "Very well. Let us suppose that someone is convicted of the most heinous misdeeds. Let us suppose he had not committed them, but that to escape torture, the accused admits he has perpetrated these acts, thereby defaming himself. Even if this confession is not made under oath, it is still an act of defamation, and if defaming a fellow human being is a mortal sin, then defaming oneself is even more wicked. And does it not then follow that he who renounces virtue to revel in sin and benefit from it will always stray from the path of righteousness?"

Alcuin shook his head. At that moment Charlemagne stood, making the two opponents look small in the shadow of his great stature. "My dear Lothar. I do not doubt that the miller is guilty, an important fact that will no doubt put an end to these terrible deaths. But do not forget who you are accusing. The accusations you are making against Alcuin are of such gravity that you must either prove that they are true or apologize to him as his rank and position warrant."

"Beloved cousin," said Lothar with exaggerated reverence to the king. "Everyone knows of your fondness for this Briton under whose charge you have placed the education of your sons. But it is precisely for this reason that I exhort you to heed my words. That my evidence might open eyes that are presently blinded to the truth."

Charlemagne took his seat and yielded the floor to Lothar.

"Alcuin of York . . . Alcuin of York . . . Until recently, I myself would bow when I heard his name, always preceded by a reputation for wisdom and honor. And yet, look at him: Behind that guarded, impassive, imperturbable face hides an egotistical soul, corrupted by vanity and envy. I ask myself how many others he must have deceived and what other crimes he must have committed." Charlemagne coughed impatiently and Lothar acquiesced. "You ask for proof? I will provide it. So much proof that you will wonder how you could have placed your trust in this instrument of the Devil. But first, allow my men to take Kohl away."

Lothar clapped his hands and immediately three servants appeared and led the mill owner out of the church. When they returned they were accompanied by Kohl's wife, dressed in mourning.

The woman seemed alarmed, but Lothar soothed her. "If you cooperate, nothing bad will happen to you. Now swear on this Bible."

She obeyed. Then after paying her respects to the king, she sat on the stool Lothar gave her.

From her hiding place, Theresa could see that the woman was trembling with fear. She remembered having seen her at the mill the day she accompanied Alcuin.

"You have sworn on the Holy Bible, so answer truthfully or so God help you. Do you recognize this man?" Lothar asked, pointing at Alcuin.

The woman looked up fearfully, then nodded yes.

"Is it true that he was at the mill a week ago?"

"Yes, Your Excellency, that's right." She started crying inconsolably.

"Do you remember the matter that brought him there?"

The woman wiped her tears away. "Not clearly. My husband asked me to prepare something to eat while they spoke business."

"What kind of business?"

"I don't remember. About buying some grain, I suppose. I beg you, Your Excellency, my husband is a good man. He has always treated me well—anyone can tell you. He has never beaten me. We have been punished enough with the death of our daughter. Please release us."

"For pity's sake, just answer the questions. Tell the truth, and perhaps the Almighty will have mercy on you."

The woman nodded, trembling. She swallowed and continued. "The monk asked my husband for a batch of wheat, but my husband told him that he only traded in rye. I heard this because, when they started talking money, I paid more attention."

"So Alcuin proposed a deal to Kohl."

"Yes, Your Excellency. He said that he needed to buy a large amount of wheat, that it was needed in the abbey. But I swear, Lord Bishop, that my husband would never have done anything unlawful."

"Very well. Now leave."

The woman kissed the bishop's ring and curtsied to Charlemagne. Then she stole a glance at Alcuin before following the same servants that had brought her there. When the woman had left the church, Lothar turned to Charlemagne. "Now it transpires that your monk trades in wheat. Were you aware of this activity?"

The king gave Alcuin a stern look. "Your Majesty," Alcuin stepped in. "I know you will think it strange, but I was merely trying to discover the source of the sickness."

"And make a tidy profit along the way," Lothar interrupted.

"In heaven's name! Of course not. I needed to earn Kohl's trust in order to obtain the wheat."

"Oh! To reach the wheat you say! So what have you concluded, Alcuin? Is Kohl guilty or innocent? Are you pursuing him or defending him? Did you lie to him at the mill, or are you lying to us now?" He turned toward Charlemagne. "This is the man you place your trust in? He who makes falsity his way of life?"

Alcuin clenched his teeth. "*Conscientia mille testes*. In God's eyes, my conscience is worth a thousand testimonies. The fact that you do not believe me does not concern me."

"Well, it should concern you, for neither your eloquence nor your contempt will free you from the dishonor with which you conduct yourself. Tell me, Alcuin, do you recognize this document?" He showed him an ink-stained *folia*, visibly crumpled.

"Let me see," he said, examining it. "May I ask where the devil you found this?"

"In your cell, naturally," he said, snatching it back from him. "Did you write it?"

"Who gave you permission to enter my cell?"

"In my congregation, I do not need it. Answer! Are you the author of this letter?"

Alcuin nodded begrudgingly.

"And do you remember its contents?" Lothar persisted.

"No, not really."

"Then pay attention," he said, and repeated the request more politely to Charlemagne before reading: "*With God's help. Third day of the calends of January, and the fourteenth since our arrival at the abbey,*" he read. "*All the evidence points toward the mill. Last night Theresa discovered several capsules among the cereal, which Kohl kept in his storehouses. Without doubt the miller is guilty. I fear that the pestilence will spread through Fulda, however, the time has not yet come to put a stop to it.*"

Lothar stuffed the parchment into his clothing with a grimace of satisfaction. "Certainly these do not seem like the devotions of a Benedictine. What does Your Majesty think?" he asked the king. "Do they not reveal clear intent to cover up a crime?"

"It would seem so," Charlemagne lamented. "Do you have anything to say in your defense, Alcuin?"

The monk hesitated before responding. He argued that he tended to write down his thoughts in order to reflect on them later, adding that nobody had the right to rummage through his belongings, and that he had never done anything that might harm a Christian. However, he did not elaborate on the text.

"And if you suspected Kohl, what compels you now to defend him?" Charlemagne asked.

"It is something I determined later. Actually, I suspect it was his red-haired assistant who—"

"You mean Rothaart, the *late* Rothaart?" Lothar interjected. "What a coincidence! Does it not seem odd to you that the person responsible for poisoning the entire town should also be poisoned to death?"

"Perhaps it was not such a coincidence," Alcuin retorted, directing a defiant look at Lothar.

Still crouching behind the choir, Theresa was torn between trusting Alcuin and believing Lothar. Hoos had warned her against the monk and now Lothar was also accusing him of misdeeds with complete conviction. Even the king himself was starting to doubt his own adviser. She wanted to believe him innocent, but then, why would he have locked her in that room?

"Do you know this woman Theresa?" she heard Lothar ask him.

"Why do you ask?" Alcuin responded. "You know her as well as I."

"Yes, but is it not true that you have spent many hours working with her?"

"I still fail to understand what you mean."

"If you do not understand, then imagine what we must think about a young, attractive girl, as I seem to remember, helping a monk at all hours of the night in matters that fall beyond a woman's abilities. If you please, Alcuin, be honest. Aside from conducting business, do you also pursue daughters of Eve?"

"Hold your tongue. I will not permit you to—"

"And now you order me to be quiet," he said, laughing affectedly. "Confess, for the love of God. And isn't it also true that you made her swear an oath? Did you or did you not order her to keep your secret? Was this how you attempted to keep your abominable plans secret? By abusing your position, using your superior knowledge, and taking advantage of the shortfalls inherent to the female intellect?"

Alcuin was now visibly grinding his teeth as he stood face-to-face with Lothar. "But what plans do you speak of? God knows that what I say is true."

"And I suppose God will also be aware of your attempted poisoning, will He not?"

"For goodness' sake, don't be ridiculous."

"Ha! And you think I am the ludicrous one! Very well. Let us see what our King Charlemagne thinks about all of this. Ludwig! Step forward."

The coadjutor obeyed wearily, looking at Alcuin with scorn.

"Beloved Ludwig, would you be so kind as to tell us what you saw last week, during the ceremony for the execution of The Swine?" Lothar requested.

The coadjutor bowed as he went before Charlemagne. Then he straightened up as if he had swallowed a stick and began speaking in a proud tone, as though his testimony alone could solve the mystery.

"There was a great sense of expectation that day," he began. "All the monks were transfixed by the gallows. Unfortunately, I do not see well at a distance, so I amused myself by sampling the food and observing the guests. However, the dignitaries were seated close enough to me, I could see them clearly. That was when I caught him," he said pointing at Alcuin. "I was surprised to see him raising a cup, for the Briton balks at drink. Yet my incredulity doubled when I noticed that, rather than his own, he was holding Lothar's cup. That was when I saw him fiddle with his ring, opening it, and emptying some powder into Lothar's cup. Lothar drank from it before I could warn him, and moments later collapsed. Fortunately we were able to tend to him before the poison could take full effect."

"Is this true?" Charlemagne asked Alcuin.

"Of course not," he answered categorically.

But at that moment Lothar grasped Alcuin's hand and pulled on the ring around his little finger. Alcuin resisted, but as they struggled, the lid came open and a cloud of white powder was strewn over Charlemagne's cloak.

"And what is this?" said the sovereign, standing up.

Alcuin stammered and retreated. This was not how he had envisioned events unfolding.

Before he could answer, Lothar responded for him. "This is what is hidden in a man with a dark soul. A man who brandishes the Word of God while his tongue spits the poison of evil. Abbadon, Asmodeus, Belial, or Leviathan: Any of them would be proud to have him as a friend. Alcuin of York—a man capable of lying to make a profit, capable of keeping quiet while people die in order to protect himself, and capable of killing—he brushed the powder from Charlemagne to prevent his true nature from being unmasked. But I will show you his true face, the face of the beast. Because he was the first to discover what Kohl was doing. Yet rather than stop him, he blackmailed him for his own gain. He lied to him to earn his trust, and he lies now, defending him in order to defend himself. It was his assistant Theresa who was unable to bear her burden of guilt. Refusing to participate in the murder that Alcuin was eager to repeat, she came to me in confession." He turned challengingly to Alcuin. "And now you can hide behind whatever falsities you can conjure, for nobody born under God's mantle will dare heed your barking."

Alcuin silently scanned the faces that had already condemned him. Finally, he took the Bible and placed his right hand on it.

"I swear before God Almighty—for the salvation of my soul— that I am innocent of the charges made against me. And if you will grant me time—"

"Time to continue killing?" Lothar interrupted.

"I have sworn on the Bible. Why don't you also swear?" challenged Alcuin.

"Your oath is worth as much as the word of that woman who helped you. No, not even that much. Catullus said that the oaths of women are written in the wind and on the surface of waves, but yours evaporate while they are still in your thoughts."

"Cease spouting old wives' tales and swear!" Alcuin demanded. "Or do you fear that Charlemagne will strip you of your position?"

"How readily you forget our laws!" he said, smiling paternally. "We bishops are not of the same class of people, who like common subjects, must consign themselves to vassalage. Nor must we make oaths of any kind. You know that the evangelical and canonical code forbids it. You know that the rank and position of bishop is one bestowed upon us by God. Our positions cannot be taken away by anyone's whim, not even the king's. Everything associated with the Church is consecrated to God. But even if I could swear an oath . . . how dare you demand that I do so? For if you believed that I am telling the truth, then what would be the point in swearing? And if you believed that my word is false, then by demanding I take an oath, you would be leading me into error, and in doing so, encouraging the perpetration of sin."

Alcuin tried to contradict him, but to his despair, the papal envoy appeared to agree with Lothar's argument.

"Well, then. It seems obvious that the mill owner is guilty," the monarch concluded. "A batch of wheat has been found in his possession containing the seed that apparently produces the poison, and that is something irrefutable, so I see no reason, Alcuin, why you continue to protect him. Unless, of course, you are involved, as Lothar suggests."

Alcuin gave him a grim look. "Since when has an innocent man been obliged to defend himself? Where are the twelve men required for the accusation to be valid? Lothar's words have been nothing more than quibbles, nonsense, and buffoonery. If you will grant me a few hours, I will prove—"

At that moment, the crash of a falling candelabra made everyone turn in surprise.

Theresa crouched behind the balustrade. In her eagerness to hear what was being said, she had leaned against the candles, and her weight had sent the entire structure plummeting to the ground.

One of the clerics caught a glimpse of her and on his command, two acolytes ran toward the choir. When they found that it was a woman, they grabbed her and shoved her in the direction of Lothar, who instructed her to kneel and beg for forgiveness.

"Well, well. If it isn't the bear hunter!" said the king in surprise. "May I ask why you were hiding?"

Theresa kissed the royal ring before begging for mercy. Stammering, she explained that she was looking for a missing friend whom she had mistakenly thought had died and was now fleeing from her for some reason. She emphasized that she had not heard what they were discussing, and that all she wanted was to know why her friend Helga was running away from her.

When the young woman finished babbling, Charlemagne looked her up and down. For a moment he thought she had lost her senses, though her explanation was so hasty and strange that he decided perhaps she was no liar.

"And you thought you might find your friend up there in the choir?"

Theresa reddened.

"She is Alcuin's assistant, my Lord," Lothar interjected. "Perhaps you would like to interrogate her."

"I don't think so. I would rather take a break now. Maybe in prayer I will find an answer."

"But, Your Majesty. You cannot . . . Alcuin needs to be punished immediately," he insisted.

"After some prayers," said the monarch. "Meanwhile, keep him under guard in his cell." He signaled to have Alcuin escorted away and then left through a side door, cutting Lothar short.

At once the bishop forgot about Theresa and addressed the sentry who was taking Alcuin to his cell, telling him to make sure he did not leave it under any circumstance.

"If he needs to relieve himself, he can do so out of the window," he blurted out.

Two guards escorted Alcuin back to his cell, flanking him on either side. Theresa followed a few steps behind. As they walked, the young woman tried to apologize, but at each attempt the monk only quickened his pace.

"I did not meant to incriminate you," she finally managed to say.

"Well, according to Lothar, it seems a little too late for that." He kept walking without looking back at her. For the entire trip back to his cell, Theresa kept apologizing for what she had done, all the while asking herself why she was doing so. For after all, the monk had used her for his own purposes. He had locked her up, and if it had been left up to him, nobody would know yet about the cause of the Plague. There was also the matter of the *folia*, in which he had accused Kohl as the culprit, something he had never mentioned to Theresa before.

As she struggled to sort through her thoughts, Alcuin went into his cell. But, before the guard locked him in, he turned to Theresa, and taking her hands into his, he said in Greek: "*Return to the episcopal scriptorium and reexamine the polyptychs.*"

Then the guard closed the door, giving Theresa an arrogant look. She turned and ran toward the kitchens, pressing against the key that Alcuin had just given her to her chest.

19

When she reached the kitchens, Theresa found Favila wrestling with a chicken. "So you heard the news of the postponed execution too? Truly, I don't know what they are waiting for to bring that murderer to justice," she said as a greeting to Theresa as she continued to pluck feathers from the bird.

Theresa nodded without making a fuss, but she felt annoyed that Favila and everyone else took for granted The Swine had killed the miller's daughter.

"Have you seen Helga?" she asked halfheartedly.

The woman shook her head no as she jointed the chicken.

"I didn't think you would have," she added, then took a piece of cheese and said good-bye to the cook.

She had to wait for the congregation to gather in the refectory before she could access the episcopal scriptorium without being seen. Though she had been in that room dozens of times, fear constricted her throat. She inserted the key in the lock and turned it until the bolt popped, then she quickly went in and closed the door behind her. She was comforted by the smell of the fire, still burning in the hearth, glad that the bishop had instructed one be built in such a cold room.

On the table she found several unfurled documents that looked as if they had been worked on recently. She ran a finger across the ink and found it still wet. Written within the hour, she estimated. She looked through them but could see nothing important. Mostly they were various *epistolae* signed by Lothar exhorting other bishops to follow the precepts of the Rule of Saint Benedict.

She put down the documents and went to the bookshelves where she found the polyptych that she had already reviewed so many times. However, when she tried to take it down, she realized that it had been chained to the shelf, so she pulled it out as far as she could and opened the cover to examine its contents. Due to the proximity of the neighboring volumes, she could barely turn the pages. Still she managed to locate the summaries of the grain transactions settled almost four years earlier with the nearby town of Magdeburg.

The text was all the same in the same handwriting—the exact same sentences as before. She read them over again without finding anything new. But on the altered page, she could only read the paragraphs that someone had tried to pass off as the original entry. She couldn't examine the hidden text that she had discovered earlier.

While she continued to study the pages, she wondered again what she was doing in the scriptorium trying to help Alcuin. She did not even know whether the monk was guilty or innocent. If they discovered her, they would think she was in cahoots with him, an accomplice in a murder, and she too would probably end up on the pyre. She decided she must leave and quickly put the whole affair behind her.

She was about to close the book when suddenly some words jumped out at her: *In nomine Pater.* She looked at the letters closely, reading them slowly over and over again. *In nomine Pater.* Why did it catch her attention? It was nothing more than the standard way to begin a letter.

In a flash, she understood. Good God! That was it! She gave a cry of joy and ran to the documents spread out on the table. She frantically searched through the epistles signed by Lothar, unfurled them with trembling hands. There it was. *In nomine Pater.*

The same inclination . . . the same stroke . . . the same handwriting!

The amendments made to the polyptych in which the grain sales were recorded had been written by Lothar's hand. She crossed herself and then shivered, taking a step back. If it was Lothar who had made the corrections . . . perhaps he was also behind the murders.

She had to take the evidence to the king.

Tidying the documents on the table, she returned to the polyptych on the bookshelf, but try as she might, she could not free it from its chain.

She was trying to figure out how to work it loose when she heard the door creak. Terrified, she crouched among the books just in time to see the stout figure of Lothar walk into the scriptorium. Theresa put down the polyptych and crawled to the end of the bookshelf. There she hid behind a large chair.

Lothar went to the table and looked at the documents before approaching the hearth. Then he walked over to the polyptych and unchained it. He hesitated for a moment, glancing from side to side as if he feared being watched. Then he leafed through the codex and finally cast it into the flames, where in the blink of an eye it burned like a parched bale of hay.

Moments after Lothar departed, Theresa left, too. She needed to speak to Alcuin to tell him all that had happened, but when she reached his cell she found it empty. On the way there she passed by the kitchens, where to her surprise, she found Helga the Black. Astonished, Theresa didn't know what to say. But Helga gestured to her to stay silent and led her to a storeroom where they could speak in private.

"I thought you were dead," Theresa said sharply. Then she gave her friend a strong embrace.

"I'm so sorry," Helga said. "I didn't want to worry you, but Alcuin made me do it."

"Made you? Made you do what? And what about your legs? Are they all right?" She remembered seeing them blue from the sickness.

"It was fake," she said, ashamed. "Alcuin made me put tincture on them. He told me that if I didn't do it, he would take my child from me when it's born."

"But why?"

"I don't know. He wanted you to see me like that, and then for me to disappear. That man is the Devil. I warned you."

Theresa slumped into a chair, dispirited. Why had Alcuin forced Helga to do something so strange? Clearly he wanted her to think she was sick, but why? Alcuin was not the type of person to do things randomly, so she tried to think of a sensible reason for his actions. She recalled that, after thinking that Helga the Black had fallen ill, her indignation had made her confess to Lothar. Had that been Alcuin's intention? And if that were the case, why had the monk wanted Lothar to know his plans? She was still confused, but determined to uncover the truth. She kissed Helga and told her to look after herself. Then she left in the direction of the church, where she assumed they had taken Alcuin.

At the entrance of the church, a guard confirmed that they were assembled there, but that she could not enter. Theresa tried to persuade him, but the guard would not yield. At that moment she felt a hand rest on her shoulder. She turned to find herself face to face with Lothar, who apparently had arrived for the conclave at that moment. She feared she may have been discovered, but to her relief the bishop gave her a friendly smile.

"Perhaps you would like to join us," he even suggested.

Theresa sensed a certain darkness in his words, but thought that it would give her an opportunity to inform Alcuin of Lothar's involvement in the falsification of the polyptych. She accepted his invitation and the bishop told her to make herself comfortable. Everyone resumed the same positions, just as they had before the break, reminding Theresa of a painting she had seen before.

The spectators whispered to each other about Alcuin's guilt, while the monk, some distance from them, paced up and down like a caged animal. When he saw Theresa, it seemed to unnerve him. He nodded to her almost imperceptibly and kept pacing as he studied his wax tablet. Moments later, Charlemagne appeared, attired in the impressive cuirass he normally wore for summary trials. They all stood until the monarch took his seat. After giving his permission for them to do the same, Charlemagne told Alcuin to resume his testimony. However, Alcuin continued to look over his tablet, until the king cleared his throat to call attention to the delay.

"Forgive me, Your Highness. I was rereading my notes."

Charlemagne gestured to him to continue as silence descended upon the hall.

"It is time to reveal the truth," Alcuin finally began. "A difficult truth, incestuous, and wicked. A truth that has on occasions led me down a path of lies, through ravines of sin that I have had to negotiate in order to reach a place of enlightenment." He paused to scrutinize the eyes of those gathered. "As you all know, strange events have afflicted the city of Fulda. All of you have most likely lost a sibling, a parent, or a friend. My own assistant, Romuald, a strong and healthy lad, died, and there was nothing I could do to prevent it. Perhaps it is for this selfish reason that I swore to uncover the truth behind what was happening. I investigated every death. I spoke to all who fell sick. I inquired about their habits, their behavior. All in vain. There was nothing connecting the deaths, which were as unjust as they were strange and sudden. Then I remembered an epidemic that ravaged York many years ago when I was a magister. On that occasion the cause of the epidemic was rye, yet here, in Fulda, many of the dead had not recently eaten rye. My inquiries led me toward wheat, surmising that if the symptoms were so similar to the rye epidemic, perhaps there could be a link." He paused to reread his notes. "Everyone knows that there are three mills in Fulda: the abbey's, the bishopric's, and Kohl's. I searched the first two mills and found nothing to confirm my suspicions. So then I went to Kohl's mill with the intention of obtaining a sample of wheat. It is true that I proposed a deal to Kohl, but it was only to see if he had the contaminated grain."

"That's all good and well," said the king, "but your account thus far doesn't alter Lothar's version of events."

"If you will allow me to continue?"

"Proceed."

"To my surprise, in a sample that my assistant Theresa provided, I discovered the capsules that caused the sickness. I must admit that I immediately blamed Kohl. However, though the wheat found at his mill suggested he was involved, in reality those tiny, poisonous bodies did not prove that he was guilty."

"Forgive me," Lothar interrupted, "but what does all of this have to do with your lies? With your attempt to poison me? With your written confession in which you recognize Kohl's guilt and with your refusal to stop the poisonings?"

"For the love of God . . . let me speak!" Alcuin sought the approval of Charlemagne, who gave his assent with an impatient gesture. "We knew that the contaminated wheat had passed through Kohl's mill."

"It was at Kohl's mill!" Lothar specified cleverly. "Are you choosing to ignore the fact that an official has found all the batches of contaminated wheat hidden on Kohl's property?"

"Oh, yes! The official! I had forgotten . . . It is this person we have before us, is it not?" said Alcuin, pointing at a timid little man. "Your name, please?"

"Ma . . . Maar . . . tin," he stammered.

"Martin. A memorable name . . . would you mind coming closer?"

The little man stepped forward.

"Tell me, Martin, have you been an official for long?"

"Not lo . . . long, sir."

"How long? A year? Two? Three, perhaps?"

"Not thaaaat long s . . . sir."

"Less? How long then?"

"Two . . . m . . . months, I don't know . . . sir."

"His brother died from the sickness, and he assumed his post," Lothar explained.

"Ah! Naturally, that is a good enough reason. And of course, you appointed him."

"I am always the one who appoints the official."

"Very good. Allow me to continue: Martin, tell me," he said, dipping his hand in his pocket to pull out a fistful of wheat, which he then appeared to divide between his two hands. Holding out both closed fists to Martin he asked, "In what hand is the wheat?"

The official smiled, revealing a row of chipped teeth. "In th . . . at one," he indicated.

Alcuin opened the hand he had indicated, showing it to be empty.

"In th . . . th . . . at one," he said, pointing to his other hand.

But once again, it was empty. Martin was left wide-eyed. His face was like that of a child whose apple had been stolen. "You . . . you're . . . a . . . demon."

Alcuin let his arms drop and from his sleeves fell the handfuls of wheat.

Martin smiled.

"May I ask what this buffoonery is about?" Lothar interrupted in indignation.

"Forgive me," said Alcuin, "Forgive me, Your Majesty . . . it was just a joke. Permit me to continue."

Charlemagne agreed with some reluctance. Alcuin bowed and turned back to the little man. "Martin, tell me . . . is it true that you found the wheat?"

"It . . . it is . . . sir."

"I see! But as I seem to recall, Lothar announced that it was very, very well hidden."

"That's right . . . s . . . sir. Ve . . . very well hiiid . . . en. It to . . . took all . . . all morn . . . ing to f . . . f . . . find it."

"But in the end you discovered its whereabouts."

"Yes . . . sir." He smiled like a young boy who had caught a very slippery eel.

"And tell me, Martin, if the wheat was so well hidden, how was it possible that you found it, if you aren't even able to find a fistful in my hands?"

Except for Lothar, everyone, including Martin, roared with laughter. However, the little man's smile froze when he noticed Lothar's cold stare. "He . . . he help . . . helped me," he said, signaling the bishop.

"Well, I never! I hadn't heard that part of the story before." He turned to Lothar. "So the bishop told you where to search for the wheat?"

"What did you expect?" the bishop retorted. "Have you not seen that he is a half-wit? What matters is not whether I helped him, but the fact that it was found."

"Of course, I don't doubt it." He paced up and down. "And tell me, my good Lothar, how did you know that the wheat was contaminated?"

The bishop hesitated for a moment, but then quickly answered: "Because of the grain that Theresa told me about."

"This grain?" said Alcuin, putting his hand in his pocket and showing him another fistful of wheat with clearly visible tiny black balls intermixed.

Lothar looked at it without much interest, then his glassy eyes looked back up at Alcuin. "Exactly like that, yes," he confirmed.

Alcuin arched his eyebrows. "How odd, because those black balls are peppercorns." He closed his hand and put the wheat grain back in his pocket.

"Not so fast," the bishop blurted out. "You have not yet explained your attempt to poison me and why, knowing what you knew, you decided to remain silent."

"Do you truly want to know?" he said with a wry smile. "First, as everyone here should comprehend, it was never my intention to poison you. It's true that I added this powder to your drink." He opened his ring and showed them the powder. "But it is no poison, just a harmless purgative." He tipped the remaining contents into his hand— and then, in full sight of the king, he swallowed it with evident disgust. "*Lactuva virosa*: unpleasant, but little more. If I had wanted to poison you, you can be sure I would have succeeded. No, dear Lothar, no. I drugged you, but it was to prevent another terrible murder. That of the poor wretch whose only crime was that he was born slow-witted."

"Are you referring to The Swine? That degenerate who slit the throat of the miller's daughter?"

"I am referring to The Swine. That man who you attempted to execute knowing that he was innocent. The simpleton you chose to blame for a murder committed by another: Rothaart, the redhead, an employee of Kohl and your accomplice."

"By God! Have you lost your mind?" Lothar roared.

"It was him, in fact, who led me to you," he said, even louder. Alcuin took a deep breath to calm himself. "The young woman was killed with a blade. I must confess that at first I too blamed the idiot with his grotesque face and the evasive look in his little pig's eyes. But then I saw his deformed hands that have been that way since birth, and I realized that he could not have even held a spoon."

"What do you know!"

"I know that Kohl's daughter died from a knife to the throat. More specifically, it was on the left side and with an upward motion. A slash made by someone left-handed, without a shadow of a doubt. The maidservant who found the body described it in detail, and a small piece of the young woman's ear was missing."

"But how did that lead you to Rothaart?" Charlemagne inquired.

"Rothaart was hotheaded. He was left-handed, and he was skilled with the knife, which he brandished frequently in the tavern. He had money. Too much of it. The day I met him, he was bragging shamelessly to a friend about his wealth. I contacted that friend not long after Rothaart's death, and his friend had no qualms admitting that, the day after the girl's murder, Rothaart had scratch marks on his face."

"That doesn't prove it was he who killed her," the monarch remarked.

"He knew the victim well. In fact, the night she was found dead, the redhead had spent the night at the mill. According to Kohl's wife, that same night their daughter awoke in discomfort, left the house to empty her stomach, and never returned. I will say it again: left-handed and skilled with a knife. We know it could not have been The Swine because he is incapable of holding any kind of implement, and we know that Rothaart, the left-handed, was there on the premises with his knife."

"But, what was his motive to kill her?" the king asked.

"His fear of Lothar, of course," Alcuin said, unblinking.

"Explain yourself," ordered Charlemagne.

"Rothaart drank frequently. He latched on to the barrel like a newborn to a teat. The night of her murder, he had to transport the contaminated wheat from the granary to the mill. When he arrived at the mill, he was drunk. As he was busy working to unload the poisoned grain, Kohl's daughter happened upon him, probably surprised to see him there at that time of night. There were a thousand excuses Rothaart could have given her, but the *aqua ardens* clouded his senses and he reacted as he would've in the tavern: He pulled out his knife and with one stroke, killed her."

"I didn't know that you had the powers of a witch," said the bishop sarcastically. "Or is it that you were there in person?"

Alcuin declined to answer, instead posing another question: "Tell me, Lothar, is it true that Rothaart regularly visited your chambers? To speak to you about the mill business, I suppose."

"I see so many people that if I had to remember all of them, I would not have room for anything else in my head." He cleared his throat.

"And yet your acolyte remembers. In fact, he told me that you would spend quite some time discussing matters of money."

Lothar gave his acolyte a stern look, then turned back to Alcuin. "And what if I did talk to Rothaart a lot? The bishopric owns a mill, and Rothaart works as a miller at Kohl's mill. Sometimes they would mill grain for us, and sometimes we did it for them."

"But the sensible thing would be to discuss these matters with the owner of the mill, not a subordinate."

"And from that you infer who the murderer is? Alcuin, stop talking nonsense and accept the truth: Whatever Rothaart did, it doesn't matter. It was Kohl who was selling the wheat."

"If you don't mind, I will continue with my nonsense." He glanced at his notes. "As I have already said, Rothaart the redhead had money: He wore sumptuous jerkins, boots of fine leather, and enough gold on his arms to buy an allodium—and all the farmhands needed to work it. This is inexplicable for a miller. It is clear that he had other means of income, which fits with what his friend Gus at the tavern told me he does on Sundays."

"What activity is this?" the monarch asked.

"I spoke to Gus after Rothaart's death at length over a couple of tankards of beer. After lamenting the loss of his friend, he told me that Rothaart obtained wheat from somewhere, which he ground at Kohl's mill on Sundays when the mill owner was attending High Mass. Once it had been milled, he transported the cereal to a clandestine storeroom where he kept it until it was ready to be sold."

"And Gus told you all of this, just like that?" asked the king.

"Well, it was easy to convince him that I already knew about his schemes. He was also shaken by the unexpected death of his friend Rothaart, which naturally I attributed to divine justice, and then there was the considerable amount of beer that I purchased for him to drink. So it is no surprise that he confessed to what at any rate he didn't consider a sin. Bear in mind that Gus was being deceived, and made to work for little more than some wine and a paltry sum of money."

"Gus, a drunk, and Rothaart, a murderer. Well, perhaps they were! But what does that have to do with me?" Lothar asked, incensed.

"Have patience, I've nearly finished. As I have already explained, I deduced that the sickness came from the grain due to the similarity of the symptoms I observed in victims during the famine in my native York. That was why I asked Lothar for the bishopric's polyptychs: to find an entry perhaps related to contaminated rye. Surprisingly, neither Theresa nor I could find any direct mention of contaminated wheat, but there was a scraped and amended page containing the information we sought. As if by magic, it strongly suggested that a shipment of wheat had been transported from Magdeburg to Fulda. A deadly shipment of wheat that was likely bought at a discounted price or traded for no cost at all by the previous abbot."

"So what are you talking about? Go to the cemetery then and accuse the late abbot," Lothar said, red in the face.

"I would have done that, were it not for the fact that I always suspect the living, particularly since I discovered that you were plowing uncultivated land, preparing for something to be sowed in the middle of January. Tell me, Lothar, since when is wheat sown in winter?"

"What rubbish! That land belongs to me, and I can do whatever I please with it. And I will say more. I am sick of your unfounded accusations and your eagerness to show how wise you are. You speak nothing but blather without a shred of evidence. You accuse Rothaart, yet he is dead. You speak of The Swine, but he is both demented and mute. You mention the old Abbot of Fulda, yet his body has been lying in his grave for several years. And finally, you claim that there is a polyptych that reveals secrets through some act of witchcraft, on a page that nobody has seen, let alone verified. Very well. Do you have this polyptych? Show it to us once—or rescind your accusations."

Alcuin tensed. He had assumed that Lothar would crumble under the weight of his arguments, but he had risen to the challenge. Now, without solid proof, it would be difficult to gain Charlemagne's support. He looked at the king, who shook his head disapprovingly.

Alcuin was about to speak up when Theresa stood and walked toward Charlemagne.

"I have that proof," she announced in a firm voice, taking from her bag a crumpled sheet.

Everyone fell silent.

Standing before the king, Theresa unfurled the page from the polyptych that she had managed to tear from the volume moments before Lothar had cast it into the fire. Alcuin looked at her in astonishment.

The king took the page from her and examined it closely. Then he showed it to Lothar, who could not believe his eyes.

"Damned witch! Where did you get this?"

The king moved the sheet away from Lothar before he could snatch it from him. Then he gave it to Alcuin. Theresa handed him some ash so he could repeat the process of rubbing, slowly in the reverse direction, before everyone present. When the hidden text emerged, the king read it out loud.

But Lothar fought back. "And who says I had a hand in it? That text was written two years ago by the previous abbot. He was in charge of all the polyptychs. Ask anyone."

Several monks confirmed Lothar's claims.

Theresa boldly intervened. "That's right. The original text that the ash reveals was written by the abbot, but the subsequent scraping and the new text that covers it was written by you, by your hand. You wrote it thinking that it would conceal the only proof that linked the wheat to the Plague."

"I never wrote that text!" Lothar cried in fury.

"Yes, you did," the young woman insisted. "I confirmed it myself by checking it against your letters. *In nomine Pater.*"

"Ha! What letters, you pathetic liar?" he said, giving her a slap in the face that echoed in the church. "There are no letters. There are no documents."

Theresa looked impotently at Alcuin, realizing that Lothar would have time to destroy any documents that could incriminate him.

However, Charlemagne stood. "Let us test her claims," he said, removing a sealed scroll that he had been keeping close to his chest. He broke the seal and carefully unrolled it. "Do you recall this epistle, Lothar? It is the missive you dispatched to me yesterday, a copy of the message you were planning to send to the rest of the bishops. You submitted it to me as evidence of your forthright Christian conduct, I suppose, as a preliminary step before requesting a higher position."

Charlemagne's eyes fell on the words: *In nomine Pater.* The handwriting was identical to the text written on the palimpsest, down to the last detail.

"Do you have anything to say?" the king asked Lothar.

The bishop was speechless with rage. Suddenly he turned toward Theresa and tried to hit her, but Alcuin stood in the way. Lothar tried again, but the monk stopped him, knocking him down with a punch.

"I have been wanting to do that for a long time," he murmured as he massaged his fist.

Four days later, Alcuin told Theresa that Lothar had been arrested and taken to a cell where he would stay until his trial. He said it had not yet been revealed when the bishop discovered the wheat was contaminated, but it was clear that, despite being aware of it, he had continued to sell the grain as if nothing had happened. Kohl was freed after it was determined his involvement in the plot wasn't intentional, as was The Swine. Although, unfortunately, his spirit was as broken and battered as a frightened puppy.

"Will they execute the bishop?" Theresa asked as she tidied away some manuscripts.

"To be honest, I don't think so. Considering Lothar is a relative of the king, and he will continue to hold the position of bishop, I fear that sooner or later he will evade his punishment."

Theresa continued to stack the codices she had been using all morning. It was the first time she had returned to the abbey scriptorium since Lothar's guilt had been uncovered.

"It doesn't seem fair," she said.

"If at times divine justice is hard to comprehend, imagine trying to understand worldly law," Alcuin responded.

"But so many people have died."

"Death is not paid for with death. In this world in which the light of life is so easily extinguished at the whim of sickness, at the mercy of hunger, war, or the inclemencies of nature, nothing will be gained from executing a criminal. Reparations for the lives of murder victims are dealt according to their wealth and the wealth of their murderer. It is wealth that determines the severity of the punishment."

"And since many of the dead are not rich . . ."

"I can see you learn quickly. For instance, the murder of a young woman of childbearing age is punishable with a fine of six hundred solidi, the same as if she were a boy under twelve. However, if the deceased is a girl under the age of twelve, the penalty could just be two hundred."

"And what do you want me to understand?"

"In the eyes of God, man and woman are equal, but in the eyes of men, evidently, they are not: A man generates money and riches, while a woman creates children and problems."

"Children that will bring wealth and labor," Theresa added. "What's more, if God created man in his image and likeness, why doesn't man take God's viewpoint?"

Alcuin raised an eyebrow, surprised at the thoughtfulness of her answer. "As I was saying, sometimes murder is punished only with a fine, while crimes that cause grave losses, such as arson or destruction, end up being punished with the execution of the perpetrator."

"So he who kills is fined, while he who steals is killed."

"More or less, that's the law."

Theresa turned her attention back to the gospel she had been working on since the early hours of the morning. After dipping her pen in the ink, she transcribed another verse so that she could complete the daily page that Alcuin required of her as soon as possible. Each page consisted of around thirty-six lines, which she usually finished in about six hours of work, half the time it would take an experienced scribe. For some time Alcuin had been working on a type of calligraphy that would enable faster and simpler writing that was easier to read and transcribe. He had developed a new kind of uncial lettering, smaller than capitals, which made it easier to copy Vulgates. Theresa was using it, and the speed at which she worked filled the monk with pride.

After the copying was complete, Alcuin turned his attention to broadening Theresa's knowledge, insisting on the *ars dictaminis*, or the art of writing epistles. "You shouldn't spend all your time thinking about how to copy—you must also think about what you want to write."

On occasion, when Alcuin left the scriptorium, Theresa would take out the parchment that her father had hidden in his bag, and study it in an attempt to decipher its contents. Sometimes she would consult the Greek codices she found on the shelves of the scriptorium. But in none of them, nor in any of the Latin texts, was there any mention of the Donation of Constantine. She was surprised to find no reference to it, but she did not dare ask Alcuin.

In addition to analyzing the parchment, Theresa spent her time studying a fascinating book: the *Liber Glossarum*, a singular codex that was a compendium of a vast body of knowledge. According to Alcuin, the copy she was reading had been made at Corbie Abbey from a Visigothic original inspired by Saint Isidore's *Etymologiae*.

On more than one occasion he had cautioned her against the paragraphs in which the pagan prose of Virgil, Orosius, Cicero, or Eutropius could be discerned, but because of contributions by Jerome, Ambrose, Augustine, and Gregory the Great, Alcuin allowed her to continue reading. That book provided Theresa with a window to a world of wisdom beyond the confines of religion.

"There are some things that I still don't understand," she said, closing the book for a moment.

"If you spent less time with that volume and made more of an effort to read the Bible . . ."

"I'm not talking about the *Liber Glossarum*. I'm referring to the incident with the poisoned wheat. I've been thinking, and I still fail to comprehend why you locked me in that room."

"Ah. That? Well. The truth is I was concerned for your well-being. And also, I must confess, I was worried what more you might tell Lothar. In fact, I am the one who made you go to him the first time, but then the situation became more dangerous."

"You? Now I really don't understand."

"After you discovered the hidden text, my suspicions centered on Lothar. He was the only person who had access to the polyptych, and the correction seemed recent. Unfortunately, Lothar began to grow wary of us, so I thought it would be beneficial to make him believe we suspected someone else. That was why I told Helga the Black to dye her legs and feign the sickness—so that you would become agitated and go to Lothar. I knew you would tell him that I suspected Kohl, which would enable me to continue with my investigations. I even wrote the letter he found in my cell to purposefully mislead him, knowing that he was watching me."

"But why didn't you tell me your plan?"

"So that you wouldn't alert Lothar for any reason. I needed him to trust you, trust your version of what was happening. In fact, the idea to dye Helga's legs is one I got from Lothar himself."

"How do you mean?"

"It was he who used it first with Rothaart, the redhead. I discovered it when I examined his body. He didn't die from the sickness, but was murdered by Lothar. Rothaart was the only person who could betray him, besides The Swine, and once the redhead died, the only suspect that remained was Kohl."

"And why didn't you tell Charlemagne all of this? Even I doubted your innocence."

"I needed time. As I said in the trial, I discovered that the bishop was plowing land outside of the bishopric's boundaries. I suppose Lothar, sowing the wheat, thought that he would free himself of the proof that incriminated him, without losing the value of the grain. But the problem isn't so easily solved. The ergot could pass from one crop to another and end up contaminating even more of the town.

"But, I didn't know where he was hiding the cereal, nor if the batches that were found at Kohl's mill, planted there of course by Lothar, accounted for all of the bishop's contaminated wheat, so I had two acolytes watch the fields. I did not want to unmask him until I was certain of his intentions. What really concerns me is that there is a batch of grain that I still haven't found."

Theresa felt stupid for having mistrusted Alcuin. She put down the book, gathered her writing implements and asked for permission to retire to think things through. After all, night had fallen some time ago.

20

When Gorgias awoke, he prayed that it had all been a dream, but around him he saw the walls that had imprisoned him for over a month. Each morning Genseric visited the crypt to check on the progress of the document that Gorgias was transcribing, bring him a stewpot containing his daily rations, and remove his bucket of waste through the hatch in the door.

Gorgias endeavored to write as carefully as his faculties would permit. But he soon realized that the coadjutor was only paying attention to the quantity of text, disregarding the accuracy of expression and the elegance of the calligraphy. At first he attributed Genseric's silence in regards to the text to his poor eyesight, but then he remembered that Genseric had never learned Greek. He was sure that Wilfred must be aware of this fact, and so it was odd that he did not demand to see the text for himself. This made him reconsider.

When the coadjutor left, Gorgias began to eat from the pot of food just delivered to him. He thought about Genseric and his pale blue eyes. After a while he stood.

His pale blue eyes.

And what if the man who had stabbed him on the day of the fire had been Genseric himself? The coadjutor did not seem the kind of individual to assault a younger man, but it had been nighttime, and it was a surprise attack. He recalled including Genseric in his list of initial suspects alongside the midget monk and the precentor—although, due to Genseric's age, he was last in line. Gorgias was sure his attacker already knew about the parchment in his bag. And Genseric had knowledge of the castle's documents and, it would appear, its secret passages.

He paced around in circles. Wilfred had always told him that he was transcribing a secret text, but if this were the case, then why did he now entrust it to Genseric? There was a stabbing pain in his arm but he ignored it. What's more, why would the count want to lock him up? And if he needed the document so badly, why was he not checking on his progress himself?

No. It made no sense. The only explanation was that Genseric was acting independently. The coadjutor attacked him and stole the copy of the parchment containing the annotations in Latin, and now he wanted to do the same with the transcription in Greek.

He pondered the events for the rest of the day, until he decided that Genseric must know the immense importance of the parchment. For Wilfred spoke of its power with fear, though he did not explain why. For some reason Genseric coveted this power, and without a doubt he would kill to obtain it.

Gorgias reexamined the text he had been translating from Latin into Greek and estimated that, continuing at the same pace, he would finish the work in around ten days. He had this long to figure out a way to save his life. Over the next few days he devised a plan of escape.

Genseric normally appeared after the Terce service, stayed a while in the antechamber and then opened the hatch to supply him with food. Sometimes he left it open while waiting for the text, which might be the opportunity Gorgias needed.

The hatch, a sort of small vertical cylinder, had a couple of partitions located between its top and bottom, forming two more receptacles. He judged that a piglet would hardly fit in either, so even if he could dismantle the partitions, he would never fit through the hole. However, he thought that if he could distract Genseric, perhaps he could grab his arm and force him to unlock the door.

It was Wednesday. He decided to attempt his ploy on the Sunday, which would give him enough time, he thought, to file through the partition mountings on the hatch.

By Thursday afternoon he managed to loosen the first one. Once he had filed through it, he concealed the damage with some bread wetted with black ink. By Friday he had dislodged the second and third, but on Saturday he had still not managed to file away the last one. He had worked without respite but the wound on his arm prevented him from continuing. That night he could not sleep peacefully.

When he heard Genseric arriving on Sunday, the last partition was still in place. For a moment he thought about giving up, but then thought he might manage to force it open. Desperate, he rested his foot against the partition and pushed with all his might. It didn't budge. Finally, with a kick, he made it jump out of its housing, just as he heard the front door of the chapel unlock.

Gorgias had just enough time to reposition the hatch and clumsily secure it in place with the putty he had prepared. When Genseric asked about the noise, Gorgias told him he had fallen against his chair.

He prayed that he would not notice the imperfections in the hatch. But soon he heard him releasing and turning the revolving hatch as usual. The plate of peas confirmed that it was Sunday. He quickly took it and then placed an old, draft parchment in the hatch to see if Genseric could distinguish it. The coadjutor turned the hatch and removed the parchment, and just as Gorgias hoped, he did not secure the mechanism.

He quickly crouched down near the hatch. Now all he had to do was wait for it to turn again so he could strike the partition and trap Genseric's arm. He started breathing so heavily that he thought he would alert the coadjutor. However, the old man was unalarmed. Gorgias thought he could hear him sliding his wrinkly fingers over the parchment. Suddenly he noticed that he was bolting the hatch.

"I must go over the text," he informed him.

Gorgias cursed his bad luck. He knew it wouldn't take long for Genseric to discover that the hatch had been tampered with. Suddenly, from behind the door, Gorgias heard an instrument scraping the housings. Then he heard a curse as a blow to the hatch almost knocked his teeth out. Gorgias stepped back while the curses continued to flow on the other side. He feared Genseric would do something stupid. However, the oaths became less frequent until they gradually disappeared like a storm in the distance before the door to the chapel slammed violently.

That night, a stranger arrived with Genseric. From inside his confinement, Gorgias could hear them arguing heatedly, their voices rising until they were shouting. The newcomer seemed highly agitated, and soon the voices were replaced by the sound of blows. Moments later, the hatch opened, and powerful arms removed the damaged partitions. Light entered the room, revealing a tattoo of a serpent.

Gorgias retreated, thinking he was about to die. Yet, nothing happened. The tattooed arm passed the old, draft parchment that Gorgias had given to Genseric back into the cell and then disappeared. Gorgias heard them reposition the partitions.

For three days, he was left alone with no news of Genseric

"Get up!" the coadjutor ordered from the other side of the door.

Gorgias obeyed, not too sure what he was doing anymore. He looked at the little window with swollen eyes and saw that it was not yet dawn. Staggering over to the door, he rested his head on it. Gorgias prayed that Genseric had forgotten the incident with the hatch, though it would have made more sense, he thought, for him to pray for the walls to fall in and crack open his head.

The hatch turned, letting in a thread of light before abruptly closing. Gorgias groped in the darkness for the pot of food. He picked it up and devoured the porridge without savoring it, for he hadn't eaten in three days.

He was swallowing the last mouthful when Genseric ordered him to prepare the parchment. Gorgias coughed. He could hardly think.

"I . . . I have not been able to make any progress," he said. "My arm . . . I'm sick."

Genseric cursed him and threatened to torture Rutgarda.

"I swear I'm not lying. Please, see for yourself."

Without giving him time to answer, Gorgias dismantled one of the partitions from the hatch. He could hear Genseric releasing the bolt on the other side. Through the hole he could see the light of a candle. Then he slowly inserted his injured arm. Suddenly he felt something crush it and he cried out in pain.

"If you try anything, I'll break it right here," Genseric declared.

Gorgias agreed and Genseric lifted his foot. When the pain subsided, Gorgias could feel the heat from the candle near his fingers while the coadjutor examined his arm.

Genseric was taken aback. If the arm had not been moving, he would've thought the limb belonged to a corpse.

The coadjutor returned at nightfall to announce that the physician Zeno was prepared to see him, but by that time Gorgias couldn't even understand, for he was consumed with fever. When he came round, he could hear Genseric on the other side of the door, striking the hatch to remove the two partitions. The beam of light expanded.

Genseric ordered him to rest his back against the door and put both arms through the hatch. Gorgias did as he was told, barely aware of his actions. He didn't even complain when his wrists were chained.

Then he felt Genseric insert a stick between his forearms to secure him against the door, making it impossible for him to pull his arms back through. A few moments went by before the coadjutor opened up, forcing him to drag himself along the ground in the direction of the door.

He barely had time to look up before Genseric covered Gorgias's head with a hood, which he cinched at the neck. Before removing the stick that kept him secured to the door, Genseric warned that he would kill him if he tried to escaped. Gorgias nodded, but he could hardly stay on his feet as Genseric pulled him up by the chains.

Gorgias didn't know for how long they were walking, only that the journey seemed endless. Finally they stopped somewhere sheltered from the wind. Before long someone arrived and greeted Genseric. By the tone of voice, Gorgias supposed it was Zeno, but it could just as easily have been the man with the tattoo. The coadjutor insisted that Zeno tend to Gorgias with the hood still on his head, but Zeno refused.

"He could die and I wouldn't know."

When his hood was finally removed, Gorgias thought he was in some abandoned stables. Two torches lit up the cubicle in which, for some reason, they had placed a table. Zeno asked Genseric to take off the chains.

"Can't you see his condition? He's not going anywhere," the physician argued.

Genseric refused. He freed the injured arm, but chained the healthy one to a ring on the table.

Zeno moved a torch close to the wound. Seeing it, he was unable to contain an expression of horror. He sniffed it and flinched. He pressed on the wound with a piece of wood, but Gorgias did not respond. Zeno shook his head.

"This arm is dead meat," he whispered to Genseric. "The rot has penetrated the lymph. You can start looking for a grave."

"Do what you must, but he cannot lose the arm."

"It's lost already. I don't even know if I can save his life."

"Do you want your money or not? I don't care if the rest of him explodes, but that arm needs to be able to write."

Zeno cursed. He handed the torch to Genseric and asked him to give him light. Then he opened his instrument bag on the table, took out a narrow blade and held it near the wound. "This might hurt," he warned Gorgias. "I have to open up your arm."

He was about to begin when Genseric reeled back. The physician noticed just in time to catch him.

"Are you all right?" he asked.

"Yes, yes. It was nothing. Continue."

Zeno raised a skeptical eyebrow before turning back to his work. He poured a little liquor on the wound and then made a cut parallel with the scar. The skin dropped off like a toad's gut, allowing a trickle of pus to escape. The stench made Genseric step back. Zeno found a needle and attempted to thread it.

"Shit!" Zeno exclaimed when it slipped through his fingers. He bent down to pick it up, but try as he might he could not find it.

"Leave it and use another one," Genseric suggested.

"I don't have any more here. You'll have to go to my house."

"Me? You go."

"Someone has to contain the hemorrhage." He released Gorgias's elbow and a stream of blood flooded onto the table. Zeno put pressure on the artery again.

Genseric nodded.

Though Gorgias was lying there helpless, the coadjutor warned Zeno not to leave his side. Before he left he made sure the chains were secure and confirmed with Zeno where he kept the needles. He was about to leave when he gave another sudden lurch.

"Are you sure you're all right?" Zeno insisted.

"Fix that arm by the time I return!" he said, squinting as he left the stables, as if he could not see.

Zeno tightened the tourniquet under Gorgias's arm until the flow of blood stopped. Examining the wound again, he noticed its brown and purple coloring and shook his head. The arm was lost, however much Genseric refused to accept it.

Gorgias suddenly came round. Seeing the physician he attempted to sit up, but the chain and tourniquet prevented him. Zeno tried to calm him.

"Where have you been? Rutgarda has given you up for dead," the physician told him. He bent down as he spotted the glint of the lost needle.

Gorgias tried to speak, but his fever prevented it. Zeno informed him that he had to amputate the arm, or he would inevitably die. Gorgias looked at him in horror.

"Even if I remove it, you could still die," the physician blurted out, as if talking about slaughtering a pig.

Gorgias understood. For a few days he had not felt his fingers. He had tried to ignore it, but from the elbow down all that remained was a lifeless limb. He pondered Zeno's words. If he lost the arm, he would lose his livelihood, but at least he could fight for Rutgarda. He looked at his pustule-covered arm miserably. It pulsated, but there was no pain. It was clear the physician was right. When Zeno explained that Genseric opposed the amputation, Gorgias could not comprehend it.

"I'm sorry, but he's the one paying," Zeno replied.

Gorgias tried to reach for something at his neck, but Zeno stopped him.

"Take it," Gorgias managed to utter. "The stones are rubies. It's more than you've ever been paid."

Zeno examined the necklace that hung from the patient's neck. He clasped it and then pulled it off him, thinking it over as he looked at the door. "Genseric will kill me."

But he spat on the ground and told Gorgias to bite into a dry stick. Then he took hold of the saw and carved through the arm like a butcher.

When Genseric returned, he found Gorgias unconscious in a great pool of blood. He looked for Zeno, but could not find him. The amputated limb lay on the floor. Where it used to be was now just a skillfully sewn stump.

Before long Zeno reappeared, doing up his trousers. When he saw Genseric he tried to explain that he had decided to do the inevitable, but the coadjutor would not heed reason. He cursed him a thousand times, condemned him to hell, insulted and attempted to hit him. But suddenly he calmed down, as if seized by a strange fatalism, before reeling again. He seemed confused. His gaze wandered around the room. Zeno managed to catch him before he collapsed onto the floor. He was coughing, his face pale as a mask of marble. The physician gave him a swig of liquor, which seemed to revive him.

"You look unwell. Would you like me to accompany you?"

Genseric nodded without conviction.

Zeno unfastened Gorgias's other arm, then brought his cart around, ushering on the coadjutor before loading Gorgias as if he were a sack of wheat. Finally he climbed on, cracked his whip, and guided the horse through the woods, following Genseric's confused directions. As they traveled, Zeno noticed that the coadjutor was repeatedly scratching the palm of his left hand. It seemed irritated, as though he had rubbed it with nettles. He mentioned it, but Genseric was oblivious.

They stopped in the oak grove near the fortress walls. Genseric clambered down from the cart and started walking, dragging his feet like a ghost until he reached a wall. In the darkness, the coadjutor groped among the climbing plants until he found a small door, took a key from his robes, and inserted it with difficultly into the lock. Then he leaned against the doorframe to rest before opening it and entering like a sleepwalker. Finally, he collapsed.

When Gorgias awoke the next day, Zeno was long gone, and Genseric's dead body lay by his side.

It was some time before Gorgias was able to stand. With his vision still cloudy, he looked at the stump that Zeno had bandaged for him with a strip of material from his own chasuble. The pain was excruciating, but at least it was not bleeding.

He turned toward Genseric's body. The monk was lying on the ground with a contorted expression, his hands clutching his stomach, the left one a strange purple color. Gorgias wanted to kick him, but contained himself.

Looking around, Gorgias saw that he was in the circular crypt where he had been imprisoned all that time. He turned toward the cell and pushed the door open with a squeak. Fear made him hesitate, but finally he went in to search through his documents. Fortunately, the truly valuable ones were still where he had hidden them. Stashing away the original and the Greek transcription, he did his best to tear up everything else he could find with his one hand. Then he took some bread that had been left there and departed for the old mine.

By midmorning he could make out the great, corroded honeycomb that the iron deposit had become. He continued along the old mining paths, among mounds of sandstone, the remains of old chests scattered around, broken lamps, and gnawed leather harnesses, which, after the mines were depleted, nobody bothered to remove.

Soon he reached the old slave huts and stopped to examine the half-ruined structures, often used by bandits and vermin, praying they were unoccupied. The rain was growing heavier, so he walked into the only hut that still had a partially preserved roof, seeking refuge among the pulleys, amphorae of caustic, tackle, and dismantled winches. Finally he found a space near some barrels full of stagnant water. He slumped against them and closed his eyes, trying to manage the searing pain. For a moment he wished he could cast off the bandage that covered the stump, but he knew it would be foolish.

He thought of his wife, Rutgarda.

He needed to know that nothing bad had happened to her, so he decided to visit her that night. He would wait for the sun to go down and then enter Würzburg through the drainage channel, which could be used to pass through the walls when the gates were locked. Trying in vain to get to sleep, he remembered his daughter Theresa. How he missed her!

He ate a little of the bread that he picked up in the crypt and pondered how Genseric had died. Over the course of his life he had witnessed many deaths, but never had he seen a face as distorted as the coadjutor's, choked on his own vomit. He wondered if he had been poisoned, perhaps by the man with the serpent tattoo.

Suddenly he could see it, like an apparition: the night when he was attacked. Those pale eyes, an arm thrusting at him, all his attempts hold his assailant off. His mind conjured the image of a snake wrapped round the dagger that had wounded him. Yes, he was certain. The man who had attacked him was same man who had argued with Genseric in the crypt. It was the man with the serpent tattoo.

At nightfall he began the journey back to Würzburg, where he arrived protected by the half-light. He found his house empty and he supposed Rutgarda was still sharing a roof with her sister, so he decided to try her home, located on the hillside. As he approached, he heard his wife humming a little tune she often sang. For a moment the pain in his shoulder disappeared. He was about to go in when he heard some men who were around the corner.

"Christ's wounds!" one of them blurted out. "I don't know what the hell we're doing here. The scribe has probably been eaten by wolves by now," said one of the men who was trying to protect himself from the downpour.

Gorgias cursed his bad luck. They were Wilfred's men, and the fact they were waiting for him suggested that Wilfred was involved. He couldn't take the risk, so he clenched his teeth and retraced, heavy-hearted that he wouldn't see Rutgarda.

On the way back to the mine, he looked up at the narrow illuminated windows above the fortress walls where Wilfred resided. The rain seemed to play with the lights, hiding and revealing them like some kind of riddle. As he speculated on the whereabouts of Wilfred's chambers, he heard clucking. The stink confirmed that the animal pens were just on the other side of the wall, which made him wonder whether he might be able to steal a chicken. He needed to eat, after all, and a bird that needed very little food could provide him with a delicious egg every day.

He looked around for a crack in the wall that would enable him to climb over, but soon realized that with just one arm, he would never manage. He made for the animal entrance, despite knowing that a guard would be posted there. As he approached, his hunch proved to be true. Behind the palisade, he could make out the image of Bernardino, the short, barrel-shaped Hispanic monk.

He stopped under a tree, undecided as to whether to continue. Briefly, he thought about speaking to the monk, but then concluded that would be a stupid thing to do. More clucking made him linger, his stomach cramped with hunger, then he heard a cart approaching. When it reached him, he could see that it was the same guards who had been at Rutgarda's sister's house moments before. As they arrived at the gate, the men called to Bernardino.

Approaching the cart to identify its occupants, he then opened up for them immediately.

"Damned rain! You've been relieved?" asked the midget, attempting to shield himself from the downpour.

The men responded listlessly and urged on the horse.

Gorgias took his opportunity. As the cart rolled past, he crouched down and ran beside it protected by the darkness. Once through the gate, he hid behind some bushes until the soldiers were out of sight. He breathed more easily after the midget had closed the gate and took shelter in the hut without spotting him.

Before long, when the monk's snoring confirmed that he was asleep, Gorgias crawled through the undergrowth in the direction of the animal pens. Where he reached the pen, he stopped for a while, determining which hen seemed the plumpest. Waiting for the chickens to calm down, he slowly opened the gate to the pen and snuck in like a stealthy fox hunting its prey. When he was close enough, he grabbed his quarry by the neck, but the bird started to cackle as if being plucked. All of a sudden, the rest of the hens woke up, making such a racket that Gorgias was sure they would wake the dead.

He kicked at them, making them scatter, then hid on the other side of the pen and waited for Bernardino to appear. The midget soon emerged, wondering what was going on, and Gorgias took the opportunity to run to the gate, escaping with the hen.

When he arrived at the mine it was still completely dark. He took shelter again in the slave hut beside the barrels. One of the barrels was empty so he used it as a cage for Blanca, his new tenant. Despite the pain in his shoulder, he soon fell into a deep sleep and was dead to the world until long after dawn. When he woke, Blanca the hen greeted him with an egg under her legs.

Gorgias repaid her with a couple of worms he found nearby, putting some spare ones in a wooden bowl, which he then covered with a stone. After drinking some fresh rainwater, he carefully unwound the bandage to examine his stump. Zeno had sawed off the bone just above the elbow and sewed up a flap of skin, which he had somehow also cauterized. The blisters from the burns were still visible. But Gorgias accepted his stump of an arm as a lesser evil, knowing that it had been the only way to prevent the rot from returning. He carefully re-bandaged himself and sat down to consider his situation.

In his head he tried to make sense of all the events that had transpired since the morning when a stranger with pale blue eyes had attacked him in order to steal the parchment in his bag. Then there was the fire and loss of his daughter. Remembering made him cry again. After the burial, Wilfred had ordered him to hand over the Donation of Constantine, but the document had gone up in flames in the parchment-maker's workshop. Then Genseric had intervened, in collusion with Wilfred himself, it would appear, to lock him away in the crypt in order to ensure he carried out his task. After a month in captivity, and without news of any imminent papal delegation, he had attempted to flee, which he managed thanks to Genseric's strange death. Then there was the man with the serpent tattoo, and the amputation of his ruined arm.

He pondered the role that Genseric had played. At first he had assumed he was acting by himself, had even assumed it was Genseric who had attacked him, but the unusual circumstances of his death and the fact that Wilfred was keeping watch over Rutgarda made him doubt those assumptions. And who was the serpent man? Certainly, it must be someone aware of what was happening. What's more, from the way he had threatened Genseric, he undoubtedly appeared to outrank him.

Resting against the barrels, Gorgias noticed that the hen was examining the bandages on his shoulder with her pea-brained curiosity, and he smiled bitterly. He had lost his right arm, his writing arm, because of a despicable document. He took the parchment out of his bag and studied it closely. For a moment he was tempted to tear it to pieces and offer it to Blanca as feed. But he resisted. After all, if it was so valuable, perhaps they would pay him to recover it.

It has stopped raining, so he got up to wander about the area and create a list of priorities. First he had to find a way to survive, a problem that was still unresolved despite the best efforts of the hen. On the way back to the mine, he had passed through a walnut grove. Nuts and berries could supplement the eggs, but even so he would need more food. He considered trying to catch some animal using Blanca as bait, but he soon decided that the idea would surely lose him his hen.

Hunting would be difficult. With just one arm, and without the necessary traps, even a duck could get away from him. But perhaps fishing would be possible. In the mine he had twine and thread, pieces of metal to bend into hooks, and enough worms to offer up a banquet. The river was close and while he waited for the fish to bite, he could make more hooks. He felt pleased to have resolved the problem of finding food. Then he remembered his wife Rutgarda, and he yearned to see her again.

He didn't know how long they would keep her under watch and he tried to think of someone who could help him, someone to tell her what he was doing and how he was faring. He would be satisfied if he could just let her know that he hadn't forgotten her. But he feared being discovered, so he decided to wait for a better opportunity. Rutgarda was doing well, and that was all that mattered.

After a while he took out the document and examined it carefully. Its transcription was perfectly finished, and he read it repeatedly, focusing on the parts that had surprised him while he made the copy. There was something dark in that parchment, something that perhaps Wilfred had not even noticed.

He put it in his bag and looked for somewhere to hide it. If he was captured, he might be able to negotiate with it. He inspected his surroundings until he found a beam that he considered suitable. Then he climbed up on to some barrels and hid the document behind it. Then he rolled away the barrels so nobody would have reason to even suspect. He looked up at the beams and was satisfied. Then he unleashed Blanca so she could go eat worms while he prepared the fishing hooks.

A week passed which Gorgias spent in terrible pain. His temperature rose, keeping him bedridden for a while, but just as quickly, the fever was gone. He amused himself with Blanca, giving her slack so she could search for worms by day, and bringing her in at night so that she would lay her eggs nearby. He found some old blankets, which he used to make himself comfortable. Sometimes he would climb to the top of the hill to look over the city, or admire the mountains in the distance, their snowy peaks beginning to thaw. He told himself that when the passes were clear, he could flee to another city with Rutgarda.

As the days went by, his arm improved. Gradually he began to move his shoulder without excruciating pain. The stitches fell out and the scar took on a pinkish tone like the rest of the shoulder. One morning the stump stopped hurting, and it never bothered him again.

At the beginning of the third week he decided to explore the tunnels that went down into the mine. In the nearest one, he found steel and enough tinder to light the torches that were mounted throughout the tunnels. Further down he found some strips of iron that he could use as cooking utensils. During his excursions he categorized the tunnels into caves, passages, and pits. The first two tunnels, which he thought had entrances prepared for moving animals and materials, he judged to be useful shelters. The rest of the tunnels were so slippery that he decided he would only use them if he were in danger.

In time he began to plan his return to Würzburg. He was growing thinner with each passing day, and was certain that if he stayed at the mine much longer, sooner or later he would be discovered. He was convinced that he could parley with Wilfred and reach some agreement. After all, the count was a cripple. Perhaps if he could find him alone, he could approach without risk. And he might be willing to exchange the document in return for guaranteeing the safety of him and his family. All he had to do was watch the count's movements in order to find the right moment.

He had spent the previous day preparing a beggar's outfit, which he easily achieved given the condition of his clothes. He had added a hat that he had found in the tunnels and a threadbare woolen cloak. He was about to don his outfit when he heard the pealing of bells in the distance sounding an alarm. It was the first time they had rung since the fire, and given that the entire city would be in a state of alert, he decided to wait until nightfall to avoid arousing suspicion.

As he descended the hill he feared the reason for the bells might have been a Saxon attack, but he continued regardless. However, when he arrived at the city gates, he found them closed. He spoke to a guard, saying he was a poor wanderer looking for some shelter, but the soldier suggested he go back to where he came from.

Despondent, he explored the unusually quiet streets of the outlying poor quarter. An old man peered out from the shack he was hiding in. When Gorgias asked him what was happening, the old man bolted his window shut, but Gorgias pressed him and he finally informed him that several young lads had been stabbed to death. Then added, "It's some man called Gorgias. The same one who murdered Genseric not long ago."

Gorgias was dumbstruck. He pulled his hat down over his ears and, without even saying thanks, fled toward the mountains.

FEBRUARY

21

The days went by and Helga the Black's belly swelled. Touching it, Theresa was surprised to find that she wished for Hoos Larsson to give her a child. However, the problems and complications of pregnancy made her push the idea from her mind, and she was content to stand by and admire the way Helga devoured every bit of food within reach.

But it was not just her belly that had changed. Pregnancy, it appeared, had transformed the slovenly woman into an industrious worker, for a few days earlier she had traded her tavern for a larger house near the chapter. She no longer caked her face in makeup and her attire began to resemble that of any respectable woman. And yet, what astonished Theresa most was the ease with which Helga labored in the kitchens. Favila said she had a gift for stewing, to the point that she had stepped back from the pots to leave that responsibility to the new cook. Theresa told herself that, ultimately, all that would remain of the old Helga was the terrible scar that her lover had left on her face.

Helga, however, only seemed to care about the future of her child. She rocked her great belly as if it were a cradle, sung made-up melodies to it softly, explained to it the secrets of a good roast pheasant. She knitted tiny hats that would keep the baby's head warm. She prayed for the child that she suspected was a girl, and she visited Nicholas, the old carpenter who, in exchange for some pastries, was building a beautiful cot for the baby in his free time.

Despite her belly, Helga did not neglect her duties in the chapter kitchen. Indeed, that night a dinner was to be held as an apology to Alcuin of York, that was to be attended by the king and his entourage. For the occasion, Helga had prepared capon and pigeon, grilled pheasant and freshly killed venison, which alongside an ox stew and the cheesecake made by Favila, would surely delight the guests. Generally dinner was served in the refectory after the None service, but on this occasion Ludwig, Lothar's secretary, had commandeered a smaller chamber located above the calefactory, for there would not be a large number of diners.

For Theresa, the banquet would have just been another dinner, were it not for the fact that she had been invited.

"The king insists," Alcuin had informed her.

From that moment, Theresa had been a bundle of nerves, trying to memorize the *Appendix Vergiliana*, Virgil's epic poems that Alcuin had told her to recite during the feast.

"You don't have to learn them by heart," the monk had explained, "but you must practice them several times so that you find the right intonation."

However, Theresa's greatest concern was whether the dress that Helga had bought for her that afternoon in the textile district would fit properly.

When she had finished her work in the scriptorium, she set off for Helga's house trembling like a chicken up until she put on the dress and saw herself transformed into a lady of refinement. She was dying to show it off, but Helga made her wait for the final touches to be made. Finally, her friend stepped back to check the fit, tightened the dress a little more, and then hugged her affectionately. "It's too close-fitting, isn't it?" Theresa said, embarrassed.

"You look beautiful," Helga the Black informed her, telling her to run along to the dinner.

When she reached the dining hall, she saw that the guests were already settled in their seats. She was received by Alcuin, who apologized for her lateness. Theresa curtsied to the monarch, then ran with dainty steps to the place that had been reserved for her, beside an elegantly dressed young woman. The girl greeted her with a smile that revealed tiny white teeth. She looked about twenty years old, though later Theresa discovered that she was around fifteen. A servant whispered to Theresa that it was Gisela, the eldest daughter of Charlemagne, and this was not the first time she had visited Fulda because, aside from the battlefield, she accompanied her father wherever he went. Theresa counted another twenty or so people, most of them the king's men, as well as five or six tonsured fellows she assumed belonged to the diocese. Charlemagne presided over the long rectangular table, which was covered in impeccable linen tablecloths and decorated with winter flowers. Several trays full of game competed abundantly for space with plates of cheese, cold meats, and fruit, while dozens of jugs of wine sat packed in among the food signaling a celebration fit for kings.

At the monarch's signal, they all raised their cups and started eating like ravenous animals. As the dinner progressed, Theresa noticed that some of the diners, their appetite for food sated, turned their attention to her curves. Embarrassed, she loosened her belt so that the dress did not cling to her so tightly and then she positioned a centerpiece of flowers between her and the ogling eyes. Gisela realized what was happening and added another couple of bunches to hide Theresa even more.

"Don't worry," the girl said with a smile. "All men are the same— except if they drink. Then they're worse."

When the desserts arrived, Alcuin approached Theresa and told her to stand, an event which some men approved of vociferously. A cleric too drunk to applaud got up from his chair and attempted to say a few words, but all he managed to do was belch before losing his footing and collapsing onto the table. After they had removed him, Charlemagne stood and asked Theresa to read.

Before beginning she prepared herself by taking a swig of wine. The long draft gave her courage. She dodged the scraps of food scattered around the floor and went over to the lectern that Alcuin had prepared for her. She opened the codex and took a deep breath. As soon as the first word left her mouth, the room fell silent. She read slowly, calmly—sometimes whispering, sometimes impassioned. When she had finished, nobody said a thing. Charlemagne was still standing, transfixed, looking at her oddly. For a moment Theresa thought he was about to reprove her, but to her surprise, the king filled his cup and offered it to her in admiration. She accepted it, but when he told her that he wanted to see her in his private chambers, the cup slipped through her fingers, causing wine to splash all over her new dress.

After the dinner, Theresa told Helga what had happened.

"Consider yourself fucked," she responded.

Theresa regretted having worn the dress. She was scared, but she didn't believe the king could force her to do anything like that. She decided to speak to Alcuin before going to meet the monarch. However, try as she might, she could not find him anywhere.

As two guards led her to Charlemagne's chamber, Theresa prayed he would be asleep. To her relief, Alcuin opened the door. The monk invited her in and stood beside her as they waited for Charlemagne to finish washing.

"Ah! You're here! Come in and take a seat," said the king.

As he dried his torso, Theresa admired him. Though he was of a mature age, he was the biggest man she had ever seen. Bigger still than the largest of the Saxons.

"Excellent. So has Alcuin informed you of my intentions?"

"No, Your Majesty," she stammered.

"He has told me that you are very clever. That it was you who discovered the contaminated wheat."

Theresa looked at Alcuin, red-faced, but he merely nodded.

"The truth is that it happened by chance," she said.

"And that you also found the hidden text in the polyptych?"

The young woman looked to Alcuin again. For a moment she thought that Charlemagne was trying to implicate her, but Alcuin reassured her.

"Well, I went over the polyptych several times, but the credit should go to Brother Alcuin. It was he who insisted on it."

"Modest as well as bold. Let's not forget your role in obtaining the final piece of evidence."

She blushed. It was true she had taken a risk when she tore out the page from the polyptych, but she hadn't expected the king to acknowledge it. She was still suspicious of the reasons for this praise.

"Thank you, Your Majesty," she managed to say.

Charlemagne grunted, finished drying himself, and then covered himself with a woolen cloak.

"I would like your behavior to serve as an example for my subjects. I have discussed it with Alcuin, and he has agreed—so I have decided to reward you in some way. Perhaps with those lands that belonged to the bishopric."

Theresa was speechless. Now she was sure he must be joking.

"After all," continued the king, "the land was only half-plowed, and if it is not cleared, then it will be a waste."

"But I . . . I don't know anything about crops or land."

"That's what Alcuin told me, so I told my engineer to take a look. He will give you the help you need. Furthermore," he added, "just the verses you recited would have earned you this reward."

Theresa left the room in a daze. She could not believe that overnight she had gone from being a poor, frightened outsider to an estate owner. And not only that: Charlemagne had assured her that she would have the grain needed to sow the fields immediately. When she told Helga, her friend said she was not convinced.

"You know what? Nor am I!" Theresa replied, and they both burst out laughing like madwomen. They curled up in front of the fire and talked, trying to guess the size and location of the land and fantasizing about the wealth that it would bring. Helga warned that, in reality, land itself was worthless. If it was to provide income, she would need laborers, oxen, seeds, equipment, and water, and even then, rarely did they yield more than the sustenance needed by the families who worked them. But Theresa preferred to close her eyes and imagine herself alongside Hoos as a powerful landowner.

Then the two friends went to bed side by side, huddled up against each other to keep the cold out. Helga soon fell asleep, but Theresa spent the night thinking, imagining what would happen if the king was good for his word.

The next morning Theresa went to the scriptorium, where she found Brother Alcuin absorbed in his texts. The monk greeted her without raising his head, but then he looked up to congratulate her on her good fortune.

"I don't think he was serious," she ventured.

"Then you had better start believing it. The king is not a man who speaks lightly."

"But I know nothing of farming. What will I do with the lands?" She waited for him to give her the answer.

"I don't know. Work them, I suppose. Reading and writing is not a trade that supports a family. You should be happy."

"I am. But I don't know . . ."

"If you don't know, then learn." He turned back to his mass of documents, signaling that their conversation had ended.

Midmorning a servant appeared in the scriptorium asking for Theresa. He informed them that one of Charlemagne's men awaited her in the main square ready to accompany her to her new land. Theresa asked Alcuin to go with her, but he refused, saying he had too much work. With the monk's permission, the young woman wrapped up warmly and went with the servant to the place where a young man was waiting for her on horseback.

The king's engineer was brown-skinned and wavy-haired. His green eyes contrasted attractively with his weather-beaten complexion. Despite his different appearance, he reminded her somehow of Hoos Larsson. He said his name was Izam of Padua.

"Can you ride?" he asked. A riderless mount was grazing beside him.

Theresa held on to the reins and with a leap she was in the saddle. The young man smiled. He turned his horse, spurred it on and started to trot slowly through Fulda's narrow streets.

They rode north, following the river through a lush forest of beech trees with the sun's tepid rays evaporating the damp earth smell that merged with the sweet aroma of the morning. After traveling in silence for some time, Theresa inquired about the meaning of the word *engineer*.

"I confess it's a little-used term," he responded with a laugh. "It's used to describe people, like me, who built *engines* for war."

The young man continued to speak as if he were discussing the matter with a colleague, enthusiastically explaining the importance of catapults and the difference between onagers and mangonels, without realizing that Theresa was yawning continually. By the time he noticed, he had already told her almost everything he knew.

"Sorry. I'm boring you."

"It's not that," Theresa said, "it's just that I don't share your passion for weapons. Plus, I don't understand what your profession has to do with my land."

Izam thought about replying, but decided not to waste his breath on a girl who didn't value his knowledge. A couple of miles on they reached a clear demarcation of hawthorn wattle that stretched into a far-off forest. A small part of the land seemed to have been plowed, but most of it was still uncultivated. The young man jumped down from his horse, opened what appeared to be a rudimentary gate, and walked into the enclosure.

"It appears the bishop knew what he was doing. Wait here a moment."

As Theresa dismounted, Izam started walking with exaggerated steps. Suddenly he turned around with an expression of astonishment. He climbed back on his horse and told Theresa to wait as he galloped off.

But soon he returned in a state of excitement. "Lass, you can't imagine what has fallen into your hands. The fief has about ten *bonniers* of arable land, of which half has already been plowed. Beyond, on the other side of the hill, there are around six arpents of vines and three or four of pasture. But that's not all: The river we left behind us branches off into a stream that runs into this area."

Theresa looked at him blankly.

"Let me explain. Do you know what a fief is?"

"Of course. It's the land that a family owns," she responded, offended that he had assumed she might not know.

"But its size does not depend on the amount of land available, but on whether the family is able to cultivate it."

"I know." She was still none the wiser, and she felt that she would never learn to cultivate the land.

They wandered around the estate on horseback, talking about plots, fiefs, arpents, and perches—and admiring the work that the bishop had already done. They found pens for animals, a newly built shepherd's hut, and timber foundations for what could be a magnificent home. Theresa was surprised that Izam knew about farming, but the young man explained that his trade was not restricted to building engines of war. In truth, he told her, battles between armies usually ended in endless sieges that required exhaustive knowledge of the surrounding land, for they had to prevent the movement of supplies, divert watercourses, assess the position of defenses, choose the right places to make camp, and, on occasion, dig saps or mines into walls. The same factors also had to be considered when an army wanted to build a new settlement.

"And that's not all. Sometimes sieges continue for years, so it's important to know which fields are appropriate, both for growing grain for the soldiers and fodder for the animals." He bent down to pick up a pebble. "For instance, see that hillock?" He tossed the stone, which flew into the tops of some fir trees. "It's to the north. It will protect the sown fields from the icy winds. And look at this soil," he said as he squashed a clod under his foot. "Light and damp, like brown bread soaked in water."

Theresa bent down and picked up another pebble.

"And that there?" she said, pointing toward a little mound. She took a step back and tried to launch the stone at it. Izam moved his head out of the way instinctively. The stone fell far short of its mark. After his initial surprise, he burst into laughter like little boy.

"Don't make fun of me," Theresa complained.

"Oh, so you did it on purpose!" he replied, laughing heartily again.

They sat down to eat lunch on some piles of wood that marked the ground plan of the house. Izam had brought a bag of freshly baked bread and cheese, which they savored as they listened to the gurgle of a nearby stream. A couple of hours had gone by, but Izam admitted that they were actually very close to the town still. "Half an hour on horseback," he told her.

"So why did we take so long?"

"I wanted to follow the course of the river, to see if it's navigable. If you can get your hands on a barge, then you'll be able to use it to transport grain. By the way, there is something that worries me." He went over to his mount and took a crossbow from a saddlebag. "Recognize it?"

"Nope," she responded without paying it much attention.

"It's the one picked up and used the other day at dinner."

"Ah! I don't know. I wouldn't know one from another."

"That's precisely what intrigues me. I don't believe there is another one like this in all Franconia."

He explained that the crossbow was a rare weapon. In fact, he had never seen any other.

"I built this following the descriptions provided by Vegetius in his work *De Re Militari*, a fourth-century manuscript on the art of war that Charlemagne showed to me. That was why I was surprised, not just that you not only chose it from the pile, but also that you knew how to use it."

She told him that a man who had helped her in the mountain possessed a similar weapon. But when she told him that he had bought it from a soldier, he shook his head in wonder.

"The first one I built was stolen from me. Perhaps it was the soldier you mention, or even the man who helped you."

They chatted for a while longer before she suggested they return. Izam agreed. He took one last look at the land and led the horses to the stream to water them. Once they had set off, Theresa spurred on her mount, for she was eager to tell Helga about all she had seen.

As they returned to Fulda, Theresa thanked the engineer again. Izam smiled, but told her that it was Charlemagne who she should be thanking. All he had done was follow his orders. When they finally went their separate ways, his green eyes lingered with her.

Back in the kitchens, Theresa found Helga plucking a pheasant. She seemed busy, but as soon as she saw Theresa, she dropped the bird and ran to meet her. Theresa suggested they go out to the well and take a break on the way. They sat on a stone bench and Helga demanded to hear every last detail. She listened to Theresa with such excitement it was as if the land belonged to her.

"And all that is yours?" she asked in disbelief.

Theresa nodded. She told her about the great expanse of the arable areas, the vineyards, the hay meadows, the river, and the house. Finally, she also mentioned the young man, Izam.

"He was very kind," she said.

"And handsome," Helga added, giving her a wink. She had seen him through the window.

Theresa smiled. Indeed, the engineer was attractive, though of course, not as handsome as Hoos. They continued to talk about the lands until Favila, fed up with their chitchat, came out to prod them back to work with a poker.

The two women laughed and ran to the kitchen to continue their conversation whenever the cook left the room. Theresa told her that she was worried about her lack of means to work the land, and Helga reassured her.

"But you can't imagine how much there is to do! The lands are only half-tilled. I'll need a plow and an ox—and someone to help me. So many things!"

"Oh! I bet you'd be less worried if you had debts instead of lands."

Theresa fell silent. Perhaps, she thought, there was a neighbor who could give her advice, but the fact was that the only person she had to turn to for help was right in front of her. Seeing her despondency, Helga put her arm around her.

"Cheer up! I still have some of the money you gave me when you sold the bear's head. You could use it to buy a young ox."

"But that money's for my lodgings."

"Don't be silly, lass. You got me this job, so don't you worry about it. Anyway, this is your opportunity: When the land starts to bear fruit, you'll pay me back with interest." She pinched her cheek.

She explained that a one-year-old ox cost twelve denarii, while an adult one ranged between forty-eight and seventy-two, or in other words, around three months' wages. To Theresa the price seemed within anyone's reach, but Helga explained that nobody can go three months without eating. When they had finished their cooking duties, Theresa continued the conversation.

"Izam said we can return to the lands tomorrow. What do you think I should call them?"

"Hmmm, let me think . . . Theresa's wonderlands!" she said, laughing.

The young woman cuffed Theresa around the head and Helga returned the gesture, making them laugh like little girls.

In the afternoon Theresa returned to the scriptorium, where she found Alcuin buried in his documents. She had hundreds of questions for him, but as she was about to start asking them, the monk stood.

"I saw Izam. He told me that your lands are excellent."

"Yes . . . though I don't know how they can be excellent if I don't even know how to work them," she lamented.

"You appear to have two good hands."

"And little else. What good are those fields to me if I have no tools, no animals?"

"In that case, you could lease it and obtain an income."

"Izam suggested the same thing. But to whom? Those who could afford it already have more than enough land."

"Find someone who will work it in exchange for part of the crop."

"Izam proposed that, too, but he explained that those folks do not possess plows or oxen, so they would not be able to work the land and generate a profit."

"All right. Then I'll tell you what we'll do. Tomorrow is Thursday. After Terce we'll go to the market, find a hardworking slave and buy him for your lands. There are tons of them, so we might get a good price."

Theresa could not believe what she was hearing. It felt like her life was growing more complicated by the moment. If she did not even have enough for herself, how could she own a slave?

Alcuin admitted to her that Charlemagne had already suggested this possibility, then Alcuin assured her that keeping a slave did not have to be expensive.

The next morning they left early for the camp that the king's men had set up on the outskirts of the city. According to Alcuin, the slave traders used the monarch's visits as an opportunity to conduct business, whether buying captured enemies who had been enslaved or selling some of their best slaves. However, after a few days, the traders reduced their prices in order to get rid of the less sought-after individuals.

"Twelve solidi?" Theresa's hands went to her mouth. "But you could buy three oxen for that!"

Alcuin explained that it was the usual price for a young, well-trained slave, but if they hunted around they might find one for cheaper. When Theresa told him how much money she had, Alcuin showed her a bulging pouch.

"I could lend you some."

As they walked toward the walls, Alcuin spoke to her of the responsibility that came with owning slaves. "It's not just a matter of giving orders and them obeying you," he explained. "Believe it or not, slaves are God's creatures, too, and as such we must ensure their well-being. And this includes feeding them, clothing them, and educating them as good Christians."

Theresa looked at him in surprise. In Constantinople she had grown up surrounded by slaves who she had always considered as creatures of God, but she had never imagined that owning one could result in so many problems. When Alcuin explained that owners were also responsible for the crimes committed by their slaves, she became even more alarmed.

"That's why it's best not to buy them young—when they are agile and strong, but also rebellious and irresponsible. Unless you are prepared to take a whip to them, you are better off finding one that is married with children—so he won't attempt to escape or cause problems. Yes, the best thing to do is find a family that will work hard and generate a profit for you."

He added that even if she found a hard worker, she would have to keep a close eye on him because, by nature, slaves were short on brains.

"I don't know if I need a slave," Theresa finally admitted. "I don't even know if I should have one."

"What do you mean?"

"I don't understand why one person should rule over the life of another. Have these poor wretches not been baptized?"

"I don't suppose most of them have, no. But even if they were, and even though original sin disappears upon baptism, it is right that God decides the life of men, making some slaves and others lords. By nature, slaves have a tendency toward evil, which is repressed by the power of their possessor. If a slave did not know fear, what would prevent him from acting treacherously?"

Theresa considered replying, but decided to put an end to the conversation in which she had no real arguments or ideas.

They soon reached the gates and the rancid smell of sweat announced their arrival at the slave market. Stalls lined the river in a succession of shabby tents of various sizes, where slaves milled around like livestock. The younger ones were chained to thick stakes driven into the ground, while the older ones submissively went about their cleaning and maintenance tasks around the camp. As the monk passed them, several traders rushed to offer him their wares.

"Take a look at this one," said a trader riddled with pockmarks. "Strong as a bull. He will carry your loads and protect you on your travels. Or would you prefer a boy?" he whispered, noting Alcuin's indifference. "Sweet as honey and willing as a puppy."

Alcuin gave him a look that the trader immediately understood, retreating with his tail between his legs. They continued to wander between the stalls, where all kinds of goods were on sale aside from the slaves.

"Ready-sharpened weapons!" cried one trader, showing off an arsenal of daggers and swords. "Send your enemies to hell in one slash."

"Ointments for boils, poultices for riding sores!" announced another whose appearance suggested he needed them himself.

They passed the first stands and arrived at the enclosure where animals were being sold. Horses, cattle, and goats wandered about with more freedom that the slaves they had just seen. Alcuin stopped to inspect an ox as big as a mountain. The animal was grazing behind a wall with a batch of cheese resting on top of it.

A dealer approached to help him make his mind up. "You have a good eye, monk! Quite an animal you're looking at."

Alcuin gave him a sidelong glance. Though he did not like to do business with dubious traders, he had to admit that the beast seemed strong as iron. He asked for the price and the man thought about it. "Since it's for the clergy . . . fifty solidi."

Alcuin's look was of such indignation that the man immediately brought the figure down to forty-five.

"That's still a lot of money."

The animal stood before them impressively.

"If you want a horned goat, I can sell you one for thirty-five," the dealer blurted out without much interest.

Alcuin told the man he would think about it. Then he and Theresa returned to the area where the slaves were sold. At the entrance, Alcuin asked Theresa to let him continue alone in order to make haste. The young woman agreed to meet him back at the same place when the sun reached its highest point.

While Alcuin bartered with the merchants, Theresa decided to take another look at the livestock. On her way there, a trader offered her a few coins for her body and she quickened her pace. When she reached the pen with the ox that had interested Alcuin, a little man hobbled up to her.

"I wouldn't pay more than ten solidi for it," he said, giving her a sideways glance.

Theresa turned in surprise to see an unkempt middle-aged man, leaning against the timber fence and staring brazenly at her. His blond hair matched his ice-blue eyes. However, his most striking feature was the fact that he was supported by just one leg. Seeing Theresa's surprise, he jumped in. "I lost it working, but I'm still useful," he explained.

"And what do you know about oxen?" she asked him haughtily. It was obvious the man was a slave, and if one day she was to own one, she thought she should know how to handle them.

"I was born in Friesland, where there is more cattle than there is pasture. Even a blind man can spot a sick ox."

While the herder was distracted, the man took the opportunity to strike the animal with his stick. The beast didn't flinch.

"See? And the same thing will happen when it's yoked. It won't move."

Theresa looked at the man in surprise. Then her eyes followed the slave's stick as he pointed at the animal's hoofs, which were encrusted in dried blood.

"If you want a good animal, see my master, Fior. He won't cheat you."

At that moment the owner of the ox returned and the slave slunk off. Theresa noticed that he used a crutch in place of his absent leg. She ran after him and asked where she could find Fior. The slave told her to follow him.

As they walked, he told her that Fior only sold small oxen.

"They're not as powerful, but strong enough to pull a light plow. However, they're resilient, they don't need much food, and they cost less. For these lands they are just what you need."

They walked among the carts, dodging the streams of detritus that zigzagged from the camp down toward the stream, until a woman and two little boys came out to meet them. One of the little boys came from the slave stands. The woman embraced the one-legged man, and the children tugged at his clothes. Theresa noticed how thin the woman and the boys were. Their eyes were like great sunken dishes on tiny skulls.

"Did you get anything?" the woman asked.

From the pocket of his trousers, the slave took a bundle of cheese and gave it to her. She smelled it and cried with joy. Then she picked up the children and carried them behind a tent to feed them. The slave hobbled over to Fior to explain to his master what the young woman needed, which is when Alcuin appeared with a cross expression on his face. He was accompanied by the owner of the giant ox.

"This trader says a crippled slave stole some cheese from him. And he says the slave was with you. Is that right?" he asked Theresa.

The young woman understood what had happened. Behind the tent, the slave's two boys were still devouring the cheese. Their punishment would undoubtedly be horrific.

"Not exactly," she lied. "It was me who told him to take it. He had no money with him so I came to find his master so that he would pay for it."

"That's theft!" cried the merchant.

"It was theft trying to sell us a sick ox," Theresa retorted fearlessly. "Here," she said, taking the pouch from Alcuin's robe and giving him a couple of coins, much to the monk's surprise. "And get out of my sight before I go to the judge."

There trader took the money and left muttering curses. Alcuin gave Theresa a stern look.

"He tried to trick us," she explained, pointing after the livestock merchant.

Alcuin's expression did not change.

"This slave took the cheese for his children. Look at them! They're on death's door!"

"He's a thief. And you were foolish to attempt to protect him."

"Very well. Then go back to that saintly ox trader and spend your money on a useless beast. All I know is that the slave warned me against that swindler and his children have perhaps not eaten for a week."

Alcuin shook his head. Then he accompanied her to go and speak with the livestock merchant and owner of the slave.

Fior turned out to be a stout man who would only do business with a glass of wine in his hand. As soon as he had greeted them, he offered them a drink and showed them several animals brimming with health and vitality. He offered them a medium-sized dappled ox, which he assured them would work like a maniac from day one.

They agreed on a price of twenty denarii, a good deal considering the animal was over three years old.

"Not unlike me," said Fior with a smile, revealing several wooden teeth. "Slender and hardworking from the moment I get out of bed."

Then he showed them some leather tack and several farming implements. Some were in need of repair, but they were needed and the merchant offered them for a good price, so Theresa and Alcuin decided to buy them. After securing the gear to the ox, they asked Fior about cheap slaves, but when he heard how much money they had, he shook his head and assured them that for that price they couldn't even buy a domesticated pig.

"For that money I could sell you Olaf. He's a hard worker, but since he lost his leg he's only brought me problems. He's yours if you want him."

Seeing her apparent interest, Alcuin took Theresa aside.

"It would just be another mouth to feed. And for the love of God! He's missing a leg. Why would he give him away if he was any use?" he blurted out.

But the young woman became obstinate. If she were going to own slaves, she would be the one to decide how many legs they had.

"His wife and children can also work," she argued.

"He won't sell them. Or he'll ask for more money. More than we can pay. Plus, you need a slave, not an entire family."

"It was you who told me that married ones are preferable, with ties that will stop them from fleeing."

"For goodness' sake! How is he going to run away if he's crippled?"

Theresa turned away and approached Fior, who was patiently waiting with the cup of wine still in his hand.

"All right, we'll take them," she said, pointing at the woman and her children who were listening in from behind a cart.

"Oh! No. The woman and children aren't included. If you want them you'll have to pay another fifty denarii."

"Fifty denarii for a family of skeletons?" she replied in indignation.

"No, no. Fifty each! In total, a hundred and fifty denarii."

Theresa looked him directly in the eyes. If he thought he was a good barterer, he didn't know who he was dealing with yet. She took out her scramasax and in one slash cut the strap that held the gear to the ox, making everything fall to the ground with a loud crash. The man looked at her in surprise.

"Forty denarii for the whole family. Take it, or you can keep your cripple, your midget ox, and your knackered old implements."

The man clenched his teeth, looked at the gear and burst into laughter, flashing his gums.

"Damned money-grubber! To hell with all you women."

He laughed again and took the pouch that the young woman was holding out to him. Then he toasted the transaction before Theresa and Alcuin set off on their return trip, with Olaf hobbling behind them and his wife pulling the ox with the two children sitting on its hindquarters, prodding it along.

On their way to the cathedral, Olaf proved to be a poor walker but able talker. His life had been a difficult one, though no more than any other slave-born man. His parents had been slaves and it was a natural state of life for him. He did not yearn for freedom, for he had never known it, and most of his masters had treated him well because he had always worked hard.

In fact, the only thing Olaf pined for was his missing leg. It had happened two years earlier while he was felling a great fir tree. It came down sooner than he expected and crushed his knee, shattering the bones. Fortunately, a butcher managed to amputate his broken limb before the rot could take him to the grave. Since then his family's situation had deteriorated to become a living hell.

At first, his master Fior had attended to him in the hope that he would be able to work just as he had before the accident. However, he soon realized that having just one leg had made Olaf a burden that was difficult to justify.

While Olaf was recovering, his knowledge of the fields and skill with his hands made up for his invalidity, but as soon as Fior appointed a new foreman, Olaf was relegated to women's tasks. So he went from overseeing the rest of the slaves to dragging himself around the storerooms searching for scraps with which to feed his children and his wife, Lucille.

"But I can still work," Olaf insisted as he stepped up the pace with his crutch. "I can ride, and I know the countryside like the palm of my hand."

"Don't buy any horses then," Alcuin whispered to Theresa, "or he'll take off on the first one we acquire."

Back in Fulda, Alcuin suggested that Olaf and his family stay in the abbey until the hut in the forest was ready. They stabled the ox and went to the monastery kitchen, where some monks provided them with onion soup and apples, the children celebrating as if they had been given cake. After dinner they were allowed to sleep near the fire, which they were all grateful for. Worn out, the mother and children soon fell asleep, but Olaf barely closed his eyes, for he had never slept on a woolen pallet.

The next morning, Theresa went to the monastery stables before taking them to their new land. At the stables they were lent a cart to transport the grain, some food, and some old implements that they would have to return within a week. Theresa thanked Alcuin for excusing her from her usual duties for the day and for his help obtaining the loan of tools. Though they went by the shortest route, it took them half the morning since Olaf insisted on traveling on foot to show Theresa that he could manage by himself.

When they reached the hut, the boys seemed delighted. They climbed up onto the roof like squirrels and ran through the fields until they collapsed with exhaustion. Olaf called them nicknames like midgets, loudmouths, and urchins, but he always called his wife his "beloved Lucille."

Together Lucille and Olaf built a rudimentary fence around the hut, cleared the area around it, and made a mound of stones where they could cook without the wind blowing the fire about. They prepared a stew of pork belly and turnips, which the boys devoured before it even hit their plates. Olaf then built some simple traps, which he set up in the surrounding area. It would mean they could add rabbit and mice to the pulses that they would have to live off of until spring.

By midafternoon, in unison the boys announced the arrival of a man on horseback. It was Izam of Padua, Charlemagne's engineer.

Olaf neared the horse so he could tend to it, but the man remained mounted. He approached Theresa and told her to jump on. She was surprised, but she obeyed.

"Alcuin told me about this foolery," he said, "but I can see it's worse than I thought. What possessed you to buy a cripple? What a way to ruin your estate."

"Well, he doesn't seem to be doing such a bad job," Theresa said, pointing at the slave. At that moment, Olaf was returning with a rabbit in his hand.

Then Izam spurred on the animal until they were some distance from the hut.

"These are lands to sweat blood into. They're not for a charity case. It rains, hails, and snows here—you'll have to plow fields, fell trees, drive oxen, build a house, saw timber, clear undergrowth, and do a thousand other things. Who is going to do all that? A one-legged man and three skeletons?"

Theresa dismounted from the horse and started walking back to the hut. Izam turned his mount and followed her.

"What a stubborn girl. Going back there won't solve anything. You'll just have to sell them again."

The young woman spun round. "Who do you think you are? These lands are mine, and I will do as I please with them."

"Oh really?" Izam said, skeptically glancing at the slaves.

She realized in that moment that the slaves were her responsibility now: As Alcuin had informed her, she had to look after them, and if they did not work hard enough, the land might become their grave.

When she asked Izam what options she had, he assured her that the few he could think of all involved selling the slaves. "I'm not saying they're useless, but they're not for this estate. Let's go back to the market. Perhaps we can return them without losing much money."

Theresa acknowledged that he was probably right. Yet when they returned to the hut and she saw the two little boys playing, she was incapable of accepting his proposal.

"Let's wait a week," she suggested. "If in that time they haven't been able to do what is necessary, I will take them to the market myself."

Izam groaned through his teeth. It would mean losing a week, but at least that madwoman would see for herself the mistake she had made. He climbed down from the horse and went into the hut to warm up. Inside, he was surprised by the neat and tidy appearance of the space, as if it had been lived in for a long time.

"Who repaired the walls?" he asked in disbelief.

"The useless cripple," Theresa answered. She then shoved him aside to straighten a board that was out of place. Olaf rushed to help.

"Here, use this," said Izam grudgingly.

Olaf took the knife Izam was holding out and used it to secure the board in place.

"Thank you." He returned it and Izam sheathed the weapon.

"It's cold out there. Tell your wife to come in. Do you have tools?" the engineer asked.

Olaf showed him the ones that the abbey had lent them: a hand axe, a pick, and an adze. He told him that in the evening he would make a good wooden mallet, and perhaps a rake. Not much more, for he had to repair the plow they had acquired.

"It's wooden," he informed Izam. "The plowshare needs replacing."

Izam said that without an iron plowshare and a good mold-board, they would not succeed in making the furrows. Then he looked at Olaf's crutch.

"Can I have a look?"

He examined the stick closely. It was a crudely carved cherry-wood branch with a leather-lined wooden support at the top. He tested its flexibility and returned it to him.

"Right. I must go," he announced.

He stood and left the hut and Theresa followed. When they were outside, she thanked him for his understanding.

"I still think it's madness . . . but there you go. If I have time, I'll see if I can make him a wooden leg."

The young man mounted his horse and took his leave. Before he was out of sight, Theresa noticed him turn to look at her.

22

All week, Theresa alternated her work at the bishopric with managing her new lands. She found that Olaf had dug a small channel from the stream leading to the hut to avoid having to continually transport heavy pails of water. He had built a gate for the fence and four stools for his family to sit on. But it was not just the fields he had taken care of. Between the efforts of both he and his wife the hut had been transformed into a proper home. Helga the Black had given them a chest and small table, as well as fabrics that Lucille had used to prevent the wind from coming in through the cracks. Olaf had dug a fireplace in the center of the hut, and on each side they had arranged sacks of straw on which to sleep at night. As for the plow, though he could repair it, he was unable to handle it. Lucille had tried, too, but by the third day her hands were covered in blisters. Olaf grumbled to Theresa.

"It's this damned leg," he said, hitting it. "Before I could have plowed these fields in two days, but God knows it's not a woman's work."

Theresa took a deep breath and grimaced. She looked at the two little lads scampering between the ox's legs, laughing and enjoying themselves, black as coal from the filth but already with a little more meat on their bones. The situation saddened her, but if Olaf could not till the soil, she would be forced to resell them.

She looked at him furtively as he cleaned the ox collar. She was about to say something when he seemed to read her thoughts. "I'm modifying the collar so that the pull is lower. That way the ox will lower its neck and press the plow into the earth."

Theresa shook her head at the futility of his efforts. Olaf didn't understand the situation she was in.

They were about to get up when they heard the sound of hooves. As they came out of the hut, they saw Izam of Padua riding toward them, and behind him, a donkey laden with wood. The engineer dismounted and went into the hut without saying a word. He measured Olaf's stump with a cord and then went out with the same determination with which he had arrived. Soon he returned carrying an armful of sticks.

"A one-legged man is like a woman without breasts," he announced.

Theresa was annoyed by the comparison, but she watched closely as Izam quickly tore off Olaf's empty trouser leg, revealing a poorly stitched stump.

"In Poitiers I had the opportunity to examine a wooden leg of extraordinary worth. Nothing like those sticks that cripples tie to their stumps in order to walk around like snails." He measured the diameter of the stump again and then measured a piece of wood. "The leg I speak of was a miracle of engineering, an articulated device that they said belonged to an Arab general who died in the terrible battle. Fortunately a monk pulled it from the body and kept it at the abbey." He measured Olaf's good leg and transposed the measurements to the wood again. Then he pulled out a strange mechanism that seemed to Theresa like some kind of knee joint. "It took me two days to make this, so I hope it works."

Olaf let Izam do his work while Lucille led away the children, who were fighting with each other over whatever pieces of wood they could get their hands on. Theresa was transfixed.

•

Izam chose a cylindrical piece of wood, adjusted it at one end to the wooden joint, and positioned it beside the good leg. Then he cut the other end until it was level with Olaf's heel.

"Now the thigh."

He took a wooden pot and pushed it onto the stump. As soon as he let go, it fell to the floor, but he picked it up as if nothing had happened and continued carving into it until it fit the limb. Then he removed it to empty it a little more and line the inside with a piece of cloth and some leather.

"Right. I think that's it." He pulled the socket over the stump and then secured it in place with some belts that he had brought with him. Then he calculated the length of the wood he would have to cut for the space between the socket and the knee mechanism.

"How does it work?" Olaf asked.

"I don't know if it will."

He helped the slave up and Olaf stood, wobbling slightly with his weight resting on the wooden limb.

"The foot still needs to go on, but I need to see if the spring holds. Now try to walk."

Olaf stepped forward unsteadily, holding on to Izam, but to his surprise the wooden leg bent at the knee and after the stride it straightened again as if by magic.

"It has a slat of yew," Izam explained, "the wood used to make good bows. When it receives the weight it flexes, allowing for articulation. When it reaches its limit, it then returns to its initial position and you can take your next stride. See these slots?" He pointed at four holes drilled into the knee. "With this pin you can select the amount of resistance. And if you take it out," he said as he demonstrated, "the mechanism will move freely, so you will be able to ride with the leg bent."

Olaf looked at him in disbelief. He was hesitant to try walking without the crutch, but Izam encouraged him. After a couple of attempts he managed to cross the room. When he reached Lucille's arms, the woman burst into tears as though he had really grown a leg.

They spent some time adjusting the mechanisms and commenting on the simplicity of the joint. Izam explained that, using slats of different thicknesses, he could calibrate the flexibility and resistance.

Then they went outside to test out the wooden leg. Olaf found that he could walk on stone without difficulty, but when he tested his footing on the fields, the leg sank into the soil.

"We'll attach a foot to solve the problem," Izam promised.

On the way back to the hut, Lucille offered Izam the rabbit she had stewed for Olaf and the boys. But Izam realized it was the only food they had, so he declined. As he whittled the foot, the young engineer had to admit to himself that he was going through all this trouble for the slave family because of his interest in Theresa. He was intrigued by how a girl so young and pretty could be capable of undertaking a task of such a magnitude, and the fact was, now that he really thought about it, from the very first moment he met her, he had tried hard to please her and be near her.

He tested the wooden foot for the last time before fixing it to the end of the leg. Once attached, he turned it backward and forward to make sure it wouldn't jam. He explained to Olaf that the foot could move freely, but if it bothered him, he could remove it himself.

Then they discussed the plow.

Izam mentioned the advantages of an iron plowshare and the use of a moldboard. Timber plows like Olaf's brake easily, he explained, and hardly penetrate the land. As for the moldboard, it would push aside the churned up earth and leave a wide furrow, aerating the land so that the seed takes a firm hold. Spring would be the sowing season, so they would have to be quick if they wanted to finish plowing the fields.

Olaf told him that as soon as he had finished plowing, he would start to clear the land that was still wild.

After praising the cleanliness of the hut and the remarkable channel that supplied it with water, Izam took his leave. He didn't say that he would return, but Theresa hoped he would.

By the second week, Olaf was certain that his new leg was far superior to his old crutch. In fact, he was so pleased with it that, despite the chafing that it caused on his stump, he wore it for several days without taking it off. He had learned to drive the plow into the earth by supporting himself with his real leg and using the rigidity of the artificial one to balance himself as he pushed. Sometimes, when he had to do heavy work, he would insert the pin to jam the knee, which would make better use of his strength.

Lucille and the children were happy. And Olaf was even happier.

At dawn they rose to plow the fields. Olaf would open up the soil and then Lucille would sow the rye, while the boys ran behind them scaring off the birds that tried to eat the seeds. After the sowing, they covered the furrows with earth that had been broken up with a mallet. In the afternoon, once they had finished their work, Theresa and Helga would travel from town to bring some implement, food, or old fabric with which to make clothes for the young lads.

Lucille and Helga soon became good friends. They spoke tirelessly of children, pregnancy, stews, and the gossip from the town. Sometimes Helga had a feeling of importance, ordering Lucille to sort out the hut.

Though she devoted less time to it, Theresa continued to help Alcuin copy and translate documents. She went early to the scriptorium and stayed there until midday, transcribing whatever texts the monk entrusted to her. However, Alcuin had moved from his calligraphy work on to theological matters that Theresa hardly participated in, which made her think that the day would come when she would no longer be needed.

Sometimes various haughty-looking priests visited the scriptorium, entering without warning and sitting with Alcuin. They were Romans and they were part of the papal delegation that always accompanied Charlemagne. Theresa decided to call them "the beetles," because they were always dressed in black. When the beetles came to the scriptorium, she had to leave the room.

"The religious men who come to the scriptorium . . . are they monks too?" she inquired one day.

"No," said Alcuin with a smile. "They might have been once, but now they're clerics of the Roman chapter."

"Monasteries . . . chapters . . . it's all the same thing isn't it?"

"Not at all. A monastery or abbey is a place where monks withdraw into solitude to pray and ask for the salvation of mankind. Generally they are closed-off places, sometimes far from the towns, with their own laws and lands, governed by a prior or abbot according to his best judgment.

"A chapter, on the other hand, is an open congregation, made up of a group of priests guided by a bishop who administrates a diocese." He saw Theresa's expression and continued. "To be clear, in Fulda there is both the abbey, with its abbot, its monks, its orders, and its walls—and the chapter, with its bishop, its clerics, and its ecclesiastical duties. The monks pray without leaving the monastery, while the chapter's priests attend to the townspeople in the churches."

"I always get the clergy mixed up: Monks, bishops, deacons . . . aren't they all priests?"

"Of course not," he laughed. "For instance, I have been ordained as a deacon, but I'm not a priest."

"How is that?"

"It might seem a little odd, but pay attention and you will understand quite easily." He picked up Theresa's wax tablet and drew a cross at the top of the rectangular space. "As you know, the Church is governed by the Holy Roman Pontiff, who we refer to as the Pope or Patriarch."

"In Byzantium there's another pope," she said, pleased with herself. It was one of the few things about these matters that she did know.

"True." And he added another four crosses to the first. "The Roman Pope governs the Patriarchate of the West. Aside from this, there are the four Eastern Patriarchs: Constantinople, Antioch, Alexandria, and Jerusalem. Each Patriarchate presides over the various kingdoms or nations that fall under their jurisdiction through the Primatial Archdioceses or Primacies, which are overseen by the most senior archbishops in each kingdom."

"So they would be the spiritual leaders of each nation," the young woman ventured.

"Guides, more than leaders."

Under the first cross he drew a circle to represent the Primacy. "Several archbishoprics are dependent on this Primatial Archdiocese." He drew some small squares to symbolize the archdioceses.

"The Papacy, the senior archdiocese, archdiocese, and then the diocese."

"Corresponding to the Pope, the senior archbishop, the archbishop, and the bishop."

"It's not so complicated," she confessed. "And these Roman clerics belong to the Papacy."

"That's right. Though it doesn't mean that they have been bishops. In fact, most of the time it is ties of kinship or friendship that determine who fills these positions." He gave Theresa a suspicious look. "Tell me—why this sudden interest in priests?"

She looked away, red-faced. In truth she was worried about her dwindling responsibilities as a scribe, and she thought that the more she knew about religious matters, the easier it would be to keep her job.

Alcuin had mentioned to Theresa that the papal mission had traveled to Fulda on its way to Würzburg. The mission was transporting some relics that Charlemagne hoped would put a stop to the continual insurrections to the north of the Elbe. Very soon the mission would continue on its way to the citadel to deposit the sacred artifacts in its cathedral.

When Alcuin told her that he would join the expedition, a blot appeared on the parchment that Theresa had been working on.

That afternoon she came across Izam on his way to the stables. The young man asked how the lands were doing, but Theresa barely paid any attention to him, her head filled with thoughts of Würzburg. When Izam said farewell, she regretted her rudeness.

That night she could hardly sleep.

She pictured her father, humiliated and dishonored. Every night since she had fled she had asked God for His forgiveness. She missed the two of them, her father and her stepmother. She pined for their hugs, their laughter, their joking banter. She longed to hear the stories that Gorgias would tell about Constantinople, his passion for reading, their nights of writing by candlelight. How many times had she wondered what had become of them, and how many times had she avoided thinking about the answer!

Sometimes she felt tempted to return and prove to everyone that she was not to blame. As the months passed she had reflected deeply on the parchment-maker's role in causing the fire, recalling his every action, his provocation, the blow he dealt to the frame and how it fell into the flames.

She should be going back to fight Korne, she thought, and would cry at her cowardice. She feared losing what by some miracle all that she had gained in Fulda: the love of Hoos Larsson, Helga the Black's friendship, Alcuin's wisdom, and the wealth from her lands. If she were condemned in Würzburg, she would lose her new life.

She estimated that it had been three months since she fled. Finally she slept, thinking that she would never have the courage to return.

The next morning, Alcuin scolded her after she chose an ink that was too fluid by mistake.

"I'm sorry," she said. "I slept poorly last night."

"Problems with your land?"

"Not exactly." She wondered whether she should tell him. "Do you remember what you were saying yesterday? About your impending trip to Würzburg?"

"Yes, of course. What about it?"

"The thing is . . . I was thinking it over, and I would like to go with you."

"Come with me?" He paused. "What kind of a foolish idea is that? It is a very dangerous expedition. There will be no women traveling, and I don't see what interest—"

"I want to go with you," she persisted. Alcuin was surprised by the brusqueness of her interruption.

"And the slaves? And your land? Is that why you slept so poorly?"

"Helga will look after Olaf and Lucille. She'll look after all of it. I beg you . . . You told me yourself that you need an assistant."

"Yes, but here in Fulda, not on board a ship."

Theresa had finally decided to take the risk. Although she could not admit to her part in causing the fire, she had to return to Würzburg and face up to her responsibilities.

"I will go all the same," she protested. Alcuin could not believe his ears.

"Excuse me? May I ask what brew have you been drinking?"

"If you don't want to help me, I'll go by myself, on foot."

The monk was taken aback by the young woman's insolence. He thought about giving her a slap, but ultimately he pitied her. "Listen to me, you pigheaded devil! You will stay in Fulda, whether you like it or not. Now, forget all this nonsense and concentrate on your work." He left the scriptorium, slamming the door violently behind him.

The next day, an acolyte informed Alcuin that the papal delegation had decided to move their departure forward to Sunday morning. It would appear that someone had arrived from Würzburg bearing ill news. When the acolyte left, Alcuin closed the door and turned to Theresa.

"Guess who has arrived?"

"I don't know, some soldier?" She feared they might be searching for her.

"It's your friend—Hoos Larsson."

Theresa didn't locate her loved one until late in the afternoon. She found out from Alcuin that he had been taken to the optimates' residence so that he could inform the papal mission of the situation in Würzburg, and since the morning he had been in a meeting with Charlemagne's soldiers. Just before None, the young man exited the meeting room with an expression of frustration.

Theresa had been waiting for him outside, numb with cold. As soon as she saw him, she stood. He looked thin and haggard, but his shaggy hair and deep blue eyes made him intensely attractive.

When the young man recognized her, he ran to her and they melted together in an endless kiss.

They spent the night at Helga the Black's house. She was more than happy to lend them her home and move to the kitchens. Theresa attempted to prepare some meat, but the stew burned. They ate frugally and spoke very little since all they wanted to do was smother each other in kisses. When they went to bed, Theresa thought that no book could fill her like Hoos did with his body.

In the morning, the young man told her the terrible news. "I wish I did not have to tell you this, Theresa, but Gorgias, your father . . . has disappeared."

She looked at him in disbelief. Then she moved away from him.

She asked him a hundred times what he was referring to, and she hated him for not telling her the night before. He could not explain why he hadn't shared the news until the next day.

He told her that, in Würzburg, Count Wilfred had informed him about the fire. It didn't take him long to figure out that the girl everyone believed to be dead was the same young woman he was in love with.

"When we met, you told me that you worked as an official parchment-maker—that you had fled Würzburg and were born in Byzantium. It all fit together."

"And you told them?"

"Of course not. But Wilfred said to me that the girl's father, or in other words, your father, had disappeared. He spoke of nothing else, as if he was desperate to find him."

"But what do you mean *has disappeared*?" Tears ran down her cheeks. "How did it happen? Have they searched very hard for him?"

"Theresa, I don't know. I wish I could tell you something more, but nobody knows. They haven't seen him, and of course they've looked all over. Wilfred ordered a house-to-house search. He issued an edict and even organized a search party to comb the surrounding area. To be honest, I think you should go back to Würzburg. Your presence might aid the search."

Theresa nodded. She was glad she had pressed Alcuin to allow her to accompany him. Then she remembered the attack on her father at the parchment-maker's workshop. That time the assailant had only managed to wound his arm, but perhaps he would attempt to do worse. Her weeping prevented her from continuing. Hoos tried to console her—and though he did not manage to, Theresa appreciated the warmth of his arms.

Midmorning, Theresa set off for the chapter. There she found Helga organizing the sacks of food. Before turning to her, the woman finished straightening a final row and then stopped for a moment. At first Theresa made small talk, but her red eyes gave away the torment that she was feeling. She recounted everything to her friend: the terrible fire, the death of the girl, her father's disappearance, and her intention to return to Würzburg.

When she had finished, Helga could not believe she was looking at a fugitive. She warmed a cup of milk for her, which Theresa drank in little sips. Helga asked her what she was going to do.

"How am I supposed to know?" she sobbed.

"Take my advice and forget your family," she said, delicately wiping her tears. "Enjoy your new life now. You've found a suitor and now have more than what I or any of my friends could ever have dreamt of. If you go back to Würzburg, you will no doubt be arrested. That Korne that you speak of sounds like an evil bastard."

Theresa nodded. In truth she was crying because she feared that her father was dead, which, as Hoos had pointed out, was quite likely.

She hugged Helga and kissed her on the cheek. When she had calmed down, her friend agreed to accompany her to the city walls, where she was to meet Olaf to give him some equipment.

They passed the time kneading spelt dough to bake some buns that they would give to Lucille's boys. After lunch, they gathered up their things and asked Favila for permission to leave for a while.

On the way to the poor quarter, they noticed a stranger who seemed to be following them. At first they didn't pay him any attention, but as they turned into a narrow street, he ran after them and stood in their path. It was Widukind, Helga's violent ex-lover.

Now that he was close, they could see he had been drinking heavily. The man didn't seem to quite know what he wanted. He was staring at them like an imbecile, with a permanent smile on his face. Suddenly he tried to grab Helga's belly, but she pulled back. Theresa stood between the drunk and her friend.

"Out of the way, whore!" he threatened her.

He tried to shove her aside but he stumbled, and Theresa took the opportunity to draw her scramasax and she pushed it against his throat. She could smell the wine on his breath.

"If you don't leave, I swear, I'll stick you like a pig."

She would have done it without hesitation, and the man sensed it. He spat on the ground and smiled again. Then he staggered off muttering to himself. When he had gone, Helga broke down in tears of desperation.

"I hadn't seen him for days. The bastard won't stop till he's killed me."

Theresa tried to console her, but there was nothing she could do. She took her back to the chapter and then returned to the walls alone, but by the time she had reached the place where she had agreed to meet Olaf, he was gone. She waited in case he came back, but finally decided to get going because the sun was going down and she wanted to give the buns to the children.

As she walked, she thought about telling Hoos about Widukind, wondering if he could scare him off since he was strong and skilled with weapons. If he had a word with Widukind, perhaps he could pacify him. As she continued down the path, she remembered the previous night, and she thought that Hoos, as well as being strong, would make the best husband anyone could hope for.

It was Saturday. As she walked, she recalled that Hoos had told her that the delegation would leave on Sunday morning. For a moment she wondered what she would do. On the one hand she longed to stay in Fulda, look after her land, and start a family, but her desire to return to Würzburg and find out what had happened to her father was even stronger.

As she progressed she admired the stream, its basin wide and peaceful. She thought to herself that in spring she would buy some nails, and instruct Olaf to build a skiff with which to sail the watercourse.

Soon, she reached the beech wood that bordered her land. The trees would give her the timber needed to build a lovely home for herself, while Olaf and his sons hunted venison with which to make nutritious stews.

She was admiring the snowcapped treetops when a noise startled her. She listened carefully but couldn't hear anything more. Preparing to set off again, another crack made her stop in her tracks. She thought it might be an animal stalking her and took hold of her scramasax. Suddenly, a figure came out from the trees. She screamed when she realized it was Widukind, his face ablaze with anger. Theresa saw a dagger in his right hand. The other held a half-empty skin full of wine.

She was scared but she tried not to show it. She hastily glanced around her. To her left there was the river, to the right, the forest. Seeing Widukind in the state he was, she thought she could probably outrun him.

Without waiting for him to attack, she darted toward the part of the forest she judged to be less dense. Behind her, Widukind took up the chase. The ground was frozen, making her think she might slip at any moment.

As she ran, the path became narrower and more difficult to negotiate. Sooner or later he would catch up to her. She looked behind, and could not see him, so she ducked down behind some bushes, just in time to see Widukind screaming like a madman. She crouched down even lower as the man lashed out at anything that came into his path, as if possessed by the Devil.

Then he stopped to drink from the wineskin, pouring its contents down his throat until the liquid brimmed over his gums. Screaming again, he thrust his dagger into the undergrowth.

With each step he moved closer to Theresa. She knew that if she hid there much longer she would undoubtedly be discovered, so she clutched her scramasax and made ready to fight. By then, Widukind was almost on top of her. At any moment he might hear her breathing.

But suddenly the man turned away and Theresa took the opportunity to resume her escape. Widukind heard her, turned, and cursed before launching himself after her. It was almost as if he were sober. His pace was quick and he moved forward with determination. Theresa scraped against the bramble as she ran. On each side of the path there were rows of trees forming a tight passage through which to escape. The faster she ran, the more she thought she could feel him breathing down her neck. She jumped over a tree stump in her way, but then she slipped. The man dodged the stump but then also stumbled, giving Theresa time to get up on her feet and flee once more. To her right she saw a small embankment and she threw herself down in the hope that she would reach the river, her behind scraping against the brambles.

Widukind did the same, always just a few paces behind her. But Theresa knew she was a good swimmer. If she could reach the river, perhaps she could get across. She ran with all her strength, praying to God to help her reach the water.

She had covered a short stretch when another figure unexpectedly appeared in front of her. They both tumbled to the ground as she crashed into him. Widukind looked at them in surprise.

As Theresa regained her composure, she saw that it was Olaf. He was lying on the ground now, and his wooden leg had come out of its socket. She tried to help him, but Widukind shoved her away. Olaf sensed the danger and told Theresa to get behind him. Widukind smiled at the young woman taking cover behind the lame man.

"A cripple and a whore . . . I'm going to enjoy ripping off your last leg—and *you* I'm going to fuck raw."

"Theresa! The scramasax!" cried Olaf, scrambling to his feet.

She didn't understand.

"The scramasax!" he insisted.

The young woman handed it to him.

Widukind laughed at the absurdity of the situation—but Olaf grasped the scramasax, quickly took aim, and threw it.

Widukind felt a sudden blow to the throat, then the warmth of the blood as it spilled down his neck. And after that, he felt nothing.

As soon as he had reattached his artificial leg, Olaf made sure Widukind had stopped breathing. He then convinced Theresa, to avoid any problems, that it would be best if they kept their mouths shut. She agreed. Ultimately, she thought she had been fortunate that Olaf had heard Widukind's screams and come to help her. Now Helga would have nothing to worry about. She could bring her child into the world without that rat ever bothering her again.

Olaf stripped him in order to burn his clothes. "If we bury him and they discover his body, they will undoubtedly know it was a murder. However, without clothes, after the wolves devour him, not a trace will remain."

After gashing the body a couple more times so that the blood would attract scavengers, he hurled it over a sheer drop. Then he gathered the dead man's clothes and shoes.

On the way back to Theresa's estate, they barely said a word to each other, though before they arrived, the young woman gave Olaf her thanks.

"Any slave would have done the same for his mistress," he said in justification.

When they reached the hut, Olaf searched the clothes before casting them in the fire. He kept the knife and shoes, which would serve him well as soon as he dyed them. He offered the dagger to Theresa, for a slave could not possess weapons, but she refused it.

"File the point and you will be able to use it without anyone accusing you," she suggested.

Olaf thanked her for the gesture as he admired the dagger. It was a crude instrument, but made of good steel. He could modify it so that it would be unrecognizable. To show his gratitude, he bowed to Theresa and Lucile did the same. Then they prepared some dinner, for night would fall soon.

By the time they had finished eating the roe deer leg, the moon was bright in the sky, so Theresa decided to spend the night in the hut. Lucille made a space for her between the two children, and Lucille slept on the floor to her right. Olaf slept outside, covered in a cloak.

That night Theresa purged her sins again. She remembered her father, Gorgias, and speculated on his whereabouts. Perhaps he was dead, but as likely as it seemed, she would not accept it as truth. She evoked memories of Alcuin, yearning for the days of learning, for his kind words and his extraordinary wisdom. Then she thought about everyone who had died because of her: the girl in the fire, the two Saxons at Hoos's house, and now Widukind . . .

For a moment she wondered whether the wealth of her land was worth all she had been through.

The howling of the wolves made Widukind's body come to mind. Then she thought of her father and cried, picturing him being devoured by vermin.

Suddenly Theresa sprang up, causing Lucille to also wake, but Theresa told her that nothing was wrong. The young woman wrapped up warm and left the hut. Olaf was surprised because it was still completely dark. The slave came out from behind the ox he was using as a shelter and gave her a confused look as he rubbed the sleep from his eyes. Theresa admired the moon in silence. In a few hours the sun would come up and then Alcuin would set off for Würzburg. She took a deep breath and looked at Olaf. Then she told him to make ready. "Come with me to Fulda. But before leaving I want to make certain arrangements."

In the early hours of Sunday morning, the abbey stables were a hive of activity. Dozens of monks ran up and down bearing food, animals, weapons, and equipment under the close scrutiny of Charlemagne's men. The cart drivers yoked their beasts, who were lowing and thrashing their heads in protest. The maidservants prepared to bring the final supplies of salted belly pork, and the soldiers stayed busy following their commanders' instructions.

Theresa found Alcuin as he was loading a cart with his belongings. All she had brought for the journey were a change of clothes and her wax tablets. Everything else she had left with Helga the Black, whom she had only woken minutes earlier to tell her that she was leaving. Helga would look after her land until she returned, and Theresa promised she would be back even if it was just to collect the rent that her friend had promised to pay her.

When Alcuin saw Theresa, he walked angrily over to her. "May I ask what you're doing here?"

"Nothing that concerns you," she responded without looking at him. She threw her bag onto the cart.

"Remove your bag at once! Do you want me to call the soldiers?"

"And do you want me to walk to Würzburg alone? Because that's what I'll do."

"You'll end up in a ditch."

"Then so be it."

Alcuin took a deep breath through clenched teeth. Never in his life had he come across such an obstinate creature. Finally he murmured something and turned away.

"Pox on you. Get in the cart!"

"What?"

"Did you not hear me? I said get in the cart!"

Theresa kissed his hand, not knowing how to thank him.

At dawn, Izam of Padua appeared, sporting a striking robe of red serge and gleaming chainmail. He was followed by a large group of soldiers that would escort the Roman delegation. When the engineer spotted Theresa, he made as if to go and greet her, but stopped when he saw another young man approach her first.

Theresa let Hoos embrace her and he kissed her on the lips. Izam looked on with a perplexed expression, which Hoos happened to notice.

"How do you know him?" Hoos asked when he saw Izam walk off.

"Who? The one in the chainmail?" she asked, trying to act normal. "He works for Charlemagne. He helped me with the slave I told you about. The one with the wooden leg."

"He seems very interested in you." He smiled and kissed her again, making sure Izam could see.

Theresa thought it odd that Hoos was not surprised to see her, for at no time had she told him of her intention to travel to

Würzburg. On the contrary, she was a little surprised to see him since she had thought that they would both stay in Fulda and continue their relationship in peace, and yet, there they were: abandoning themselves to whatever fate awaited them without any kind of plan. Hoos explained to Theresa that her friend the engineer had hired him as a guide.

"You should have seen their faces when I told them that snow still blocked the passes. They screamed and shouted like madmen. That's when I suggested they travel to Frankfurt first and sail upriver from there. The thaw has already begun down there, so with a bit of luck we'll be able to reach Würzburg by ship."

"And you were going to leave without telling me?"

"I was certain you would come," he said with a smile. "And anyway . . ."

Theresa gave him a wary look.

"Anyway what?"

"If necessary I would have dragged you myself." He laughed and lifted her into the air.

Theresa smiled, happy in Hoos's strong arms. She felt that while he was near, nothing bad could happen to her.

Theresa counted around seventy people who had assembled for the journey. A dozen or so belonged to the papal mission, around twenty looked like men-at-arms, and the rest were cart drivers, servants, and townspeople. As she expected, she was the only woman, but it didn't concern her. Aside from the men, the delegation was furnished with eight ox-driven wagons and as many lighter carts pulled by mules.

At Izam's signal, the whips cracked against the beasts, which lowed in pain and then laboriously set off in the direction of the city walls. Alcuin traveled on the first wagon with the papal mission. Theresa sat swaying on the second cart with her attention on

Hoos, who navigated the march, while Izam brought up the rear of the convoy along with the main body of soldiers, setting course for Frankfurt.

During the journey, Hoos and Theresa traded news. He told her that in Würzburg folks were dying of hunger, which was why twelve carts were transporting grain, and that in Frankfurt they would gather whatever provisions they could fit on the ship. She spoke to him of Alcuin and how he had solved the case of the poisoned wheat.

"I'll say it again: Don't trust him. That monk's sharp as a needle, but as shady as the Devil."

"I don't know . . . he's been good to Helga. And he's given me work."

"It makes no difference. When this is over and they pay me, you won't have to work anymore."

Theresa nodded unenthusiastically and admitted to him that all that mattered to her was finding her father alive. When Hoos pointed out how difficult it would be to fulfill her wish, she refused to listen to him and curled up under a blanket.

The delegation trudged on wearily all morning. Two riders equipped with torches led the way in front, ensuring the carts could negotiate any obstacles in their path. Just ahead, four servants wearing gloves removed the stones that would hinder the progress of the convoy, while the cart drivers, with whip and oath, toiled to keep the oxen away from the sheer drops in the embankments. Alert to any dangers, another pair of well-equipped outriders guarded the rear.

After passing a muddy section where the men had to do as much pulling as the beasts, Izam called a halt. He judged that the road had opened up sufficiently to provide a safe place to make camp, so the men positioned the wagons in a row along the bank of the stream before tethering the horses to the first cart and unloading the fodder for the animals. A servant lit a fire over which he arranged several joints of venison, while Izam assembled the rest of them into organized watches.

Once all the arrangements for their camp were complete, they made themselves comfortable around the fire and drank until the meat was well roasted. Theresa helped the cooks, who celebrated the presence of a woman who was skilled with the pots. A couple of lookouts returned with some rabbits, much to the delight of the papal mission. The less fortunate had to make do with oatmeal porridge and salt pork—but the wine was shared with all, and the men gabbed and laughed as they emptied their tankards.

As Theresa cleared up some bowls, Izam came up behind her. "You're not drinking wine?" he said, offering her some.

She turned around, startled. "No, thank you. I prefer water," she said, taking a sip from her cup.

Izam was surprised. While traveling most people chose to drink watered-down wine, or failing that, beer, for both were less likely to cause illness than contaminated water.

He insisted. "This stream can't be trusted. Its bed is not stony, and it flows from west to east. Plus, we passed a settlement of tenant farmers a couple of miles back—no doubt all their waste is flowing downstream."

Upon hearing that, Theresa spat the water out and accepted Izam's cup. The wine was strong and hot.

"I tried to say hello to you earlier, but you were busy."

She responded with a forced smile. She saw Hoos eating venison and was worried he might see them.

"Is he your betrothed?" he asked.

"Not yet." She blushed, without quite knowing why.

"It's a shame I'm engaged," he lied.

For some reason she didn't like his comment, but they spoke for a while about the difficulties of the journey.

Finally, she gave in to her curiosity. "You know what? I don't believe you really are engaged," she said, smiling, and instantly she regretted her boldness.

Izam burst into laughter.

At that moment Alcuin arrived to congratulate them. "For your cooking, Theresa, and you, Izam, for your skill guiding the delegation," he said.

Izam thanked him and left to attend to a couple of soldiers who were demanding his presence. Theresa took the opportunity to interrogate Alcuin about Izam of Padua.

"I really don't know whether he has a maiden," the monk answered, surprised he was being asked such a question.

They arrived in Frankfurt early the next day. Hoos and Izam used the morning to scour the port in search of the most appropriate ships. At the wharf they found solid Frankish sailing boats, Danish ships with spacious holds, and broad-bellied Frisian vessels. Izam was keen on strong and capacious hulls, while Hoos preferred light craft.

"If we come across ice, we might have to tug them," Hoos remarked.

They finally decided on two heavy boats, well furnished with oars, and a light ship that could be dragged up the river if necessary.

At midday they began loading the vessels. They all ate together in a nearby warehouse, and a couple of hours later, the three boats were cleaving through the Main River crammed with animals, soldiers, and priests.

23

Alcuin of York could never have imagined that such a string of blasphemies could come from the mouth of a prelate. However, when Flavio Diacono heard the creaking of the hull, he didn't stop cursing until the ship became completely stuck in the ice.

"We should never have embarked on this voyage!" Flavio blurted out as he climbed down from the boat with his arms full of belongings. "What is this wretch trying to do? Kill us all?"

Izam scowled back at him as he spat out the piece of meat he had been chewing for some time. He had enough on his plate trying to free the hull, without having to worry about the complaints of a couple of fussy priests. He looked ahead and swore. A completely frozen river stretched out in front of him.

Since they had set sail from Frankfurt, the voyage had been without incident and they had seen nothing more than the random plaque of ice to concern them. Fortunately the ships that were following them had managed to avoid crashing their stern and they were bobbing tamely behind. He quickly positioned a couple of beams at the bow, ordered the crew to empty the hold, and made sure the provisions and animals were located on the most solid part of the ice floe. Hoos led a group across the ice to the bank.

Flavio could not be calmed. "I'll be damned if I know what's going on! Now what is that man doing?"

"I don't know," replied Alcuin. "Getting us out of here, I suppose. That's what we're paying him for," he said, continuing to gather up his books. "Please hold this Bible for me with care. It's a very valuable specimen."

Flavio grabbed the Bible and threw it heedlessly onto a stack of bales. He was annoyed by Theresa's presence and the carefree attitude with which Alcuin was responding to the serious situation.

"Perhaps we are preparing to go back?" Theresa ventured.

"I don't think so. In fact, I could swear they are intending to lift the boat out of the water and drag it across the ice," said Alcuin.

"Have you lost your senses? How is someone going to drag a boat to Würzburg?" the Roman interjected again.

"My dear Flavio, look around you," he said without lifting his gaze. "If Izam wanted to turn back, he would've used one of the other ships to tug us out. However, he has tied the ropes to the cutwater at the prow, not the stern, and then he yoked the oxen, which can only mean he intends to lift it up out of the ice."

"But that is insane. How are thirty men going to pull a boat?"

"Thirty-one, Father," said Theresa, who had already counted them.

"And you will be party to this foolishness?" he asked Alcuin.

"If we hope to reach Würzburg, of course," said Alcuin, putting away some bottles. "And since it doesn't appear like you are intending to push or pull, you could at least help me with these quills. Secure them in place there, alongside the inkwells."

"But it's impossible!" he insisted as he handled the instruments. "Thirty men dragging a boat—or thirty-one, unless they want to die pulling. Look at the size of the hull: It's over twenty paces wide. And the provisions? What will happen with the provisions that we're unloading now?"

"Maybe you should ask the commander."

"Izam of Padua? Perhaps that upstart has spoken to you, but since we set sail from Frankfurt, he hasn't said a word to me." He put down the items he was holding and turned to face Alcuin. "Do you know what I think? That you're delirious. What you're saying is the ravings of an old monk who thinks he knows more than a prelate. What we should be doing is continuing on foot, following the course of the river. We have oxen, and well-armed men."

"Well, here is what I think," said Alcuin, "I think if you spoke less and helped more, we would have already finished unloading the ship."

"Alcuin! Remember that I warrant respect."

"And you remember that I deserve rest. As you say, I am not young. If I am to pull the ship, I need repose."

"My God, you persist with that ludicrous idea? Thirty-one men cannot—"

"Granted, more might be needed. As you were speaking, ten crewmembers from the second boat climbed down a ladder to come and join us," Theresa pointed out.

Flavio didn't even look at her. "Then permit me to inform you that you are not the only one who can speculate. If we are unable to refloat the ship, then we must transfer our cargo to one of the other boats and return to Frankfurt to wait for the ice to thaw. Those men who are crossing over now must be coming to help us unload our cargo onto their boat."

"Is that why they are coming with all of their belongings?" Alcuin asked. "They will indeed help us, but in the manner in which I have already explained. Incidentally, if it seems such a bad idea to you, then surely you should board the other returning ships."

"You know as well as I do that we need to reach Würzburg."

"Well, then, stop complaining and get your belongings off the boat so that we may lift it a little easier. Theresa, help me with this volume. Look." He pointed at the crew. "Two of the men onshore have already begun to head upriver, no doubt to see the extent of the ice. As you can see, the rest have started to cut and prepare logs."

"Timber to repair the ship?" the young woman suggested.

"Actually, it looks like they are making levers for moving the boat. Observe the terrain: In this area, the river pools—and this fact, along with the shade from that great mountain," he said, pointing at it, "are the likely causes of this unexpected freeze. However, farther up, where there is no shade and the slope of the river steepens, I warrant that the water flows without hindrance."

At that moment Hoos returned with a satisfied expression. He left his weapons on the ice and boarded the boat to talk with Izam. "As I suspected, we'll have to go upriver for a couple of miles. But farther up, the ice begins to break up and we'll be able to continue the voyage."

"And the bank?" asked the commander.

"There are two or three places where it narrows, but the rest of the passage shouldn't be difficult."

"All right. And the lookout?"

"I posted him up high, like you ordered."

"Then all we have to do is lift this bastard up and drag her upriver over the ice."

Wrapped in rigging, the crew pulled in unison, clenching and straining every muscle fiber in their bodies. On the first attempt, the boat merely creaked. At each signal, the men lurched forward, jolting the ship forward with an almost imperceptible rattle. Then the creaking turned into a groan, and finally, the keel lifted into the air and dropped down onto the frozen surface. Slowly, as progress was made, the pulling became more constant. With the oxen out front, twelve oarsmen pulled the ropes at the prow. Helping were another eight located on each side of the hull and straining to steer it. Theresa and Alcuin joined in where they could. Only four men remained on the second boat, guarding the supplies and equipment, with everyone else helping. Gradually the ship was dragged up out of the ice like a dying beast, revealing a deep scar in the ice when it finally slid forward all the way.

In the middle of the afternoon, causing a string of oaths, the ice cracked as clear as a bell under the hull.

"Stop! Stop, you damned bastards, or the ice will give way and we'll all drown!" shouted Izam.

The men quickly released the ropes and took a few steps back. By that point the ice was thinner, and farther on it began to break up into a labyrinth of ice plaques.

"Gather in the rope and the animals. Make a hole in the ice and let the animals drink a little. You two, when the oxen have recuperated go back for the provisions," Izam ordered.

Flavio, who had taken no part in the pulling, took a few steps away from the ship. Soon Theresa and Alcuin appeared, their faces flushed from their effort. The monk attempted to say something, but all he could manage was a groan. Then he let himself drop to the ground and closed his eyes, trying to catch his breath.

"You shouldn't have been helping," Flavio rebuked. "The men look at me as if I were from another planet. People like us aren't expected to help."

"A little exercise raises the spirits," Alcuin panted in retort.

"You are wrong there. Leave the work to those who are obliged to do it. We *oratores* devote ourselves to prayer, the role that God has given to us." He helped him shift the lightest bundle.

"Ah, yes." Alcuin said. "The rules that govern the world: The *oratores* pray for the salvation of mankind, the *bellatores* fight for the Church, and the *laboratores* do everyone else's work. I'm sorry, I had forgotten," said Alcuin with a sarcastic smile.

"So you should not—" Flavio raised his voice, but Alcuin cut him off.

"However, you will agree that even peasants must pray once in a while. Pass me a little water, for pity's sake."

"Of course, and not just once in a while."

"And additionally you will also acknowledge that the *bellatores*, in addition to training for battle, must not forget their spiritual obligations." He took a swig of water.

"Naturally," Flavio admitted.

"Then I don't see why we should not do some work from time to time," he said, feeling a little better.

"You forget that I am not a monk like you. I'm a papal chancellor. The Primicerius of the Lateran."

"With two arms and two legs," Alcuin reminded him, pulling himself up. "And now, if you will excuse me, there is still work to do."

The monk looked over toward the bank. Then he stole a glance at Izam, leaning against the parapet on the ship.

"No doubt he's worried about that lookout who left some time ago and hasn't yet returned," Theresa said looking at Izam.

"By God, lass, don't be so dramatic. The scout is probably emptying his bowels somewhere or still exploring the terrain," said Flavio.

"But look at Izam: He's staring at the woods with such concern."

Flavio realized she was right. The engineer was pacing up and down like a caged animal, giving orders one after the other, and his hand was positioned firmly on his bow.

Alcuin left Flavio and approached Izam. "I estimate we still have a day and half's journey ahead of us. Am I wrong?" he probed.

Izam gave him a sidelong look. "Sorry but I don't have time for confessions right now," he said, walking away.

"I understand. You're not the only one wondering about that lookout. I, too, would be alarmed."

Izam looked at him in surprise. He hadn't yet shared his concerns with the crew, but this priest seemed to have guessed. He fixed his gaze on the trees and stroked his chin. "I don't know why they haven't attacked us already. Waiting for nightfall, perhaps," he observed, taking it for granted that they both knew what he was talking about.

"I think the same," Hoos interjected, joining the conversation. "There can't be many, or they would've already struck."

Alcuin and the commander turned to look at the newcomer. "When I need an opinion I'll ask for it. Stick to your tasks," Izam replied.

"Right you are," said Hoos, withdrawing.

"Do you know him?" asked Alcuin.

"From Aquis-Granum, though not well. All I know is that he knows these parts better than all those soldiers put together. And now, if you don't mind, I must prepare my men."

Alcuin nodded and made for the place where the oxen were resting. At that moment all he cared about was protecting his belongings, and there would be more opportunities to do that near the animals. He noticed that Izam was dividing the crew into two groups. It appeared he had changed his mind about the number of men who should fetch the provisions. Hoos and Theresa were instructed to stay.

"Listen carefully," the engineer requested. "It is possible that there are bandits behind those trees, and if there are, we must hurry. Those of you going back for the cargo, keep your eyes open and walk on the ice in the middle of the river. You three take care of the equipment. The rest of you the provisions. If you have not returned in one hour, we will leave without you."

The men selected to retrieve the provisions set off. Alcuin and Flavio went with them. The rest tried to return the ship to the water, but with several shoves they barely moved it the width of a hand. Izam organized their defenses with barrels of arrows on each side of the ship. Then he positioned himself at the prow, ensuring that Theresa was onboard, taking cover behind a pile of sacks.

He was pondering the situation when suddenly he made out a dark object upriver floating among the ice plaques. He was unable to identify it, for the current quickly dragged it under, but gradually the blot slid toward the prow of the ship.

Izam took a harpoon, jumped overboard and stood on one of the ice plaques until the blot floated near. Then he thrust the harpoon at it, feeling it sink into something. Sharply pulling on the shaft, he cried out in horror when he realized the blot was the head of the lookout, horribly mutilated.

The hour was almost up when the first crewmen appeared in the distance carrying the provisions. They were slowly trudging along when one of the oxen gave out a low bellow and then collapsed as if it had been struck by lightning.

Izam knew the attack had begun. He immediately ordered his men to ready themselves in their positions behind their bows. The returning group took cover behind their sleds. Izam's archers released a volley that crossed paths with another volley launched by their assailants from the banks. A couple of men left the cover provided by the oxen and started running toward the ship, but both were brought down within a few paces. Alcuin and Flavio crouched behind the sled. Hoos managed to crawl from the ship over to them. "Stay here until I say otherwise," he ordered.

Alcuin and Flavio nodded.

Hoos ducked down behind the wounded ox and cut the tether that bound it to the healthy one. Then he called to the clerics. "Let's go! Get behind the ox. When I strike it, run alongside it, using it as your barricade."

"Flavio won't be able to," Alcuin objected.

Hoos looked at Flavio and saw that an arrow had pierced his thigh. "Don't worry, I'll take care of him," he said, handing Alcuin the rope that was attached to the ox. "Let's go, quickly."

"And the provisions? asked Alcuin, seeing that Hoos had cut the harnesses.

Hoos crouched behind the sacks as arrows rained down on them from all sides. "I'll drag them with us. Now run," he said, and he struck the beast on the back.

The animal bolted off with Alcuin hanging on to its rope. Hoos shouted to him to take cover and the monk obeyed. One of the oarsmen tried to follow the animal, too, but just as he was about to reach it, a spear knocked him off his feet.

Hoos called to another man to help him. Flavio lay on the sled, protected by some wooden boards. Then, crouching down, the remaining men started pushing it in the direction of the ship.

"Those bastards are bombarding us!" bellowed Hoos as they approached the boat.

"Is Flavio all right?" asked Izam from the deck.

"Just a scratch on the thigh."

"And the provisions?"

"In the carts," he said, pointing behind him toward another group of men now arriving under the cover of two wagons.

"Good. Make haste! Load up the supplies and let's push the boat off."

Though he was exhausted, Alcuin joined the men who were trying to refloat the boat from the port side. Hoos and the rest of the group soon joined them.

"Get Flavio onboard! He's badly wounded," cried Izam, with the arrows continuing to rain down on them.

Some oarsmen hoisted the provisions on board, made Flavio comfortable on the deck, then went below to continue to push the boat.

"For God's sake! Push, you wretched bastards!" screamed Izam.

The men heeded his instruction and on the second attempt, the ship moved.

"Again! Harder! Push!"

Suddenly the ice started breaking up with a deafening crunch. The men leapt away, terrified, and the boat began sinking as though the Devil were dragging it to hell.

"Get back quickly! Get away!"

At that moment the surface opened up and the boat plunged into the water down to the gunwale. Several oarsmen fell into the river, tangled in the ropes.

"On the boat! Get on, you wretches, get on!" Izam ordered with arrows showering down around him.

Hoos managed to clamber up first. The other survivors dropped their bows and clung to the gunwale. Alcuin hung on for his life, half his body submerged in the river.

"There are men trapped down here," said Alcuin, holding on to a wounded oarsman.

"There's no time, get on." Hoos held out his arm from the parapet.

"We cannot just leave them there," he insisted, still gripping tightly to the one he held.

"Get on, damn it, or I swear I'll come down and hoist you up myself!"

But Alcuin didn't budge.

Hoos jumped overboard and onto the ice alongside Alcuin. He drew his sword and ran it through the man the monk was help-ing. Then he stood up to finish off another oarsmen who had been struggling to escape the freezing water.

"No need to wait now. We're off!" Hoos announced.

Alcuin looked at him in a daze. He held out his arm, and a cou-ple of oarsmen helped him clamber onboard.

The ship progressed upriver until the sun hid behind the moun-tains. Before long, it stopped in a small pool.

"We'll drop anchor here," Izam declared.

Alcuin took the opportunity to tend to the wounded, but since he had no ointments he was limited to cleaning and bandaging arrow wounds.

A weak voice came from behind him. "Can I help?"

Alcuin looked at Theresa with a concerned expression. He accepted her offer with a grim face and the young woman crouched down to assist him. When they had finished with the wounded, Theresa withdrew to a corner to pray for the dead.

Hoos approached Alcuin with a piece of bread in his hand. "Here, eat something," he offered.

"I'm not hungry. Thank you."

"Alcuin, for the love of God. You saw it yourself. The boat was already on its way and those poor wretches were trapped. There was nothing else I could do."

"You might not have thought the same had it been you trapped there," he responded angrily.

"Don't fool yourself. I might not be the kind of person you would share an evening of poetry with, but I saved your life."

Alcuin nodded and walked away in irritation.

As soon as the sun came up, one of the oarsmen was lowered from the prow to assess the damage. After a while he reappeared, sour faced. "The hull's ruined," he informed them as they dried him off. "I doubt we'll be able to repair it here."

Izam shook his head. He could moor the boat to the bank to procure some timber, but it was an unnecessary risk.

"We'll keep going for as long as the ship lasts."

Alcuin awoke to the splashing of the oars. Beside him slept Flavio, half-covered in a blanket, and Theresa, curled up beside her father's bag. Alcuin decided to wake them lest they freeze to death. While Flavio woke up, the young woman fetched a little wine and a slice of rye bread.

"They've rationed the provisions," she informed them. "It would appear that much of the food was lost in the attack."

"My leg hurts," Flavio complained.

Alcuin lifted his robe. Fortunately, the Roman was a stout man and the arrow had embedded itself almost entirely in fat.

"We'll have to remove it."

"The leg?" he asked, alarmed.

"No, good Lord, the arrow."

"Best we wait until we reach Würzburg," Flavio suggested.

"All right. In the meantime try this cheese."

Flavio took the cheese and bit into it. Suddenly Alcuin grabbed the arrow and pulled it out in one jerk. Flavio's scream echoed around the mountains. Alcuin paid no attention, proceeding to pour a little wine on the wound. Then he covered it with some bandages that he had ready.

"Damned novice of a surgeon."

"That wound could have developed complications," he argued calmly. "Now get up and try to walk a little."

Flavio obeyed begrudgingly, and soon he was staggering over to his belongings, dragging his feet as if they were in chains. He noticed one of his chests sitting in a puddle of water. He screamed hysterically and, with Alcuin's help, moved the chest to a higher position.

"Judging by your face, it must contain something important," Alcuin remarked, slapping the chest.

"*Lignum crucis* . . . a relic that travels with me," an anguished Flavio explained.

"*Lignum crucis*? The wood from the Cross of Golgotha? The relic kept at the Sessorian Basilica?"

"I see you know what I speak of."

"Indeed. Though in truth I'm pretty skeptical."

"What? Are you implying—"

"Good God, no. I apologize," he cut in. "Naturally I believe the authenticity of the *lignum crucis*, in the same way that I give credence to the bodies of Gervasius and Protasius, or the cape of Martin of Tours. But you will recall that there are many abbeys and bishoprics where all kinds of little bones have by chance been found."

"*Breve confinium veratis et falsi.* It will not be me who disputes the authenticity of relics that contribute to drawing souls to the Kingdom of Heaven."

"I don't know. Where matters of God are concerned, perhaps we should trust more in His commandments."

"I see you have a gift for controversy." Flavio tried to dry the chest with a damp cloth. "The talent of someone who wastes his breath without knowing the reason for his arguments. Do you know the true power of relics? Are you able to distinguish between the Lance of Longinus, the Holy Shroud, and the blood of a martyr?"

"I know that classification—but in any event, I repeat my apology. I did not wish to question—"

"If you do not wish it, then do not do it," Flavio said loudly.

"I'm sorry, Father," Alcuin responded, taken aback. "But, if it is no trouble, permit me to ask a final question."

Flavio looked at him wearily, as if he could not be bothered to answer. "Yes?"

"Why are you taking the relic to Würzburg?"

The prelate seemed to think it over. Finally he responded. "As you will know, for years Charlemagne has been trying to subjugate the pagan Obodrites, Pannonians, and Bavarians. However, neither his continual campaigns nor his exemplary punishments have altered the fact that they remain Godless in the depths of their souls. The pagans are crude folks, stuck in the ways of polytheism, of heresy, of concubinage . . . with these people, the force of arms is necessary, though sometimes it is not enough."

"Please continue." Alcuin was already not sure he agreed with Flavio's premise.

"Damned wound." He paused to reposition his bandages. "Well, eight years ago Charlemagne and his host went to Italy in response to the Holy Pontiff's entreaty. As you might know, the Lombards, not satisfied with ruling over the former Byzantine duchies, had invaded the cities of Faenza and Comacchio, besieged Ravenna, and subjugated Urbino, Montefeltro, and Sinigaglia."

"You speak of Desiderius, the Lombard king."

"That man, a king? For the love of God, don't make me laugh. He might have called himself one, but he was nothing more than a serpent in human form. The king of treachery. That should have been his title."

"But didn't a daughter of Desiderius marry Charlemagne himself?"

"Indeed. Could you imagine a more heinous offense? The Lombard took it upon himself to wed his pup to Charlemagne and then, believing himself immune, attack the Vatican territories. However, Pope Adrian persuaded Charlemagne that he needed his help, and the king, after crossing the Great Saint Bernard Pass with his troops, surrounded the traitor at this lair in Pavia."

"Without question the gesture of a good Christian."

"In part, yes. But do not be fooled. Charlemagne wishes to contain the expansionist ambitions of the Lombard king as much as the pope did. After all, following his foreseeable victory, not only would Charlemagne return to the papacy the usurped territories under the *liber pontificalis*, but also benefit himself by appropriating the Lombard duchies of Spoleto and Benevento."

"Interesting, to be sure. Please, do continue."

Theresa was listening attentively.

"The rest you will know. Desiderius refused to leave Pavia, forcing Charlemagne to begin a siege. However, after nine months, Charlemagne's host grew impatient. It would appear that they feared for their crops—and there was news of another revolt in the Saxon lands. Meanwhile, Desiderius remained trapped, so Charlemagne started to consider how he would end the siege."

"But Charlemagne was victorious," Theresa cut in, proud that she knew the story.

"That's right, but not thanks to his troops. As soon as he learned of the situation, Pope Adrian ordered the *lignum crucis*—kept until then at the Roman Basilica of the Holy Cross in Jerusalem—to be taken to Charlemagne's camp. And within a week of its arrival, a sudden epidemic began to decimate the Lombards. Desiderius surrendered, and Charlemagne took the city without shedding a single drop of blood."

"And now Charlemagne plans to use the power of the *lignum crucis* in his war with the Saxons."

"Indeed. The monarch asked the pope for his help, and the pope did not hesitate to send him the relic. And now that he has it, he intends to deposit it in a safe city."

"It's curious," said Alcuin. "Please forgive my forwardness, but as the guardian of such an important relic, why have you embarked on this dangerous and unnecessary journey? You could have waited in Aquis-Granum until Charlemagne began the next campaign."

"And leave the inhabitants of Würzburg at the mercy of their ill fate? I don't know about you, but I would consider that neither charitable nor Christian."

"Viewed in that way, you are right. Incidentally, shouldn't you open the chest to check its condition?" Alcuin remarked as he started to lift the lid.

Flavio swooped down on the chest and slammed it shut again. "I don't think that's necessary," he hastened to say. "The chest is lined with greased leather. What's more, the *lignum crucis* is protected by a lead coffer that acts as a reliquary."

"Ah! Then we have nothing to worry about. Particularly if the coffer you speak of is large and with thick panels."

"It is. And now, if you will allow me, I will rest a while."

Alcuin watched Flavio as he leaned back against the chest. He wondered whether his abrupt behavior was due to his lack of sleep or the recent attack, but the question still remained how such a light chest could contain a heavy lead coffer.

By midafternoon, the water was flooding the ship quicker than the oarsmen could bail it out, so Izam ordered them to moor the boat immediately. After positioning the lookouts, he divided the men into two groups, one that would guard the ship and another that would disembark. Then he approached Flavio and Alcuin to inquire after the health of the Roman prelate.

"We'll remain anchored for four hours," he informed them. "Enough to carry out some repairs. How is your injury?"

"It still hurts," Flavio responded.

"If you wish, you can wait on board. We have work to do on land."

"I'll go down," Alcuin announced. "And you should do the same," he said to Flavio. "That leg needs some movement."

"I would rather wait here," he said plaintively.

Theresa joined the group disembarking, for she needed a few moments of privacy that she wasn't afforded while on the ship.

On land, Izam divided the responsibilities among the men into those responsible for the repairs and those who would carry out guard duties. The first group patched up the hull with planks taken from the deck itself and caulked it with pitch that they had onboard. The rest established a defensive perimeter around the boat to prevent another attack.

Theresa took the opportunity to go off and wash in peace—something she hadn't been able to do since they'd set sail. She was still squatting when Hoos appeared. She stood up, embarrassed, but he tried to take her in his arms anyway. Theresa protested, but Hoos persisted, laughing stupidly. When she moved away, he shoved her unceremoniously. At that moment Izam appeared.

"The lookouts need you," he said to Hoos drily.

Hoos looked at him out of the corner of his eye and reluctantly obeyed, though not before stealing a kiss from Theresa and slapping her on the behind. When he had gone, she finished straightening her skirt, visibly angered. Izam picked up a clasp from the ground for her and she thanked him. Then she apologized for Hoos, as though she were responsible for his behavior. They walked for a while in silence, until Theresa noticed that Izam seemed perturbed.

"We've never talked about it," she said, "but you're not from these parts."

"No, I'm not. I was born in Padua—I'm Italian."

She was glad he had finally said something. "Would you believe me if I told you that I suspected it?" she joked. "I met some Roman monks on their pilgrimage to Constantinople. Their Latin was similar to yours, though their accent was sloppier. I was born there. Did you know?"

"In Constantinople! Well, I never! A beautiful city, by Januarius!"

"I don't believe it—you've been there?" she asked in astonishment.

"I have indeed. I spent a few years there. My parents sent me to learn the art of war. A magnificent metropolis in which to buy, sell, and love. Though it's not so good for solitary pursuits and meditation. I have never known such talkative folks."

"That's true," she laughed. "They say a Byzantine can speak for several hours even after death. Do you not like a good conversation?"

"I wouldn't prefer to say except that I can count with the fingers on one hand the number of times a discussion has proved to be edifying."

"Sorry. I didn't mean to bother you." She reddened.

"No. I don't mean you," he hastened to add. "And you, what are you doing here? I mean, in Franconia, and now here with us on the ship."

She looked at him. He wore his hair gathered up under a beaver-skin hat that contrasted with his green eyes. She surprised herself by staring at him without answering, so she quickly responded somewhat clumsily recounting the events that had led her to this point. She intentionally left out the events in Würzburg and the reason for her being on the boat, but she spoke of her childhood and flight from Constantinople. Izam, meanwhile, paid her little attention. He was busy looking from side to side like an animal stalking prey.

"A busy life," he finally said.

Suddenly, he swooped down on her, violently pinning her to the ground. She didn't even have time to scream. She just heard a swarm of arrows whistling around her and felt a throbbing at her temple.

Izam raised the alarm as several men dropped to the ground. The young man rose and readied his bow, but another volley of arrows forced him to take cover. He noticed that Theresa had hit her head and was lying unconscious. All around him people were crying out in pain.

He called for his men to cover him. On his signal, they all fired. Then, he picked up Theresa and ran like a madman toward the ship. Flavio and Alcuin pulled the young woman on board. The rest of the men jumped on board however they could, then they all fell upon the oars. Under a barrage of arrows, the boat started to move. Finally it gathered momentum, and gradually it made headway upriver away from the danger.

24

The oarsmen rowed the battered ship toward the breakwater at Würzburg's port, turned it clumsily to the side, and, after pitching a couple of times, drove it abruptly into the riverbed at the wharf. Immediately, a throng of peasants threw themselves into the water wanting to help with the disembarkation.

Izam positioned himself at the prow to oversee the mooring, while the rest of the crew jumped into the river and pushed from the stern to refloat the hull. When the ship finally dropped anchor, the cries of jubilation drowned out the church bells that welcomed the newcomers to Würzburg.

Gradually the arriving trickle of people turned into a stream of desperate scavengers, prepared to kill for a piece of bread. The crowd grew on the bank, competing for the highest and best spots. Children climbed trees and the elderly made do with cursing whoever shoved them aside. Some sang in joy and everyone thanked the heavens. Suddenly, it was as though the days of hunger and hardship were already melting away.

A boy went too close to the provisions and was jostled away by a crew member. Another youngster saw this and laughed and the first lad threw a stone at him.

Soon Wilfred's soldiers arrived. A peasant jeered at them and then had to run off before he was discovered. The rest of the townspeople respectfully made way for the soldiers.

Wilfred's men roughly made way through the crowd, opening up a path for the carts. Once they reached the wharf, they positioned archers along a corridor from the ship to the wagons.

Then Wilfred appeared on his wooden chair, pulled by his dogs. "Listen carefully, you bunch of scavengers!" he called out to the impatient crowd. "The first person to touch a single grain will be executed. The provisions will be taken to the royal granaries, where they will be inspected, and once they have been inventoried, they will be distributed, so move aside and let these men do their job."

The count's words riled some of those present, but they were soon appeased when the first supplies were unloaded.

Wilfred whipped the dogs and they pulled his contraption. The crowd stepped back even further as if that cripple could decide the fate of all those present with a mere glance.

As he reached the gangplank, Wilfred ordered two of his men to take him onboard, which they did by lifting him into the air and carrying him onto the deck of the ship. There he greeted Alcuin and Flavio, inquired about events during the voyage, checked the condition of the provisions, and looked sidelong at the wounded, instructing his servants to tend to them. It was some time before Izam approached him. He hadn't known that the count of Würzburg was a cripple.

"Würzburg, at last. *Deum gratia*," said Alcuin, and he passed his hand across Theresa's brow. The young woman had not yet regained consciousness.

"No change?" Flavio Diacono asked him.

"I'm afraid so. Let's get her off the ship. I hope her family is waiting for her."

"She's from Würzburg?"

"She's the daughter of Gorgias, a Byzantine scribe."

One of the peasants helping with the unloading stopped and
looked at them openmouthed. He began to tremble. The bale of
grain he was carrying slipped through his fingers overboard and
into the water.

"Useless fool!" Wilfred bellowed. "That grain is worth more
than your life."

The peasant fell to his knees and crossed himself. Visibly shaken,
he pointed to where the monks were standing.

"Lord help us! The scribe's daughter! The dead girl has been
resurrected!"

Not even the Volz woman's cow giving birth to a two-headed calf
had caused such a huge stir in Würzburg. When the calf was born,
folks spoke of the Devil's intervention, and there were those who
attempted to burn the farmer along with her bicephalous monster.
A resurrection was something that even the most fervent believers
could not have imagined.

Tidings of the miracle spread like seeds to the wind. Before
long, whispers turned into murmurs, which rippled through the
crowd to every corner of the city. The boldest milled around the
ship to try to see her with their own eyes, while others jostled for a
spot near the gangplank.

Hearing the rumor left Alcuin feeling stone cold. He was still
wondering what had caused all the commotion when the feverish
crowd forgot about Wilfred's threat and began to climb onto the
ship. Wilfred deployed his men, but the mob ignored his soldiers.
It was as though some collective madness had taken hold of them.
At the count's orders, an archer fired. The peasant at the front of

the mob staggered and fell overboard as the arrow hit him. The rest of them stepped back. When a second arrow was released, they all left the boat.

Yet Wilfred felt just as disconcerted. He had walked over to where the girl lay so he could confirm her identity. At first he didn't recognize her, but as he came closer, his eyes widened as though he were looking at the Devil himself. He was in no doubt. The young woman was Theresa, the scribe's daughter.

He was so riled that when he attempted to cross himself, his nerves prevented him. When he finally calmed down, Alcuin suggested they take Theresa on land and Wilfred agreed. Between them Hoos and Alcuin improvised a stretcher on which to bear the young woman.

Wilfred had his servants unload him and his wooden carriage, ordering his men to make way for them as they began their return. As they proceeded, the people started going down on their knees, begging for mercy in the wake of the miracle. Some tried to touch the resurrected woman, while others prayed that her reappearance was not the work of the Devil. The procession traveled along the town's streets in the direction of Wilfred's fortress. Once they had arrived, the crowds once again thronged the walls.

A group of skeptics led by Korne the parchment-maker went to the cemetery to exhume Theresa's body. They did not know exactly where she had been buried, so they dug up the most recent graves, but could not find her. Then they returned to the fortress and demanded to be allowed to join the deliberations that Izam, Flavio, Alcuin, and the count had begun.

By then Wilfred had informed Alcuin of the fire. He also spoke of Korne's obsession with avenging the accidental death of his son. Without telling anyone, Alcuin hatched a plan to protect Theresa.

Wilfred eventually allowed Korne's presence in order to prevent a disturbance outside. The parchment-maker asked to see the revenant, but Alcuin objected. The monk argued that Theresa was unconscious and that he would answer any of his questions. He explained what his relationship with the young woman was and informed them that, thanks be to God, he could explain the miracle.

Wilfred tapped his fingers nervously. Then he cracked his whip and the two dogs pulled the mobile contraption toward one of the windows so he could look out and contemplate the mob.

Alcuin continued to stare at him, still taken aback that a cripple could move around with the help of nothing more than a couple of dogs. Then he realized that everyone was staring at him, waiting for his explanation. "First we must verify that this young woman really is who she appears to be," he said. "I know those present say they recognize her, but what do the young woman's relatives say? Can we be sure when she hasn't confirmed it herself?"

"For the love of God! Try to be sensible," Korne suddenly cut in. "How is the young woman going to confirm her own identity if she is unconscious? We'll have to wait for the stepmother to arrive and see if she can clarify anything."

"And her father, the scribe?" Alcuin inquired.

"He disappeared a couple of months ago. We haven't found him yet."

For a moment there was silence, then Zeno appeared after having examined her condition.

"How is she?" Izam asked the physician.

"Cold as ice, but the warmth from the hearth will soon revive her."

Izam turned to the fireplace, a sort of oven adjoining the wall of one of the rooms, instead of the usual fireplace dug into the ground.

Korne cleared his throat. Nobody wished to bring up the subject of resurrection.

"Well," the parchment-maker announced, "it seems obvious that the girl never died in the fire."

Alcuin stood. His great height projected a long shadow that slid toward the parchment-maker. "Let's get one thing clear. The only undeniable thing is that the young woman here now lives. Whether the woman you refer to died in the fire is what we want to ascertain. Remember that, after the disaster, her parents recognized the body."

"It was an unrecognizable body. Zeno can confirm it," Korne said adamantly.

Alcuin looked at Zeno, but the physician took a swig of wine and looked away. Alcuin pulled a Vulgate from among his belongings and his skinny fingers slowly opened the cover and traced the volume as if he were reading something. Then he closed the book, lifted his gaze, and fixed his eyes on Korne. "Before beginning this discussion, I briefly made my way to the fortress chapel to pray to God to enlighten me. I prayed after touching the relics of the Santa Croce and suddenly I had a vision. An angel appeared before me from the darkness. From his neck came a resplendent crown that bordered his long and immaculate head of hair. He was floating gently, like a leaf on still water and his eyes emanated the eternal peace of the Almighty. The harbinger showed me Theresa's body consumed by flames, and beside her another perfect body was formed by a whirl of blinding light, which swelled and gleamed until a new Theresa was fashioned, alive and without sin."

"Another Theresa? Are you suggesting that it is not the same one?" a frightened Wilfred asked.

"Yes and no. Imagine for a moment a little caterpillar. Imagine this little caterpillar of imperfection leaving the cocoon of sin to become a virtuous butterfly. The caterpillar and the butterfly are the same creature, but one lies consumed while the other is reborn before it flies up to the heavens. The truth of the matter is that Theresa died. Perhaps she sinned, and her body burned for it. But sometimes God, in his infinite wisdom, reveals the path to redemption by bestowing upon us a miracle. A wonder that shows us the way of repentance." He gave Wilfred a grim look. "The Creator might have allowed Theresa's soul to suffer in the Acheron, the Phlegethon, and the Cocytus of the Greeks, in order to purge her sins in the place where the Lord cleanses the foulness of the daughters of Zion. But, what good would it have been if none of us learned from her torment?"

Wilfred and Flavio were captivated. They hardly breathed and remained silent for a few moments, until they realized that Alcuin had finished. However, Korne's eyes were blinking stupidly. Though he didn't understand the full meaning behind Alcuin's words or know for certain whether God had a hand in it, he wasn't about to admit there had been miracle. "And what does that prove? The Devil might have resuscitated her," he sputtered.

Alcuin took a triumphant breath. He had managed to make Korne fall into heresy. Now it would be easy to divert his attention, accusing him of blasphemy. "Are you denying this divine inter-vention?" he said, raising his voice. "Do you dare contradict God? To compare His infinite power with the degradation of the Devil? Kneel, blasphemer! Show your remorse and accept the ways of the Lord—or prepare for immediate torment."

Alcuin snatched Izam's sword from him and held it against Korne's throat.

"Swear before God!" he commanded him, holding out the Bible. "Swear before God that you renounce the Devil!"

Sweat appeared on Korne's brow while he swore as ordered. Then he stood and left the room, biting his lip.

Once they were left alone, Flavio remonstrated with Alcuin. He was the papal envoy and, therefore, the only person authorized to pass judgment on a divine intervention. "I'm sorry to have to tell you this, but perhaps you have been too hasty. Sometimes, aston-ishing events are caused by the most trivial circumstances. After all, Zeno says that the body that burned in the fire was unrecognizable."

"Look, Flavio: Zeno wouldn't even recognize his own mother," Alcuin retorted, pointing at the sixth cup of wine that he had emptied.

"But, damn it! You could at least have waited to share your vision until after Theresa woke up, so she could tell us what happened. I assure you that if the miracle is real, I will be the first to celebrate it."

"You heard Wilfred say what kind of a man that Korne is. He's driven to do away with Theresa. The young woman was in danger, so if a miracle will help me save her life, why not welcome it?"

"What are you saying? That you made it up? You didn't have that vision?"

"No, I'm afraid not."

"God Almighty! And could you not think of anything else aside from inventing a miracle?"

"Flavio, after what happened in the fire, it is a miracle indeed that the young woman lives. It's just as if she had been resurrected. What's more, God assists us in different ways. You with your relics, and me with my visions," he declared.

At that moment a disheveled and frightened maidservant came into the room.

"The girl's waking up," she announced.

They both rushed to where Theresa was resting. Alcuin saw that her face was beaded with sweat. He removed the blankets that covered her and asked for a candle to be brought over. Then he soaked a cloth in warm water and carefully cleaned the girl's face. Next, as he normally did with his students suffering from exposure to the elements, he rubbed down both of her arms, concentrating on the joints.

Gradually the color returned to her cheeks. Her eyelids fluttered and—following a few moments of uncertainty—they opened, revealing reddened eyes with irises reflecting a beautiful syrupy hue.

Alcuin smiled and said hello to the young woman before tracing the sign of the cross on her forehead. Then he helped her lift her head, placing a cushion under it.

"Theresa," Alcuin whispered.

She acknowledged him with a breath. In front of her she saw the bony figure of a man at peace.

"Welcome home," said the monk.

Alcuin endeavored to explain all that happened since their arrival, but Theresa did not understand. Her head felt as if it had been kicked by a horse, and the story of a miracle was so confusing it seem like it had been taken from the dream of a lunatic. She lifted her head and asked for a little water. Then, when she heard the tale again, she looked at Alcuin as though he were a stranger. At that moment Wilfred came in and Alcuin whispered to Theresa to play along.

"Theresa, do you recognize me?" the count asked, pleased to have found her awake.

The young woman looked at the dogs and nodded.

"God rejoices at your return, as do we, of course. It has been a sad time, but you have nothing to worry about now. Soon everything will go back to how it was."

Theresa smiled timidly.

In response Wilfred gave her a forced grin. "I would like you to try to remember. Do you recall what happened in the fire?"

Theresa looked at Alcuin as if seeking his approval. The monk said nothing, so she responded with a stammer.

"Then I imagine you will want to tell us about it," he said, his face moving closer to hers. "Did you see the Redeemer? Did you discern His appearance? Do not worry if you can't respond—it was He who returned you to us."

Theresa thought the question odd and wasn't sure how to respond.

Alcuin stepped in. "Perhaps she needs to rest. She's confused. She hit her head and hardly remembers anything," he declared.

"Very well . . . that's understandable. But as soon as she recovers, let me know. Remember that it was me who buried her charred remains."

Wilfred said a halfhearted good-bye before leaving the room. Meanwhile, Alcuin examined the contraption that transported him. He handled the dog chair like a seasoned cart driver, easily negotiating the thresholds and loose tiles that got in his way. He noticed that the contraption had a chamber pot housed in the rear to assist his bowel movements. The skill with which he handled the hounds told him that he had been in that condition for some years.

Alcuin turned to Theresa. The young woman was giving him an inquisitive look.

"Look," he said, sitting beside her. "The ways of the Lord take strange twists and turns: tortuous paths that sometimes confuse the foolish, but not those who have devoted their lives to following His doctrine. It is obvious that your time has not come yet. Perhaps because you have not yet made yourself worthy of the Kingdom of Heaven, though this does not mean you cannot achieve it."

Theresa was feeling increasingly confused. She did not comprehend what was happening, nor why they were insisting she had been resurrected.

"And my parents?" she asked.

"Your stepmother awaits in the antechamber. You will see her soon."

Theresa slowly lifted herself up. Her head was pounding.

She recognized Wilfred's room. She had been there on occasion to meet her father, but it had never seemed so cold and desolate.

Alcuin helped her sit up. She touched her head, noticing a painful bump. Alcuin explained that she had hit her head during a skirmish with bandits. As the memory came back to her, Theresa inquired after Izam and Hoos. Alcuin informed her they were both busy unloading the ship.

"I want to see my parents," she insisted.

Alcuin asked her to be patient. He told her that Rutgarda seemed traumatized, and they still had not found Gorgias. Theresa became agitated, but Alcuin soothed her, saying that he would speak to Wilfred to learn what had happened. As for the miracle, he confessed that he had been forced to make it up.

"Korne would not have accepted any other explanation. I know it was blasphemous, but at that moment, I could not think of anything more suitable."

"But why a miracle?"

"Because, in the words of Wilfred, they had found your charred remains."

"My remains?"

"A body they thought was yours, and which apparently still wore a blue dress that Gorgias recognized as the one you had on that day."

"That poor girl." She recalled again how she had not been able to do anything to save her. "I tried to protect her with my wet dress," she explained, relating the details of what had happened during the fire.

"I imagined that's what anyone with half a brain would have done, but not the notables that inhabit this town. That was why I thought it would be helpful if these *notables* saw the hand of God in your return. And I also considered the fact that Korne the parchment-maker is eager to avenge his son's death. For the time being, he has sworn to respect you, but I do not believe that will stop him for long."

He informed her that he would tell her stepmother to come in and see her. "One last thing." He gave Theresa a grim look. "If you want to live, don't speak to anyone about the miracle."

25

Alcuin was settled into a cell in the southern wing of the fortress, near Izam's room and adjoining Flavio's. From his window he could see the Main Valley, with the foothills of the Rhön Mountains in the background. On the fields, the snow was beginning to thin, but on the peaks it continued to gleam as if the mountains had been given a coat of paint. He noticed the strange formations scattered around the landscape wherever the forests became sparse. Observing them more closely, he noted the presence of a myriad of cavities bored into brownish mounds. They were similar to mining tunnels, and as he dressed he wondered whether they were, in fact, mining tunnels and if they were in use.

He went down to dinner after None and met with Wilfred in the armory, accompanied by Theodor, the giant he used as a draft animal when the dogs were locked away.

The count seemed pleased to see him and impatient to learn more about the miracle, but Alcuin was only interested in talking about the parchment that Charlemagne had commissioned Wilfred to prepare. He decided to wait until the giant retired to his chambers before raising the subject. However, Theodor remained impassive behind the chair for a long time until Wilfred finally ordered him to leave.

"A veritable mountain in trousers! I have never seen a man so large," said Alcuin.

"And loyal as a dog. All he's missing is the wagging tail. So tell me, are your chambers to your liking?"

"Certainly. The views are excellent."

"Some wine?"

Alcuin declined the offer and sat down in front of the count, waiting for the right moment to bring up the subject that pressed on his mind. "Do you lock away the dogs at night?" he asked.

Wilfred explained that he only used them in the morning—for certain routes free of stairs. He also liked to go out with them into Würzburg's streets, particularly the best kept ones.

"Sometimes I even venture out of the city," he said with a smile. "You should see how they understand my expressions. One blink from me and they will set upon the first person I signal."

"With the carriage still harnessed to their backs?"

"I will tell you a secret," he said, still smiling.

Wilfred activated a device on one of the armrests and a spring released the rings used to harness the hounds to the contraption.

"Very clever."

"Indeed," he said with pride. "I had it installed myself. The most difficult thing was hardening the strip of metal so that it could be used as a spring, but our blacksmith is talented enough he could build a harp and make it play itself." He reinserted the rings into their housing and reset the spring. "But that's enough about dogs—let's talk about Theresa. I don't think any other matter is more significant now."

They spoke of the celestial apparition, which Alcuin repeated from top to bottom, adding one or two more fabricated details.

When he had finished, Wilfred seemed perplexed, but without stopping to reflect, the count seemed to accept Alcuin's theory and insisted again that he try the wine. This time the monk accepted.

When he had finished his cup, he inquired again about the parchment.

"It's almost complete. You will be able to see it soon," said Wilfred apologetically.

"If you don't mind, I'd rather see it now."

Wilfred cleared his throat and shook his head. Then he nodded toward his contraption. "Help me, please."

Alcuin positioned himself behind the wheelchair and pushed Wilfred in the direction he indicated. As they reached a chest of drawers in his room, the count asked Alcuin to pass him a coffer that the monk estimated to be one cubit long by half a cubit wide. Wilfred opened it, revealing its interior, which was empty. Then he lifted a false bottom and took from it a document that he held out nervously to Alcuin. The monk took it and held it in the candlelight.

"But this is just a draft."

"As I said, it is not ready yet."

"I know that's what you told me, but Charlemagne will not accept that answer. It has been several months. Why is it not ready yet?"

"There was only enough parchment left for two trial runs. It is a special parchment. Uterine vellum: you know, the one made from unborn calf's skin."

"Everyone knows what vellum is," he murmured.

"This is different, brought in from Byzantium. Anyhow, the only copy was lost in the fire, so Gorgias started another. But a few weeks ago the scribe disappeared from the scriptorium along with the document."

"I don't understand—what do you mean?"

"About two months ago I met with him in my chambers, and he assured me that he would have it finished within a few days. However, that same morning he vanished as if by magic."

"And since then?"

"Nobody has seen him," he lamented. "As far as I know, Genseric was the last person to see him. He accompanied him to the scriptorium to collect a few things and was never seen again."

When Alcuin suggested they go to speak to Genseric, Wilfred fell silent for a moment. Then he downed his wine and looked at the monk with glazed eyes.

"I'm afraid that will not be possible. Genseric is dead. They found his body last week in the middle of the forest, run through with a stylus."

Alcuin coughed when he heard this last part, but his astonishment turned to stupor when he heard that, according to Wilfred, Gorgias was the murderer.

The next morning Alcuin went to the kitchens early. As in other fortresses, they were located in a separate building so that, in the event of a kitchen fire, the flames would be contained. Indeed, as soon as he entered, he noticed the blackened walls—a clear sign of repeated fires. He asked a maidservant for the head cook, who turned out to be Bernardino, a stout monk the size of a wine barrel. The squat man greeted him without a glance as he dashed about as nimbly as a squirrel organizing the supplies. When he finally stopped, he gladly turned his attention to Alcuin. "Sorry about the rush, but we were in desperate need of the provisions you brought." He handed him a hot cup of milk. "It's an honor to meet you. Everyone is talking about you."

Alcuin accepted the milk with pleasure. Since he had left Fulda he had drunk nothing but watered-down wine. Then Alcuin asked Bernardino about Genseric. Wilfred had told him that it was the cook who had found the coadjutor's body.

"That's right." With difficulty he perched on a chair. "I discovered the old man in the middle of the forest, lying face-up with froth at the mouth. He couldn't have been dead long, for the vermin had not yet devoured him."

He told him about the stylus sunk into his belly. It was of the type used by scribes to write on wax tablets, he explained. It had been driven deep into him.

"And you think it was Gorgias?"

The midget shrugged.

"The stylus undoubtedly belonged to Gorgias, but I would never have attributed an act like that to him. We all thought him a good man," he added, "though lately some strange events have taken place." He explained to him that, in addition to Genseric, several young boys had turned up dead, and it was rumored that the scribe was also behind those murders.

When Alcuin asked him about the coadjutor's body, Bernardino informed him where it had been buried. The midget was surprised at the monk's interest in the whereabouts of the clothes that Genseric had been wearing, for normally they washed the garments of the dead and if they were in good condition they were reused.

"But Genseric's stank of urine, so we decided to bury him in his habit."

Alcuin finished his cup of milk and asked the cook if the young boys had also been stabbed.

"They were. Strange goings-on."

Alcuin nodded, disconcerted. He thanked Bernardino for the information and wiped the remnants of milk from his mouth. Then he asked when they could examine the place where he had found Genseric. They agreed they would meet that afternoon following the Sext service. So he said farewell and returned to his chambers. On the way he decided to ask Wilfred to exhume the coadjutor's body, for something did not add up.

In the corridor that led to his room, he bumped into Flavio Diacono, with bleary eyes and disheveled hair. It was late to be rising and the prelate behaved as if there was no work to be done. Alcuin had the impression that Flavio Diacono—with his puffy flesh and perfumed clothes—was the kind of priest who was less concerned with abiding by the precepts than in fulfilling his own desires. In a moment of drunkenness, he had even admitted that in Rome he used to enjoy the company of young girls, suggesting that Alcuin should try it. But Alcuin naturally chose celibacy. The Church, of course, condemned concubinage, but it was not uncommon for some men of the cloth to succumb to the pleasures of cohabitation, living with women they bought or coerced with the threat of eternal damnation.

He returned Flavio's greeting and accompanied him to the dining hall. It was not his place to judge his behavior, but as Saint Augustine had declared in his *De Civitate Dei*, though men were born with the freedom to choose, there was no doubt that for some, such a faculty only allowed them to make poor decisions.

At breakfast, everyone present discussed Theresa's miracle.

Izam did not give an opinion, but several clerics suggested setting up an altar on the ashes of the old workshop, and one even suggested building a chapel there. Wilfred was in agreement, but listened to Alcuin's objection when he proposed that they wait for an ecumenical council to comment on the matter.

When they inquired after the whereabouts of the young woman, Wilfred responded that Theresa had spent the night in the fortress storerooms, after Zeno had given her an infusion of willow and lemon balm. Rutgarda had stayed by her side, waiting for her to awaken. It would appear that Rutgarda had barely slept between praying, weeping, and tending to Theresa, hoping that the miraculous appearance of her stepdaughter was an omen that her husband would return.

At that moment Wilfred's young daughters burst into the room. The two little girls laughed playfully, evading the wet nurse who tried to grab them. Ignoring her warnings, they scampered through the legs of the guests. Finally the devoted maidservant let herself fall to the floor and threatened the girls with a spanking, but they stuck out their little tongues and with a mischievous expression hid behind Flavio and Alcuin's robes.

Wilfred celebrated his twins' capers by clapping his hands, to which the girls responded by running over to him. He took them in his arms and kissed their heads until their hair was wild. The children laughed again, their little eyes dancing, then pulled away when he galloped his fingers across their round tummies. Wilfred was laughing, too. The two curly-haired and red-cheeked cherubs had brought him joy again. He kissed them once more and after asking them to behave like well-mannered little ladies, he handed them over to the exhausted wet nurse.

"Quite the little devils. Just like their mother," he said with a smile. He picked up the rag doll they'd left on his lap and placed it on the table.

Most of those present knew that Wilfred's wife had died the year before from a wicked fever. Some had immediately advised him to remarry, but he was not partial to the idea of cohabiting with a woman again, except for the occasional dalliance.

"Refresh my memory," Flavio Diacono cut in. "Did you say that Theresa started the fire?"

"That's right," answered Wilfred. "Apparently the girl flew into a rage and set fire to the workshop where she was employed. Several people died."

"And yet, yesterday you were of the opinion that Theresa could do no harm."

"I did say that," he confirmed. "One of the victims later confessed to me that it was Korne who'd caused the fire when he pushed the young woman. But I also believed her father to be an upright man, and look at him now: He is wanted for murder."

After breakfast, Alcuin went to the fortress stables, where Bernardino, mounted on a donkey, waited for him. The midget bade him a good morning and invited him to also mount the animal. But the monk decided he would rather accompany him on foot.

As they walked, Alcuin pressed Bernardino for details of the froth that he discovered on Genseric's face. The little man confirmed that the body lay face up, with the eyes open and a mass of bubbles on the face.

"Bubbles? You mean a froth on the lips?"

"How should I know! The man was stiff, like all corpses."

They arrived at the place along a clear path that wound through an oak wood near the fortress. The sun was shining warmly and the patches of snow were beginning to thaw. Alcuin examined the footprints on the path.

"It was right here," Bernardino announced, stopping the donkey. The midget jumped down from the animal and skipped off into the forest like a kid. He stopped behind some rocks, where he triumphantly indicated the place where the body had lain.

"Do you remember the exact day?"

"Of course. I had gone out in search of nuts to make a cake for Wilfred's daughters. There are some walnut trees down there. I was passing through here when the donkey stopped and—"

"And that was what day?"

"Sorry, yes . . . it was last Friday. Saint Benedict's Day."

Alcuin crouched down at the spot Bernardino indicated. The grass was flattened down in some places where the body had lain. Then he examined the surroundings.

"How did you transport the corpse? I mean . . . did you drag it or put it on the donkey?"

"I know what you're thinking," he said with a laugh. "You think that because I'm a midget, I couldn't have lifted him."

"Well, yes, I suspected as much."

Bernardino went over to the animal and struck it with his stick, making it lie down flat with a hee-haw. Then he skillfully mounted the donkey and, holding the mane tightly, he gave it another blow, making it give a start. When the animal stood up, Bernardino laughed proudly, baring his yellowing teeth.

On his return, Alcuin went to the storerooms to see how Theresa was faring. There he found Rutgarda, who went out of her way to praise him for the way he had behaved with her. Alcuin dismissed it as a minor thing and asked to speak to the young woman.

"Alone, if possible."

Rutgarda and Hoos, who was also present, left the storeroom. Then Alcuin approached the bed. "It's cold here. How are you feeling?"

"Awful. Nobody knows where my father is." She had tears in her eyes.

Alcuin pursed his lips. He could tell that nothing he could say would do much to console her. He wondered whether she knew that her father had been accused of murder.

"Have you spoken to anyone about the miracle?"

She shook her head no. Then, answering Alcuin's question without being asked, she said that her father would never have done anything like what a maidservant had told her he had done. Alcuin said he didn't doubt it.

"It's all lies," Theresa insisted. "He would never—" Her sobbing prevented her from continuing.

"I'm certain of it—so now the important thing is to find him. We don't know why he disappeared, but I promise I will solve the mystery."

He waited for Theresa to dry her tears. Then he helped her wrap up warm, alerted Rutgarda, and they all left together through a back door that led into the fortress. There he requested that Wilfred accommodate them in the main building, which was warmer and safer, instructing Theresa to stay in the room for a few days.

In the middle of the afternoon, Alcuin found Wilfred in the scriptorium. His dogs growled as soon as they saw him, but the count soothed them. He flicked the reins and the animals pulled him toward Alcuin, who offered them two pieces of meat that he had pilfered from the kitchens. The hounds devoured the fillets as if they hadn't eaten for months.

He noticed that Wilfred still had the rag doll that his daughters had left behind. It had curious white eyes made from pebbles, on which someone had painted rough blue irises.

"How do you open doors?" the monk inquired.

"Either I use this hook," he said, showing him a sort of harpoon attached to a hazel branch, "or the dogs pull me close. What brings you here?"

"A delicate matter. You said that Genseric was stabbed to death."

"That's right. Run through with a stylus." He urged on the hounds, which turned around and dragged him to a small alcove. Opening a drawer, he removed a stylus of the type used by scribes, and showed it to him. "With this one to be precise."

The monk studied it closely. "It's of high quality," he remarked. "Did it belong to Gorgias?"

Wilfred nodded and then returned it to the same place.

Alcuin examined the table that was used as a writing desk. He asked whether it was where Gorgias wrote, and the count confirmed that it was. There were several other styluses lined up neatly alongside some inkwells and a little jar of pounce. A thick layer of dust covered the instruments, with the exception of two long, thin areas that were cleaner. Upon noticing this, Alcuin grew suspicious, but he kept his thoughts to himself, continuing his examination as if he hadn't noticed anything amiss. He was surprised not to find the texts in Greek that Gorgias would undoubtedly have needed to prepare the manuscript. When he brought up the matter of exhuming Genseric's body, Wilfred arched an eyebrow.

"Disinter him? Whatever for?"

"I would like to grant him the blessing of the holy relics," the monk lied. "Flavio is the guardian of the *lignum crucis*, the wood from Christ's cross."

"Yes, I know, but I don't understand."

"Genseric died unexpectedly, perhaps with some sin on his conscience. Since we have these relics, it would be uncharitable not to use them to sanctify his body."

"And to do that we have to take him from his grave?"

Alcuin assured him that it was necessary.

After a few moments' hesitation, Wilfred agreed. However, he did not accompany him, but summoned the giant Theodor to show him to Genseric's resting place.

In addition to being half a body bigger than any other person, Theodor was also half-mute. As he tirelessly removed spadesful of earth, all he mumbled was that the grave stank of dung. Alcuin thought he would be lying if he said Theodor smelled any better.

After some puffing and panting, Theodor's spade struck the coffin. Alcuin was pleased to see they had used a timber casket, for otherwise the earth would have ruined any clues left by the murderer. Using another spade, Alcuin scraped away the remnants of soil and asked Theodor to help him pull the coffin up and out, which he did. But when he ordered him to lift the lid, the blue-eyed giant told him it was not his business and stepped away, leaving Alcuin alone with the casket. On the third attempt, the lid came open.

As soon as he lifted it, the stench made them both vomit. Theodor moved farther away while Alcuin contended with the creatures swarming over Genseric's corpse. The monk protected his nose with a rag as he brushed away the worms that had amassed on the half-rotten face. Then he searched the body's habit for the place where the stylus had been thrust into him. He found the opening over the stomach: a small, clean incision. He noted the ring of dried blood around it, guessing that the diameter of the stain was about that of a candle. Next he observed the worm-eaten face, with no sign of the froth Bernardino had mentioned. However, he did find traces of it on the neckline of the habit, so taking a knife he cut off a piece of the fabric, shaking off the larvae, and put it in a pouch. Then he carefully examined the palms. The right one seemed bruised, with two strange cavities. When he had finished, he took out a piece of wood and pretended it was the *lignum crucis*, placing it in the coffin while saying a prayer. Finally he replaced the lid and asked the giant to help him rebury the casket.

In the evening some dishes of fish were served in the refectory that seemed to offend Flavio Diacono. Wilfred apologized for the food, but there were not enough provisions for elaborate feasts or celebrations, as even his own reserves were almost depleted.

"It is a shame some of the supplies were lost under the ice," Wilfred lamented. "The townspeople were desperate for that food."

"Are the provisions from the ship not sufficient?" Flavio asked.

"Ha! A half-dead ox, six pecks of wheat, and three sacks of oatmeal. You call those provisions? They won't even reach their plates."

"There are still two ships loaded with provisions downriver. If necessary we could repair our boat and sail down to them," Izam suggested.

"And how have you fed yourselves until now?" Alcuin inquired. "I mean . . . apparently you have suffered from a severe famine."

Wilfred confessed that they held out until the last of their reserves, but when the dead started to pile up, they had to resort to using the royal granaries. "The victuals were not arriving, and people were dying," he explained. "As you know, the royal grain is kept to feed troops in the event of combat, but the situation became unsustainable, so I proceeded with rationing."

"At any rate, it does not look like you are destitute," Flavio pointed out. "Even the hard of hearing would be deafened by the mooing of your cows and the clucking of your hens," he said, pointing toward the area of the courtyard where the animal pens were.

Wilfred reversed his carriage, pulling away from the table. "Is this how a guest thanks me for my generosity? Since when do Romans concern themselves with the troubles of mere country folks?" the offended count protested. "Shut away in your cathedrals as you are, you know nothing of the hardships of your congregation. You have orchards and vegetable gardens, livestock and poultry, lands that you lease out, serfs who in exchange for food clear the fields and repair the walls. You receive tithes from everyone around you and collect taxes for the use of your roads, but you are exempt from paying any yourselves. And still you come here and judge me? Of course I have food. I am no fool. I'm a cleric, but I also govern. What will happen when the townspeople can bear it no longer? When they grow desperate and hunger overcomes them? They will arm themselves with whatever they can find and raid our stores."

Alcuin hastened to intervene.

"Please, accept our apologies. The severity of the situation has taken us by surprise, but I assure you we are as grateful for your hospitality as we are for your generosity. Tell me, do you truly believe the supplies brought on the ship are insufficient?"

Flavio was annoyed at what he considered to be Alcuin's inter-
ference. Yet, he had to admit that his intervention had come at the
right moment.

"Do the numbers yourself," Wilfred grumbled. "Not counting
priests and monks, about three hundred families live in Würzburg.
But at this rate, by next month perhaps, there will be none."

"And the market gardens?" asked Alcuin. "You must have garlic, shallots, leeks, cabbages, radishes, turnips . . ."

"The ice killed off every last thistle. Have you not seen how desperate the townsfolk are?" he responded, pointing at the mob of
people in the lower part of the city. "They can't tell the difference
between an apple and an onion anymore."

"And your reserves?"

"In the granary we still have around a hundred pecks of wheat,
plus another thirty of spelt, but that grain is pure poison and we
only use it to feed to what animals remain. Even so some desperate
souls were bold enough to break into the storehouses and steal a
couple of sacks. The next day we found the thieves outside Zeno's
house with their guts spilling out their mouths. Unfortunately,
death took them before we could hang them."

Alcuin shook his head. If Wilfred's estimations were accurate,
they were faced with a sizable problem.

"And the relics?" the count asked Alcuin hopefully, "will they
not help us to find food?"

"Undoubtedly, Wilfred. Undoubtedly."

MARCH

26

Since his arrival in Würzburg, Hoos Larsson hadn't had a moment's rest. Wilfred had assigned him to the troop led by Izam, who, foreseeing more attacks, was scouting the surrounding area every day. In the mornings they would inspect the walled perimeter. At twilight scouting parties would set off to circle the town from east to west before climbing to the top of the outcrop on which the fortress perched. Men, women, and children had to keep watch over streams and roads, shore up the defenses, and repair the walls.

In the second week, Hoos was charged with leading an expedition to the old mines. A shepherd with little work to do had apparently seen a fire there and Wilfred had decided to comb the area and turn the tunnels into a trap.

In the early morning, twelve men set off equipped with leather jerkins, shields, and bows. Izam sported the chainmail that he had brought on the ship. Hoos had never used it, but Izam insisted on its usefulness.

"I agree that on water they are a liability, for if you fall in you will be dragged to the bottom. But on land it's like wearing an iron bell."

Hoos looked at Izam with disdain, then tried to estimate the remaining distance to the mine. He thought to himself that if bandits appeared, Izam wouldn't even have time to count his arrow wounds.

"Perhaps we'll bump into Gorgias," Izam ventured. "The mine wouldn't be a bad hideaway."

"Well, if we do, you heard Wilfred's orders: 'If you find him, riddle him with arrows.' He killed Genseric and also some young boys with a stylus."

"It seems that the count has been badly affected by the loss of his coadjutor, but Alcuin has other ideas around what may have happened. If we find him, I think we should take him alive."

Hoos rode on. If it came to it, he thought, he wouldn't waver.

They reached the mine by midmorning. The scouts had reached it first, reporting that the place seemed deserted, but as a precaution Izam divided his men into two groups. The first headed for the slave huts and the second made for the tunnels. During the search, Hoos discovered some fresh fish bones and eggshells in a shed. The scraps seemed recent, but rather than tell Izam he hid them by dispersing them with his boot. They combed the place without finding anything significant, so after a final look around, Izam and his men joined those exploring the mine.

In the first tunnel the darkness was pitch black. As they progressed, the passages became narrower and narrower, forcing them to bend down as they walked. In one of the tunnels, one of their men stumbled, falling through the ground. There was little his friends could do except listen to his body tumble into the chasm. They deliberated whether to continue on or get out of that rat hole as soon as possible when a deafening rockslide threatened to bury them alive, dust filling their lungs. One of the men ran for the exit and the rest followed, feeling half-suffocated. Collapsing outside with bodies battered and spirits broken, they decided to call off the search and return to the town.

Only when there was complete silence in the tunnel did Gorgias push aside the rickety old corves he had hidden behind, and coughing and spluttering, he gave thanks to the heavens for helping him. With difficulty he came out of his hiding place and lifted away the timber from the rock fall he had provoked. He was glad he had foreseen that situation and prepared adequately.

A few days before, while he had been searching the mine, he discovered a beam that was not properly shored up to the ceiling. At first it worried him, but he soon hatched a plan to make use of it by tinkering with its support, turning it into a trap. He dug under the base of the pile and replaced the earth with small stones. Selecting a long, thin stone, with great care, he managed to position it vertically in the cavity under the base of the beam. Then he tied a string to the stone, covered it up, and retreated to a nearby cavity. From there he checked that, if he pulled the rope, the stone would come away, and the beam would collapse along with the tunnel roof.

Once he had returned to his hut, he reflected on the moments leading up to the soldiers' arrival. That morning he had been in the huts when he heard the neighing of a horse. Gobbling down his fish, he went outside immediately and found that a group of men were approaching the mine. He quickly picked up Blanca and ran toward the tunnel, where he ducked down and prayed to God they would not enter. However, when he saw the first torch, he fled to the cavity near the trap, moved a corf in the way to conceal him and waited until the men were close enough. Before long, he saw them approaching. If they went any farther they would surely discover him. When one of the men came up to the corf, Gorgias gripped the rope and braced himself. He had to attempt it quickly. He rolled the rope around his arm and pulled with all his might. The stone moved and the pillar toppled to the ground, causing the rockslide.

After the collapse, he had searched the place for any wounded, hoping that he might find the man with the serpent tattoo among the rubble. But no such luck. When he had reached the exit, there was no trace of the men who had been looking for him. He was relieved by his good fortune. But he mourned Blanca, for in order to keep her from clucking, he'd had to wring her neck.

On Hoos's return to Würzburg, a maidservant informed him that Theresa had gone out in the company of her stepmother, who wanted to pick up some clothes, and the young woman talked of taking a stroll in the fortress gardens. Hoos took off his weapons, washed his face, and went out to find her.

He discovered her sitting on a tree stump in one of the orchards. Coming up behind her, he gently stroked her hair. She turned in surprise, revealing a sad smile on her face. When she told him that she needed to find her father, he promised to help her.

They crossed the cloister under the arcades to protect themselves from the wind. Hoos picked some flowers and made a clumsy adornment for her hair. Theresa smelled of clean, damp grass. As they walked she huddled up to him, and he slid an arm around her waist and whispered that he loved her. Theresa closed her eyes so that she would never forget those words.

They ran to the bedroom that had been allotted to her, hoping that nobody would interrupt them, but they didn't come across a soul. She went in first and he closed the door behind them.

Hoos kissed her passionately, exploring her throat, her neck, her chin. He held her in his arms as if he wanted to keep her there forever. Theresa felt the heat of his body, his excited breathing, his confident lips discovering another trembling place to kiss— and she liked all of it. Hoos caressed her brazenly, noticing the goose bumps on the girl's skin, her desire growing with each of his kisses. He felt the firmness of her nipples, throbbing under her clothes. He slid his lips across her body, feeling her almost shameful softness.

She allowed him to undress her, to envelop her with his tongue, to warm her with his whispering. With each moment she wanted him more, and with each caress she longed for another, more forbidden touch.

She shuddered when his manhood brushed against her, feeling ashamed as she asked him, moaning, to penetrate her. He entered her slowly, pushing his way into her, overcome with lust. She held him tight, wrapping her legs about him, feeling his excitement, his movements, every pore of his skin. She rocked in time with his hips, wanting him inside her, faster and faster, harder and harder. She whispered for more, for it to never end, as her cheeks flushed, making her look like a harlot. Then, gradually, waves of pleasure radiated through her belly, time and time again, until she felt like she would lose her mind.

He loved her, and she loved him back. When Hoos pulled away, she stroked his shoulders, his strong arms, and the strange serpent tattooed on his wrist.

When Theresa woke, she saw that Hoos was already dressed and was smiling at her. She thought to herself that the leather jerkin and dyed woolen trousers made him look like a prince. The young man told her that he had to go to the royal storehouses to help share out the rations, but as soon as he finished, he would be back to kiss her again. She stretched and asked him to hold her. Hoos planted a kiss on her lips, then stroked her cheek before leaving the room.

A moment later someone knocked on the door. Theresa supposed it would be Hoos, so she ran to open it still half-naked, but before her appeared Alcuin's face, with a grim expression on it. The monk asked to come in, and she assented as she covered herself.

The willowy figure paced up and down the room before stopping to give her a slap.

"May I ask what you think you're doing?" he blurted out in indignation. "Do you think anyone will believe the miracle if you go about merrymaking with the first person who crosses your path?"

Theresa reddened from shame, looking at him with trepidation. She had never seen him so worked up.

"What if somebody saw you? Or if that Hoos opens his big mouth?"

"I . . . I didn't."

"For goodness' sake, Theresa! Your mother has just confessed to me that she saw him leaving your room, so don't start acting all prudish now."

"I'm sorry!" She burst into tears. "I love him."

"Oh! You love him do you? So marry him and start having children! In fact, why not go the market first and announce to all and sundry that you have carnal knowledge of Hoos—that the revenant has found a more pleasurable angel, and they should devote the chapel they want to build in your honor to the Devil himself!"

Alcuin sat down, his nerves in shreds.

Theresa didn't know what to say.

He drummed his fingers on the chair, looking her up and down. Finally, he stood. "You must stop seeing him. At least for a while. Until people have calmed down and forgotten about the fire."

Theresa agreed, red-faced.

Alcuin nodded several times, then blessed her before leaving the room without another word.

Moments later her stepmother appeared. Rutgarda, who had stayed overnight at her sister's house, had been waiting outside for Alcuin to leave. She walked in without a greeting, her eyes fixed on her stepdaughter. Though Rutgarda was much shorter than her, she took Theresa by the shoulders and shook her hard, telling her that she was a brainless little tart. With her behavior, Rutgarda assured her, she wasn't only putting herself in danger, but also giving ammunition to those who were accusing Gorgias of murder. She gave her such a talking to that Theresa wished she were deaf. She loved her father, but the situation was becoming unbearable. She wanted Würzburg to disappear from the face of the earth, for every last inhabitant to vanish, so she could be alone with Hoos. She didn't care what they would say, or what they thought would happen to them. She just wanted to be beside him. She would leave the fortress and ask Hoos to take her away from that awful place, to go with her to Fulda, where her lands and her slaves would give them a new life. There they could grow old together in peace, with no more fear or lies.

Without stopping to reflect, she left Rutgarda standing there and ran outside, covering herself with an old habit. As a group of servants were leaving the fortress, she mingled with them to pass through the gates and head to the granaries.

The royal storehouses stood on a hilltop in the northernmost part of the city, protected by a thick wall and connected to the fortress via an underground passage. Access was normally gained through that passage, and the gates that opened onto the streets of the citadel were only used when needed. When Theresa arrived in the area, a crowd had gathered at the entrance, waiting for the rations to be distributed.

However, it was too late to go back. Hoos would be inside the storehouse, and the only way to get in would be to wait until the gate was opened. Without realizing what was happening she found herself dragged along by the swarms of people pressing toward the entrance. Equipped with bags and sacks, the mass was shouting and threatening to break down the gates. Now and then, violent shoves created gaps in the crowd that were quickly filled in again by the mob. At one point, Theresa felt herself a mere rag doll at the mercy of the jostling. She thought she might be crushed to death. Then all of a sudden her hood came off and someone recognized her.

As if by magic, a space opened up around her. The townspeople stopped pushing and stared at the figure of Theresa. She didn't know what to do, until suddenly from within the crowd came an ominous voice. The head parchment-maker screamed at the crowd to make way for him as he approached Theresa, who had frozen like a mouse faced with a snake.

When he reached her, Korne bent down as if he were bowing to her, but instead he picked up a stone and hit her round the head with it. Fortunately a group of townsfolk stopped him from doing it again, while some women took Theresa to the storehouse gate. There two soldiers took over and it wasn't long before Hoos appeared, accompanied by Zeno, who had been called for because Theresa's head wouldn't stop bleeding.

The physician took some filthy scissors from his bag and attempted to cut her hair, but Theresa wouldn't allow it. So he used a carved comb to separate her hair, which revealed a small gash. Zeno confirmed that it wasn't serious, but applied some liquor, which made her cry out in pain. Then he covered the wound with a compress of cold water.

While the physician pressed the cloth against her head, a necklace of gems that Theresa had seen before flashed in front of her eyes. She waited for Zeno to move away before she tried to confirm what she had seen, but the man was fidgeting and she was unable to get a clear view of the jewelry. Finally, bending down to pick up his instruments, the rubies were revealed again. Theresa's heart missed a beat: It was her father's necklace.

After Zeno had finished and was walking away, Theresa waited for Hoos to be distracted before running after him. She reached Zeno in the corridor that connected the storehouse to the fortress.

In the underground passage, the light flickered intermittently from torch to torch. The physician was distractedly ambling along with his usual air of drunkenness and apathy. When Theresa approached him, Zeno turned in surprise, but his surprise turned into astonishment when Theresa grabbed him by the front of his shirt.

"Where did you get it?" she blurted out.

"What in the Devil's name?" He shoved her away, making her fall to the ground.

The young woman stood up and threatened him once more.

"Damned madwoman! Has that stone to your head un-hinged you?"

"Where did you get that necklace?" she repeated.

"It's mine. Now get out of the way or you'll be picking up your teeth off the floor."

Theresa fixed her eyes on him. "You know Hoos Larsson, right? He's there, right at the other end of the tunnel." Then she tore violently at her dress until one of her breasts was exposed. "Answer me now or I'll scream until he comes and kills you."

"For God's sake! Cover yourself. You'll have us both burnt at the stake."

Theresa tried to scream, but Zeno covered her mouth. However, the physician was trembling like a beaten dog and he looked the young woman in the eyes, begging her to be quiet. He did not let go until she had signaled she wouldn't scream.

Removing his hand cautiously he admitted, "Your father gave it to me. Now leave me in peace, wretched girl."

But, before he could leave, Theresa made him explain the circumstances of his meeting with her father. Reluctantly, Zeno told her that, at the request of Genseric, he had attended to Gorgias at an abandoned granary. He added that he merely wished to help, and he promised Theresa that her father had given him the necklace as payment for his services. He refrained from mentioning the amputated arm, however. When Theresa asked where her father was, he didn't have an answer. So she demanded that he take her to the place where he had tended to him. Zeno tried to wriggle out of it, but the young woman wouldn't let him.

Suddenly the physician's expression changed. "Nice tits," he said with a silly little laugh.

Theresa stepped back, covering up her chest. She would have slapped him if she could. "Listen to me carefully, you filthy goat turd! You will take me to that place now, and if you dare touch me, I swear to God I will have you burned alive."

Theresa doubted the weight of her threats, but when she added that she would accuse him of having robbed her father, the physician stood up straight as if someone had just impaled him. The stupid smile was quickly wiped off his face and he agreed to escort her.

After tidying up her habit, the young woman snatched Zeno's bag from him so she could pretend to be his assistant. She followed the physician and they left the fortress through a side door without any more trouble.

She walked along behind Zeno in a state of anxiety, as if she only wanted to return to the granary and put an end to the whole pantomime once and for all. When they were in the vicinity of the abandoned stables the physician stopped. He waved his arm at it and made as if to go back, but Theresa made him wait.

The young woman approached the shelter that was half-devoured by the undergrowth and looking as if it would collapse at any moment. When she pushed the door open, a swarm of flies accompanied the stench that wafted out from inside. She entered slowly, waving her arm at the cloud of insects buzzing around her. Her stomach turned and she retched. Feeling unable to contain her nausea, she vomited, yet continued into the darkness in search of a clue that would lead her to her father.

Suddenly she stumbled on something. She looked down and her heart pounded. Among the fallen leaves, a putrefying arm, peppered with insects, was propped upright as though baying for vengeance.

Theresa left the building in horror and vomited again. Hatred and pain overcame her. "You killed him, you bastard." She thumped against Zeno's chest with her fists. "You killed and robbed him," she said, crying inconsolably.

Zeno tried to calm her down. He had forgotten that they had left the amputated arm on the ground, so he was left with no choice but to tell her the truth. While he recounted the events, Theresa listened in bewilderment.

"I don't know what might have happened afterward," he said apologetically, "but Gorgias was still alive. Genseric asked me to take them somewhere else. I obeyed and then went back to town."

"Where did you take him?"

Zeno spat and looked fixedly at Theresa.

"I'll take you, then I'm off."

They skirted the walls of the fortress until they reached the point where the defenses adjusted to the quirks of a rocky outcrop. Zeno pointed to the place where the thick ivy obscured an entrance. On the other side of the wall, the outline of a building could be seen and Theresa guessed that it must be part of the fortress. At that moment the physician turned, leaving her alone in front of the door.

She struggled to force her way in since the damp had made the wood swell until it pressed against the stone jamb. On the third attempt, however, the door gave way, opening into a chapel room that was in such disarray it looked like a fight had taken place. The light from the entrance spilled onto the furniture, which was strewn across the floor, while the draft from the open door lifted scraps of parchment into the air in little eddies as if they were dead leaves. She examined every nook and cranny without finding anything of use, until suddenly she noticed the small door to the cell where her father had been imprisoned. Cautiously she went in, and there she found an untidy pile of writing equipment, which she quickly recognized as belonging to her father.

On tenterhooks, she rushed over to the codex with the emerald cover, where her father would keep important documents. *If anything ever happens to me, look inside it*, he had often said to her.

She took it without looking closely at it, then gathered all the pieces of parchment she could find in the room. She also took a stylus, pens, and a wax tablet. Then she took a last look around and ran out of there as if the Devil were after her soul.

When she arrived at the fortress entrance she had to notify Alcuin to let her in. When the monk asked her where she had been, she lowered her head and tried to slip away, but he took her by the arm and led her to a quiet corner.

"Looking for my father! That's where!" the girl responded, shaking his hand off.

Alcuin believed her. He knew he wouldn't be able to keep her in one spot for long.

"And what have you found?"

She shook her head. Alcuin then noticed the wound on her head. And Theresa told him about the stone Korne had thrown at her.

Alcuin asked her to follow him to the scriptorium. He waited for her sit down, then paced back and forth in silence, as if debating whether to tell her everything that was going on.

"All right," said Monk, having made up his mind. "I made you promise something once and you went against your word. Now I need to know whether you are prepared to keep an extraordinary secret."

"Another miracle? Sorry, but I'm sick of your lies."

"Listen to me." He sat down. "There are certain things you do not understand yet. Love is neither pure, as you imagine it, nor tainted, just because I say it is. Men are not wicked and sinful, nor innocent and compassionate. Their actions depend upon their ambitions, their desires and longings, and sometimes, more often than you can imagine, on the presence of evil." He stood again and wandered around the scriptorium. "There are as many nuances as there are variations in the sky. Sometimes it is warm and bright, sometimes icy and tempestuous—like one's mortal enemy. What is real and what is a lie? The accusations Korne makes against you, confirmed by his relatives and friends, or your claim that you possess the absolute truth and are blameless? Tell me, Theresa, is there not a little bitterness within you? Does your soul not harbor a shadow of resentment?"

Theresa knew full well who was to blame, but she decided to keep silent.

"As for the miracles," Alcuin continued, "I can safely say that I have never witnessed one. Or at least, not of the kind these fools imagine. But think about this: How can we be sure you were not resurrected? How can we ignore the fact that a protective force got you out of that inferno and guided you through the mountains? And sent you to Hoos, who saved you once, and then to that trapper who saved you again? Or even to the prostitute who took you in, or to me, when you sought a healer?" He looked fixedly at her. "Ultimately, all that I have done was done to protect you. The miracle was technically a lie, yes, but I assure you that I was guided by the hand of the Almighty. He has designed a fate for you that you are unaware of and that will now be revealed to you. A fate that Gorgias, your father, has been involved with since the beginning."

Theresa listened, absorbed. He spoke of things she didn't understand, but his words seemed sincere.

Alcuin approached the desk that her father used and pressed both of his palms to its surface. When he lifted them, his handprints were visible in the dust.

"Your father worked here, in this very spot. Here he spent his final weeks preparing a document of inestimable value to Christendom. Now answer me: Are you prepared to swear an oath?"

Theresa was frightened, but she agreed. She repeated after Alcuin that she would never, under pain of eternal damnation, reveal what she would soon learn about the document. She swore it on a Vulgate that she then kissed reverently. She promised that Hoos would never learn anything about it.

Alcuin took the Bible and placed it near his handprints. Then he eyed the prints in the dust left by Gorgias's styluses and asked Theresa to look at them closely.

"According to Wilfred, your father disappeared a couple of months or so ago, and Genseric was found dead two weeks ago. Now, look at these marks. What do you see?"

Theresa examined them carefully. There were Alcuin's handprints on the table, a row of styluses, and two small elongated marks.

"I don't know . . . prints in the dust."

"Yes, but look closely: The handprints I have just made are fresh, and yet the other two," he said, pointing at the elongated marks, "whose shape undoubtedly corresponds to two styluses—they are already covered with a thin layer of dust. And even then . . ."

"Yes?"

"They are not identical. Not only in their shape, which is obvious, but also in the quantity of dust they have accumulated. The one on the left, which is a little bigger, has more than the one on the right."

He walked over to the drawer where Wilfred kept the stylus they had found driven into Genseric's stomach. He picked it up and positioned it perfectly over the smaller print. "As you can see, this print was made from this stylus, but the veil of dust over it is finer than the dust covering the print left from the bigger stylus. This tells us that the stylus I am holding—the one that ended Genseric's life—was taken from the desk later than the bigger one, which lay in this other mark."

He then went over to a nearby table where there were several books and picked one up. "The marks from these books, on the other hand, display a similar amount of dust to the mark left by the bigger stylus. Wilfred assured me that on the day your father disappeared, so did the codices and styluses. However, the thinner layer of dust that has settled over the print of the smaller stylus, again, the one found stuck in Genseric, suggests that it was actually taken from the scriptorium quite a few days later."

"And that means . . . ?"

"Think about it. Books aren't the only things missing from the scriptorium. Also gone are inkwells, pounce, pens . . . everything that your father would need to prepare a document. And curiously, all the prints left behind from this equipment display a similar amount of dust as the large stylus, which allows us to deduce that the equipment and the large stylus were taken at the same time. So, it doesn't make sense that the other stylus would disappear later, especially considering that, after your father's disappearance, Wilfred closed the scriptorium. So, someone other than Gorgias took that stylus that was found in Genseric."

"But why?"

"To frame your father, of course. And not only that. I am certain that Genseric did not die from the stabbing. Rather, the suspected murderer drove the stylus into him after he was killed."

"But, how can you be so sure?" Theresa asked in surprise.

"Well, with the far-fetched excuse that I wanted to bless the coadjutor's body with some relics, I was allowed to exhume his coffin, and was able to examine his habit. I must confess that if

Genseric had not been of weak bladder, they would have buried him in other clothes, and his habit would be lost by now, so I was fortunate that he was. During my examination I found the entry wound, with the corresponding hole in his clothes at stomach level. An injury like that would have made him bleed to death. But interestingly there was nothing more than a small ring of blood on the habit."

"I don't understand."

"Well, a living heart pumps the blood through the wound, causing death by exsanguination, which never happens when a body is already dead."

Theresa was still trying to grasp the meaning of his words. "So what you are saying is that Genseric died some other way, and then someone tried to feign a murder?"

"He didn't die another way—he was killed another way!" he exclaimed.

He told her how he had examined the remains of vomit found on Genseric's front, and without being able to establish the nature of the poison, he was still absolutely certain that some kind of bane had finished him off.

Theresa breathed a sigh of relief. She considered telling Alcuin what she had found on her excursion with Zeno, but without knowing why, she decided to wait a while.

Meanwhile, the monk, who was gathering together codices and tidying the scriptorium, continued to ponder his theories. "Wherefore, whoever gained entry to the scriptorium was in all likelihood the same person who murdered Genseric," he concluded.

"You mean Wilfred?"

"Poor Wilfred is a cripple. What's more, he's not the only person who had keys. Genseric also had some."

"So what does that mean?"

"This is what I intend to find out."

He explained that, before disappearing, Gorgias had been working on a document of vital importance to the interests of Charlemagne and the Papacy. A fourth century testament in which the Emperor Constantine yielded the Roman Church to the Papal States, acknowledging the Pope's entitlement to govern the Christian world.

"Gorgias did not finish the document. In fact he was working on a replica of the original. I have the original with me, but it is in a deteriorated state. The fact is we need to complete it, and to do so, we need your father."

"What do you mean?" Theresa interrupted.

"He is the only person who can finish it. Hence, I would like to propose a deal: You stay here in the scriptorium, working on this draft—and in the meantime, I will search for Gorgias."

"And what will I have to do with it?"

"Go over the draft. We might be able to use it, if necessary. The truth is nobody else should know about this matter. And under these circumstances, finding a scribe I can trust—and with a good enough command of Greek to transcribe correctly in it—would be difficult, to say the least."

Alcuin then explained in more detail what the work would consist of, and reiterated the importance of keeping it secret.

"Not even Wilfred can know?"

"Not Wilfred, nor anyone else. You will work alone in this scriptorium, and if anyone asks, you say you're transcribing a Psalter. You will continue to sleep in the fortress, come here in the morning, and not stop until nightfall. While you make headway, I will look for your father. He cannot have gone far."

Theresa agreed. Finally she decided she must tell him about Zeno. Hesitantly, she told him of her discovery of the amputated arm and the crypt in the wall.

"Amputated, you say? Good God, Theresa! Why did you not tell me immediately?" he cried, despairing.

Theresa tried to apologize, but it seemed as if the Devil himself had suddenly taken hold of Alcuin as he swore and cursed, scattering the parchments across the floor, before slumping into the chair like a defeated, old rag doll.

Stunned by his outburst, Theresa didn't know what to say.

After recovering his normal composure, the monk stood up with an absent look in his eyes. "We have a problem, then. A big problem," he said, his voice unnervingly tranquil.

"What problem?" a fearful Theresa asked.

"The problem, Theresa, is that even if we find your father, he will not be able to finish the job!" he screamed again like a man possessed.

Theresa's quill slipped from her hand.

"And you know why?" he added, still roaring. "Because he is an invalid now. A useless one-armed scribe incapable of writing a docket."

At that moment Theresa saw everything clearly. The monk had never intended to help her father. His only intention was to help himself, and now that her father was of no further use to him, he would no longer look for him and would only focus on the document.

Instantly, she hated him with every fiber of her being and suddenly had the urge to plunge her own stylus into *his* stomach. But then, just as suddenly, she remembered the parchment hidden in her father's bag. Perhaps she could still defeat this devil.

She mustered the courage to offer a deal. "Find my father and you'll have your parchment ready for you."

Alcuin gave her a sidelong glance and turned back to continue brooding.

"Did you not hear me?" She boldly grabbed him by his habit. "I can finish it, I tell you."

The monk smiled sardonically, but then Theresa took a quill and quickly began to write.

IN-NOMINE-SANCTAE-ET-INDIVIDUAL-TRINITATIS-
PATRIS-SCILICET-ET-FILII-ET-SPIRITUS-SANCTI

- - -

IMPERATOR-CAESAR-FLAVIUS-CONSTANTINUS

Alcuin turned pale. "But, how the hell?"

The script was as crisp as her father's, and the copied text was an exact replica.

"I know it by memory," she lied. "Find my father, and I will finish it."

Astounded, Alcuin accepted. He asked her to write a list of what she would need to write it and then ordered her to return to her chamber.

Alcuin found Zeno at the tavern in the main square, his face buried in a whore's chest, drunk with wine. Seeing him arrive, the prostitute rummaged through the physician's pockets and after appropriating a coin she left the table without a word. It was not the right place to talk about such serious affairs, so Alcuin convinced Zeno to exit the inn. As soon as they stepped out into the street, Alcuin threw a bucket of water over the physician, which sobered him up enough so that he could confirm what Theresa had said.

"I swear I had no dealings with Genseric. I removed Gorgias's arm, and that was it," he said defensively.

Alcuin clenched his teeth. He had hoped Theresa had been wrong, but if Zeno had truly operated on Gorgias, then he would surely die. The physician confirmed that it was Genseric who hired him to tend to the scribe.

"Genseric, who incidentally was found dead the next day," Alcuin pointed out.

Zeno acknowledged it, though he doubted that Gorgias was the murderer. "He lost so much blood when I cut off his arm," he said, shaking his head.

Alcuin understood.

"Now that you mention it, Genseric was behaving strangely, as if he were intoxicated, which I thought odd because he never drank. I recall that he mentioned something about an itchy hand. It was red and looked to be covered in bites."

Zeno couldn't provide Alcuin with much more information, only the location of the stables where he had operated on Gorgias and also the entrance to the crypt. After telling him these things, he walked unsteadily back into the tavern.

Alcuin had no difficulty finding the two places Zeno had mentioned. In the stables he found nothing of interest, but in the crypt he gathered several clues that improved his understanding of the situation.

On his return to the fortress, he found that there was a great stir at the gate. When he asked what was happening, a woman told him that the guards had closed the gates, locking them outside.

"I am Alcuin of York," he said, identifying himself to a sentry. The guard paid him as much attention as he would a junk merchant.

"You can shout as much as you want—they won't let anybody in," a boy assured him, pushing and shoving.

"Neither in nor out. Not even their own soldiers are allowed through," said another boy who seemed a little more informed.

Alcuin attempted to climb the hillock on which the sentry was posted, but the guard dealt him a blow with his stick. As he fell to the ground, Alcuin realized that he had just cursed out loud the man who hit him. Several peasants laughed at his unholy outburst.

Though there were rumors, nobody really knew what was happening. Some were saying that a pestilence had broken out. Others claimed the Saxons were attacking. There were even those who purported that more dead boys had been found.

Alcuin was about to head to the nearest church when he noticed Izam on the wall. Without giving it a second thought he clambered onto a barrel and waved his arms. Izam recognized him and ordered his men to allow him through.

"May I ask what is going on?" Alcuin protested once inside. "That idiot struck me," he said, pointing at the sentry at the gate.

In response Izam took him by the arm and asked Alcuin to follow him. On the way to the armory he informed him that the Devil had taken over the fortress.

"I don't understand. You said Wilfred's little girls are missing? What happened?"

"Nobody has seen them since this morning."

"God's wounds! Is that what all this fuss is about? They're probably somewhere in the fortress playing with their dolls. Have you spoken to the wet nurse?"

"We can't find her, either," the distressed young man responded.

When they reached the hall, it was abuzz with servants, soldiers, and monks. Most were murmuring to each other in small groups, trying to find out the latest bit of news, while others stood about distraught. Izam and Alcuin continued on to the armory, where Wilfred awaited them. He was thrashing about on his stumps in his wheelchair.

"Anything to report?" he asked Izam.

The young man clenched his teeth. He informed him that his men were guarding all the entrances and he had organized thorough searches of the stables, storehouses, orchards, and latrines . . . if the girls were in the fortress, they would undoubtedly be found. Wilfred nodded begrudgingly, then looked at Alcuin in hope he brought news.

"I have only just found out," he apologized. "You have searched their rooms I suppose?"

"Even behind the walls. Lord Almighty! Last night they seemed so happy, so relaxed."

He remarked that the girls always slept with their wet nurse, a spinster who had never given cause for concern.

"Until now," he added, and he smashed his cup against the hearth.

Izam decided they would interrogate all who were in the fortress, particularly the servants and those close to the wet nurse. Alcuin asked for permission to inspect the rooms, and Wilfred ordered a minion to accompany him.

When Alcuin arrived at the girls' cell he found it a terrible mess. He asked the servant if the chaos was due to Wilfred's men searching the room, which the servant confirmed, adding that the wet nurse was a very meticulous woman.

"You were present when they searched the cell?"

"I stood at this very door."

"And how did it look before they came in?"

"Neat and tidy, as it is every morning."

Alcuin asked the servant to help him pick up some of the clothes that were scattered around, seemingly most from two chests that Wilfred's men had emptied in their frantic search. The biggest chest belonged to the girls, and the other was the wet nurse's. They paired up shoes and dresses, dividing according to whether they belonged to the twins or the wet nurse. Then Alcuin stopped to examine some objects that were on a crudely built dresser. There was a polished metal plate to use as a mirror, a bone comb, several cords, a couple of fibulae, two little vials that seemed to contain makeup, another smaller one of rose perfume, a piece of soap, and a small washbowl. They were all perfectly arranged, which confirmed the tidy nature of the nanny. There were also two generously sized square beds in the room: one for the woman, located beside the window, and another for the two girls on the other side of the room. Alcuin paused at the former, smelling it and examining it as if he were a hunting dog.

"Do you know whether the wet nurse had relations with anyone? What I mean is, was there a man?" he asked, as he extracted some hair from between the blankets.

"Not that I know of," the servant answered, a little surprised.

"All right," he said gratefully. "You can lock up the room now."

On the way to the scriptorium he bumped into Theresa, who was in such a state that he barely recognized her. Apparently some soldiers had come into her room and turned it upside down. Alcuin informed her that the twins were missing and that they had sealed off the fortress.

"But my stepmother is out there."

"I suppose they will allow people through once the girls have been found. Now let's go to the scriptorium. I need your help with something."

They found that the scriptorium had also been searched. Alcuin gathered up the scattered codices while Theresa moved the furniture back into place. When they had finished, the monk sat down and asked Theresa to bring him a candle. He told her what he had learned about her father.

"It's not much, but I'll keep at it," he said apologetically. "And you? Have you made any progress?"

She showed him the text with two new paragraphs. Each night, before she went to sleep, she would read the parchment hidden in her father's bag and memorize the next few lines.

"It's not much, but I'm making progress."

Alcuin grumbled, then took a cloth from his bag and placed it on the table.

Theresa examined its contents closely. "Hair?" she asked.

"Indeed. I can't see the strands very clearly in this light." He cleared his throat as if he was embarrassed to admit it. "But they all seem different."

Theresa moved the candle so close that a drop of wax fell onto the hairs. Alcuin told her to be careful, and she apologized for her carelessness.

She could distinguish three types of hair: some fine and brown; some curly, shorter, and darker; and finally, some similar to the latter, but grayer in tone.

"The short ones are—" she reddened.

"Yes, I think so," Alcuin confirmed.

After Theresa returned from washing her hands, she still felt disgusted. As she dried her hands, the monk offered his conclusions: "By all appearances the wet nurse was a tidy, meticulous woman, with no known romances and concerned only for the well-being of Wilfred's daughters. This impression was reinforced by her plain attire, her clean face, and the care and attention she gave the little girls. However, the room that she shared with the twins tells a different story. Inside I found adornments, makeup, and perfume, as well as an expensive dress, more suitable for a young lady of means and of a marriageable age. The wet nurse was a mature woman and her pay wouldn't have allowed her to buy those items. She must have acquired them by engaging in illicit activities."

"That, or they were gifts," Theresa suggested.

"At any rate," he added, "she was a woman who was not so devoted to the children as would appear, especially considering that she had no qualms about sharing a room and bed with a graying man who was no doubt very old and a member of the clergy."

"But, how can you be so sure?"

"From the smell of church incense on the blankets. His habit must have been impregnated with it."

Theresa nodded, surprised. However, Alcuin did not attach much importance to it. He continued to tell her about his encounter with Zeno, explaining that, somehow, the crypt where they had taken Gorgias must have been connected to the inside of the fortress. He added that—due to the plates and food scraps he found—he was convinced that it was used to imprison her father.

At that moment someone banged on the door. When Alcuin opened it, a soldier was there to inform him that his presence was required.

"What's happening?"

"They've found the wet nurse drowned in the cloister well."

When Alcuin arrived at the well, several men were lifting the body out using pikes. Finally the woman's bloated corpse surfaced, collapsing like a sack of pork belly onto the cloister paving. Her clothes had come undone, revealing an immense pair of breasts, flaccid from feeding the girls. Then, Izam was lowered down to inspect the bottom of the well and make sure there were no other bodies. When he came back up, he assured Wilfred that his daughters were not there.

They took the body to the kitchens, where after a superficial examination, Alcuin determined that she had been strangled to death before being deposited in the well. Her fingernails were chipped, but there was no trace of skin embedded under them, which meant they may have been damaged when the body was retrieved. He then examined the genitals, verifying that the pubic hair matched what he'd found on her pallet. Among her clothes he found nothing of significance. Her outfit befitted her role, a dark habit protected by an apron. Her face, though swollen, seemed clean, with no creams or makeup. When he had finished, he gave permission for her shrouding. Then he asked to speak to Wilfred alone.

In private he informed the count of his findings, which suggested that a member of the clergy had seduced the woman in order to kidnap the girls. However, he added that in his opinion, it was likely the wet nurse wasn't aware of her lover's intentions.

"How can you be so sure?"

"Because otherwise she would have prepared to make her escape, yet her belongings were found in her cell."

"Perhaps they attacked her. We don't know for sure, for goodness' sake. And the man that you speak of? Do you have any clues?"

"The blankets stank of incense," he explained.

"I will order every priest be detained. If anyone has touched the children, I will string them up by their own entrails."

"Calm yourself, my Lord. Bear in mind that if they wanted to kill your daughters, they would have done so already. No, the twins are safe. And as for some other perverted or ghoulish intentions, I would rule that out, too. If that were the case, it would have been easier to take any other little girl. There are dozens astray on every corner."

"Calm myself? With my daughters at the mercy of some fiend?"

"I repeat: If they wanted to harm them, we would already know about it."

"If *they* wanted? Why do you speak in the plural?"

Alcuin pointed out that it would have been difficult for one man to carry and hide two little girls. As for the motive, excluding despicable acts, and ruling out revenge, there could only be one reason.

"Stop speaking in riddles, man."

"Blackmail, my esteemed Wilfred. In exchange for their lives, they intend to obtain something that you possess: power . . . money . . . land."

"I'm going to make those rats eat their own balls," the count bellowed, touching his testicles. The two dogs became agitated, making the chair shake.

"In any event," Alcuin reflected, "it could well be that the suspected cleric only amused himself with the nanny and played no part in the kidnapping."

"So what do you suggest—that I stay here with my arms crossed?"

"Be patient and get on with the search. Put the priests under watch and have them take oaths. Block the movement of people and goods. Make a list of those who enjoy your complete trust and another of those you believe capable of blackmailing you. But above all, wait for the kidnappers to communicate their intentions to you—for once they do, time will be of the essence."

Wilfred nodded.

They agreed to report back to each other as soon as they had any news. Then the count cracked his whip and left the kitchens. Alone in the room, Alcuin looked at the poor naked woman. He covered her with a sack and made the sign of the cross over her, thinking it lamentable that her carnal desires had led to her demise.

27

The day passed by slowly for Wilfred. Izam and his subordinates scoured granaries, barns, storehouses, towers, wells, tunnels, moats, passages, attics, cellars, carts, bales of straw, barrels, chests, and even cupboards. Nowhere went unchecked. Every man was questioned and searched from head to toe. Wilfred offered fifty arpents of vineyards to anyone who could provide information on the whereabouts of his daughters, and thirty more for the heads of their abductors. He locked himself in the armory and demanded hourly reports on the progress of the investigations.

Meanwhile, with Theodor's help, he made a list of loyal subjects and another of adversaries. In the first, he wrote down only four names, then one by one decided to removed them. In the second, he included so many names that he did not wish to tell Alcuin. Wilfred excluded all newcomers from his list of suspects, for he believed that the abduction of his daughters had been a long time in the planning. In fact, he had accepted Alcuin's suggestion to double the search party by forming two groups: one of his own men and another made up of the ship's crew, led by Izam.

At sundown, Wilfred sent his men to scour the area. Violent exchanges and shouting could be heard throughout the night as soldiers interrogated townsfolk. Several priests were tortured, but at dawn, the soldiers returned with empty hands.

The next day was identical to the previous one. First thing in the morning, Wilfred decreed that the rationing of grain should be put on hold until the twins were found. He also sealed off the city walls so that no inhabitant could leave or enter without his knowledge. Alcuin advised him against indiscriminate reprisals, but the count assured him that as soon as the rabble were beset by hunger, the kidnappers would be turned in.

Since the girls had been abducted, Hoos had been very involved in the search. At first he had assisted Izam. Then, making the most of Wilfred's trust in him, he put himself forward to inspect the royal granaries and their adjoining tunnels. Wilfred then placed Hoos in charge of his own men.

Theresa longed for Hoos's caresses. She could still feel the intensity of his kisses, still taste his skin. Sometimes she caught herself pressing her legs together as if she could keep him there. Nonetheless, since their last encounter, she had hardly seen him. He was always busy, and she would rise early to go to the scriptorium, which she left only to eat in the kitchens. It even crossed her mind that he had taken up with another woman, and when she saw him she told him as much. He seemed hard-pressed, but even so, it bothered her when he said good-bye without even giving her a kiss.

While Theresa made progress in the scriptorium, Alcuin assessed the reports on the kidnapping that reached the fortress. Among them, there were several who claimed they had seen the late wet nurse practicing witchcraft, and others who blamed wolves for the little girls' disappearance. Some seemed well intentioned, but most were from unscrupulous townsfolk lured by the reward. Several men had been thrashed for making up lies, but one of them mentioned the theft of some booties from the laundry.

Alcuin questioned the midget monk in charge of domestic services. He confirmed they were missing. "Sometimes clothes are mislaid, but with the twins' garments, we were always quite careful."

He assured him that it had been four booties, plus a couple of the cloths used in the kitchens. Alcuin thanked him and returned to the scriptorium, convinced that the twins were still in the fortress. In a meeting with Izam, Alcuin suggested they keep watch over the storehouses and kitchens.

"If, like I suspect, they are still here, their abductors might need food."

"That's impossible. We've left no stone unturned."

"I don't doubt that, but there are more stones here than in a quarry."

Alcuin asked Izam to post a guard at the door of the scriptorium day and night, which Izam agreed to readily. He also agreed to keep watch over the kitchens and report anything new to Wilfred in the morning.

That night, taking advantage of the moon's absence, several hungry townspeople clambered over the wall that protected the royal granaries. The assailants were driven away, but it became very clear that Wilfred's restrictive measures would soon bring serious consequences.

The next day at breakfast, Wilfred hardly ate. He was not interested in Alcuin's discoveries and paid no attention when he was informed about the assault on the granaries. He seemed absent, as if some potion had clouded his mind. Fortunately, in a moment of lucidity he agreed to resume the distribution of provisions and allow for the transportation of goods. Izam applauded the decision, for it would prevent further incidents, although, like many others, he wondered what had triggered the change of heart. When Alcuin queried Wilfred on the matter, he refused to answer. The monk continued to prod him, but the count suggested that Alcuin concentrate on the parchment and step back from the kidnapping investigation. From now on, he said, he would lead the search for his daughters himself.

Over the course of the afternoon, normality returned to the fortress. Gradually the servants went back to their tasks, the grain was distributed to the townsfolk, and preparations began for the first hunt, which would take place with the arrival of spring. Izam and his men continued the repairs to the ship, which they had only half finished when they arrived in the city, and Wilfred's soldiers returned to man the defenses.

The congregation attending the Sext service plodded into the Church of Saint John Chrysostom as unhurried as a herd of grazing sheep. The procession was led by Flavio Diacono wearing a striking purple biretta similar to a pope's. He was followed by a retinue of clerics dressed like peacocks, followed by the minor orders, and then the choir boys. At the rear of the procession were a throng of curious townsfolk, worshippers, and starvelings wanting to attend a Eucharist to pray for the safe return of the twins.

The church soon filled like a packed sheepfold. When the great doors were closed, Cassiano, the precentor, had the boys warm up their voices. Then, with Flavio's permission, he opened his arms like an angel to commence the miracle of Gregorian chant. Those in attendance, most of them clerics, bowed their heads when the first antiphon rang out in a symphony of celestial notes that made the ashlars vibrate. Cassiano swung his arms directing the swirl of voices up into the vaults, where they enveloped the pillars and reverberated until hairs stood on end. The music kept dancing, flowing from those cherubs like the melodic prayers of goldfinches

Then, abruptly, one of the voices fractured into a howl of terror. The rest of the children fell silent and everyone in the church turned toward the choir to see the boys retreating as if fleeing from a bad smell.

Lying on the ground before them, Korne the parchment-maker convulsed and vomited what little life he had left. By the time Alcuin reached him, the old man was dead.

They took the body to the sacristy, where Flavio anointed him with holy oil in a final attempt to resuscitate him. But despite his efforts, the body remained motionless. Alcuin noticed that Korne's head had been shaved, that he had gray hairs on his pubis, and that he reeked of incense. Korne's eyes seemed askew, and his mouth continued to issue a whitish froth. When Alcuin examined his hands, he found two puncture holes on the right palm.

When he informed Wilfred of what happened, the count merely continued to munch on the chicken thigh he was holding. After throwing the bones to the dogs, he looked at Alcuin indifferently as he wiped his mouth with his sleeve. The monk told him that he had found a snakebite on Korne's right hand.

"Have him buried outside of the cloister," was all he said in response.

"You don't understand," he persisted. "At this time of year there are no reptiles."

"Würzburg is full of serpents," he answered, turning to look elsewhere.

Alcuin could not comprehend his indifference after he had pointed out the strange, identical nature of Genseric's and the parchment-maker's deaths. And not only that, but he had also informed him of Korne's gray hairs, the fact that his head was shaven, and—more important—that each morning, after breakfasting in the kitchens, Korne had accompanied the twins to their singing lessons. It seemed useless to explain that, in all likelihood, it was Korne who had abducted the twins. Anyone else in his place, crippled or otherwise, would have jumped with joy, and yet Wilfred remained impassive, as if his fate had already been decided.

Wilfred dismissed him without looking up. But as Alcuin left, the monk saw tears in the count's eyes.

On the way to his chambers, Alcuin wondered what might be behind Wilfred's strange reaction. In his mind, such melancholy could only be explained by temporary dementia caused by the loss of his daughters, even if, curiously, his delirium did not seem to be affecting the rest of his faculties. Consequently, it would be sensible to assume that his behavior was not random but premeditated, as if he had prior knowledge of a link between the deaths of Genseric and the parchment-maker.

He decided to visit Korne's room in the fortress, for since the workshops had burnt down that was where he resided. The chamber was not unlike the one Alcuin was staying in. It had an old bed, a crude table with a stone bench under the window, some shelves with a work habit on top, some skins, and the usual bucket for emptying the bowels. He looked inside the container and recoiled in disgust. Then he crouched down to scour the floor, both examining it with his eyes and with his hands until he came across what seemed like a necklace bead. However, in the light he could see that the little white pebble with a blue circle painted on it was in fact an eye from one of the twins' dolls. He was at pains to admit that the smell of incense had led him down the wrong path, believing the culprit to be a man of the church.

He immediately made for the scriptorium, where he found Theresa working in an uncharacteristically clumsy manner. Normally the young woman would practice the text she had to copy on some old parchment before doing the final version, but that afternoon she was smudging her writing as if she were painting with a brush. Although Alcuin reprimanded her, he sensed that her mistakes were owed not to incompetence, but because of something worrying her.

"It's Hoos," she finally confessed. "I don't know if it's because you reproached him, but ever since the night we were together . . ." She reddened. "I don't know, he seems different."

"I didn't say anything to him. What do you mean by different?"

Tears rolled down the young woman's face, and she told him that Hoos had been shunning her. That morning, after bumping into him, he had snubbed her cruelly.

"I even fear he might strike me," she sobbed.

"Sometimes we men behave coarsely," he said, trying to console her. "It's a question of nature. If circumstances sometimes mar the souls of those at peace and cloud the minds of the learned, who knows what they might do to men who give in to their most sordid desires?"

"It's not that," she complained, as if Alcuin understood nothing. "There was something strange in his expression."

Alcuin relented, patting her on the back. As he gathered up his notes, he thought to himself that he had enough on his plate with the disappearance of the twins to also have to try to reason with a young woman in love. Instead, he asked her how the parchment was progressing.

"I've almost finished it," she answered. "But I must admit there is something that has me worried."

"I'm listening."

Theresa went to find something and returned with an emerald-colored codex, which she placed in front of Alcuin.

"Aha! A Vulgate," said the friar as he leafed through it.

"It's my father's Bible," she said, stroking it with tenderness. "I found it in the crypt where he was imprisoned."

"A nice copy."

"That's not all." She picked up the Vulgate and opened it approximately from the middle. "Before the fire my father told me that if anything happened to him, I should look inside his book. I didn't know what he was referring to at the time, in fact, I couldn't even imagine that anything would happen to him. But now I believe that, while he was working for Wilfred, he began to fear for his life."

"I don't understand. What do you mean?"

She lifted the codex and forced the spine until a gap appeared between the gatherings. Then she inserted her fingers and pulled out a piece of parchment that she unfolded, and read from: "*Ad Thessalonicenses epistula i Sancti Pauli Apostoli. 5.21. Omnia autem probate, quod bonum est tenete.*" She translated: "Examine it all, retain the good."

"Yes, but what does it mean?" he asked in surprise.

"On the face of it, nothing, so I did what it said in the quotation: I examined the Bible until my eyes hurt. Now look at this," she said, pointing at a paragraph.

"What is it? I can't see it."

"It's barely visible. My father must have diluted the ink with water so that it would barely leave a mark, but if you look carefully, you can see that between each line, as faint as morning dew, there are notes."

Alcuin pressed his nose against the page but still could not make out a thing.

"Interesting. And what do the notes say?"

"I'm still confused. They provide information on the Donation of Constantine. But I believe my father discovered something strange in the text."

Alcuin coughed and looked taken aback. "In that case it's best I deal with this codex," he decided. "And now, try to finish your work. I will keep searching for your father."

When the monk left, she felt abandoned, and longed for a shoulder to lean on, for someone she could trust. Without intending to, she thought of Izam. He was so different than Hoos! Ever attentive and polite, always willing to help. She felt a little dirty thinking of him in such a way, but it was not the first time her thoughts had turned to him. His deliberate way of speaking, his warm voice, his kind eyes . . . Though she loved Hoos, sometimes she caught herself thinking of Izam, and it made her feel uncomfortable.

She considered Hoos's strange conduct again, wondering why he was behaving in such a way. She trusted him. She truly loved him. She thought they would go to Fulda together, where they would start a family, and have strong and healthy children who she would raise and educate. Perhaps they would buy a large stone house, with stables outside, even. She even thought about decorating it with drapes so that Hoos would find it comfortable, and perfuming the rooms with rosemary and lavender. She wondered whether he had thought about such things, or if there was another woman, and that perhaps he had forgotten about Theresa's love. Finally she turned to her parchments to continue copying, but she only got to the second line before thinking of Hoos again, and she knew that until she spoke to him, she would not be able to do anything well. She stopped writing, cleaned her instruments, and left the scriptorium intent on reclaiming the man she loved.

The soldier guarding the scriptorium informed her that Hoos Larsson could be found in the tunnel that connected the storehouses to the fortress. When Theresa arrived, she found him loading sacks of wheat onto a cart. At first Hoos appeared reticent to talk, but when she insisted, he stopped what he was doing and turned to her.

She spoke of her hopes and her needs. She told him that she dreamed of waking up beside him each morning, sewing his clothes, cleaning the house, and tending the vegetable garden, learning to cook so she could serve him as he deserved. She even asked him to forgive her, lest—without intending it—she had done something wrong.

Hoos acted distant, however, and impatient for her to finish. When she demanded a response, he said only that he had slept too few hours because he had been searching for her father. He told her he had interrogated half the city, scoured every nook and cranny, but it was as if he had been swallowed by the earth.

His words moved her. "So, you still love me?"

His only response was to kiss her, making all her fears fade away. Theresa felt happy. Still in his arms, she told him what had happened with Zeno and how he'd shown her to the crypt.

"Why didn't you tell me before?" he said, stepping back in surprise.

Theresa argued that he was always busy. And she was terrified that someone might overhear and attempt to capture her father.

"He's accused of murder," she added as a reminder.

Hoos nodded, but Theresa insisted that her father was innocent. Zeno had amputated his arm and could testify to it. Then she began to cry inconsolably. Hoos was attentive, embracing her tenderly. He stroked her hair and promised her that from that moment on everything would change, he even asked her to forgive him for his foolish behavior. He explained that events had overwhelmed him, but that he loved her with all his soul and would help her find Gorgias.

"I'll visit the crypt you speak of. Does anyone else know its location?"

She told him that only Alcuin was aware of its existence.

Hoos shook his head, repeating to her that she should not trust the monk. Then he asked her to go back to the scriptorium, promising that as soon as he discovered anything, he would come for her.

On the way to the scriptorium, Theresa recalled that, according to Alcuin, Genseric was already dead when he was stabbed, and she thought to herself that Hoos should be made aware of this fact. She had sworn to Alcuin that she would not tell anyone, but in reality that oath concerned the document, and not a matter that might prove vital for finding her father.

Turning around, she returned to the part of the tunnel where she had left Hoos, but all she discovered were a few abandoned sacks of grain. Surprised, she looked around and saw a side door, through which she could hear voices. She pushed the door open and walked down a narrow corridor, at the end of which she thought she could make out two faintly illuminated figures. One of the appeared to be a cleric. The other was Hoos Larsson. She continued until, to her surprise, she heard them arguing about her.

"I'm telling you, that girl is a problem. If she knows where the crypt is, she could tell anyone. We must eliminate her," the cassocked man asserted.

Theresa's heart thumped.

"And the rest of them? The girl trusts me and will do what I say. She doesn't know about the twins—or about her father and the mine," said Hoos. "When she has finished the document, then we'll get rid of her."

The cleric shook his head, but then agreed.

Hoos Larsson brought their conversation to a close, and without saying good-bye he made for the door.

When Theresa realized he was heading her way, she ran down the corridor toward the exit. But as she ran, she tripped over a sack of grain and fell to the floor. When she tried to stand up, Hoos was there.

He reached down and grabbed hold of her arm. "What are you doing here?" he asked without releasing her.

"I came back to tell you I love you," she lied, trembling.

"From the floor?" Hoos had noticed the door that she had left ajar, but he said nothing.

"In the darkness, I tripped."

"Tell me then."

"Tell you what?" she asked, red-faced.

"That you love me. Wasn't that why you came back?"

"Ah, yes!" She was shaking as she forced a smile.

Hoos pulled her to him without letting go of her arm. He kissed her on the lips, and she didn't protest.

"Now get back to the scriptorium."

When at last he released her, Theresa's soul was filled with hatred for that man and his serpent tattoo.

She could not comprehend it. The idea that Hoos—the man she had given herself to—intended to murder her made it impossible to think straight. She ran to the scriptorium without looking where she was going, like an outlaw pursued by a pack of wolves. She tried to understand how it could have happened, but she could not find an explanation. Images of her father at the mine swirled around with the images of Hoos making love to her. As she ran, tears clouded her vision. Who was the cleric she had seen from the back? Alcuin himself, perhaps?

When she reached the scriptorium she found it empty, but the sentry allowed her in because he knew her. She searched for the document she had been working on but couldn't find it, so she assumed that Alcuin or Wilfred had gone off with it. However, under some parchments, she found her father's emerald-colored Vulgate. She took it along with a couple of pens and left, intending to flee the fortress.

Avoiding dark corners, she moved along the corridors as if she feared someone would jump on her at any moment. As she passed the armory, a cassocked man suddenly stood in her way. Theresa's blood froze, but the cleric merely pointed to a pen that she had just dropped. The young woman picked up, thanked him, and walked on, her pace quickening with every step. She went down the stairs and turned down the passage that connected the entrance hall to the cloister. From there she would go out into the courtyard and then to the fortress walls.

She walked with her head bowed, trying to conceal herself with her cloak, when suddenly she saw Hoos and Alcuin talking on the other side of the cloister.

Hoos saw her, too.

She quickly averted her gaze and kept walking, but she saw him take his leave and quickly head toward her. Theresa was almost at the exit. She went out into the courtyard and broke into a run, but as she reached the fortress wall she realized in horror that the gates were closed. She looked behind her and saw Hoos in the distance advancing slowly but deliberately. Her heart pounded. She turned again, desperately seeking another way out.

At that moment she saw Izam on horseback by the stables. She ran toward him and asked him to lift her up. Izam was puzzled but gave her his arm and hoisted her onto the hindquarters. Crying, she begged him to take her away from the fortress. Izam asked no questions. He spurred on the horse and shouted an order for the gates to be opened. Moments later, with Hoos cursing his bad luck, they had left the walls and the citadel behind.

Izam guided his mount through the ant's nest of narrow streets until they reached some abandoned shacks in the poor quarter outside the walls. He dismounted next to some abandoned-looking stables. Leading the horse inside, he tethered it to a rail. Then he piled up some straw and offered it to Theresa to sit on. When he thought she had calmed down, he asked her what was going on. She tried to speak, but her weeping prevented her. As much as he tried, Izam was unable to console her. After a while Theresa ran out of tears and she abandoned herself to melancholy. Without knowing why, he took the liberty of holding her, and she was comforted to think that someone was protecting her.

When at last she could speak, she told him what she had witnessed in the tunnel. She explained that she had heard Hoos promising to kill her, and also that he knew the whereabouts of her father. She had to persuade Izam that Gorgias was no murderer, that they had to find him, for he was undoubtedly in danger. However, Izam urged her to continue her story. She told him all she knew, leaving out Constantine's document. The young man listened closely and inquired about Alcuin's role, though Theresa could not give him a clear answer. Izam pondered it all and finally decided to help.

"But it will have to be tomorrow. It's getting dark, and going down into the mine now would be an open invitation to bandits."

Theresa cursed those Saxons a thousand times. She hated them with all her being. She remembered again her assailants after she had fled Würzburg, the brutal attack during their voyage on the ship, and how the one person they should have killed—that bastard Hoos Larsson—remained alive. She was surprised when Izam corrected her assumption.

"I don't think they were Saxons. They were just outlaws. The rabble doesn't distinguish between the two because they identify pagans with evil, and evil with the Saxons. But the Saxons that are still resisting are hiding out in the north, beyond the Rhine."

"It doesn't matter whether they're bandits or Saxons. They're all our enemies."

"Of course, and I fight them with everything I have, but as strange as it may seem, I have never hated the Saxons. They're only defending their lands, their children, their beliefs. They're rough, yes. And cruel. But how would you behave if one morning you got out of bed to find an army laying waste to everything you know and love? Those pagans are fighting for what they've had since they were born, for a way of life that some foreigners from far off lands have come to take from them. I must admit that on occasions I have admired their valor and aspired to their energy. I even believe they truly hate God, for they often fight like demons. But I can assure you that they are only guilty of having been born in the wrong place and wrong time."

Theresa looked at him disconcertedly. In her mind, like all humans, the Saxons were children of God. So how could they be guided toward the Truth if they refused to accept it? At any rate, she thought, her anger returning, who in hell cares about the Saxons? Hoos, now he was a real servant of the Devil—the worst kind anyone could meet. The only man who had ever made her feel truly happy was nothing more than a con artist she now hated with such venom that she would gladly tear him apart with her bare hands. She kicked herself for having been so naive, for having wanted to marry him and give her life to an animal like that.

Her anger clouded her senses, making her incapable of distinguishing between rage and cold. She put Hoos out of her mind and laid her head against Izam's chest. His warmth comforted her. When she asked where they would spend the night, she was surprised to hear him say they would stay in the shack. He didn't trust anyone in the fortress anymore. The young man covered her with his cloak and took some cheese from his bag. When he offered her some, Theresa refused, but Izam broke off a piece and made her eat it. Her mouth brushed against his fingers.

As the young woman savored the food, Izam regretted not having any more cheese so that he might touch her lips again. He recalled the day they met. He had been attracted by her polite demeanor, her honey-colored eyes, and her messy hair. She was so different from the plump, rosy-cheeked girls that populated Fulda. But later it had been her bold and impetuous character that had captivated him. Curiously, the fact that she could read—something that would unnerve any normal man—fascinated him. He loved the interest with which she listened to him, and in turn he enjoyed listening to her stories about her native Constantinople. And now he was beside her, protecting her amid so many strange events, and not knowing what was real and what was fantasy.

28

When the voices woke Gorgias, it was already nightfall at the mine. He had just enough time to roll to one side and pull the pallet over himself. Pain shot through him as he fell on the stump of his arm. He crouched down and waited in silence, praying to God that the darkness would protect him.

Before long, hidden in the shadows inside the miner's hut, he listened to the approaching voices until finally he could see two individuals bearing torches. One of them was tall and blond, and the other appeared to be a priest. The strangers separated and began to sniff around the shacks, kicking aside the discarded junk. At one point the blond one came near his hiding place while the other waited at a distance. For a moment Gorgias thought he would be discovered, but in the end the man turned around, signaled to the clergyman, and they each deposited a bundle just a few paces from where he was hiding. Then they turned around and, as quickly as they had arrived, disappeared into the darkness.

Gorgias hid until he was sure they were not coming back. After a while he poked out his head and rested his gaze on the abandoned bundles. Suddenly one of them moved, making Gorgias give a start. He thought it might be some kind of wounded beast, so when the movements stopped, he decided to investigate.

With difficulty he left his hiding place and dragged himself toward the two bundles. He could barely manage to do even this. In the last week his arm had taken a turn for the worse—so much so that he had spent several days lying down without eating a thing. His fever told him that he was dying. If he had been able to find the strength, he would have returned to Würzburg, but for some time he had been breathless from his shivering.

He reached the first bundle and probed it with a stick. Squeezing it, he noted that it yielded and wriggled, and he flinched when it let out its first groan. He kept silent, and immediately heard it again. This time it faltered, making almost a moaning sound. Frightened, he slowly approached and unwrapped the bundle and, stunned, he did the same with the second one. When he had finished, he couldn't believe his eyes, which were the size of two great plates. Before him, gagged with kitchen cloth, lay Wilfred's twins.

He quickly undid the ligatures that bound them, lifted up the one that was breathing and nervously slapped the cheeks of the one that he hoped was sleeping. But she gave no reaction. He assumed she was dead, but when he tipped her chin up, the little girl coughed and began to cry, spluttering and asking for her father. Gorgias thought to himself that if those men heard the girls they would come back and kill them all, so he dragged the twins as quickly as he could to one of the tunnels, where he hid and hoped that the stone would muffle their crying. However, once inside, they sank into a strange torpor that made them sleep.

As on the preceding days, Gorgias struggled to get to sleep. Though still consumed by fever, the presence of the girls had given him back a little of the lucidity that he had lacked for so long. He stood and contemplated them. Their faces seemed a little blue, so he woke them up by timidly nudging them. When they were awake, he lifted up the one that was most alert, tidied her curls and sat her down like a rag doll. The little girl teetered a little but managed to keep her balance, even after hitting her head against the corf he had leaned her against. She seemed dazed, for she made no complaint. The other girl was in a stupor. He could barely feel her pulse. He poured a little of the water he kept in the tunnel on her head, but still there was no reaction. He did not know if their condition was the reason for their abandonment, but he knew that if he did not get them to Würzburg soon they would undoubtedly perish.

With the sun coming up, Gorgias decided to take them outside. It felt cold out in the open, auguring a storm. He wondered how he would transport them if he could barely stand himself. Searching the area, he found a wooden chest to which he tied a rope. He knotted this to his belt and then dragged it through the mud to where he had left the twins. Carefully, he placed them inside, explaining that it was a little carriage, but the little girls remained in a daze. He stroked their heads and then pulled on the rope. The chest didn't budge. He removed the stones that were in its path and then pulled again. The chest slid along heavily behind Gorgias as he set off for Würzburg.

He had not gone even half a mile when he sank into the mud. The first time he got up again. The second time, he passed out and fell to the ground.

He stayed there, lying flat on his face until the weeping of one of the children prompted him to continue, but he could not find the strength to stand up. He merely panted like a wounded animal. He dragged himself to the side of the road. There, as he got his breath back, he realized he would never accomplish what he had set out to do. His stump was hurting again, with the pain reaching to his lungs, though he no longer cared. He rested against the side of a rock and wept in despair. He was not concerned for his own life, but he was desperate to protect the two little girls.

From the bend in the road where he was sitting, he contemplated Würzburg in the distance. He admired the cluster of hovels packed behind the walls in the valley with the towers of the fortress watching over them from the hilltop. He looked longingly at the clear sky between the little columns of smoke rising up from the houses, and the first greenery appearing on the fields in the distance that seemed unreachable. It comforted him to think that his daughter already rested there under those lands, and that soon he would be reunited with her.

As he noticed the plumes of smoke, he suddenly had an idea. He lifted the twins out of the chest and put them to one side. Then, with the last of his strength, he smashed it into a heap of splinters with his foot. He took out his steel and held the flint between his feet to direct the sparks toward the dry cloth he'd positioned on top of the wood. Then he scraped the steel, praying to God the canvas would catch. But as much as he pleaded, it would not ignite. He tried again and again, but eventually his strength left him. Exhausted, he threw away the steel, cursing his bad luck.

After a while, he remembered the document he had hidden behind the beam in the slave hut. He thought the parchment would make ideal tinder, but when he stood up with the intention of retrieving it, everything started spinning.

He realized then that he would never leave that place. The twins were silent, as if they'd been drugged. He dragged himself over to the steel to try again. Taking it in his hand with all his strength, he unleashed it on the flint. To his surprise, the sparks burst forth in a luminous torrent, raining down onto the woolen mesh. He repeated the process vigorously, blowing on the sparks, rubbing the steel against the flint with all his might. Suddenly a dot of cloth caught. Gorgias blew on it again until another speck of gold appeared, immediately turning into an intense red. Revitalized, he continued to rub the steel as the incandescent particles multiplied.

Thin threads of smoke gradually grew denser, until at last a lively flame took hold of the mesh of wood.

Now he prayed that somebody in Würzburg would spot the fire. He planned to wait until someone approached—and then, once he was sure they had found the girls, he would flee again into the mountains. At that moment he noticed the fire beginning to wane, so he fed the flames with some of the wood that had scattered. Still, the fire devoured the wood as quickly as he added it, and gradually it faded until it was reduced to a pile of embers.

When all that remained was ash, Gorgias looked at it bitterly. Driven by a foolish idea, he had destroyed the only means he had to transport the little girls. So now all he could do was wait for the cold and the wild animals to take them to their graves. He took off his cloak and wrapped the twins in it. For a moment he thought the most alert one smiled at him. Then he huddled up close to them to protect them with his body and fell asleep, dreaming of his daughter.

He knew he must be dead, for when he opened his eyes, the first thing he saw was Theresa. He saw her enveloped in a white halo, radiant with joy, her honey-colored eyes big and shining, her messy hair that she never tidied, her warm, affectionate voice. He thought he could feel her arms and hear her encouraging words. She was in the company of a kind-looking dark-haired angel.

He tried to speak to her but could only let out a groan. Suddenly he felt them lifting him. In the darkness, he could see that the two little girls were still with him, then he noticed the remains of the fire. Confused, he looked at Theresa before she took him in her arms. Then he lost consciousness again.

As much as he tried, Izam could not put Theresa at ease. The young woman had been so desperate to find her father that when she spotted the fire in the vicinity of the mines that morning, she had cried, certain that she would find him alive. Then, after reaching the top of the path and discovering Gorgias huddled up to the girls, she had run toward him sobbing with joy, and when she saw that he was still breathing, she had embraced him a thousand times before Izam suggested they return to the town immediately.

They set off back to the city with Theresa guiding the horse, Gorgias's unconscious body slumped over the back of the mount, and Izam on foot carrying the twins in his arms. At first Theresa was brimming with happiness. She spoke to her father, explaining where she had been, what had happened in Fulda, how much she had missed him. However, as they traveled, she noticed not only could he not hear her, but also that his wounded stump stank like a dead animal. She told Izam and he pursed his lips, shaking his head.

"We'll have to take him to the physician," he said, realizing too late what effect this statement might have on Theresa. "I'm sure this time he'll make him better."

His addendum did not prevent Theresa from being alarmed, so to distract her he spoke about the twins. "Someone must have left them in the mine," he remarked.

Theresa did not answer, for it was obvious to her that her father could not have kidnapped a chicken.

* * *

They were halfway back when suddenly, upon reaching the top of a slope, they saw a mob of peasants heading toward them brandishing hay forks and scythes. The mob was led by a group of soldiers who told them to halt. Izam assumed they sought Wilfred's reward. What he didn't understand was how they had found them so quickly.

Fortunately Izam spotted Gratz, one of his trusted men. When Gratz recognized Izam, he shouted for the archers to lower their weapons. But several peasants, blinded by greed, were already running toward them. Izam quickly put down the children and drew his sword, but before he could use it, an arrow knocked down the first peasant. Izam looked at Gratz, who was still holding the bow. The other peasants stopped dead in their tracks. One of the townspeople dropped his weapon on the ground and the rest copied him. Then a few of the solders overtook them, shoving aside the group of hotheads and offering their horses to Izam and the twins.

On the way back to Würzburg, Gratz revealed to Izam that someone had anonymously revealed the girls' whereabouts.

"Apparently a hooded man confessed it to a priest, who in turn informed Wilfred. This morning they ordered us to organize a search party."

Izam was surprised to hear that the informer had known where they were—and that he had blamed Gorgias for abducting the twins. He thanked Gratz for his intervention and they rode on to the citadel gates, where another angry crowd had gathered.

As soon as the gates were opened, they saw Wilfred on his wooden carriage. The count cracked his whip and the dogs pulled the contraption, which moved clumsily down the road, leaving behind Alcuin, Zeno, and Rutgarda, who were standing behind him watching the events. When the cripple reached the walls, Izam met him with the two little girls. As Wilfred embraced them, the whole town celebrated the end of their nightmare.

Back in the fortress, Theresa bit her nails as she waited for Zeno and a midwife to examine the twins. When they had finished, both the physician and the midwife declared there had been no physical violence. They would soon be back to normal. But when Zeno went to tend to Gorgias, Wilfred stopped him. He ordered that Gorgias be taken to the dungeons.

Theresa begged him again and again not to condemn her father, but Wilfred would not budge. He warned that if she continued to insist, he would imprison her as well. The young woman told him she didn't care, but Izam dragged her to another room by force.

"Let go of me!" she screamed, sobbing.

Izam held her and tried to calm her down. "Don't you see that you won't achieve anything like this? I'll get them to tend to him later, I promise."

Theresa gave in, her nerves on edge. On the way back to the chapter house, she saw Hoos talking to Alcuin. Instinctively she pressed herself against Izam as they walked toward Hoos, but the young man simply turned around and left the room.

Izam and Theresa ate together in one of the stables, surrounded by hay and straw. While they shared a stew, Izam confessed to her. He told her that apart from two or three of his subordinates, he didn't know who to trust.

"Not even that Alcuin. I know him from court, yes. He is a wise and highly regarded man, but I don't know. With all that you've told me . . ."

Theresa nodded, not paying too much attention, for at that moment all she cared about was that her father received help as soon as possible. When she reminded Izam, he promised to look for Zeno after they had eaten. He said he had already made inquiries and it was just a matter of paying the man enough.

"If I say that I need to interrogate your father," Izam thought out loud, "I don't think they will get in my way."

Theresa begged to go with him, but Izam told her it would raise suspicion.

"Then bribe the guards—or say I need to be present when you talk to him."

"Sure! You, me, Zeno . . . anyone else? It's not a welcome banquet."

Theresa looked at him, dumbfounded. Suddenly she dropped her plate and ran toward the exit. Izam realized he had been too brusque, so he caught up to her and apologized for his stupidity. He admitted he was nervous because he didn't know who or what they were up against.

"Did you not see Wilfred? If looks could kill, your father would be dead," he said.

"If it's a question of money, for the love of God, tell me. In Fulda I have lands." She had forgotten that Izam already knew that.

"It's not a matter of . . . damn it, Theresa! Whoever they are, they've already killed two people—three, including the parchment-maker. And the two little girls were sick with God knows what. If we're not careful, next it will be us."

Theresa bit her lip but still insisted on seeing her father. Izam knew she would not give up, so he made her promise that she would stay by his side until everything became clear.

"And the scriptorium? I promised Alcuin I'd help him."

"Jesus Christ! Forget the scriptorium! Forget Hoos and forget that accursed Alcuin! Now let's find that physician before he drains all the wine in the cellars."

They located Zeno in a hovel, tending to a townsman who had lost three teeth in a fight. While the physician finished with him, he asked what they wanted, but Izam pretended they were concerned about the twins. Only after the wounded man left did Izam reveal his true intentions.

"I'm sorry, but Wilfred has prohibited me from tending to him," said Zeno apologetically as he wiped blood from his hands. "I still don't understand why: That scribe is going to kick the bucket any moment either way."

Hearing his prognosis, Izam was glad that Theresa was waiting outside.

"If he's going to die anyway, what difference will it make if you see him?" He made his coin pouch jingle.

In the end, he managed to convince him by promising that he would replace Wilfred's guard with one of his own men who could be trusted not to open his mouth. Zeno asked for payment in advance, but Izam offered him just a couple of coins. When Zeno reached for them, Izam seized his wrist.

"A warning: Make sure you are sober, or it'll be you who needs his mouth fixed."

Zeno gave him a stupid smile. Before parting, they agreed to meet after the Sext service, by which time Izam hoped he would have persuaded Wilfred to increase security at the dungeons with his own men. Then he went with Theresa to collect her belongings from her room, for he didn't want her to stay there any longer. The young woman took some clothes, a burin, and her wax tablets before they continued to Izam's cell.

"What do you intend to do?" she asked once the door was closed.

Izam removed his sword and threw it on the table. He said he would advise Wilfred to increase the watch with some of his men, then wait for Wilfred's sentry to leave.

"I'll find a way to have Gratz watch the door."

He told her to wait there and not to leave the room under any circumstances. Then he equipped himself with a dagger that he hid under his cloak. When he was about to leave, Theresa stopped him. She was scared Hoos would attack her, but Izam assured her he wouldn't. He went out into the corridor and called to the soldier on guard. The youngster, a beardless, pock-faced kid, promptly accepted his order to stop anyone from entering the room.

When Izam had gone, Theresa curled up on the straw mattress to await his return.

Theresa lay there staring at the ceiling, wondering why Wilfred had been compelled to send Gorgias to the dungeons. After a while she decided to take a look at the Vulgate she still had in her bag. She took the codex to the window and, after finding the verse from the Thessalonian Epistles, she went over the notes that her father had made in diluted ink.

In total she counted sixty-four phrases—or rather, sixty-four lines, for they did not form clear sentences or paragraphs, but strings of unconnected words, all related to the famous parchment. It was no use. But she knew those words must have some significance, so she went about transcribing each one to her wax tablets. When she had finished, she placed the tablets on the mattress and with the dagger that Izam had given her, scraped away the hidden text in the Vulgate. Then she closed the codex, hid Gorgias's parchment under her skirt, and waited for Izam to return.

Within moments there was some banging on the door. Hearing it, Theresa gave a start and backed into the wall, right into an icy stone that stabbed her between her shoulders and made her yelp. She put her hand over her mouth, hoping she hadn't given herself away. She clambered onto the window ledge as a pool of blood seeped under the door.

Someone lifted the door latch and Theresa turned to look outside. She saw a moat beneath her. If she fell, she would die. Suddenly, a crashing sound made the latch jump. Theresa crossed herself and grabbed on to some projections on the outer wall, praying to God for help, as her body hung over a void.

She could hear that on the other side of the window, someone was smashing up the room. Soon her arms began to tremble and she knew she wouldn't last long. She looked around and saw the nail under the windowsill for airing food. If she grabbed it, she would tear her hand, but perhaps she would be able to hook her clothes to it.

Attempting it, her hand slipped. Then, just as her other hand lost its hold, the front of her robe caught on the nail. For a moment she felt herself falling into the void, but suddenly a hand grabbed her, hoisting her toward the window. She thought she was about to be run through with a blade, but her fear vanished when Izam's kind face appeared. After pulling her into the room, he held her tight and urged her to be calm.

Still confused, the young woman gathered up the objects that were scattered all over the place, while Izam tended to the sentry who was lying flat under the doorjamb. Theresa hoped he was just wounded, but the pool of blood told her he had been killed. She let herself drop to the ground, sobbing and feeling defeated. Izam asked her who it had been, but she hadn't seen them. After searching all over the place, Theresa discovered that they had stolen her father's Vulgate.

Izam and Theresa explained to a pair of servants what happened and they took care of the body. Then, they gathered their belongings in order to go somewhere safe. Though Theresa lamented the loss of the Bible, she was grateful that the thief had disregarded the tablets on which she had reproduced the phrases from the Vulgate.

While they walked in the direction of one of the courtyards, Theresa attributed the attack to Alcuin, for he was the only person who knew of the hidden message in her father's Bible.

"It must have been him," she repeated to Izam.

They decided to ask the monk for an explanation, but when they arrived at the scriptorium, the door was locked.

Theresa shared with Izam the hidden message she had transcribed and they wasted some time in one of the atriums, pondering its significance. Theresa admitted that she had not been able to decipher a single word.

"But my father will help us," she asserted.

Izam nodded. Then he looked up to the sky. Soon it would be time to meet the physician and try to help Gorgias.

A few minutes after the agreed time, Zeno appeared with his bag. He smelled of wine, though no more than he had when Izam first spoke to him that morning. He paid the agreed sum, and then Izam, Theresa, and the physician headed to the dungeons.

Theresa was surprised to hear that they used some old meat safes to lock away prisoners. The safes consisted of holes resembling silos cut into the rock, which when filled with snow preserved food until summer. Since they were not needed in winter, on occasion they were used as storerooms and, if necessary, as improvised cells.

"Elsewhere they only use them for thieves, but we put other criminals in there, too," Zeno boasted as if he were responsible for the idea. "We throw them into these ditches and they don't come out till they're dead. Sometimes, depending on the crime, we'll throw them bread from up top just to see them kill each other for a few crumbs. But in the end, they all rot like vermin."

Izam asked him to spare them the details, but Zeno prattled on as if Theresa wasn't there. Only when Izam grabbed him by the shirtfront did he finally hold his tongue.

The meat safes were located in a basement under the kitchens that could be reached either from the wine cellar or from an entrance near the stables. They entered through the kitchens, for the passage near the stables was very narrow and primarily used to shovel snow through.

When they reached the meat safe, they met Gratz, the sentry posted there by Izam. The man urged them to be quick, for he did not know when the other guard, who he had distracted with a prostitute, would return.

Zeno and Izam went down into the meat safe using a wooden ladder that Gratz had found. Theresa waited at the top because Zeno said she would only get in the way. From the edge, Theresa could see her father. She watched as the physician, shaking his head, inspected the scar on Gorgias's shoulder.

Her father was barely able to stammer a few words, though she heard a loud groan when Izam sat him up so that the physician could better examine him. Zeno took out a tonic, which he had Gorgias drink, but he coughed it up, making the physician curse. Then he clambered up the ladder.

"Go down if you want," he told Theresa.

"How is he?" she asked.

Zeno spat on the ground. Without answering, he took a swig of the tonic himself and then moved away from the meat safe. Theresa wanted the physician to vomit, too. At that moment Izam pressed her to climb down.

Once she was by her father's side, he looked at her oddly.

"Is it you?" he whispered.

Theresa embraced him, trying not to let him see the tears running down her face.

"Is it you, little one?"

"Yes, it's me. Theresa." She kissed him, wetting him with her tears. Gorgias hardly looked at her. It was as if his eyes no longer belonged to him.

"I'll get you out of here. Everything will be fine," she promised as she kissed him.

"The document . . ."

"What are you saying, Father?"

"The parchment." Gorgias repeated in a whisper, his pupils contracted.

Theresa burst into tears. Her father's eyes were like a pair of opaque beads.

"I hear someone coming," Izam warned her.

She didn't listen to him. Izam took her arm, but she resisted.

"*Sic erunt novissimi primi, et primi novissimi,*" Gorgias uttered in a thin voice.

"Come, or we'll be discovered!" Izam insisted.

"I can't leave him here!" Theresa sobbed.

Izam lifted her into the air and made her go back up. At the top, he promised they would return, but right now they had to run for it.

Gratz removed the ladder just as Wilfred's guard returned, humming to himself and scratching his crotch. He was surprised to find visitors, but a few coins convinced him that Izam and Theresa had just come from the kitchens. When they left, Theresa knew that her father would never make it out of the meat safe alive.

Izam decided that they would stay on one of the boats moored at the wharf so they would have the protection of his own men. Once there, they ate from the soldiers' rations before retreating to the benches at the stern. Izam wrapped Theresa in a blanket and she accepted a sip of strong wine to combat the cold out on deck. She was comforted by his embrace, and almost without intending to, she rested her head against him.

She spoke to him of her father: his dedication to his work and how he had instilled a love of reading in her. She described the nights when she would get up to prepare some broth for him while he wrote by the light of a candle; his efforts to teach her not just Latin but also Greek, the Commandments, and the Holy Scriptures. She told him about his efforts to ensure that she remembered her native Byzantium.

She cried.

Then she asked Izam to free her father. When he said he would have to speak to Alcuin, Theresa moved away in surprise. "Alcuin? What has he got to do with my father's imprisonment?"

Izam told her that during his conversation with Wilfred, the count had assured him that, if it were up to him, he would have already executed the scribe.

"But, it would seem, Alcuin stopped him, at least until the mystery is solved."

"What mystery?" She rested her head back on his chest.

"That's what I asked, but Wilfred stammered and changed the subject. Anyway, the important thing is that your father's still alive—a miracle when you bear in mind that we found him with the twins."

"But you know—"

"It matters not what you or I know. What matters is what Alcuin believes. He's the one in charge, and it's him we should convince if we want to get Gorgias out of the meat safe."

Theresa regretted having completed the parchment. She had finished it the same afternoon they imprisoned her father. Izam explained that Alcuin was a powerful man, much more powerful than she could even imagine.

"Only the king outranks him," he added. "Under his guise as a lowly monk, his skinny and ungainly appearance, and his prudish affectations and simple way of life, there is actually a man who holds the reins of power in the church—and he rules with an iron hand. He who rules the church also controls the intricate workings of the empire. He guides Charlemagne—he is his light, his sustenance, his anchor. Who else could have formulated the *Admonitio generallis*, the compendium of canonical legislation to which every subject is bound, whether priest or peasant? It was Alcuin who prohibited revenge killings, who ordered penitents to give up their delirium, who forbade working, hunting, markets, and even trials on a Sunday. Alcuin of York: a fine ally, but a terrible enemy to have."

Theresa was surprised by the revelation. Despite his intelligence, Alcuin had always seemed little more than a simple man of the cloth. She now understood the willingness with which the monk had helped her, and the readiness of Charlemagne to grant her the lands in Fulda.

While she continued thinking, Izam went off to organize the night watches. Theresa curled up under the blanket and drank down a long draft of wine, hoping its effect would clear her mind. But instead the drink made her head spin. Since she had known Alcuin, her view of him had changed direction like a walnut in a waterfall. Sometimes he had helped her; often he had confounded her; and lately, he had frightened her no less than if he were some terrible demonic being. For that was what she thought of him: He must be an evil monster. She was certain that—after recovering the emerald Vulgate—he had murdered the young sentry. Only he was aware of its contents, for he was the only person she had told.

Hoos a traitor, and Alcuin a murderer. Or maybe it was the other way around—it made no difference.

When Izam returned, he thought Theresa seemed more attractive than ever. He finished his wine and took her hand, not knowing why he felt so good when he was by her side. He hugged her while she closed her eyes. She dreamed that he would protect her from strife, from uncertainty, from all her fears . . . Then drowsiness filled her. She felt herself flush with warmth before unintentionally falling asleep with her head on Izam's chest.

In the early hours she awoke with a fierce headache. It was cold, and the slow swaying of the ship made her feel sick. She managed to hold it together as she negotiated the cargo on the deck, trying to locate Izam. At the other end of the boat she found Gratz, who informed her that the engineer had gone off to check the situation with the other ships.

"He told me to make sure you stay here until his return."

Theresa acquiesced. She took the loaf of bread that Gratz offered her and went back to the stern. There she chewed on the bread while contemplating the fortress's silhouette. The bread tasted rancid, but she swallowed it without reservation. Then, with the first light of morning, she went over the wax tablets again.

By the time the sun had climbed high in the sky, not even the tossing and pitching of the boat or the ruckus of the seamen with their tools could prevent her from poring over the strange phrases transcribed from the Vulgate. However, the words still jumbled into gibberish. The only certainty was that all the phrases repeatedly alluded to Constantine's document.

She decided to arrange the four tablets on top of a barrel—as if merely the act of looking at them could reveal their secrets. Then her father's words sprang to mind: *Sic erunt novissimi primi, et primi novissimi.*

What was he trying to say? She stood and asked Gratz for a Bible and he gave her the one they kept on the ship to protect them on voyages. Once alone again, she looked for the twentieth chapter in the *Evangelium Secundum Matthaeum*: *Sic erunt novissimi primi, et primi novissimi.* The last will be the first, and the first will be the last.

She read the previous and subsequent chapters through, without finding anything to help her understand. She looked at the tablets again while repeating the verse: *The last will be the first.* She slid her fingers over the scores in the wax.

Suddenly she understood. She tried to read the tablets in reverse order, from the last word to the first. As if by magic, neat sentences formed, combining to create clear paragraphs. When she finished reading, she understood what her father had discovered. Quickly, she hid the tablets under the bench and went to ask Gratz when Izam would return.

"Actually, he was supposed have returned by now," he said, unconcerned.

Theresa paced up and down the boat until she had learned the contents of the tablets by heart. When she grew impatient she went to see Gratz again and asked him to accompany her on land, but he told her he couldn't do that until Izam returned.

"And what if he doesn't?"

"He will. He always returns."

Theresa was not convinced by his answer, so she decided that if Izam did not come back by midday she would go alone to the fortress.

29

As the sun reached its peak and there was still no sign of Izam, Theresa made up her mind. She covered herself in a sailor's cloak, appropriated a bundle so that she could blend in, and with Gratz distracted mending a sail, she went down to the jetty and set off toward the fortress walls. An openwork woolen cap helped her go unnoticed. At the first entrance to the city they paid no attention to her, but to gain entry into the fortress itself, she had to wait for a diligent guard to be distracted by some passing carts.

Once inside, she skirted the outer courtyards with the intention of entering the building from the maze of kitchens. A couple of dogs barked as she went past, but she stroked their heads to soothe them. She crossed an atrium and from there made for the corridor that led to Alcuin's cell. When she found it locked, she went directly to the scriptorium, where she found the monk reading her stolen Vulgate. When he saw her, Alcuin stood up. "Where the devil have you been? I've been searching for you all morning." He set aside the Bible, making sure he closed the cover.

Theresa took a deep breath and walked in. She was scared, but determined that the murderous monk would release her father from the meat safe. He bolted the door behind her and offered her a chair, which she accepted. Then the monk took out the parchment that Theresa had been working on and placed it in front of her as if nothing had happened.

"You still have to clean the text and go over it again, so you may as well get on with it," he said, turning his attention back to the Vulgate.

"You're not going to ask about my father?"

Alcuin stopped reading and coughed, a little embarrassed. "I'm sorry, it's just with so much going on, I'm a bit distracted. I don't know if you heard, but a sentry had his throat cut in the fortress yesterday."

Theresa was surprised at the monk's peevish tone. He swallowed and took Constantine's document from her.

"I won't touch it," the young woman blurted out.

Alcuin arched an eyebrow. "I can understand why you're upset, but—"

"I've finished it—what more do you want? Have your damned document!" she exclaimed, rising from her chair in a rage.

Alcuin looked at her as if he didn't understand. "What in the Devil's name is wrong with you? There are still the conclusions," he said, trying to calm her down.

"Do you think that I don't know about your schemes? My father, the twins . . . that poor sentry."

Alcuin froze as if he had seen a ghost. With a faltering step he went over to the door and bolted it shut. Then he slumped into a chair. He gave her a puzzled look and asked her to continue. Theresa gripped the stylus she had hidden under the folds of her dress.

"I caught you talking to Hoos. Two days ago, in the tunnel. I heard you proposing that he should kill me. I heard everything. I heard you discussing my father, the mine, the crypt, and the twins."

"God Almighty, Theresa. What foolery is this?"

"Oh! You deny it? And what about this Vulgate?" she said.

"What about it? What's your issue with this Bible?"

Theresa clenched her teeth, exasperated. When she told him that the Vulgate was the reason he had killed the sentry, the monk smiled.

"I see! So I agreed with Hoos that I should murder you—only after you've finished the document."

"Exactly," she responded.

"Of course!" The monk stood up with an air of indifference. "But if what you say is true, what would stop me from killing you right now? After all, the document is done," he added, resting a hand on Theresa's shoulder—near her throat. The monk felt her trembling. Then he went to the door and unbolted it. "If you want to know the truth, you'll have to trust me. Otherwise, you can leave the scriptorium."

Theresa's hand clamped around the stylus under her dress. She did not trust Alcuin. But if she had to risk her life to save her father, she wouldn't hesitate, so she nodded and sat down again. The monk was pleased with her decision and sat himself at the other end of the table. Then he tidied several documents before looking at Theresa.

"Biscuit?" he offered.

She declined with a grim expression. He gulped it down in one mouthful, then he held out the document she had been working on.

"As you know, you've been transcribing a reproduction of the original document that was lost many years ago, a parchment with the Emperor Constantine's seal granting lands and rights to the Roman Papacy."

Theresa nodded, but she didn't release the stylus.

"The parchment legitimized Rome's power in the face of the Byzantine Empire. Perhaps you are not aware of the current situation of the Papacy, but forty years ago, following the conquest of Ravenna by the Lombards, Pope Stephen II requested assistance from Byzantium to defend himself against the pagans." He poured a little milk into a badly washed chalice. "When he received no response from Byzantium, the pope crossed the Alps and appeared before the king of the Franks at the time, Charlemagne's father, Pepin. Pope Stephen II anointed Pepin and his sons, bestowing upon them the title of Patrician of the Romans, and in exchange he asked for their protection in the fight against the Lombards. Are you sure you don't want a biscuit?"

Theresa declined again with a gesture. Though she could not yet understand the relationship between Alcuin's story and the recent spate of murders, she patiently waited for him to finish.

"At the pope's request, Pepin and his troops traveled to Italy, where they crushed the Lombards," he continued. "Their victory won the Exarchate of Ravenna for the Papacy, comprising the cities of Bologna and Ferrara, among others. It also secured the March of Ancona, with the Pentapolis, Rome itself, and the recovery of the rest of the duchy occupied by the Lombards. In short: The Lombards attacked Rome, and Rome asked Byzantium for help. When they did not obtain it, they turned to Pepin again, who after defeating the Lombards returned the occupied territories to Rome."

He looked at Theresa to make sure she was following him. Then he continued, "Up to this point, all would have been well if Byzantium had not demanded that the pope hand over the Exarchate of Ravenna, a territory that prior to the Lombard invasion had belonged to them. Rome wanted to enforce the Donation of Constantine, the document that allocated these lands to the Papacy, but Byzantium took no notice of their demand and maintained their claim on the territories. And not only that: Constantinople itself supported the Barbarians in their re-conquering of the lands that the Frankish king had taken from them."

"You're saying Byzantium helped the Lombards to defeat the Romans?"

"Christians against Christians—a tragedy, is it not? Yet, what is politics if not a thirst for power? Just look at the envy that drove Cain to kill his brother. With the support of the Greeks, the Lombards defeated the pope, confining him to a few arpents of land. However, Rome still had the parchment—the document that legitimized their demands—so the recently appointed Roman Pope Adrian I went to France to brandish the document before Charlemagne."

Alcuin left and returned with more biscuits. He bit into one and offered the other to Theresa, who finally accepted.

"Charlemagne led his army to Italy, where he swept aside the Lombards, restoring the lands to the Papacy and warning the Byzantines of their obligations to the Papal States. The restitutions included the donation of Bologna, Ferrara, other cities of the lower Po and the north of Tuscany such as Parma, Reggio, and Mantua, and even Venice and Istria in the north, and the Duchies of Spoleto and Benevento. He gave the Papacy practically all of southern Italy with the exception of Apulia, Calabria, and Sicily and the enclaves of Naples, Gaeta, and Amalfi, which were under Byzantine rule at the time, as well as the island of Corsica, Sabina, and levies in Tuscany and Spoleto. A few years later, Charlemagne added some cities to the south of Tuscany—like Orvieto and Viterbo. And in Campania, he added Aquino, Arpino, and Capua. All of this, evidently, did not sit well with Byzantium."

Theresa was silent, but from her face Alcuin could tell he was overdoing it.

"Sorry," he apologized. He rummaged through his papers, pretending to arrange them. "In short, the important thing is that Charlemagne managed to enforce the terms stated in the Donation of Constantine, thereby earning the eternal gratitude of the Papacy."

Theresa drummed her fingers on the table. Alcuin looked at her and nodded. "Allow me to finish and perhaps you will understand the reasons for what is happening now." He smoothed his hair and took a deep breath before continuing. "Byzantium begrudgingly accepted their losses, in part because of the indolence of their emperor, Constantine VI—and in part for fear of Charlemagne's host. Things stayed calm until a couple of years ago. Then, Irene of Athens, Constantine VI's mother, and a relative of the Devil I would say, ordered that her son be arrested and have his eyes gouged out so that she could be crowned Empress of Byzantium."

"She murdered her son?"

"No, all she did was imprison and blind him. A caring mother, don't you think? Well, as you can imagine, the harpy soon started plotting against the Papacy. Not long after she ascended to the throne she sent an assassin to Rome with the intention of stealing the document in which the legacy was recognized."

"The Donation of Constantine."

"Exactly."

Theresa looked at the parchment with the feeling that the enigma was slowly revealing itself. Yet, she was still confounded by Alcuin's behavior.

The monk continued. "Through bribery, the empress's assassin gained access to the document, which he managed to destroy before he was caught by the papal custodian. The thief was executed, but the document lay charred on the Vatican floor. Since then Irene has questioned the validity of the Donation through diplomatic missions, particularly after finding out that Pope Leo III wants to crown Charlemagne as the Holy Roman Emperor."

Theresa could not hide her astonishment. Everyone knew that the emperor was the Byzantine monarch.

"Well, the pope doesn't think so," Alcuin continued. "Rome wishes to strengthen its relationship with an emperor who is both energetic and understanding, a monarch who has demonstrated his valor and generosity. But Irene sees this decision as a maneuver that will drain Byzantium's power, thus she wants to prevent it. By destroying the document, the empress has got rid of the proof of the legitimacy of the Papacy's possessions, and without physical proof to validate it, nothing can prevent her from attacking Rome to stop Charlemagne being named emperor."

"But it makes no sense. How can the existence of the document be so significant? It's nothing more than parchment." She was beginning to grow weary of Alcuin's lecture, never forgetting that all the while her father was dying in a meat safe.

"You might think so, but sooner or later Irene will die, just as we all will. And those who will follow us will have the same desires, the same ambitions. It's not just a question of the whim of one powerful woman: The very future of humanity is at stake. To win this battle the Papal States must secure legal ownership of their possessions, which will in turn protect Charlemagne's ascension to Holy Roman Emperor. Charlemagne will guide the Western Empire along the path of Our Lord, promote learning, fight heresy, crush the pagans and the infidels, spread the Word of God, unify believers, and subjugate blasphemers. This is the real reason why the document must be finished. Otherwise, we will witness endless battles that will continue for centuries until Christendom is destroyed."

He fell silent, pleased with himself, as though his explanation would have convinced even the most foolish.

However, Theresa gave him a look of indifference.

"This is why the copy must be finished before the council that the pope will call in the middle of June," he added. "Do you understand?"

"What I understand is that Rome yearns for the power that Byzantium claims as its own, and that your primary desire is to see Charlemagne crowned. Now tell me: Why should I believe a man who keeps my father in a hole? A man who has manipulated, lied, and murdered? Tell me why I should help you." The fact that the conclusions still had to be added to the parchment gave her a strong bargaining chip that she thought she had lost. "Still, I'll repeat my offer: Free my father, and I will finish the document."

Alcuin stood. He approached the window and looked outside. He could smell the aroma of resin from a little forest nearby.

"Nice day," he said, then turned back around to face Theresa. "When I chose you, I clearly knew what I was doing. All right, lass. I'll tell you what I know, but keep in mind your oath—for if you dare to break it, I will personally make sure that every last one of your nightmares comes true."

Theresa wasn't intimidated. The stylus under her dress gave her courage.

"My father is dying," she pressed.

"All right, all right." He came away from the window and, grim-faced, he paced around the perimeter of the room. He walked upright, slowly, meditating on his words. "The first thing you should be aware of is that I have known Gorgias for a long time," he said, "and I assure you that I am fond of him and admire him. We met in Pavia, when you were still a little girl. He was fleeing from Constantinople with you and, seeking help, he came to the abbey where I was resting on my journey to Rome. Your father was an educated man with extensive knowledge, and of course alien to the corruptions of the court or the Vatican. He had an excellent command of Greek and Latin, he had read the classics, and he seemed like a good Christian. So, not without some self-interest, I suggested he accompany me to Aquis-Granum. I needed a Greek translator at the time and Gorgias needed work, so we returned together and he settled here in Würzburg to await the completion of the palatine schools that were being built in Aquis-Granum. Here he met Rutgarda, your stepmother, and very soon they married, no doubt with your future in mind. I would have preferred him to have established himself within the court, but Rutgarda had her family here, so in the end we agreed that he should work for Wilfred translating any codices I sent to him."

Though she nodded with interest, Theresa still didn't understand the connection to the series of murders. When she told him as much, Alcuin asked her to be patient.

"All right. Let's move on to the murders, then. On the one hand there is the death of Genseric. And also the wet nurse, and the death of her likely lover and murderer, the parchment-maker."

"And the young sentry," Theresa added.

"Ah, yes! That poor lad." He shook his head with an expression of disapproval. "Not to mention the other youngsters who were stabbed to death. But we'll talk about them and the sentry later. As for Genseric, ruling out the stylus as the cause of his demise, I am inclined to think it was a potion, some deadly poison that was administered to him. Zeno spoke of his trembling and the itching in his arm, which tallies with what happened to the parchment-maker, who if I remember rightly, also complained of a strange prickling in his hand. I think I even drew a picture."

Alcuin retrieved a parchment with a picture of a hand with two little circular marks in the center. "I drew this after his death," he pointed out. "Look closely. Doesn't it remind you of something?"

"I don't know. A sting?"

"With two puncture holes? No. I would suggest it's more like a snakebite."

"A serpent? Are you implying they weren't murdered?"

"I didn't say that. As for the hand wounds, I consulted with Zeno and he agreed that the diameter and appearance of the perforations were similar to those made by a viper. But let us consider the position of the marks." He pointed to them carefully. "It would be difficult for a snake to bite a palm unless someone was stupid enough to try to grab it. Perhaps the snake might go for the back of the hand or even a finger—but not the palm. Look, give me your hand," he requested. "Now use your fingers to simulate a serpent's jaw and strike at my hand."

The friar held out his hand and Theresa pinched the back of his hand with her index and middle fingers, with her thumb going into his palm. Alcuin told her to squeeze and she did so until her nails dug in. Only when the monk cried out did the young woman ease the pressure.

Retrieving his hand, he showed her his palm and then the marks she had left vertically lengthwise across of the back of his hand: one red mark near his wrist, another close to his fingers. Then he compared his hand to the picture he had drawn, depicting the puncture holes aligned horizontally across the width of the hand.

"An animal would have struck exactly as you did, on the back or on the palm, but in the direction of the arm. And yet, Korne's wounds," he said, placing the picture beside his hand, "appear across the palm, perpendicular to the marks you've made on me."

"And what does that mean?"

"That the murderer is a skilled man who is able to kill in an unhurried manner, allowing some time to pass—a useful skill to employ if you don't want to be associated with the murder. It's even possible that his victims weren't even aware of what was happening. And it must be someone with a knowledge of venoms."

"Zeno?"

"That drunk? What would he gain from these murders? No, Theresa dear. *Ad panitendum properat, cito qui iudicat.* To find a criminal, one must establish the motive. What connection might there be between Genseric and the parchment-maker?"

"They were both men. They lived in Würzburg."

"And they both had feet and a head. Try to sharpen up, for the love of God!"

Theresa made it known she was in no mood for guessing games.

"All right," he conceded. "They both worked for Wilfred. I know that everyone in Würzburg works for Wilfred, but Genseric was his coadjutor, his right-hand man, abreast of all that concerned his superior. Korne, the parchment-maker, was a close friend of Wilfred's. This connection might seem irrelevant when it comes to finding a motive for their murders, but let us continue to speculate. We can agree that the twins were abducted in order to blackmail the count, and that their kidnapper was undoubtedly the parchment-maker."

"How do we know that? From the curly hairs we found?" Theresa suggested.

"And this doll's eye that I found in Korne's cell." He took a little pebble from a small box and showed it to Theresa proudly. "It belongs to the toy that the twins were playing with on the day of the kidnapping."

Theresa examined it, impressed. The blue paint stood out crudely on the white of the pebble.

"We can deduce, therefore," Alcuin continued, snatching it back, "that the parchment-maker must have wanted something that he judged to be impossible to obtain by less risky means. For surely, he would have done that before resorting to abducting the children. He must have been after something of such value that he was willing to risk his own life, and even do away with his poor lover."

"Constantine's document?"

"Exactly: the document again. And if both Genseric and Korne died in the same manner—poisoned, that is—it would be logical to infer that they were both killed by the same hand."

Theresa knocked an inkwell to the floor, splattering Alcuin, but she was not sorry about it. "You know what I think?" she blurted out. "That in reality, you are the culprit. You knew the importance of the parchment. You seem to know how Genseric and Korne were murdered. I only told you about the hidden lines between the verses of the Vulgate, and soon after, I think you killed the sentry in order to get it." She pointed at the emerald codex. "And I saw you speaking to Hoos Larsson."

"With Hoos? When? In the tunnel? I can assure you that wasn't me."

"And later in the cloister."

"I think you're raving." He went to put his hand on Theresa's shoulder, but she fended it off violently. "Stop taking me for a fool," she warned.

"I will repeat that I never met Hoos in the tunnel, so you can forget about that. It's true that I saw him in the cloister—as I did Wilfred, a couple of servants, and two prelates. But to conjecture that from my presence there that I am involved? For God's sake, woman! When Genseric died, we were still on the ship. What's more, why would I have told you how they were murdered?"

"Then why won't you release my father now?" she cried. "Or are you hiding something?"

Alcuin looked at her sadly, smoothed his gray hair, and clenched his teeth. Then he asked her to sit down, using a tone she had never heard him use. The young woman refused, but she sensed he was about to confess something big.

"Sit down," he insisted as he wiped the sweat from his brow with a cloth. He fell silent for a moment. "I think I can safely assert that Wilfred murdered Korne, as he did Genseric."

"I don't believe you. Wilfred's a cripple."

"He is, and his misfortune is his best ally. Nobody would suspect him . . . nor any of his devices."

"What do you mean?"

"Four days ago, Wilfred showed me how one of his contraptions works. He did so when I showed an interest in how the dogs are attached to the chair. He triggered a spring that released their reins as if by magic. I had already noticed that the chamber pot was also equipped with an ingenious mechanism, so I went to see the blacksmith who admitted that he had built them. At first he refused to say anything more, but a few coins were enough to get him to tell me that he had installed an astonishing device in the rear handrail on the chair. Specifically, two small curved nails that were inserted in the grip, which when operated, shoot into the palm like two little darts. The blacksmith swore he never knew their purpose, which is understandable given how unusual the task was."

"And Wilfred uses this mechanism . . ."

"To administer the poison. The nails must have been soaked in some evil solution. Viper's poison, perhaps. I imagine that was how he killed Genseric—and also the parchment-maker."

"But why would Wilfred commit these crimes? He has access to the document. And the murdered boys? Why would he accuse my father of killing them?"

"I don't have all the answers yet, though I hope to have them soon. And now that you know the truth, and you know that I know your father is no murderer, I would ask you to please get back to work."

Theresa looked at the document, with just three paragraphs left to complete. Then she fixed her eyes on Alcuin's.

"I'll finish it when you release my father."

The monk looked away, then suddenly turned back to her, with an expression full of menace. "Your father, your father! There are more important things than your father!" he shouted. "Do you not understand that those who seek the parchment might still get their hands on it? To catch them I need them to think that I already have a culprit. Your poor father is innocent, yes, but so was Jesus Christ, and he give his life to save us from ourselves, did he not? Now answer me this: Do you think Gorgias is better than Christ? Is that what you think? Have you by any chance asked him whether he accepts his sacrifice? If he could speak, I am certain he would be grateful and more than willing. Moreover, let's stop being frivolous. We both know he is inevitably, and imminently, going to die. How long has he got left? Two? Three days? What does it matter if he dies in a bed or in a dungeon?"

Theresa sprang to her feet and slapped him.

Alcuin was immobile as his cheek flushed red. He reacted as if he had just been woken up. Standing, he went to the window, his hand going to his face.

"I'm sorry, I should not have said those things," he said. "But even so, take a step back. It's difficult to hear, I know, but your father will die soon either way. Zeno has confirmed it, and nothing we can do will alter that fact. The future of this document depends on us. I have already explained its significance, and for those reasons I implore you to accept my stance."

Theresa held back her tears. "I will tell you what," she said, finally breaking down, "I don't care what you do. I don't care if they steal the parchment from you and we all end up in hell. I will not stand by and allow my father to perish in that hole."

"You don't understand, Theresa. I'm about to—"

"You're about to kill him, and sooner or later you will do the same to me. Do you think I'm stupid? Neither my father nor I have ever mattered to you."

"You're wrong."

"Really? Then tell me—where did you get the Vulgate? Or did it fly here?"

Alcuin looked at her with a distressed expression. "Flavio Diacono found it left in the middle of the cloister." He closed the Vulgate and handed it back to Theresa. "If you don't believe me, you can go and ask him yourself."

"So why will you not release my father?"

"For God's sake! I've explained that already! I need to find out who is after the document."

"A document as false as Judas," she replied, standing her ground.

"False? What do you mean?" His tone changed again.

"I know full well what you're scheming. You, Wilfred, and the Papal States—a deluge of fraud and trickery. I know everything, Brother Alcuin. The document you go to such lengths to extol, on which you have placed hopes, ambitions, and desires . . . my father uncovered its duplicity. That's why you want him to die—so that your secret will go with him."

"You don't know what you're talking about," he stammered.

"Are you sure?" She took the tablets from her bag and flung them on the table in front of him. "They're copies of the text written between the lines in his Vulgate. Don't bother trying to find it in the Vulgate because I scraped them out with a knife."

"What do they say?" he asked, his expression hardening.

"You know as well as I do."

"What do they say?" he repeated as if consumed by fire.

Theresa pushed the tablets closer to him. Alcuin contemplated them and then looked back at her.

Theresa continued. "My father knew about Byzantine diplomacy. He knew about epistles, speeches, exordiums, and panegyrics. Perhaps that's why you hired him, but also you say because he was a good Christian. And as such, he discovered that Constantine never wrote the document. That none of the donations are legitimate and that the lands in fact belong to Byzantium."

"Silence!" the monk bellowed.

"If the document is authentic, tell me, Alcuin, why is it that the document refers to Byzantium as a province, when it was just a city in the fourth century? Why does it mention Judea when that didn't exist at that time? Not to mention the use of terms like *synclitus* instead of *senatus*, *banda* rather than *vexillum*, *censura* in place of *diploma*, *constitutum* for *decretum*, *largitas* for *possessio*, *consul* instead of *patricus* . . ."

"Quiet, woman! What do those mere details prove?"

"And that's not all," she continued. "In the *introductio* and the *conclusio* the handwriting of the imperial era is poorly imitated, and the *formulae* are from another time. How would you explain the fact that in a fourth-century document, the passage on Constantine's conversation is based on the *Acta o Gesta Sylvestri*, or explain the references to the decrees of the Iconoclastic Synod of Constantinople against the veneration of images, which you know was held several centuries later?"

"The fact that the document contains errors does not prove that the donation is false," he retorted, striking the table. "The difference between real and genuine is as slight as it is between false and spurious. How could you, a descendant of the sinner Eve, have the authority to judge the morality of an act guided by the Holy Spirit?"

"Do you truly believe that is what they will say in Byzantium?"

"You are playing with fire," he warned her. "I would never harm you, but there are many who would. Remember Korne."

The chiming of bells sounding an alarm interrupted them.

"Release my father, and I will finish the document. Make something up. Whatever you want—another miracle, whatever springs to mind. After all, you're a real expert at inventing lies." Then she gathered her tablets and told him to send his answer to Izam's boat. And she left without giving Alcuin a chance to argue.

On the way to the wharf, a crowd of townsfolk swarmed around her, leaping and dancing and shouting "Supplies!" Surprised, she followed a family until she realized that the commotion was due to four newly arrived boats that were at that moment mooring at the docks. One of them, painted red and lined with shields, was notably bigger than the rest, making the other boats look like mere shallops by comparison. She looked for Izam and finally found him on the last boat. She tried to board, but was stopped. However, as soon as Izam spotted her, he came down to meet her. As he approached, Theresa noticed he was limping.

"What happened?" she asked, alarmed. Without thinking about it, she threw herself into his arms. He stroked her hair and soothed her.

They moved away from the crowd to a solitary rock. Izam explained that he had gone out to meet the *missus dominicus* since a scout had informed him of his arrival.

"Unfortunately, it seems they also warned the owner of this arrow," he joked, pointing at his leg.

Theresa saw they had cut off the end of the arrow, but a hand's width of the shaft still protruded. She asked him if it was serious, though it didn't seem so.

"If an arrow doesn't kill you straightaway, rarely does anything come of it. It's curious, but the opposite is true of a sword wound. And you? Where have you been? I told Gratz to keep you on the ship."

Theresa told him what had happened with Alcuin. When she finished, Izam looked uneasy but didn't respond right away. Instead he pulled out the arrow with some pincers. He placed the bloody arrowhead to one side and then sealed the wound in his leg with some herbs.

"I always carry them with me," he explained. "They're better than bandages."

He held the herbs in place with his fingers and asked why she had disobeyed his orders. She told him she feared he would not return.

"Well, you weren't far off the mark," he said with a smile, casting the piece of arrow into the river. However, when Izam learned the details of her conversation with Alcuin, his smile quickly turned to concern. He insisted that the English monk enjoyed Charlemagne's favor, and that going against him was suicide.

When the commotion on land subsided, they went back to the first ship so that his wound could be cauterized. He was limping a little, so she helped him by putting her arms around his shoulders. While they were preparing the iron, Izam confessed that he had spoken to the *missus* about her.

"Well, not about you, exactly. About your father and his predicament. He didn't promise anything, but he told me that he would speak to Alcuin to find out more about the crime he's accused of."

He explained that the *missi dominici* were officials that Charlemagne sent throughout his lands to supervise the administration of justice. They tended to travel in pairs, but on this occasion there was just one. His name was Drogo and he seemed an upright man.

"I'm sure he will agree to our requests."

30

The man responsible for cauterizing the wound handed Izam a stick to chew on before sinking the red-hot iron into his thigh. After withdrawing the iron, he applied a dark ointment, and finally wrapped the wound in some fresh bandages.

Izam and Theresa ate fresh fish and pork sausages while the seamen unloaded the supplies from the hold. In total the supplies consisted of four oxen, some goats, a few chickens, dozens of game, plenty of fish, and several consignments of wheat, barley, chickpeas, and lentils, which they loaded onto carts to transport to the fortress. When the unloading was complete, a mob of peasants followed Drogo and his men down the twisting narrow streets.

Izam stayed on board, for his leg was still uncomfortable. He also felt safer knowing that Theresa was on the ship instead of surrounded by strangers on land. He was pondering how best to help her when a servant sent by Alcuin appeared at the wharf, asking for the young woman.

With the gangplank removed, the servant had no way to board, so he called out a request that she disembark. Izam advised her to stay onboard, but Theresa kissed him on the cheek and, without giving him a chance to object, she climbed down a ladder.

On land, the servant informed her that Alcuin had agreed to her demands and had sent him to escort her to the citadel. Theresa thought about telling this to Izam, but she decided not to, for fear he would try to prevent her.

At the fortress, the servant showed her through the kitchens, a hive of activity with people preparing food for the feast to be held that night in honor of the *missus dominicus*. Theresa felt like she was somewhere new, for all around her were people she didn't recognize. They left the storehouses behind them and headed for the meat safes. There, the guard dropped the ladder into the hole where Gorgias was captive. Theresa carefully climbed down. She found her father shivering, lying under a rotten animal skin. The guard pulled up the ladder, but Theresa didn't care. She crouched alongside her father and kissed him tenderly. His face burned like a lit torch.

"Can you hear me, Father? It's Theresa."

He half opened his rheumy eyes. Although he was looking at her, Theresa knew he could not see her.

Gorgias raised his trembling hand to stroke the crying angel's face, and as his fingers brushed against her, he seemed to recognize her. "My child?" he sputtered.

She wet his hot forehead with dirty water she found in a jar. Gorgias thanked her in a whisper. Then he forced a smile.

Theresa promised they would soon free him. She spoke to him of Rutgarda and his nephews, the four little urchins he adored so much. She invented a story in which Alcuin had sworn he would give him back his position with all manner of honors. And she also lied about what Zeno had said, telling him he would recover from his wounds. She cried when she realized that the life was draining out of him before her eyes.

"My little one," he murmured.

Theresa squeezed his hand. She combed his thin hair with her fingers and Gorgias thanked her. Suddenly he began to cough. In a moment of lucidity he remembered Constantine's document. He wanted to tell Theresa that he had hidden it on a beam in the slave huts at the mine. He had worked so hard, but the words did not come. His vision was fading. "Where are my books? Why aren't they bringing my inks?"

He was dying.

"They're here. Just as you like them," she lied as she stroked his forehead.

Gorgias looked around him and his face lit up as if he could truly see them. Then he held Theresa's hand tight.

"Writing is wonderful, isn't it?"

"Very much so, Father."

Then his hand went limp as his final breath left his body.

* * *

Two men pulled Theresa out of the hole. Then they hoisted Gorgias's body up with a rope and took him to the kitchen as if he were a sack of broad beans. More and more people were gathering around her, murmuring and whispering with no consideration for her terrible pain. Before long, barking announced Count Wilfred's arrival. Theresa clumsily wiped her tears away, then stood face to face with the dogs, their breath on her face.

"Is he dead?" inquired Wilfred without an ounce of compassion.

Theresa bit her lip, throwing a look of hatred at that cripple who seemed to be enjoying the bitterness that overwhelmed her. Out of respect for her father she chose to be quiet, but at that moment, one of the dogs nuzzled its snout against her father's body and started to lick him. Theresa gave it a swift kick that resounded around the kitchen. The dog spun about and bared its fangs, but Wilfred held it back, grimacing sardonically. "Careful, lass. My hounds are worth more than the lives of many people."

The livid young woman contained herself. She would have slapped him had she not known that the dogs, without a doubt, would tear her apart. The count laughed at her. "Take her to the meat safe," he ordered, his expression changing.

Theresa didn't understand, until suddenly two soldiers grabbed her and started dragging her toward the dungeons. She demanded an explanation, but not only did the men not listen to her, but they hit her with a stick to force her down into the hole. After the ladder was removed, Theresa looked up and estimated it would take the height of three men standing on each other's shoulders to reach the hole, making escape impossible. Soon she saw the dogs' snouts poking over the edge—and moments later, she saw Wilfred's face.

"Do you know, lass, I am truly sorry about your father. But you should not have threatened Alcuin, and—more important—you should not have stolen his parchment."

"What are you talking about? I haven't taken anything," she responded with surprise.

"As you wish. But I must warn you: If you haven't confessed by dawn, you will be charged with theft and blasphemy, meaning you will be tortured, and then burned to death."

"Damned cripple! I'm telling you I haven't stolen anything." She threw an empty bowl at him, which ricocheted off the wall with a hollow thud before falling back down on her.

Wilfred didn't respond. Instead he cracked his whip and the dogs dragged the chair back until he disappeared from sight.

When she was sure he had gone, Theresa slumped onto the same piece of ground where her father had died only moments earlier. She could hardly think, but she didn't care about the accusations. She had returned to Würzburg for Gorgias. She had fought for him and even been bold enough to challenge Alcuin. But now that he was dead, nothing mattered. Crying bitterly, she lay on the scraps of straw that felt like needles and wondered which cemetery they would bury him in.

She cursed the document. It had caused the death of Genseric, Korne, a young sentry whose name she did not even know, the wet nurse . . . and Gorgias, a father for whom any daughter would give her own life. She cried inconsolably, and with the pain came the cold, until she was frozen numb.

Sometime in the middle of the night, a pebble hit her on the cheek. She thought it had just crumbled away from the edge, but another blow to her leg made her sit up. She looked skyward but couldn't see a soul. Again a stone came in through the hole in the wall up above where the snow was poured in from the stables. She examined the duct: It had the diameter of a small barrel and was protected by bars. She pricked up her ears and heard a "Psst."

"Yes?" she whispered.

"It's me, Izam," she heard in the distance. "Are you all right?"

Theresa lay down and went quiet as a sentry poked his head over the edge. The guard glanced at her a couple of times and then went away.

She sat up again, picked up a little stone, and threw it at the opening.

"Listen," Izam said. "There are guards out here." He paused. "I'm going to get you out of this place. Can you hear me?"

"Yes," she responded, and she waited for him to continue. But he didn't speak again.

She could no longer sleep, so she stayed awake waiting for the cocks to announce the arrival of dawn. A faint glow seeped through the snow duct, reminding her where her only hope lay. She looked at the opening, willing Izam to appear, but he never came. Then she noticed some marks on the rock that seemed to illustrate a collection of buildings. Looking closely, she couldn't recall seeing them on the day that Zeno tended to her father. She looked closer at the illustration, and noticed a repeated horizontal line that looked like it might represent a crossbeam.

Before long, the ladder was lowered and two sentries ordered her to climb out. Theresa obeyed. As soon as she emerged from the hole, they gagged and blindfolded her. Then, after tying her hands, they led her through the kitchens, which she recognized from the smell of baked bread and apple cake. From there they went to the atrium—where she felt the biting cold of the morning—and then they continued to the main hall where Wilfred was waiting. She assumed it was him, for the dogs were growling as if they wanted to devour her. Suddenly a blow from a stick tore her shoulder. The sentries demanded to know where the parchment was, and she repeated that she did not know. They lashed her several times and continued to interrogate her until they grew tired.

Theresa awoke in a pool of her own blood, the blindfold no longer covering her eyes. She looked around and saw that she had been taken to the scriptorium, where a guard was staring at her with a stupid smile. She realized that her hands and feet were chained. At that moment Hoos Larsson came into the room. He handed some coins to the sentry, who then left. He crouched down beside Theresa. He looked at her with such contempt that it seemed as if there had never been anything between them. "The lashes look good on you," he whispered, touching her earlobe with his tongue.

She spat in his face.

He laughed and gave her a slap that left her cheek bright red. "Come on, be a good girl," he continued. "Don't you remember what a lovely time we had?" He ran his tongue across her face. Then he tied her hands together and gagged her so she couldn't speak. He lowered his mouth to her ear again. "They're saying that you stole the parchment. Is it true?" he asked with a smile. "Funny how things turn out. A few months ago I had to stab your father in order to get it—and now you've gone and stolen it, just like that."

Theresa wriggled as though she had been bitten by a snake, but Hoos kept laughing. He informed her that, from what they had told him, she would not even have a trial.

"It looks like you've really fucked up. They've already prepared the gallows for you."

As the door opened, Hoos immediately moved away. Alcuin, Wilfred, and Drogo—the *missus dominicus*—appeared in the room. Wilfred was surprised to see Hoos beside Theresa.

"I wanted to see her alone one last time," explained the young man. "She and I . . ."

Alcuin attested to the fact that the couple had been in a rather unchristian relationship. Wilfred nodded and ordered Hoos to leave the room. When he had gone, he urged on the dogs, which pulled him near Theresa. "In the name of God and His son Jesus Christ, for the last time, I exhort you to reveal to us the whereabouts of the document. We know that you understand its significance—so confess, and we will be generous enough to end your suffering. But persist in your attitude and you will feel the torment of fire on your flesh," he threatened.

He noticed that Theresa wished to speak. He requested that the gag be removed, but Alcuin objected. "If she wanted to, she would have confessed already." He pulled down her dress to reveal the bloody slashes on her back. "Let us wait until the flames lick at her feet, then we'll see whether her tongue remains idle."

Drogo agreed. Alcuin had informed him of everything that had happened, and they decided to burn the young woman following dinner, straight after the None service. Then they left the room, leaving her in the company of a sentry who was instructed to prevent anyone from approaching her.

Izam heard what was happening from Gundrada, a barrel-bellied cook who had confided in Gratz when he had helped with the provisions for the kitchens. In addition to preparing the order for the ship, the woman sent a gourd pie for Izam. While wrapping it, she told Izam that the execution would take place at the fortress, for according to Alcuin, the townspeople would not approve of the execution of a young woman who had been resurrected only a few days earlier.

"I heard the last bit when I hid behind a curtain," she said with a laugh, pleased with herself, while she added an extra apple. "I for one don't understand it. If she was such a miracle, how can she now be such a criminal? I like that lass, though of course, all I know about is cooking. Try the pie." And she laughed again raucously, proud of what she knew.

Izam bit into the pie, which he found to be hard and tasteless. He paid her for the food and calculated the time. Then he prayed that his plan would be better than the cook's gourd pie.

He left the food in the storehouse and made for the tower, where—according to Urginda—they would burn the young woman. The imposing stone tower sat on a crag at the top of the fortress, making it the last stronghold. From the tower one could see not only Würzburg but also the entrances to the town, the Main Valley, and the ravines in the hills. Once he was at the foot of the tower, he discovered that its age and insufficient maintenance meant that the watchtower was propped up against a great timber beam, the top end of which rested against the inside of the fortress wall.

He grimaced when he saw a pyre in the entrance courtyard. The area was difficult to access, surrounded as it was by a precipice with the fortress moat at the bottom. Izam crouched behind a stack of firewood and waited for the procession to arrive.

It started to rain. He wrapped himself in his cloak and consoled himself with the thought that the water would make lighting the pyre more difficult. Soon the bells rang to signal the end of Vespers. While he waited, he examined the strange tree trunk that shored up the tower, bridging the gap. He thought to himself that one could use it to climb right over the huge hole between the tower and the walls.

After a while Wilfred's carriage appeared. He was followed by Drogo, Alcuin, and Flavio Diacono, richly attired. Behind them trudged Theresa, who was guarded by a pair of sentries. Izam crouched lower when the dogs pulled the contraption closer to the pyre. The servants assisting Wilfred drove their torches into the ground. The rain continued to grow heavier. At the count's signal, the guards grabbed Theresa, who seemed half-asleep. They were about to lift her on to the pyre when Izam stood up.

"What in hell's name!" sputtered Wilfred when he saw him. The sentries took up their weapons, but Drogo stopped them.

"Izam, is that you?" the *missus* asked in surprise.

The young man bowed to him.

"Magistrate, this young woman is innocent. You cannot allow this."

When he tried to approach Theresa, the guards blocked his path. Wilfred roused his dogs, who barked as if possessed. Then he ordered his soldiers to light the pyre. But Izam pulled out a dagger and threw it. The weapon cleaved through the air and thumped into the chair directly under Wilfred's genitals. He took another dagger from his belt and took aim again. "I assure you that if you have a heart, my dagger will find it," he threatened.

"Izam, don't be a fool," the *missus* warned. "This young woman has stolen a document of vital importance. I don't know what force is guiding you, but I have already decided that she will pay for her crime with her life."

"She has not stolen anything. She has been by my side since she left the scriptorium," the engineer replied without lowering his weapon.

"That is not what Alcuin has told me."

"Then Alcuin lies," he emphatically declared.

"Heretic!" bellowed the monk.

The rain continued to pour insistently while the men stood unsure of what would happen next. Izam took a deep breath. It was time for his final ploy. He took a few steps forward, gripped the crucifix that hung from his neck, and fell on his knees before Drogo.

"I call for a trial by ordeal!"

They all fell silent, amazed. A trial by ordeal invariably ended in death.

"If you are trying to save her . . ." Wilfred warned him.

"I demand it!" He pulled his crucifix from his neck and held it up to the heavens.

Drogo cleared his throat. The *missus* looked at Wilfred, then Flavio, and finally to Alcuin. The first two shook their heads, but Alcuin argued that it was impossible to survive an ordeal.

"So, you will be judged by God, will you? Approach," Drogo ordered. "Do you know what you are getting yourself into?"

Izam nodded. He knew that the usual way these trials went was to force the accused to walk barefoot on red-hot bars: If his feet burned, he was guilty, but if by divine mediation they were unharmed, then he would be proclaimed innocent. Or, they might cast him into the river with bound feet and hands: If he floated, he would be absolved of his sins. However, Izam's plan was to insist on trial by combat, which was a possible option when there were two opponents. He challenged Alcuin.

"But he is not being accused," Wilfred objected.

"Alcuin claims that Theresa stole from him, but I say that he is lying. In which case, only God can decide who is the lost sheep."

"What utter nonsense! Have you forgotten that Alcuin is the shepherd and Theresa is the sheep?"

At that moment, Alcuin approached Izam, looked him in the eyes, and snatched the crucifix from him.

"I accept the ordeal."

After agreeing that they would meet at the pyre at dawn, they all went back inside. Izam returned to the ship having been promised by the *missus* that nothing would happen to Theresa. Meanwhile Wilfred, Flavio, and Alcuin discussed the ordeal.

"You should not have accepted," Wilfred repeated, incensed. "There was no reason why you—"

"I know what I'm doing, I promise you. Think about it. In reality, what you believe to be an act of insanity is the perfect way to justify an execution, which, in the eyes of the populace, would be controversial."

"What do you mean?"

"The masses idolize Theresa. They believe she has come back from the dead. To put her to death now makes no sense, especially if we are accusing her of a crime that we can't really talk about. A trial by ordeal, on other hand, would mean that God has justified it."

"But you know nothing of arms. Izam will send you to hell."

"That may be, but God is on my side."

"Don't be a fool, Alcuin!" Flavio Diacono cut in. "Izam is a skilled soldier. At the first thrust, he will strew your intestines across the yard."

"I trust in God."

"For goodness' sake! Perhaps you shouldn't trust Him quite so much."

Alcuin seemed to ponder it. After a while, he stood up, newly animated. "A champion. That's what I need."

He reminded them that in an ordeal, the offended party could designate a defender. "Theodor, perhaps," he suggested. "He's strong as a bull and a full head taller than Izam."

"Theodor's useless. If he had to peel an onion, he would lose his fingers with the first cut," Wilfred said. "We have to think of someone else."

"What about Hoos Larsson?" Flavio Diacono suggested.

"Hoos?" said Wilfred, surprised. "I agree he is able, but why would he want to help us?"

"For money," Flavio declared.

Alcuin admitted that the young man in question had the required vigor and skill for the duel, but he was not confident that he would willingly take on the risk. However, not only was Flavio sure of it, but he offered to be the one to convince him, so Wilfred and Alcuin agreed.

Before the dawn of the next day, an emissary appeared at Izam's ship to inform him that he was required at the fortress walls. The order was confirmed by a tablet with Drogo's seal, so Izam picked up his crossbow and several darts, belted his scramasax, protected himself from the rain with a fur overcoat, and followed the envoy to the gates. Inside, the emissary led him around the moat until they reached the point nearest the parade ground at the foot of the tower.

At the base of the tower, the remains of the scaffolding climbed steeply up to the trunk of the beam that acted as a support between the tower and the walls. When the servant informed Izam that he was to climb the scaffolding, Izam didn't believe him.

"Why should we have to fight up there?" he inquired.

The emissary shrugged and pointed to the top. Izam looked up to see Drogo looking down onto the parade ground from a considerable height. The *missus* signaled to him to climb the scaffolding. But before he began, the emissary asked him to hand over his crossbow. Izam complied, then crossed himself before beginning the climb.

At first the scaffolding seemed solid, but as he ascended, the framework of poles and ropes creaked as if on the verge of collapse, so he made sure to step on only the most secure joints. His wounded leg throbbed, but his hands clasped the projections like claws. The higher he ascended, the more it swayed. Two-thirds of the way up, he stopped to catch his breath, with the rain and wind lashing against his face. Far below in the moat, a bed of rock seemed to be waiting for his strength to fail. He sucked in some air and continued to climb to the top, right to where the wooden trunk buttressed the watchtower to the wall.

When he reached the top, he had no time to recover. On the other side stood Wilfred, Flavio Diacono, Drogo, and Alcuin.

Far below them Izam could see two soldiers guarding Theresa, who was not hooded but still gagged. Despite the distance, he could see the terror in her eyes. Standing next to Izam was a tall man carrying an axe. His heart skipped a beat. At that moment Drogo stepped forward and asked Izam to swear.

"In the name of the Lord, cross yourself and prepare for combat. Alcuin puts forward a champion," he shouted, pointing to the man with the axe. "Because he is the offended party, this is his right. Now swear loyalty to God. May He guide your weapons."

Izam swore. Then Drogo turned to the champion, and told him to make ready. "Honor for the winner, and hell for he who falls!"

Izam realized that they had intended for the duel to take place on the trunk that spanned the void. He quickly studied the trunk, observing that the top had been crudely planed. It looked as though some time ago it had served as a bridge between tower and wall. Even so, keeping balance would be difficult in the pouring rain. He also noticed that halfway along the trunk, secured to its flat surface, were several small wineskins. He couldn't think what their purpose might be, nor what they could be possibly be filled with that made them bulge the way they did.

He lifted his gaze and saw his opponent preparing to climb over the tower's parapet to reach the trunk. The man used his axe as an aid. His torso was protected with a leather jerkin, and he wore studded boots. Without a doubt, Izam could tell that it was Hoos Larsson. The tattoos gave him away.

But Izam was swifter than Hoos and reached the trunk first. He made his way along it toward the wall, withdrawing his dagger and preparing for combat.

The others quickly made their way to the bottom of the tower. From the parade ground, Drogo ordered Hoos to lose the axe. With one blow, Hoos Larsson drove it into the trunk and then drew his scramasax. He advanced toward Izam without even looking where he trod. Izam moved forward, too, noting with concern the stabbing pain in his leg.

They approached each other like two cornered beasts. Izam's face was wet with rain. Hoos was unperturbed, as if going hunting. The trunk creaked as they both drew close to its center. Hoos made the first feint, but Izam parried the thrust without stepping back, responding with a jab that Hoos easily blocked.

Hoos smiled. He was an expert with the knife, and his studded boots kept him steady on the trunk. He lunged again, making his opponent retreat. Izam readied himself, but Hoos suddenly stepped back, too, as if he wanted to enjoy what was about to happen. At that moment, Drogo ordered his archers to shoot, and a number of arrows flew through the air, piercing the little wineskins between the combatants.

"What do you reckon?" snickered Hoos. "Will it hurt when you hit the rocks down below?"

This time Hoos treaded more carefully, for the perforated wineskins oozed oil onto the trunk, turning it into a deadly trap. Taking advantage of Izam's surprise, Hoos launched another attack, and though Izam managed to avoid it, he slipped and dropped his weapon into the abyss. Fortunately, he recovered his balance before Hoos could reach him with his knife. Izam quickly removed his belt and used it as a whip to stop Hoos from getting any closer.

Behind Izam, the trunk suddenly gave a loud creak and he turned in horror to see the scaffolding that secured the trunk to the wall giving way, a shower of timber falling into the moat. He had no time to react. As the scaffolding creaked and snapped, the trunk slid down at the wall end. Both combatants could see that the whole structure was about to collapse and they quickly moved toward the tower. Despite the sloping trunk, Hoos, who was closer, reached the tower with relative ease. But Izam slipped as he attempted to cross the greased area. However, he managed to grasp a protruding branch as his body hung over the void.

Izam heard Theresa scream and he tried desperately to lift himself up. Groping with one free hand, he found an arrow that had passed through a wineskin and embedded itself into the wood. Both the arrow and the branch enabled him to hang on. Hoos watched the entire scene and roared with laughter to see Izam struggling like a bird in a trap.

"Do you need help?" he mocked.

Izam hung helplessly from the trunk, unable to clamber to the top.

Hoos dislodged the axe and started swinging it. "You know what, Izam? I liked shafting her. Theresa loved it," he added, squeezing his groin.

Hoos was about to throw the axe at Izam when unexpectedly the trunk slipped a little, this time at the end jammed against the tower. The shudder made Hoos fall backward, before pitching forward, so that he ended up close to where Izam was hanging. Fortunately, the trunk straightened, allowing Izam to grab hold of another branch and swing one leg over the top.

Hoos smiled. In the rain, his expression was like that of a wild beast that knows its prey is powerless. He inched forward, watching Izam struggle over the abyss below. When he knew he was close enough, he dealt a two-handed blow that Izam evaded, moving away the leg he had swung over the trunk. Once again he was dangling over the void.

While Hoos worked to dislodge the axe, Izam was able to sway his legs and get enough momentum to swing back on top of the trunk.

For a moment, they both looked at each other. Hoos was crouched down, brandishing his weapon and enjoying the hunt. And Izam was unarmed and on the defensive. Suddenly, the axe whistled through the air, missing Izam's face by a hand's breadth. Izam knew this would be his only opportunity. Grabbing the axe by the handle where it had lodged in the trunk, he pulled it violently out, and without thinking twice, launched an attack.

Hoos dodged it with feline agility.

At that moment a succession of cracking sounds followed by a great din alerted them that everything was about to collapse. The wall end of the trunk suddenly started to drop, while the other end held fast. Izam and Hoos grabbed hold, but another shudder made Hoos lose his grip and he began to slip into the void. At the last possible moment, Izam caught his arm.

The trunk shook again and tilted even farther. Izam tried to lift Hoos, who was now pleading to be saved. He knew that in order to successfully lift him up, he would have to cast the axe into the moat. Izam dropped the axe, grabbing some branches to steady himself. With a final effort, he pulled Hoos up far enough to where he was able to grab hold of the trunk and scramble onto it.

Now Hoos was behind Izam, who was closer to the tower. The two of them carefully crawled toward the tower, trying to prevent the precariously situated trunk from slipping any farther, when the wall side suddenly dropped dramatically. It was on the verge of complete collapse.

Izam continued crawling forward and Hoos followed. When Hoos came to one of the arrows embedded in the timber, he pulled it out and continued to climb with it. Just as Izam was about to reach the safety of the tower, Hoos drove the arrow into his back.

Theresa cried out in desperation. She had been trying to free herself for some time, but now the rain had lubricated her wrists and soaked the ligatures.

The guards, absorbed in the fight overhead, paid her no attention. Theresa pulled with all her might and was able to free one
arm, and then the other. She rubbed her wrists, which she could
hardly feel, and picking up a heavy stick from the pyre she went up
behind the guards, with her eye on Izam's crossbow.

She was about to commandeer it when one of the soldiers
turned around. Without hesitating Theresa slammed the stick into
his head with all her might and he fell unconscious to the ground.
She picked up the bow and a dart and ran toward the tower. Seeing
her, the other guard tried to stop her, but Theresa was faster and
went in through the tower door, bolting it behind her. Then she
bounded up the stairs two at a time, her heart in her mouth. When
she reached a window near the top, she could see Hoos striking
Izam in an attempt to knock him off the trunk.

She aimed the already loaded crossbow out the window and
fired. But the dart whistled through the air and disappeared into
the distance. She cursed herself for rushing it. Once more she saw
Hoos strike Izam, who clutched the trunk for dear life. Theresa was
determined not to miss with her last remaining dart. She pulled on
the lever to draw the bowstring, but all she managed to do was
hurt her hand. Glancing toward Izam, she saw that he was about to
fall. She pulled on the lever again and looked at Hoos. She thought
about his false caresses and pulled . . . She thought of her father
and pulled . . . She thought of Izam and pulled until the lever gave
and she drew the string. Then she placed the dart in the groove and
took aim, knowing she would only have one final shot.

Theresa gripped the crossbow until her arms stopped trembling. She closed one eye and, calmly, she fired. Hoos was about
to thrust his dagger into Izam when he felt something thump into
his back. He looked down toward his chest and suddenly his vision
clouded. In utter disbelief he saw a bloody dart poking through his
jacket. He turned in the direction of the arrow and saw Theresa's

face through the window wearing an expression of pure vengeance. It was the last thing he saw before falling into the void.

Izam didn't stop to look. He quickly crawled up to the tower just as the trunk broke off and plummeted into the moat, taking the parade ground wall with it.

As soon as he got to his feet he embraced Theresa, who was crying inconsolably. Without a second thought he kissed her. They were both soaked to the bone. Slowly, they descended the stairs, in silence.

Down below, the soldiers were beating away at the door, but the thick timber and solid bar held. Izam drew aside the bar. On the other side Drogo, Alcuin, Flavio Diacono, and the two guards awaited them. Wilfred was some distance behind them, near the wall that had just been destroyed.

"Thank you," Alcuin said to Izam.

Theresa did not understand. Izam had just defeated his champion and Alcuin was praising him. She was even more confused when the monk turned to her and shielded her with his cassock. At that moment, Drogo ordered the soldiers to leave the parade ground."

"All will become clear," Alcuin declared serenely.

The rain subsided. The monk approached Flavio, who curiously retreated toward the crumbling parapet. "I must admit it wasn't easy," he said. "You, Flavio Diacono, papal envoy of Rome. Who could have imagined you were the cause of so much adversity?"

Theresa made as if to say something, but Izam made her wait.

"The attack on Gorgias," Alcuin continued, "the death of the poor wet nurse, the abduction of the little girls, the murder of the young sentry . . . tell me, Flavio, how far would you have gone?"

"You're raving mad," he said with an awkward smile. "The outcome of the trial by ordeal clearly proves your guilt. The defeat of your champion discredits you."

"Defeat? It was you who chose Hoos Larsson."

"To defend *your* honor," Flavio argued.

"To save yourself is more likely. If Hoos died, you would rid yourself of your henchman, the only person who could give you away. Hoos always acted under your orders. And what do you say about Genseric, your other ally? You paid both very well with gold solidi minted in Byzantium." Alcuin took out a pouch and showed it to him. "A coin whose circulation, as everyone knows, is prohibited in Frankish lands. Where did you get them?"

"I gave that money to Hoos so he would fight," the nuncio blurted out. "You approved the payment yourself."

"Flavio, Flavio! For the love of God. I found these coins before Izam challenged me. To be precise, it was the same day Theresa discovered you conspiring in the tunnel with Hoos Larsson."

Flavio fell silent. Then suddenly he positioned himself behind Wilfred's carriage and threatened to push it into the void.

"You can go ahead as far as I'm concerned," Alcuin said without turning a hair. "It's no less than he deserves."

The count's eyes, already a picture of terror, opened even wider as he heard Alcuin's words.

The monk continued. "Because it was Wilfred who eliminated Genseric," he declared. "When he discovered that his coadjutor had betrayed him, that Genseric had been responsible for Gorgias's disappearance in order to take possession of the parchment, he had no qualms about murdering him. And later he did the same with Korne," Alcuin added. Then he looked Wilfred in the eye and discreetly pointed to the handrail on the chair.

Wilfred understood. Aware that Flavio Diacono was holding the rail, he triggered the spring and there was a metallic click. The Roman nuncio felt a prick in his palm, but paid no attention to it.

"Have you forgotten to whom you are speaking? I am an emissary of the pope," Flavio stressed again.

"And you are a follower of Irene of Byzantium, the traitorous empress who blinded her own son and hates the Papacy. The woman who corrupted you and whom you now serve. You intended to deliver the document to prevent Charlemagne's coronation. And now let go of Wilfred, and tell us where you have hidden the document that you stole from the scriptorium."

Flavio reeled. The venom was already taking effect. He put his hand in his robe and pulled out a folded parchment.

"Is this what you're looking for? A false document? Tell me, Alcuin, who is most . . . ?" He shook his head as if something was echoing around it. "Who is most at fault? He who, like me, fights to ensure that the truth prevails, or he who, like you, uses covetous lies to achieve his ends."

"The only truth is God's truth. It is He who wants the Papacy to live on."

"The Byzantine or the Roman?" Flavio blinked nervously, as though trying to see clearly.

Alcuin made as if to approach him, but Flavio warned him against it. "One step closer and I'll tear the parchment to pieces."

The monk stopped immediately, knowing that all he had to do to get his hands on the document was wait until the venom took full effect. However, Wilfred did not wait. When he saw that the papal nuncio was staggering, he released his hounds. The dogs, loyal executors of his commands, threw themselves at the Roman's throat.

One dog latched onto Flavio's arm, while another tore at his robe. In the struggle, he dropped the parchment and one of the animals ravaged it until it was destroyed. Flavio, even under attack, attempted to retrieve it, but another hound leaped at his face, making him lose his footing. The man teetered on the edge of the precipice. For a second, he looked at Alcuin in disbelief, then both dog and man tilted backward into the void.

When Alcuin looked over the edge, he saw Flavio Diacono's body together with Hoos Larsson's at the bottom of the precipice.

After picking up the remains of the parchment, Alcuin realized with a heavy heart that it could never be reconstructed. He crossed himself slowly and turned to Drogo. Theresa thought she could even see the sparkle from a tear in Alcuin's eye.

31

Gorgias's funeral was held in the main church in the presence of Drogo, the rest of the papal delegation, and a choir of boys. To Theresa, the antiphons they intoned sounded like the antechamber to heaven itself. Her stepmother, Rutgarda, accompanied by her sister, Lotharia, and her husband and their children, could not refrain from sobbing inconsolably.

Standing farther back, Izam offered Theresa a seat, but she preferred to stand. Although Theresa felt that this Saturday in March was the saddest of her life, the young woman listened to the homily feeling strong and proud of her father.

Rutgarda, on the other hand, cried until she ran out of tears. When the service was over, they carried the coffin in procession to the cemetery. At the express desire of Alcuin, Gorgias's remains were buried alongside the region's most distinguished deceased, those who through their sanctity or courage had defended Würzburg and its Christian values.

On the following Sunday morning, Theresa went to see Alcuin at his request. She didn't feel like seeing him, but Izam insisted that she go. When she arrived at the scriptorium for their meeting, she found Izam also waiting for her. She greeted both of them warmly and sat in the chair they had ready for her. Alcuin offered her some hot buns, but Theresa declined. Then there was a moment's silence, broken when Alcuin cleared his throat. "Are you sure you don't want one?" he asked again, but she shook her head no. He moved the buns out of the way and spread the remains of the chewed parchment over the table. "So much work, and for nothing," he grumbled.

Theresa could only think about her dead father.

"How are you feeling?" Izam asked her.

In a thin voice Theresa said she was fine. It was obvious that she was lying, for her eyes were wet. Alcuin bit his lip, breathed deeply, and took the young woman's hand in his. But she pulled it away, so Izam took her hand in his own. Alcuin finished gathering up the remains of the parchment and then set them aside as if they were any old pile of scrap.

"I don't know where to begin," said the monk. "First, I pray to God that He may be the one to judge me for my rights and wrongs. On the one hand, I feel honored to have served Him, and on the other, I regret my wrongdoings, even if I did commit them in His name. He knows everything, and I commend myself to Him." He paused and looked at the two of them. "It is easy to pass judgment in hindsight. I may have erred by using lies, but I am consoled to think that I was guided only by what I felt inside to be just and Christian. *Accidere ex una cintilla incendia passim.* On occasions, a tiny spark can cause a great fire. I must accept that I'm ultimately responsible for all that has happened here, and even if because of the bitter consequences, I offer you my apologies. That said, you must know the events that led to how your father ended up in a grave in the cemetery."

Theresa looked at Izam and he squeezed her hands. She trusted him. She turned back to Alcuin and listened.

"As I have already said, I met your father in Italy. There I convinced him to come with me to Würzburg, where he worked for me for many years. His knowledge of Latin and Greek were providential for me for translations of codices and epistles. He always told me he liked to write as much or more than he liked a good roast dinner," he said with a sad smile. "Perhaps that was why, when at the beginning of the winter I proposed that he copy the parchment, your father immediately accepted. He knew its significance, but not its falsity, something which, I repeat, I have no qualms about." He stood and continued his account pacing around the room. "Wilfred, His Holiness the Pope, and, of course, Charlemagne, knew about his activity. Unfortunately, Flavio found out, too, and the empress of Byzantium must have deceived him and corrupted him with money.

"That's when Flavio devised a plan worthy of the Devil's own son. He knew Genseric, who had lived in Rome before settling in Würzburg, so he persuaded the pope to send him to Aquis-Granum with the relics of the Santa Croce. Through an emissary, he convinced Genseric with bribes to keep him informed, and he traveled to Fulda with the chest containing the *lignum crucis*, which he intended to use as a hiding place for Constantine's parchment when he transported it to Byzantium. Genseric, meanwhile, sought the assistance of Hoos Larsson, an unscrupulous young man he did not hesitate to hire in order to help him get his hands on the document."

Theresa did not know why she was still listening to him. This saintly monk had falsely accused her of stealing the parchment, and if it were not for Izam's victory, he would have insisted on her being burned alive. But she stayed because of Izam.

"Genseric enjoyed Wilfred's favor," Alcuin continued. "He had access to the scriptorium, and he knew the progress your father was making. I imagine that back in January, because of the amount of time that had passed since Gorgias first began his work on the document, he assumed that it was finished, so he ordered Hoos to get hold of the parchment through whatever means necessary.

Hoos attacked Gorgias and wounded him. But he did not get what he wanted, because, fortunately for your father, he went off with only a partial draft."

Fortunately for your father. Inwardly, Theresa cursed him.

"That is when the seal of Constantine enters the stage." Alcuin went over to a cupboard and took from it a beautifully carved dagger. Theresa recognized it as the one Hoos Larsson had. "We found it on Hoos in the gorge," he explained. With some effort he rotated the handle until it clicked. From inside he removed a cylinder with a face carved into one end. Alcuin soaked it in ink and pressed it onto a parchment. "Constantine's seal," he announced. "After stealing it from Wilfred, Genseric gave it to Hoos to keep hidden."

"Wilfred had the seal?" Izam asked.

"Indeed. As you know, the parchment had three components: the medium itself, made from extremely fine vellum of unborn calf; the text in Latin and Greek, which Gorgias had to transcribe; and Constantine's seal. Without all three things, it would be worthless. When Genseric saw that the stolen document was incomplete, he decided to snatch the seal."

"But what did Flavio want? The seal or the parchment?" Theresa cut in.

"Sorry if I'm confusing you," the monk said. "Flavio wanted to prevent the document from being presented to the council. He had various options: steal the document, take possession of the seal, or eliminate your father. They attempted them in that order. Bear in mind that, if they could get their hands on an original, they could demonstrate that the document was a fake in the event that it was transcribed onto another parchment."

"And that's why they kept my father alive."

"Undoubtedly they would have killed him had he finished the document. But now let us return to Constantine's seal." Alcuin stopped to pick up a piece of cake, finishing it in just a few bites. Then he cleaned the seal and screwed it back into the dagger.

"Hoos retreated to his cabin looking for somewhere to hide the dagger. There, as you told me, he found you in trouble."

"Though it pains me to admit it, he saved me from two Saxons."

"And you repaid him by running off with his dagger?"

Theresa nodded. She knew then why Hoos had been so keen to find her.

"When you went to Fulda, naturally I recognized you. I didn't recall your face, but aside from Gorgias's daughter, I don't think there's another young woman in all Franconia who can read Greek written on a jar."

Theresa recalled that day at the apothecary when he had offered her work.

"Because of who your father was," the monk acknowledged. "Then Hoos got better after having recovered his dagger with the seal, and he disappeared without a trace." Alcuin sat opposite Theresa and took one last mouthful. "Hoos went back to Würzburg, where he met Genseric, and together they hatched a plan to kidnap your father to force him to finish the parchment. Fortunately, Gorgias managed to escape. Following Genseric's death, Hoos must not have known what to do. He returned to Fulda to speak with Flavio Diacono, who no doubt suggested that he use you as a hostage to find your father, or if it came to it, replace him as a scribe. Wilfred had suspected Genseric for some time. Gorgias had vanished, but curiously his belongings didn't disappear until two days later. By then, Wilfred had already ordered Theodor to watch the scriptorium, and it was the giant who discovered that the thief was Genseric."

"But why didn't Theodor just follow him? Or force him to disclose my father's whereabouts?"

"Who says he didn't? No doubt he attempted to, but a child could put that big oaf off the scent. I suppose that, in his rage, Wilfred poisoned Genseric when he next saw him. Then he must have had Theodor follow him to discover the hiding place. He returned to

the fortress to inform Wilfred, who immediately ordered him back
to the crypt to free Gorgias. But by then the coadjutor was dead
and Gorgias had disappeared."

"So, it was Theodor who dragged Genseric's body off and stuck
the stylus in him."

"Precisely. Wilfred ordered him to take Gorgias's stylus and fake
the murder so there would be a reason to find him quickly. From
that point forward, you know the rest of the story: the voyage on
the river, your falsified resurrection, and the disappearance of the
twins."

"Now that, I still don't understand."

"It's not difficult to deduce. With Genseric dead, Flavio needed
another agent. So he moved onto Korne, a man of loose morals,
which his love affair with the wet nurse confirms. No doubt Hoos
informed Flavio of Korne's weaknesses, so by offering him titles,
and no doubt Gorgias's head, too, he persuaded the parchment-
maker to abduct Wilfred's daughters."

"Intending to blackmail him to retrieve the parchment?"
Theresa asked, still trying to fit the pieces together.

"I would imagine so. The document written by your father
he had given up for lost. However, he knew that at that time you
were working on transcribing another one. Flavio decided that by
extorting Wilfred he could obtain the document that you were
working on. At any rate, it did him little good, because Wilfred
then poisoned Korne with the mechanism in his chair."

"But that doesn't make sense. What would Wilfred have to gain
from killing Korne?"

"The knowledge of where he was keeping his daughters, I suppose. He was sure that he could get that information from him in
exchange for giving him the antidote to the venom. However, it
didn't work out as planned. Korne, who did not know where the
girls were, ran off in fear and soon died during the singing in the
service."

"So why did Flavio and Hoos leave the little girls at the mine?"

"I can't answer that. Perhaps they were alarmed by Korne's strange death. Or maybe they thought someone might discover them there. I don't know. Bear in mind it's not easy to watch over two girls. How could they feed, hide, and guard them in secret? To do this, they were counting on the parchment-maker, who was now dead. In fact, I believe they drugged them to make it easier."

"And they took them to the mine—not to abandon them, but so they could be found?"

"That must have been their intention. Remember that the next day they organized a search, from which they emerged as heroes instead of outlaws."

"And incriminating my father while they were at it."

Alcuin nodded and gestured for Theresa to wait. He went to the door and asked for more food.

"I don't know why, but all this talking is making me hungry," he said upon returning. "Where were we? Ah, yes! I remember now. They tried to implicate your father from the beginning. I discovered, you should know, that Hoos did not just work for Flavio. He worked for himself and his own benefit first and foremost. Do you recall those youngsters who were stabbed to death? I had the opportunity to speak to their families, and they told me that when they enshrouded them, they found that they had black hands and feet. Does that remind you of anything?"

"The grain in Fulda?" she suggested incredulously.

"That's right. The poisoned grain. Although Lothar never admitted to it, after I tried to account for all the poisoned grain, I realized there was still a batch hidden somewhere. Do you recall that when Hoos disappeared from Fulda, he was still wounded— and he was traveling on horseback, wasn't he?"

Theresa lowered her head and admitted she had found him the horse.

"Helga the Black told me," Alcuin continued, "but according to Wilfred, Hoos arrived in Würzburg in a wagon. So it would appear that someone else also helped him escape Fulda: Rothaart the redhead, maybe, or Lothar."

"Why do you assume that?"

Alcuin rummaged through his pockets and pulled out a handful of grain. "Because in the stables where they amputated your father's arm, I found the missing batch of contaminated wheat."

He explained that it wasn't a stretch of the imagination to think that Hoos would attempt to do business with it, taking advantage of the famine in Würzburg. "The youngsters who died were hired by Hoos for various tasks," he informed Theresa. "He must have paid them in wheat, which he did not eat himself having been warned by Lothar not to. Perhaps he didn't know that the poison would take effect so quickly, but suddenly he found himself with two very sick young lads threatening to expose him, so on the spur of the moment he decided to murder them."

"And again incriminate my father."

"Indeed. He had to find him, and if he was held responsible for several deaths in Würzburg they would help to find him. I don't know whether Hoos found out that your father was hiding at the mine. Perhaps he suspected it, or maybe it was fate. The fact is that his presence no longer suited anyone. Flavio and Hoos wanted him dead, for if Gorgias survived, he could transcribe another parchment."

"And you, too, in order to cover up his discovery."

"What do you mean?" asked the monk, surprised.

"I bet you wanted him dead, too, since my father had uncovered the hypocrisy of the document."

Alcuin frowned. At that moment the servant returned with his requested food, but Alcuin shooed him away with an irritable gesture.

"I have told you that I was fond of your father. But let's not talk about that. Whatever I could have done for him, or didn't do for him, I could not have prevented his death."

"But he didn't have to die like a dog."

Alcuin didn't blink. He picked up a Bible and found the Book of Job. He began to read it out loud as if to justify his behavior. Then he added, "God demands sacrifice from us. He sends us afflictions that perhaps we do not understand. Your father offered his life, and you should be grateful to him for it."

Theresa looked him in the eyes with steely determination. "If there is something I should thank him for, it is that he lived long enough to show me that you two are as different as night and day."

She left the room, leaving Alcuin standing there.

On the way to the ship, Izam told her why the monk had accused her of stealing the parchment. "To buy you a little more time," he explained. "If he hadn't, Flavio would have done away with you in an instant. It was Flavio that you heard in the tunnel. Hoos killed the young sentry, but it was you he was looking to kill. He found the emerald Vulgate and took it, believing it contained the parchment you were working on. Then, realizing it was just a Bible, he discarded it in the cloister so nobody would know he had stolen it."

"And that's why Alcuin had me imprisoned in the meat safe? Why he allowed me to be thrashed? Why he intended to have me burned alive?"

"Try to stay calm," said Izam. "Alcuin thought that in the meat safe, awaiting the execution, at least you would be safe for a little while. Wilfred was the one responsible for thrashing you. And Alcuin couldn't intervene without arousing suspicion of his plan, of which Wilfred was completely unaware."

"Plan? What plan?" Theresa asked, taken aback.

"For me to challenge Alcuin himself."

Theresa didn't understand, but Izam continued. "He's the one who came to me with the idea," he said, referring to the monk. "He came to see me and informed me of everything I have already told you about. Alcuin didn't know how to protect you and at the same time unmask the murderers, so he asked me to challenge him to a trial by ordeal. When I did so and Alcuin requested a champion, Flavio gave his connection to Hoos away by suggesting him as the champion."

"And you believed Alcuin? In God's name, Izam! Think about it. If Hoos had defeated you, you would be dead and they would've burned me alive."

"That never would've happened. Drogo knew everything. Even if I had died, he still would have freed you."

"Then . . . why did you fight?"

"For you, Theresa. Hoos is in large part responsible for the death of your father, and he hurt you. He deserved to be punished."

"You could have died," she said, bursting into the tears.

"It was a trial by ordeal—God's judgment. That wouldn't have happened."

Three days after the funeral, a conclave exonerated Wilfred of the charges against him. Drogo, as supreme judge, ruled that Korne and Genseric had paid fair punishment for the wickedness of their deeds with their deaths, and all present applauded the verdict. But Alcuin could not let Wilfred go completely without blame—and he condemned the ambition that had driven his Christian, yet murderous, aspirations.

Coming out of the meeting, Alcuin found Theresa surrounded by bundles of clothes and books. They had arranged to meet to say farewell. Alcuin once again proposed that she transcribe Constantine's document in exchange for money, but she flatly refused, and the monk had to finally accept her answer.

"So . . . are you sure you wish to leave?" he asked.

Theresa hesitated. The night before, Izam had asked her to go with him to Aquis-Granum, but she had not answered him yet. On the one hand, she wanted to begin a new life, to forget everything and follow him on the ship bound to set sail the next day. But on the other hand, her heart told her to stay with Rutgarda and her nephews. It felt as though all that she had learned to value from her father—his eagerness for her to become an educated and independent woman—had died with him. For a moment she saw herself following Rutgarda's advice: staying in Würzburg to marry and have children.

"You could still stay and work with me," Alcuin suggested. "I will be at the fortress for a while to organize the scriptorium and wrap up certain matters. As punishment, Wilfred will be sent to live in a monastery, so you could help me for now, and decide later about your future."

But she had already made up her mind. Working among parchments was what she had always wanted, but now she longed for a different world, the world Izam told her about and that she yearned to discover for herself. Alcuin understood.

As he helped her pack up her bundles, he asked her again about Constantine's document. "I am interested in the first transcription," he explained. "The one your father made while he was held captive. He must have nearly completed it."

"I never saw such a document," the young woman lied, recalling the parchment she had found in her father's bag. But it didn't matter. She had long since destroyed it.

"It would be monumental if it exists. If we found it, we could still present it to the chapter's council," he insisted.

"I'm telling you that I don't know anything about it." She reflected before adding: "And even if I did know its location, I would never deliver it to you. In my mind there's no place for lies, or death, or ambition, or greed—even if you wield it in the name of Christianity. So you stick with your God, and I'll stick with mine."

Theresa said a polite farewell without another thought of the parchment.

As she walked to the wharf, she recalled the strange symbols that she guessed her father had drawn in the meat safe and she wondered for a moment about the intensity with which he had etched those beams.

She found Izam on the riverbank helping his men caulk the ship. As soon as he saw her, he dropped his bucket of pitch and, with his hands still black, ran to help her with her belongings. She laughed when he took her face in his hands, leaving streaks of black across her cheeks. Cleaning herself with a cloth, she kissed him, then rubbed the pitch on his clean, dark hair.

APRIL

32

The day's voyage passed pleasantly, with the quacking of ducks and wildflowers festooning the banks as if they had been arranged by a welcoming committee. They disembarked in Frankfurt, where they parted company with Drogo to join a caravan leaving for Fulda.

When they arrived back in Fulda, they found Helga the Black with her belly rounder than any Theresa had ever seen. Recognizing them, Helga dropped the haystack she was carrying and tried to run to meet her friend, wobbling like a cantharus. She hugged Theresa so hard that the girl thought she would burst. When Helga heard that they planned to settle in Fulda, she gave so many leaps of joy that it seemed as if she might give birth right there.

On the way to Theresa's lands, Helga asked her surreptitiously whether she was going to marry Izam. The young woman gave a nervous laugh. He had not asked her, but she knew that one day he would. She spoke to her of her plans to plow more lands and build a large, solid house, like those constructed in Byzantium, with several rooms and a separate latrine. Izam was a resourceful man and had some funds saved, so she thought it would be well within their means.

When Olaf saw Theresa and Izam arriving, he ran to them like a little boy. Izam was surprised at how well the slave moved with his wooden leg, and he asked how the joint was working. While they became engrossed discussing contraptions, horses, and land, Theresa and Helga went to the rudimentary hut that Olaf and his family had transformed into a cozy home. The children had put on weight and Lucille greeted them with food on the table.

That night, crammed together, they did not sleep well, despite Olaf spending the night outside. The next day they surveyed the sown fields, which were already beginning to germinate, as well as the uncultivated land. In the afternoon, they went down to Fulda to buy timber and tools, and over the next few days they began to build what would become the family home.

On the fourth day, while Olaf and Lucille were in town, Izam took the opportunity to speak to Theresa alone. He put down the firewood he was carrying and approached her from behind, tenderly embracing her. She could feel the sweat of his brow on her neck, and she turned to kiss his sweet, plump lips.

Izam stroked her hands, which were now covered in blisters. "They used to be so delicate," he lamented.

"But I didn't have you before," she replied, kissing him again.

Izam looked around him as he wiped the perspiration from his eyebrows. The house was progressing slowly, and it was not going to be as large as Theresa had wanted. What's more, the virgin soil required more work than they had calculated—perhaps too much for the meager yield they hoped to gain from it. However, he admired the pride with which Theresa confronted every undertaking.

Together, they walked beside the stream. Izam kicked the odd pebble. When Theresa asked what he was thinking about, his response was that all they had was not what he wanted for her.

"What do you mean?"

"This kind of life. You deserve more," he responded.

Theresa didn't understand. She told him that she was happy simply to know he loved her.

"And your reading and writing? I have seen you rereading your tablet every night."

She tried to hide the tears welling up in her eyes.

"We could go to Nantes," Izam suggested. "I have fertile lands there, inherited from a relative. The climate's mild, and in summer the beaches are filled with gulls. I know the local bishop, a good and simple man. I'm sure he'll lend you books and you'll be able to write again."

Theresa's face lit up. She asked him what would happen to Olaf and his family, but to her astonishment, Izam had already thought of it.

"They will travel with us," he said, "and serve us in our new home."

Over the next few days, they made their final preparations. They sold the land, sending a portion of the money to Rutgarda and giving several arpents to Helga the Black.

Then on the first Sunday of May, they set off for Nantes to join some traders who were making the journey as far as Paris. Holding her husband-to-be close to her, Theresa looked up at the sky that turned a darker shade of blue with each passing moment. Remembering her father, she celebrated her twists of fate with a kiss.

EPILOGUE

A lthough "Dirty Eric" had lost a tooth in his last fight, he could still spit farther than the rest of the boys, and this meant— along with the fact that he had the quickest fists in Würzburg— that he was still the undisputed leader of the urchins. He guided their motley group from the poor quarter everywhere about town, always on the lookout for new hiding places.

When they returned to the slave huts that spring, they were amazed at how dilapidated they had become since the winter. Exploring the mine tunnels, they gathered all sorts of sticks, stones, and other things they would need for their games. Eric decided they should set up camp in the best-preserved hut. He told little Thomas to climb the roof beams so he could better keep watch for bandits and threatened to leave him up there if he didn't stop crying.

After a while, Dirty Eric noticed that Thomas had stopped sobbing and was crawling up a beam.

"There's something hidden here," the little boy announced. He sat up on the crossbeam and lifted up a carefully tied leather package.

Eric ordered him to hand it over.

The others crowded round. "What is it?" one of the boys asked.

Eric told them to be quiet and gave one boy a slap for trying to touch the package. He untied the cord with the care of someone unwrapping treasure. But when he discovered that it only contained a few parchments, he screwed up his face and cast the package into a corner.

The boys laughed at Eric's disappointment, but he lashed out at the nearest ones until they regretted having mocked him. Then he gazed for a while at the documents he had just thrown aside before going over and carefully picking them up.

"Why do you think that I'm the boss?" he boasted. "I'll go to the fortress and swap these for quince cakes."

At the fortress gates, Eric tried to get one of the guards to let him through, but the man shoved him aside, telling him to scram and go play with the other urchins. He was thinking about destroying the documents when he bumped into a tall monk who appeared interested in what he had. The monk said his name was Alcuin.

Eric was wary, but he summoned some courage. That was why he was the boss after all, he reminded himself. He licked his hands and smoothed down his hair before offering Alcuin the parchments in exchange for some cakes. When the monk examined the documents, he fell to his knees. Covering Eric with kisses, he blessed the child. Then he ran to the scriptorium to give thanks to God for returning the Donation of Constantine.

That afternoon, the gang of boys hailed Dirty Eric as the best boss in the world, for aside from the quince cakes, he had also managed to obtain four barrels of wine.

ABOUT THE AUTHOR

A native of Spain, a former educator, and an industrial engineer, Antonio Garrido has received acclaim for the darkly compelling storytelling and nuanced historical details that shape his novels. Each is a reflection of the author's years of research into cultural, social, legal, and political aspects of ancient life. Garrido's *The Corpse Reader,* a fictionalized account of the early life of Song Cí, the Chinese founding father of forensic science, received the Zaragoza International Prize (Premio Internacional de Novela Histórica Ciudad de Zaragoza) for best historical novel published in Spain. His work has been translated into eighteen languages, and *The Scribe* is his second publication in English. Garrido currently resides in Valencia, Spain.

ABOUT THE TRANSLATOR

Photo copyright © Thomas Frogbrooke 2013

B orn in Britain to an English mother and Italian father, Simon Bruni first fell in love with Spain and its language as a teenager. After graduating in Spanish and Linguistics, he established himself as a freelance translator in Spain, where his interest turned to literary translation. Awarded a distinction in his Master's in Literary Translation, he won a John Dryden Prize for his dissertation piece, a translation of the novel *Celda 211* by Francisco Pérez Gandul. His first published literary translation was *At the Even Hour*, a collection of autobiographical short stories in the magical realism tradition by Uruguayan author Julio Figueredo.